Praise

"Fascinating, harrowing [The] tale of a young emotional crisis...A ter... .... an extremely talented new writer." - **Charles Salzberg, author of** *Devil in the Hole*

"A riveting story...of a woman playing on the edge of insanity as she twirls madly through the hyped-up, supercharged world of New York dating...A great read." - **Julia Scully, author** *Outside Passage: A Memoir of an Alaskan Childhood*

THE MANY
LOVES OF MILA

THE MANY LOVES OF MILA

A Novel

Inna Swinton

Matchgirl Press * New York * 2013

Copyright © 2013 by Inna Swinton

All rights reserved. No part of this book may be reproduced, scanned, distributed, transmitted, or stored in any printed or electronic form, using any means or method now known or hereafter devised, without the prior written permission of the copyright holder except in the case of brief quotations embodied in critical articles and reviews.

If you would like to use material from the book (other than for review purposes), prior written permission must be obtained by contacting: inna.swinton@gmail.com

Please do not participate in or encourage piracy of copyrighted materials in violation of the author's rights. Purchase only authorized editions.

This is a work of fiction. Names, characters, places, and incidents are either the product of the author's imagination or used fictitiously, and any resemblance to actual persons, living or dead, businesses, events, or locales is entirely coincidental.

ISBN: 978-0-9899930-2-9

For My Parents: Because I am always a daughter

and

For Rolfe: Because you are my honey-daddy and you are nice to my parents (see above)

She was always fond of someone, and could not exist without loving
- **Anton Chekov,** *The Darling*

It was as if a surplus of something so overflowed her being that it expressed itself beyond her will, now in the brightness of her glance, now in her smile.
- **Leo Tolstoy,** *Anna Karenina*

Resolution number one: obviously, will lose twenty pounds. Number two: will find nice sensible boyfriend and not continue to form romantic attachments to alcoholics, workaholics, peeping-toms, megalomaniacs, emotional fuckwits or perverts.
- **Helen Fielding,** *Bridget Jones' Diary*

Family is family
- **Mama, from** *The Many Loves of Mila*

CONTENTS

Prologue	1
Chapter 1 – The Short Straw	9
Chapter 2 – Sex With Poets	19
Chapter 3 – In Theory	24
Chapter 4 – Tango	26
Chapter 5 – Home Again	42
Chapter 6 – Awash in Misery	55
Chapter 7 – Sportsguy	62
Chapter 8 – The Ring	67
Chapter 9 – Sleeping Over	71
Chapter 10 – Following Doctor's Orders	75
Chapter 11 – Daddy's Girl	77
Chapter 12 – My Prince?	81
Chapter 13 – Drama Queen	86
Chapter 14 – The Show Must Go On	94
Chapter 15 – Hating Sundays	101
Chapter 16 – Go Brazilian!	105

Chapter 17 – The Naked Island	117
Chapter 18 – Emergency	128
Chapter 19 – Fifteen Minutes	130
Chapter 20 – You, You, You	138
Chapter 21 – The Long Weekend	149
Chapter 22 – The Impasse	156
Chapter 23 – Family	159
Chapter 24 – The Birthday Watch	163
Chapter 25 – Dr. Gold	168
Chapter 26 – The Do-Over	170
Chapter 27 – The Dating Prescription	172
Chapter 28 – No Dating	175
Chapter 29 – Frigid	181
Chapter 30 – No Substitutes	189
Chapter 31 – The Eyes Have It	191
Chapter 32 – Home for the Holidays	197
Chapter 33 – The Eve Before	202
Chapter 34 – Heavy	210
Chapter 35 – Swimming with Papa	221
Chapter 36 – Hyper and Anxious	225
Chapter 37 – The Forest	228
Chapter 38 – 911	232

Chapter 39 – At Bellevue 240

Chapter 40 – Mazel Tov! 245

Chapter 41 – Riga 252

Epilogue 256

Acknowledgments 259

About the Author 261

Prologue

New York City.

Bellevue. March.

When the paramedics pushed me in a wheelchair for the second time today — this time, at the emergency room — I didn't think I would be staying long. Exhausted by the day's events, I barely struggled as two nurses took off my boots and watch, and wrapped a thin white hospital robe around me.

There was a lot to take in here: Gurney — check. Wrists and ankles tied to four corners of said gurney — check. Concerned medical professionals taking pulse and making notes — check.

Bellevue looked no different from an ordinary hospital. It had that hospital feel and smell — a mix of antiseptic, perspiration, and the vague odor of heated food. Somewhere, here, it was time for dinner.

My thoughts were still racing. *Why was I here?* Dr. Gold, my psychiatrist, suggested I go somewhere. Somewhere, yes. But not here. Not here.

I struggled to recall the past few hours. Where did he actually tell me to go, then? *Uptown.* Yes, that's right; I was supposed to go see him at his office uptown. Then why did the ambulance dump me at Bellevue?

I recalled screaming a lot about my problems earlier in the afternoon on the phone to Dr. G. When I paused to take a breath, he said, "Mila, take your Klonopin and come see me. Do you understand? Tell me what you will do."

"Sure, Dr. G. Take my Klonopin, then get to your office on Madison. ASAP."

I took my medicine, but when I got outside of my apartment and stopped a cab, I drew a blank about Dr. Gold's exact address. I rifled through my purse in vain, hoping for some clue of what I was supposed to say to the cab driver. Trident, tubes of lip gloss, mascara, brown sugar packets from Starbucks; all of it spilled out onto the street. *Darn,* I thought. *Why didn't I write down his address!*

"Sorry, lady," the cabby shouted out before he took off, and I had no choice but to go back to my apartment. Upstairs, I threw down my purse and sat on the floor, frustrated and confused. My phone rang then.

"Mila, where are you?" the male voice on the other end said.

I recognized it immediately: Dr. G. was speaking.

"Home. I'm still home, Dr. Gold. I went downstairs, and the cab driver asked, 'Where to?' but I didn't know. I mean, I knew, but I couldn't tell him. Is that strange? I said I needed to get to my doctor, but the driver, he didn't know where you were, and I forgot, and I couldn't reach you."

I started sobbing then.

Someone must have called 911 then. Dr. G., I think. He must have.

Yes, I now recalled Dr. G. saying he would. He wanted the ambulance to get me to him. But, it was up to me to tell that to the ambulance drivers when they arrived. Except I forgot this very important detail, and then I didn't notice the ambulance heading to the wrong destination. The very wrong one. Bellevue-wrong.

Strapped to a gurney now in this place, I lifted my head to look around. I saw there were many, many people here. I heard my voice emerge from an odd reservoir inside of me; my ephemeral thoughts verbalized instantaneously, with no hesitation, judgments, or restrictions on my part.

"Hello! Wow, I am so happy to see all of you. You know, Papa always says I don't pay attention to people, and if I paid more attention to people, I would see the world was full of them!"

I proclaimed this greeting in a grandiose manner to nobody in particular. A heavy Irish-looking nurse rolled her eyes. A gray-faced man in a gray robe stared at me blankly. *Good job, Mila,* I thought as I shook my head. *You're making an excellent start in this fine establishment.*

But, even as I realized how self-absorbed I sounded to these strangers, I – or my voice – persisted: "My life is hard, but not necessarily harder than yours. I mean, you all have your own problems! But you are humanity, and I love humanity." As I finished speaking, I wondered whether Dr. G orchestrated this over-the-top hospital extravaganza to teach me something. Except that I couldn't figure out what this something was. Things were flitting in and out of my mind so rapidly that I felt like I was in a movie about myself watching scene cut to scene cut to scene.

A frowning young doctor in a white coat approached. "Here, hold still for a sec," he muttered. He grabbed my arm and rubbed it with alcohol before holding up a syringe.

"Hey! What the…," I breathed and pulled away.

He tightened his grip and stabbed me. I flinched. "Deep breath," he instructed. "One more should do it." He hit me. Again. "This is a sedative. It will calm…"

But already I was fading, losing consciousness.

When I next opened my eyes, I was laying on a cot on wheels in a brightly lit aqua hallway, my legs covered by a gray hospital blanket. I sat up. I felt as if I had been drenched in cold water – I was awake and alert. I looked around.

At one end of the hall was a tired-looking sitting area. A cooking show played through static on an ancient-looking television set suspended off a wall in the corner of the room. The bright lights made the bed, the hall, and the nurses – everything – look harsh and ugly.

A hospital. Ah yes, of course. The day before was coming back to me – my anxiety attack, the emergency workers, my resisting and crying and screaming, a wheelchair, an ambulance. Oh. And the restraints.

I looked down at my wrists and ankles. *They were gone now. So was the wheelchair. I was in a bed, and I was free to move. Progress. Glass half full.*

With new vigor, I hopped off the bed. I noticed that under my hospital gown, I was wearing my beige Theory suit. That meant I needed to get to work and go do the antitrust memo for Matt, the new partner.

Hey – I just thought these thoughts without saying them aloud! Good; more progress. My mind and voice were under control, and united in real time. Now, what was next?

Shivering, I wondered how long I'd slept in this hallway. Yesterday seemed surreal, like it all happened to someone else. The harshness of the surrounding lights, however, reminded me how real everything was.

I conjured up the dim, moody lighting at Saigon, the hot new restaurant in the Meatpacking District where I'd met Alexander for dinner on Saturday. No, Bellevue was no Manhattan hotspot. I couldn't leave this hospital, couldn't just walk away. I would be here until someone let me go.

I shook my head. If my situation weren't so scary, it would be almost funny, or at the very least, interesting. I made a mental note to write down whatever I could remember the minute I could find something with which to write. Dr. G. would want to know the details – but of course, *they* took away all my pens and electronic devices.

Ahh... Dr. G. – he must be wondering why I never got to his office uptown.

Memories were surfacing now – I recalled that back in the midst of this bizarre happening, I actually thought he *planned* this whole extravaganza to teach me, his patient, a much-needed lesson about herself. *Ha. Pretty crazy, Mila.* But let's not go there.

What time was it now? I looked down at my watch. Only it wasn't there. Oh yes – *they* took it too. I wondered who *they* truly were, the-powers-that-be.

My watch was the one Mama and Papa gave me in October, when we celebrated my last birthday. It had clusters of diamonds on a pearl face, and a shiny black lizard strap. It was an expensive watch from Neiman Marcus, Mama's favorite store, a store that indicated with each purchase, that she, a formerly poor Russian Jewish immigrant, arrived – even if that arrival was on credit.

The watch was a gift because I was turning thirty-three. I was now definitely into my thirties. And oh, yes; did I mention I was divorced, without a husband or baby in sight? A failure, Russian-community-wise.

At the celebration brunch when my parents gave me the watch, I cried into my mimosa. "You shouldn't have," I said to my mother. "I don't need it."

I collapsed into tears because I knew the watch represented Mama's new hopes for me – that there would be work appointments to keep, clients to impress, and a new husband to meet. But although I was a lawyer at a big firm, the only appointments I cared about now were the dates that kept me on a roller coaster of romance highs and lows.

Here in this place, I yearned for the presence of my watch. Mama's logic was not exactly obvious, but she did believe in willing things to happen.

So, could I will my getting out of here? I looked around. Patients slept on beds around me. The TV droned in the distance, and a nurse read a book in a chair nearby. Nobody looked eager to help.

Searching for the bathroom, I saw my reflection in a hall window: A petite woman, 5'3" thanks to Pilates, pale, with longish brown hair (now messy), smeared mascara, and an upturned nose – the nose of a Shiksa, as my beloved Babushka Rosa used to say.

My stomach growled. Was it past dinner? Or just before breakfast? I felt for my purse, and then realized *they* had taken it too. I felt my chest tighten and my eyes starting to water. *Enough crying, Mila,* I commanded myself. *I will call someone.*

I reached for my phone. *Darn! Of course, gone...* Now, I panicked: Was anyone trying to text me? What if Alexander called last night? What if Matt, the partner at my firm, emailed about my progress on the horrific antitrust research memo I had left on my desk, right before I told my secretary I was taking the rest of the day off because my head was hurting?

Hurting – certainly that word was an understatement on my part. My head had not been working correctly. But at least I had covered that fact well.

It was quiet in this hall, the only sound that of the nurse's book pages turning. I made my way down to the lounge, where there seemed to be some activity. Two female patients and a nurse/guard sat at a long table. I slid into an empty metal chair across from a skinny woman with a mass of dark curls tied back with a purple leopard-print bandana. The woman was talking softly to herself. The nurse to her left sat reading the *New York Daily News* while a blonde lady to her right doodled on a scrap of paper.

"Hi, I'm Mila," I said, introducing myself as if it were the first day of school.

The only one who looked up was the purple bandana lady.

"Pam," she said. She had dark circles under her eyes and a small broken-heart tattoo on her hand. She looked haggard, as if she hadn't slept in weeks. On her feet were furry bear slippers. "Did they get you too?" she said, narrowing her eyes.

"Excuse me?" I asked.

"I was making soup. Broccoli. When they burst in."

"They?" I questioned, although I was sure her "they" were not my "they."

"The cops; they had been out to get me. They came before."

"Why?" I asked.

She looked happy now, as if grateful that someone had even asked. "It was like a movie," she continued, smiling too widely and looking at me with gleaming eyes that glistened too brightly. "You see, I uncovered a scandal, an outrageous scandal, in my neighborhood."

I nodded. "Neighborhood?" I inquired, just to be polite. Funny how I was acting as if we were at a cocktail party, and not at Bellevue.

The unfiltered thoughts I had expressed during my grand entrance to Bellevue floated in and out of my mind: *People, Mila, there are people everywhere, people whose problems are important to them.* Yes, there was that, uh, small instant verbalization problem I had earlier....

Pam went on. "East Village. My landlord or slumlord — the ass — he's paying off the cops, and I was complaining about this bar next door, the noise level, and sure as shit I wrote to Bloomberg, and they investigated. But then I wait, and wait, and nothing, and would you believe it? Two times they got me. Last week I was here, in the very same place; the very same cop brought me in."

Her story was hard to follow. Crazy. *Had I sounded crazy too?* I now recalled yesterday more clearly than I wanted to, my earlier words of "I love humanity" flashing over and over again in my mind.

I bet Pam believed she made sense to herself. The line between crazy and not crazy was fluid, it seemed. Sometimes. Just yesterday, I had been concerned about the placing of a comma in a memo. Today, I was concerned about being locked up in a psycho ward by mistake.

The doodling woman stopped drawing her Christmas trees. She was doing them in orange; there were no green crayons here.

This woman wore a navy blazer, patent ballet flats, and white pants — she was dressed up for the emergency ward. Sporting a short blonde bob, she looked like she could be Martha Stewart's sister. She should be holding a martini on a yacht rather than biting on a crayon at Bellevue.

She looked up, and whispered over to me, "Oh please, don't pay too much mind to those paranoids. Just don't get admitted."

"Admitted?"

"If you stay, it's much harder to get out. And they medicate you. If you get out now, it's no biggie. I don't expect they'll make me stay, actually."

But she looked less certain than she sounded. Her eyes seemed sad and vacant. I wondered about her story.

"They can't make me stay," she repeated. "He wouldn't ever stand for that."

"He?" I asked, being polite again.

"My husband; we were just married," she smiled, but her smile trembled just a bit.

"Oh, I see." But I didn't see anything.

"He didn't know I was sick," she continued. "And then, the stress of the wedding got to me. And his ex-wife. We were in Greece, on a honeymoon cruise, when it started. I couldn't get up out of the cabin. My doctor fedexed my meds to the next port in Venice. My husband was surprised I was so bad. We managed to get back home, but my husband didn't know it can swing the other way – the mania – so he freaked out. We were in Central Park when I lost it."

"Sorry, that's rough," I said. We stayed silent for a bit. "So, what about this admitting thing?" I asked.

"Don't worry; if you're fine, they can tell. They are very good." Then, after a long pause, she said, "Except, of course, when they are not." She laughed nervously at her own joke.

I didn't find it at all funny; it sounded ominous, in fact. My heart beat a bit faster in my chest. I wondered about the higher dose of Lexapro I had taken since January. Dr. G. prescribed it after I'd gone through a romantic debacle – when my latest romance had gone bust, I went into a deeper funk than usual. The Lexapro had helped immediately with the sadness, but it made me hyper. It also kept me thin though – and thin was good for dating. *A fair trade,* I had thought. So that's why I didn't ask Dr. Gold to lower the dose.

And, Lynn, my therapist; did she know where I was? Had Dr. G. told her? Chances are I would miss our appointment today. But maybe she wouldn't charge me. It would be good to save some cash: I'd been eyeing a pair of Chanel sunglasses, and I could put the savings toward that.

Oh, God, my parents must be losing their minds just about now. Poor Mama.

I imagined her – big in my mind, Mama always seemed taller than her 5'6". She had these great green almond-shaped eyes, which she emphasized with bright red frizzy hair that long ago had lost any shred of natural color. She always wanted to lose ten pounds, and then that became twenty and even thirty. My father always looked so slight next to her, just a few inches taller and quite a bit thinner. Thinking of my parents reminded me I had a purpose here, and I scanned the room to plan my escape. Who were the *they* whom I needed to convince I belonged *out*side rather than *in*side?

A thin young nurse – there must have been a shift change – came up to our table. "Mila Simon?" she questioned. When I nodded to confirm my identity, she went on. "Dr. Kahn can see you now."

My palms became sweaty. It was the moment of truth. Could I convince this Dr. Kahn I was fine to go?

"Later, ladies," I said crisply, hoping to sound business-like.

I nodded at Pam – now telling her story to a new coffee-klatch arrival – and at Martha's lookalike – now pushing green Jell-O around a paper plate. And I stood up to go face my sentence.

In or out – it would be decided.

TWO YEARS EARLIER

Chapter 1 – The Short Straw

Fair Lawn, New Jersey.

June.

I was spending the summer in the backyard of my parents' three-bedroom ranch following the abrupt demise of my marriage to Cliff, a handsome lawyer/investment banker and my former best friend.
It was supposed to be a trial separation.

That June, my mind melted into a myriad scribbles – and I drafted hundreds of illegible letters on topics as diverse as: the grave mistake I had made, my current woeful state, my eternal devotion, and the trials true love had endured throughout history, with its cast of characters such as Romeo and Juliet, Rhett and Scarlett, Ruslan and Ludmila.

I never mailed the letters. And that meant Cliff never opened any of them.

My "new" room in my parents' house was my old teenage bedroom, the very same one where I had gossiped with friends on a landline phone with no call-waiting fifteen years earlier. In other words – it had been a lifetime since I had lived in it.

My mama had had the room redone when I was in college. Gone was the heavy wood furniture of my teens, purchased during a family shopping outing to Levitz Furniture on Route 17. The room was now the usual Russian-style mix of European lacquered furniture with gold accents and pink Italian-villa faux-wallpaper paint. Except for the bed – my mother hadn't gotten around to changing out my old twin bed for the sleek Italian couch that would complete the remodel. I knew this was on her wish list.

My parents' home was located in Fair Lawn, New Jersey, an enclave of assimilated Russian Jews. Geographically located only thirty minutes from New York City, it was, in feel, culture, and style, worlds apart from my most recent home of Manhattan, where I had spent the last six years after my graduation from law school.

While living with Cliff in the big city, I would divvy up my time between tutoring wealthy children for their SATs (two or three hours per day); studying lines for acting roles (twenty minutes instead of the required hours); writing stand-up comedy (one hour); practicing my downward dog (thirty minutes); visiting famous diet doctors (once a week); writing in my food diary (all day long); and calling my husband Cliff to make dinner plans (up to ten times per day).

In the mornings, I would field my mama's panicked calls relaying her "Bad News Is Happening on Your Corner" report: "Mila, a woman was raped in the Bronx projects yesterday. Do you have to go out tonight?" she would plead in her Russian-accented English.

"But Mama, I live in Manhattan on the Upper East Side. In a doorman building."

"That's close enough," she would retort, full of strong opinions as per her usual.

On Tuesdays, I would go to a weekly appointment with Elsa, my psychologist. Elsa was a full-time Swedish poet and a therapist only part-time. I started going to Elsa for help with figuring out what to do with my career after I had graduated from law school and taken some time off, doing odd jobs here and there to pay the bills. I knew I didn't want to practice law, but was afraid to admit to myself what it was that I really wanted – to do something in the arts. Elsa would barely speak during our sessions, usually only uttering a single spare sentence at the very end of our fifty minutes. That line would always be something like, "Fear means…go slow."

Monthly, I would join my former law-school girlfriends for lunch on the Upper West Side. We would drink rooibos tea, pick at cherry scones, and endlessly discuss what to do with our lives.

But those days of relative leisure in Manhattan were now in the past. These days I wallowed in misery, raw with grief over the disaster my marriage had become. At night I screamed and cried about the baby room Cliff and I had started to plan for. And somewhere, somehow, I had picked up smoking as a habit.

My father would only look on in horror at as I puffed away: "*Milaya* (darling), we came to this country for this? Ladies don't smoke."

"'Ladies'?" I would question.

These days I felt more like a beaten-down, drenched squirrel.

....

My parents and I had come to America from Riga, Latvia in the early 1980s, when I was eight. We were part of a Jewish immigration *volna* (wave) that had come to escape life behind the Iron Curtain.

In Riga, we had lived in a fifth-floor walk-up *communalka*, a shared apartment for two families. My family then consisted of five people for our allotted two rooms: my parents and I in the bedroom, and my Babushka Rosa – my father's mother – and my uncle Boris, my mother's thirty-year-old bachelor brother, sharing the living room.

We shared that cold-water-only and one-toilet-for-all hovel with a young Russian couple – Tonya and Vova. "Alcoholics," my mother would whisper. "*Goyim*," Baba Rosa would say loudly back, shrugging her shoulders. "Goyim" meant "Gentiles." Non-Jews. Yes, we were most definitely Jewish.

My parents and I became one of the first Russian-Jewish families to settle in Fair Lawn, a nondescript suburb in Bergen County, New Jersey. We had found the local humanitarian-minded American Jews there eager to help out their downtrodden counterparts. These Americans found they could feel good about themselves by giving away to us their children's cheesy '70s jeans and old Farah Fawcett notebooks; we were grateful, newly arrived Jewish refugees. When I was in high school, we celebrated receiving our American citizenship by drinking vodka (OK, *my parents did; I sipped cranberry juice*) and changing our last name from Simonovsky to Simon. My mother thought a less Jewish-sounding name would help us succeed in this land of opportunity.

Within fifteen years of my family's arrival, the town of Fair Lawn had grown increasingly Russian in character, a sort of Brighton-Beach-by-the-mall. Fair Lawn had its own style though: a mix of Russian bling and middle-American plainness.

Garden State Plaza shopping center was the sacred heart of the area, equally beloved by both the middle-class American locals and their new striving neighbors, the glitzy Russian immigrants. There were Russian grocery stores, marbled *banyas* (steam baths), manicurists, accountants, general contractors, doctors, and nursery schools. Gaudy remodeled mansions had sprung up next to sedate Capes, and Lexus SUVs had replaced Ford station wagons.

The Russians injected energy and drama into this nice but somewhat boring American town. At least my friends and I found it boring when we were in high school, faced as we were on a typical Friday night with the unattractive entertainment options of: Greek diner, movies, or the local CVS. One day, an unusually exciting event interrupted the rhythm of our regular middle-class teenage lives: A Russian woman, the mother of a girl in our class, was run over by a New-York-City-bound train right in the center of town. Our classmate left school in the middle of the semester. The gossip was that the woman must have thrown herself under the train. The adults whispered about reasons, usual ones, but my friends and I were too busy planning what to wear to the prom to wonder about the savagery of adult passion.

And so, when I headed off to Columbia University for college and law school, I scoffed at the thought of ever having to live in this place again.

Over time, the idea of my eventual return became even more unlikely: In law school, I bumped a guy in the elevator, a fellow student. Cliff was striking: tall with jet-black hair, a perfect nose, and large blue eyes.

We became friends. We discussed philosophy and psychology; went to the Film Forum and law school parties together; ate my mother's turkey meatball soup; and crammed for exams together. One day, during a game of drunken truth-or-dare, we kissed. From that point on, we were dating.

In many ways, we were opposites: I was impulsive, and Cliff was cautious. I was optimistic; Cliff was pessimistic. I was picked last at kickball; Cliff was a star athlete. My parents were still married, arguments and all; his were divorced. I saw my parents once a week, and Cliff had moved far away from his and been independent for years. He had few possessions; I collected knickknacks from around the world.

After law school, we traveled together in Europe, and when we got back to New York, I invited Cliff to share my studio because the rent was cheap, and he had no place to live. He took me up on it.

But when the two of us had been dating for six years but were still not talking marriage, my mother, being a mother, pressed me about the lack of what she called "progress": "Milochka (little Mila), you are not a child anymore. What are your plans?"

I shrugged. "Who needs a piece of paper to say two people love each other? We don't."

"That's not what I am saying, *solnyshko* (little sun). All women want marriage. The world is simple: You meet, you marry, you have a house, children, friends. What you're saying – it's all theory. You're too young to know how things really work."

"Mama, I *am* happy," I insisted.

But, when I really thought about it, I realized I did want to get married – it was the next thing, as normal as going to college, having a job, and brushing your teeth. So I started pressing Cliff. Then, Cliff and I went to Italy for a vacation, and he bought me a lovely hammered gold ring. It wasn't an engagement ring, but I could parlay it into one, I was sure. But afterwards, when I hinted and cried and told him six years was too long and all of our friends were married, Cliff stayed silent.

I showed the ring to my mother one night, but told her it was a secret.

"*Mazel Tov*, my darling," she said, embracing me.

"It's not yet a proposal, Mama," I pointed out.

"It will be," my mama reassured me.

The next day, at our weekly family dinner, Mama took matters into her own hands. Speaking directly to Cliff, she said, "So, you and Mila are getting married!" and smiled sweetly. He stared at her, confused.

"Mama! What are you saying!" I burst out in total surprise.

"Cliff, I saw the ring. When is the date?" she persisted.

"This summer," Cliff replied and looked over at me.

I gasped. *Finally*.

Our wedding was at a Russian nightclub in Brighton Beach. It seemed the entire Russian community of Fair Lawn showed up to celebrate with my mother, who never forgot the birthdays of either her friends or their children, and gave generous dinner parties. The vodka flowed freely, and tuxedoed waiters carried out huge platters of Russian celebration staples: meat-filled *piroshki* (pastries), herring, potato salad, and beef stroganoff. My parents had saved for years for this occasion. And what they hadn't saved? Well, Mama always managed to engineer cash flow by moving things around on her credit cards.

The rabbi who officiated at the ceremony, Rabbi Shuster, was a portly opera singer. His moving rendition of "Sunrise, Sunset," made my mother's immigrant friends tear up. They had come here only twenty years ago, and were conquering this new strange land: Their children were assimilating, marrying, having children, and becoming part of the fabric of American society.

There were no relatives or family friends present from Cliff's side other than his mother, a golf-playing, frosted-blonde retiree, and her best friend, a large special-ed teacher with a buzz cut. Cliff's father had not come; he was claustrophobic, and unable to fly cross-country from L.A. The Russians present whispered: "The groom's mother is with a lady date, and his father didn't show up! *This is America!*" Then they toasted Cliff and me, the happy couple, before they downed their shots of vodka.

A year later, my parents were watching *60 Minutes* when they saw a familiar face: It turned out that Rabbi Shuster, the man who had blessed my union with Cliff so eloquently, was not a rabbi after all, but a Volvo salesman. This fact made the thousands of marriages he had officiated at invalid (although ultimately, a law was passed to legalize all the unions).

Mama cried as she told me the news. "Milochka, how terrible! God was not with us this time. It means your marriage has a weak blessing. But we will overcome even this. We are strong."

"Mama, I don't believe in signs," I assured her.

Perhaps I should have.

Only a few months after the wedding, I convinced Cliff that we should start trying for a baby. He agreed, but was hardly enthusiastic about doubling up his efforts. My coterie of girlfriend advisors and I attributed this to his divorce-scarred childhood and general fear of responsibility. Or perhaps Cliff was simply nervous that suddenly, we would have to grow up, and say goodbye to movie marathons on Friday nights and three a.m. discussions of Kant and Hume with friends in SoHo. I was too excited about finally being married to pay much attention to any part of my own trepidation about crossing that next threshold. And as for my rapidly-becoming-less-frequent sex life with Cliff? Well, I pushed thoughts of that firmly away. I didn't want any clouds over my sunny horizon.

A year to the date after the wedding, there was still no pregnancy. And sex had become rarer and rarer. Cliff, now an investment banker, was preoccupied with an enormous merger in Hong Kong, and I was feeling the strain of my stop-and-go acting career. Or, my "non-career," as my father referred to it.

There were so many "almosts" for me. I was cast as a young Russian mother on an episode of *Law & Order*, in a scene during which my toddler had a full-blown tantrum at a Queens diner while Detective Ed Green, played by the very handsome actor Jesse L. Martin, ate dinner with another detective at a nearby table. "I MADE IT!" I screamed to Cliff on the phone when my agent called to tell me the good news — only to find out the next morning that the location was changed to a Chinese restaurant in Midtown and my role was written out. I filmed a role in a new James Bond movie, only to be edited out post-production. An independent film with an up-and-coming director fell off that director's to-do list when he was invited to be the second assistant director on a Kate Winslet movie.

Just to make sure, though, that there wasn't anything, well, really *wrong*, I started going to fertility doctors, acupuncturists, and herbalists, none of whom could find anything actually wrong. They suggested exercise, tonics, juicing, and Transcendental Meditation for mood improvement. "Malaise," pronounced a leading colonics expert who regularly appeared on Oprah. "Clary sage essential oil," suggested a Feng Shui expert whom I met at a party and confided in after a few glasses of wine. "Gives better energy in the bedroom," she smiled. Elsa, the silent therapist, stayed mostly silent, advising no adjustments to either my mental state or any part of my daily routine. She simply asked me what I would suggest to myself if I were she. I had no idea, but I nodded thoughtfully in response.

Mama was certain the curse of the false rabbi was responsible for the non-appearance of a joyful bump. "It is all our fault," she wept, "because we wanted to impress our guests with an opera-quality rendition of a song from *Fiddler on the Roof*!"

I needed to stop thinking about it, quit the obsessing over the lack of a baby. It was time to change focus. So I decided to throw myself into creating theater material rather than creating babies. And that's when I started I looking for someone – someone to direct a play I had just written about my first Halloween costume in America.

The Halloween I was writing about had taken place during my elementary school days. On the very morning of my school's Halloween parade, I had mentioned to my mother that I needed a "costume." She didn't think too much about the holiday, and had to call in late to her engineering job in New York City so we could purchase a last-minute costume. We drove in a panic to our local CVS; what we found there sealed my fate. The $4.99 special – a costume about which I would be inspired years later to write an entire play – consisted of a gigantic yellow balloon cat head, a plastic cape, and a t-shirt with the words "Kooky Spook" on it.

We left the store, and I put it on. The first "o" in Kooky and the last "o" in Spook framed my tiny nipples. The huge balloon head waved in the wind and made it difficult for me to walk into the school. The cape flared out behind me.

The costume proved, of course, to be entirely inappropriate; all the other girls were dressed as Pocahontases and Cinderellas, and I soon found I hated the itchy yellow plastic, and how ugly the costume made me feel. Adding insult to injury, a rough older boy who lived nearby tormented me during the parade, calling out, "Commy Kook!" whenever he spied me. It made me feel like an outsider, more of an unadjusted immigrant than I was already.

So, years after this tragicomic event, I wrote a play to illustrate the challenges of assimilating from the point-of-view of a Russian-Jewish immigrant girl. The play was to be produced by a Jewish arts organization.

The show's producer suggested some possible directors; I picked Dominic's name from the list. No particular reason other than I liked the name's flow – double Ds and the R. Dominic de Rossi.

The names of five directors were on that list, so my chances of walking away with my life intact were four out of five. It didn't happen; I had drawn the short straw. But, I'm getting ahead of the story.

When I met Dominic, I found him to be physically unimpressive: You would never notice Dominic in a crowded room. He had close-set brown eyes and wavy brown hair, and since he was of average height, he wore platform shoes. He spent his days working as a temp at Chase, but he yearned to become a professional critic, and spent the rest of his time contributing play and book reviews to various free magazines. His tendency to criticize spilled over into his personal life: he loved to find fault with anything and everything. At restaurants, the bread was stale, the wine rancid. He was never happy with entertainment – that play was mediocre, this movie just average.

The most distinctive thing though about Dominic was his energy: He had an excess of it. He went to the theater almost every night, belonged to several arts organizations, and played on a hockey league. He also was a struggling, unrecognized, uncompensated artist, working late into the night on writing what he called his "breakthrough" play.

So in this city, where investment bankers and celebrities ruled, Dominic was an outsider. Something about his outsider mentality drew me in. Like he was similar to the "Kooky Spook" I used to be.

Dominic became my theater mentor, opening up the downtown theatre scene to me: Front-row seats at the puppet reenactment of the Triangle Shirtwaist Factory Fire. Invitations to dingy Brooklyn lofts for readings of prose plays about water conservation and global warming. Operas about hostage-taking on cruise ships.

I welcomed the resulting flurry of activity; running around the city to avant-garde arts events made me feel passionate and driven. Trying for a baby and tracking my fertility in a notebook had been a bummer, and I was depressed and anxious about what I perceived as the failure of my hormones. Besides, Cliff was up for a promotion at his company, so he was working later and later, and we were spending less time together.

Dominic ushered in a lighter time for me. He and I collaborated on several short plays in which we acted that summer, and to his downtown friends, Dominic introduced me as, "Mila, a writer."

When Dominic wrote a play about a poet stealing away the wife of an investment banker, I did not see the irony; get the foreshadowing. I even critiqued it, telling Dominic it needed "…more of an arc."

One day, Dominic and I went for drinks after a rehearsal. And then off for some salsa dancing. Drunk, laughing and stumbling out of the dance club, Dominic and I were saying goodbye in Union Square Park. A cab stopped, and he opened the door for me. He leaned in close, and

I felt his sweat and smelled his strong cologne. Suddenly our hug turned into a kiss.

By the time Dominic waltzed – or rather tangoed – into my life, Cliff and I had been together for years.

So yes, there was a one-word explanation for my sudden move from Manhattan: an affair. Actually, that's two words, if you count the article. In Russian, where there are no articles and people speak directly, the proper word is *Izmena* – it means "betrayal." The word *izmena* is related to the word *meniat* – to exchange.

I had "exchanged" Cliff for an Off-Off-Broadway theater director named Dominic de Rossi. It had been a stupid choice, in Mama's opinion: "A diamond for a pebble," as she put it. Well, she had a right to her opinion. For me though, it wasn't about the men; it was about circumstance. And that made the whole thing frightening.

Life is like that. A chance act of minimal significance sets off a chain of events of enormous consequence not just to one person's life, but to the lives of many. And, perhaps, if that act or thing never happened at that precise moment, it never would have happened at all.

But, in some lives, at some moment, something of some consequence in the flow of time and chain of events does happen. And when it does, nothing is ever the same. This is the story I am going to tell.

Chapter 2 – Sex With Poets

It got worse. Or better. Worse for my marriage. Better for my sex life – which had been non-existent.

Truth was, the sex between me and Cliff had never been that great: We had never figured out why we didn't connect sexually, although we both had many theories. I thought Cliff was a bad kisser: He closed his eyes and pursed his lips and touched me as if I had all the appeal of plastic. And he held me awkwardly, like I would break. Cliff once admitted he didn't like kissing; he thought people kissed only for show.

Cliff did like sex, but only if it was athletic and intense, almost violent. He said people were just animals, and sex should be animalistic, not tender. And he loved to look at porn. It had put his home, where he had been born – the San Fernando Valley – on the map. Porn was in his blood, he explained once.

Cliff knew the names and filmographies of the porn stars by heart. He and his dad had watched porn together starting when Cliff was a pre-teen; they had bonded over *Playboy* and *Hustler*. His family had told stories of the sexual prowess of Cliff's grandfather, a dapper Los Angeles actor-type whose claim to fame was a romance with Ava Gardner. Or perhaps it was Rita Hayworth or some other great Hollywood starlet.

I admired Cliff's honesty – *Other men just didn't say what they really think*, I thought, and so Cliff was letting me in on this big male secret. But it did frustrate me. Especially as online porn was Cliff's favorite late-night activity.

One night, as we lay there next to each other in our pajamas – me reading a play, and Cliff reading a merger agreement – he reached over and embraced me. I hugged him back hard and put my nose at his temples. He smelled sweet and musky; I loved his smell. And he was my favorite person. Our lack of sexual chemistry continued to puzzle me.

"Babe..." Cliff said.

"Yeah?" I murmured.

"Do you think you're a lesbian?"

My body froze. Completely.

"What?"

"I... It's just that..." Cliff stuttered, obviously ascertaining from my paralysis that I wasn't going to agree with what he had just said.

"Oh. My. God. Did you just ask me if I'm a lesbian?"

"I didn't mean anything by it," he said quickly. Too quickly.

I laughed, but the sound coming from my mouth was abrupt and hard. "How could you not mean anything? You said ... that you think I'm a *lesbian?* Wow, that is really an odd question, Cliff. For my husband to ask."

"Cliff, what made you think that now, specifically?"

"Let's just drop it."

"*Drop it?* You just came out in the middle of nowhere and asked me if I'm a lesbian, and then you don't want to talk about it? Gosh, that's crazy. Hmmm, would that turn you on?"

"It was just a thought. Calm down," he instructed, as if I were a pet dog.

"I don't know; it doesn't sound like 'just a thought' to me," I yelped back, horrified.

"Mila, forget it."

I couldn't.

....

I continued to make attempts to meet Cliff's needs. But I felt stupid lying on my stomach and reading while Cliff masturbated on my back. This act was so impersonal; it was as if I could have been anybody – another woman; a sex doll; a slit in the ground.

If I had been Jenna Jameson – one of Cliff's favorite porn stars – I'd beg him to keep on "...fucking my ass." I could imagine it: "Fuck my ass, baby," I'd whisper over my shoulder as I arched my back. I'd flip my blonde extensions and pucker my glossy lips seductively. "Harder, baby, harder! Faster! Yes, yes!!" Jenna would yelp.

Into the quiet of the room, I uttered,"...Cliff...?"

"Yes?"

"Here; let's do it, if you want," I offered, touching his pajama clad leg tentatively. So much for channeling Jenna.

"I want you to attack me, not just try to play a part," Cliff responded, genuinely hurt.

I got up out of bed and went into the kitchen for a pint of ice cream. Tears streamed down my face as I tasted the cold, creamy chocolate. What a cliché I was.

....

"Yes, yes, yes – that's right, that's perfect," Dominic moaned. He lay on top of me, his eyes wide open and staring into mine. "And how is it for you? Is it too much?" he pressed.

I shook my head no.

"I am so in love with you, my darling," Dominic whispered into my ear.

This man's confidence, and his openness about his feelings, scared me. And drew me in.

We were in a small, dark room at Chase, Dominic's workplace. It was a supply closet, and it was full of notepads and boxes of staples. If someone walked in on us, Dominic would lose his job. But there would also be a certain cachet to it – other men would be impressed by his sexual exploits. Talk for the water cooler, to be sure.

And what would I lose? Just then, I didn't want to think about it. By crossing the line of infidelity, I'd lost the protection of being part of a unit: man-and-wife against the world. I had entered the uncertain territory of the unfaithful. And wasn't there a ring for the unfaithful in *The Inferno*? I felt the jab of something in my back – a tape dispenser – bringing me back to the closet floor.

There were other locations – two months' worth of them. Bathrooms. Many bathrooms. We met for Japanese food in a funky restaurant in Chelsea; in the din of the techno music and with crowds present, nobody ever noticed us going to the back together. There were hotel bathrooms – the single "handicapped" ones in the four-star hotels on Park Avenue. There were taxis. There were outdoor spaces on the river, and in Central Park. And there was his room in Brooklyn, inside a third-floor walk-up he shared with a married couple.

It all seemed so artsy and free-spirited to me: Dominic made love as if he were directing a theater production. He would light candles, and give massages. "Just relax and enjoy. Feel the energy we're a part of; it's all meant to be. What is, is," he'd whisper.

At these words, I didn't know whether to laugh or cry: The man didn't recognize his own grandiosity. I knew he was flying high, yes, but I didn't mind the ride.

Dominic simply loved to preach, to inspire. "Fear; everyone is motivated by fear, Mila, and this is a disaster for art," Dominic told me one day. "Artists must only act from a place of courage and passion. Don't you see?" he challenged. "You must; you are an artist."

"I think so," I murmured back, only vaguely understanding. By this point, we had been seeing each other for several weeks. And – I was afraid. Afraid of the compulsion I felt to keep up the charade.

But I also wanted out of this charade – I just didn't know how to stop. And did I only desire to end it because I was afraid to see where this choice would take me? And too, what should I do about Cliff? Was the only courageous choice the truth? Should I tell him of the affair?

That day as I stood in my bathroom, I brushed my teeth and thought about fear. Fear was certainly familiar to me: My father was always afraid of being fired by one of his American bosses who did "not understand him." My mother was afraid of exotic tropical viruses finding their way to my New York City apartment. And as for me – wasn't I afraid when I decided to go to law school? Wasn't I afraid of uncertainty when I asked that Cliff buy me a ring? Were all my decisions wrong? Had I lived a life lacking in authenticity? And was I afraid now to face the fact that I was having an affair? Was I afraid to admit to myself that there was no turning back, that I couldn't undo the facts?

I put down the toothbrush and turned away from the bathroom mirror, my cheeks hot. I went out to my bedroom and climbed under the covers; I was alone, as Cliff was still at work. I thought back to college, to my favorite seminar, "Adultery and the Russian Novel." The class's professor, Svetlana Maximova, was six feet tall and rail-thin. I remembered how she would speak in a thick Russian accent: "And Tolstoy vaz breeliant! You see, Anna had to die; zere vas never anover ending for an adulteress, condemned forrrrever to live a life vizout paaassion. And vaaat is live vizout paaassion?? Naasing, I propose to you, absolutely naasing!" Svetlana would say with conviction, taking a deep drag of her clove cigarette to punctuate her analysis.

When I read about Anna and Emma Bovary, and the Lady from the Chekhov story, I had gotten them. Perhaps that was because of my Russian blood: Russians got darkness. The characters in the stories wanted romance because they wanted to feel alive. They needed romance because they needed to feel alive. I too had felt the tragedy of the desire for romance, although I knew that breaking structures led to tragedy. I understood the precipice of emotion always beckoned, and it could be like standing on a balcony or a moving train and having that urge to jump. Life was really like that — you could leap off into the unknown at any moment. And the people who did not leap, who would not leap, and who never understood the inevitable pull of an abyss, would say you were mad if you did.

After years of being afraid of this exact possibility inside of myself, I jumped. To Dominic.

CHAPTER 3 – IN THEORY

One day, Dominic told me that his ex-girlfriend Sara had broken his heart. They were college sweethearts who had dated for ten years. She was a dancer; he was an actor. She had left him for an investment banker. Her choice had devastated Dominic – and made him angry. He thought Sara was shallow; that her choice had been about money.

This plot sounded familiar. The play he had given me to read was his thinly veiled revenge fantasy – where the poet gets the investment banker's girl.

As I got to know Dominic better, I learned more. Because we weren't "officially" dating – he referred to me as his "married girlfriend" – he was actively looking for a relationship. And during our time together, he'd had several dates with one particular woman he'd met online. Dominic told me although the two of them were falling in love, her ex-fiancée would not disappear from her life. "Is he really an ex?" I asked. Dominic said he wasn't so sure. Eventually, the man threatened to hurt Dominic if he wouldn't quit writing love letters to the woman. That was when she broke things off with Dominic.

"Her loss," Dominic said to me.

I felt jealous of her. She was available – I was not – so I couldn't expect Dominic not to date. And yet I bristled at the mention of other women.

Yet another ex had recently called Dominic out of the blue. Turned out they too had broken up because of a jealous boyfriend.

"But Dominic, did she also already have a boyfriend when you first met?" I asked, incredulous.

"Yes; we had such a special magnetism, my sweet," he explained. "You can't deny love's truth."

Despite Dominic's proclivity for unavailable girlfriends – I was at least his third – I was impressed with his pronouncements. He was a person of faith, I thought; love was his religion. And romantics made their own rules.

....

Another time, Dominic showed me a book of poems he had self-published. The title was, *A Tune From the Outside: Poems D'Amour and Emptiness*. I kept the book on my bedside table and poured over it late at night as Cliff sat at the computer in the other room working on a screenplay in the little free time he had.

Alas, Dominic's poems were meandering – and sometime nonsensical – compilations of words and images. There seemed to be a central theme though: The writer was a vessel of love and purity traveling through a cold and unappreciative world. Seemed to me Dominic had a chip on his shoulder.

I didn't tell Dominic that's what I thought. Instead, I wrote appreciative notes in the margins: "So raw. Your voice is important!"

One poem in particular called out to me: *"I'm your Superman lover – better get me while you can. Don't walk by, your head held high. Better be free."*

If I had been taking one of my English lit classes, I would have critiqued, "The poet is enamored of love and of himself. The work shows hubris; narcissism, perhaps. The instability of the images may reflect some inner instability of the author."

I might have concluded this, had I taken just a moment to think. But I was too busy. Busy phoning Dominic, seeing Dominic, writing Dominic, reading Dominic's work. My critical faculties were suspended, held hostage to mounds of florid verse and sweaty lovemaking in a twin bed in a Brooklyn walk-up.

CHAPTER 4 – TANGO

So much for living authentically: The two months of sneaking around had made me miserable.

I had never lied to Cliff about anything. *Anything.* I felt ashamed, and wanted the secret meetings with Dominic to end. And yet I couldn't stop. The affair, the passion, the intensity, had a life of its own. And, after so many years of not-right or non-existent sex, it was a relief to feel sexy, to be sexual. Unlike Cliff, Dominic didn't love porn, and he didn't think there was something wrong with me the way Cliff did.

As my life increasingly became gray instead of black-and-white when it came to men, I defended each man to the other. When Dominic spoke with derision about lawyers and bankers, I said he was bitter, and that they weren't all the same. I told him Cliff was sweet and caring and sensitive, a great friend and a supportive partner. I mentioned that our sex life was not great, but did not say more. I did not want to embarrass Cliff.

When Cliff began to bristle at the mention of yet another example of the wondrousness of the poor poet I knew, I explained earnestly that Dominic was a hardworking artist, a generous mentor.

A few weeks after Dominic and I started to tango, Cliff sensed my aloofness. He asked me to go to the Bronx zoo for a day.

"The zoo, Cliff?" I asked. "Why?" Cliff did not particularly like zoos or animals, and had never wanted a dog – a creature that would depend on him for food and vital functions.

"I thought it would be nice to do something romantic."

"Let's think about it," I said flatly. But when I heard the lack of enthusiasm in my voice, I cringed. *When did I get so mean?* I made sure we planned a day to the zoo – but then it rained.

And when it did, it was like an icicle had landed in my heart. Like in Hans Christian Andersen's *The Snow Queen*, a book I loved as a child, the evil mirror broke, and a small piece lodged inside, distorting sight and freezing the heart. Everything I saw from then on was crooked.

....

Things with Dominic intensified. I felt like I was almost sleepwalking through my life — as the affair had a life and rhythm of its own. Dominic called me six times a day and left long messages about how much he missed me. And yet we saw each other daily. Had sex daily.

We would meet for lunch during Dominic's break from Chase, at a diner way on the East side, almost at the river. We ordered the same thing every time: a grilled cheese for him and half a Greek salad for me. We'd split the check. I would look around us and imagine everyone knew we were having an affair. And then I imagined all the men and women around us were also having affairs; who else went for lunch in such an out-of-the-way place?

At 5:00 p.m., when the temps at Chase left for the day, I'd meet Dominic near Bloomingdales and we'd take the subway to Brooklyn together. We'd kiss on the train. This was reckless behavior, yes, but who would I know on the after-work train to Brooklyn? All the people Cliff and I socialized with would still be at work, or they would take taxis instead of the subway. Dominic and I would spend an hour at his place, and I would rush home to meet Cliff for dinner.

I was getting tired of the busyness. Something needed to change, but nothing did by itself, and so I was caught in this new routine. Then Dominic left. He went to Paris for a few weeks. He'd lived there on a grant after grad school, and considered it his spiritual home. While he was there, Dominic created a multimedia theater piece about Sartre. The piece became popular, and he got some critical acclaim. In Paris, he felt appreciated as an artist.

With Dominic gone, a weight lifted. I felt happier than I had in months. Out of sight, out of mind. I felt as if I were breathing again; that breathlessness resulting from our afternoon trysts was gone. The stress of watching time —the end of Dominic's lunch break; the start of my dinner hour with Cliff — was gone too.

I began to feel close to Cliff again. What a relief: We could make it. We'd figure out the sex thing together. *Cliff and I had just needed some time,* I thought. I now had hope for our relationship.

Then Dominic reached out to me from across the ocean: A postcard from Paris arrived — a beautiful card, with a painting of rows of foxes drinking tea in mid-air. "It's magical here!" the card proclaimed.

I hid the card from Cliff; I wanted him to think that Dominic and I had just grown apart, and not that we were no longer speaking just because he was out of town. Cliff had become more uncomfortable with the presence of Dominic in my life, in my mind. He no longer cared to discuss projects I was doing with Dominic, or my thoughts about Dominic's latest production or article. I sensed he was becoming suspicious. Even for Cliff, so preoccupied with his work, there was suddenly too much Dominic in my life. Too much, too often.

When Dominic called and said he was considering staying in Paris for the year, I realized I wanted him to. But then he texted — "change of plans, back on 10/17, your b-day!"

I decided that would be the day I would end our affair. So I agreed to meet Dominic at our diner for lunch, to tell him in person.

When we met, he was ecstatic. "I've missed you terribly, my butterfly! Here, open this." He handed me a small gift wrapped in pink tissue. The card said: "Life with you is technicolored." And inside the tissue was a glass mosaic butterfly.

"Thanks, Dominic. This is sweet," I responded, thinking to myself that Cliff never brought me little sweet things. He wasn't romantic like that. No, Cliff would say, "Just tell me what you want, Mila, and I'll get it." And he would. He was generous — he just needed to be prompted. So what that he hated Valentine's day and other forced displays of affection? Cliff was romantic when it counted. He was there for the big things — supporting my acting career; spending more time with my parents than maybe he would have liked.

"Dominic, I've been wanting to talk with you," I started.

"Let's not talk seriously now, my sweet," Dominic said sternly, his voice tight and his eyes narrowed. "I've just had a long flight. I'm tired."

I knew he knew what I was going to say, and he disapproved of my idea. I bit my lip; I didn't want to hurt him on my birthday. We decided to meet up at 5:00 p.m. that afternoon, as had been our routine before Paris.

When we met at his place, I couldn't find the words. I was miserable when he first touched me: "Dominic, this has to stop. I cannot go on. I feel just..."

But I didn't finish the sentence. Dominic was slipping off a bra strap and massaging my neck. I closed my eyes. His touch felt good. Warm, confident, and masculine. He wanted me, and he let me know that. And I wanted him. I enjoyed our physical interludes.

After, we lay together, spent and satiated.

"Oh, I have the most wonderful news!" he exclaimed. My friend Peter is producing an evening of theater about love, loss, and tragedy. I would love to be able to direct the piece you showed me."

Dominic was referring to an experimental poem play I had written about a couple separated by the 9/11 tragedy – the boyfriend perishes in the collapse of the twin towers, and the woman is left to mourn and wonder what could have been. The play came from a deep place within me, and was the kind of work I yearned to create. Inspired by Dominic's love for poetry, if not by his actual mediocre poems, I had made the piece more experimental – with the voices speaking in the dark. It was a monologue for two people, and I was proud of the piece.

"Wow, Dominic, that's great. Who would act in it?"

"You and me, naturally."

"Well... I'm not sure, Dominic. I don't think that's right. The male voice is based on Cliff. And anyway, I thought it may be good for us to take a break from working together for a while," I gulped out.

Dominic's mouth curved down slightly, and his eyes narrowed. He said in a quiet, measured voice, "Do whatever you want. But it's a great opportunity, and you're talented, Mila. Your work should be seen." He stared at me then with a slight smile, and he put his hand on my heart. "Courage, Mila, courage," he whispered into my ear.

I didn't believe Dominic cared only about my work now. I was aware he didn't like rejection.

Suddenly, I noticed the time: It was almost 8:30 p.m. It was time for my birthday dinner with my parents and Cliff! I threw on my clothes and ran out to find a cab.

I arrived at the restaurant, an intimate Italian in Tudor City, just as Cliff pulled up in his car from work. He kissed me on the cheek. "You look wonderful, babe," he said.

It must have been the sex making me glow. I excused myself to run into the bathroom; were my stockings inside out? They were. *Good catch, Mila*, I said to myself.

At the white linen table over their plates of fancy pasta, my parents beamed. They adored Cliff, and were grateful to him for giving me a good life and for being a great son-in-law. "To our beautiful children!" my mother said as she raised a toast.

The dinner went on, as per the usual: My father claimed he did not understand the fancy descriptions on the menu, and so Cliff reviewed the choices with him. My father pointed out that he liked simple food, like that he had had in Belarus after the war. And I reminded him, as always, that there was actually no food after the war, only potatoes. The four of us laughed as if I had never said that before. Cliff then ordered pasta with three types of mushrooms for my father, as he always did. We were a family.

Over dessert, Cliff gave me a birthday card. This was a first. He never got me cards; he always said they were too sentimental. I was touched.

It was a child's birthday card, of a dog holding balloons. "You are Special!" the front said. Inside the card, Cliff wrote, "To my wonderful best friend and wife! I am so proud of you and your many talents. I know you will succeed in whatever you choose." My head ached. It was all too much.

The next day, I broached the possibility of Dominic doing my experimental play to Cliff. Dominic's words had stayed with me: I *was* talented. I *deserved* to have my work seen. And Dominic could help me become the artist I knew I was.

Cliff winced at the mention. "I thought you and Dominic were done working together, Mila," he said, looking straight into my eyes.

I saw his pain. But I couldn't let his feelings in at that moment. Suddenly, I was desperate to do the play with Dominic, and nothing else could exist.

....

The day of the theater event came. The play was a success, and a woman from the audience approached me after the applause. "Thank you. It was lovely." She hesitated. "I – I lost my close friend. Your piece captured something very real – the longing…" She choked up.

My eyes welled up. Instinctively, I reached for her hands. "I am so sorry," I offered.

I felt that this moment was the reason I wrote the piece: to touch someone like this, to create stories that resonated with an audience. I felt very connected to the world in that moment – and to my purpose, which had really eluded me at times.

I was proud of my writing, and had wanted Cliff to see the performance, as he always did. This time, though, he had refused to come: "I don't want to see him on stage with you," Cliff had said, shaking his head, and looking tired and sad.

In response, I had hugged him. I felt sad too, but I was also excited to show my work. I promised Cliff that this would be the last project with Dominic. I promised him I meant it this time. I promised myself the same thing.

It was my mother who came to the production, in a show of support of me. She always came. Although she had been devastated when I hadn't pursued a full-time law career right after graduation, once she saw I was serious about pursuing acting, she did what she could to help.

I had been telling Mama about Dominic for a few months now: how talented he was, how interested he was in my work. I knew, though, she did not approve of the amount of time I had been spending with him, or the fact that we kept on finding ways to work together. But this did not stop her from coming.

"That man, this… he is Dominic?" she whispered to me after the performance, revealing some negative feelings through her tone and furrowed brow.

I gulped. "Mama, if you came to criticize me, please don't," I begged. I couldn't take any more pressure. Not now. I wanted to enjoy my excitement about the play. I knew she was upset there was no baby; that instead, there were plays in East Village basements and late-night taxis from Brooklyn acting rehearsals. It seemed Mama's only child, the perfect child, the straight-A student who had needed no curfew, was failing where it counted most: in real life. I didn't want to hear criticism of Dominic, because I was already ashamed enough that I had let this weird and decidedly scary relationship continue.

"Milochka, I love you. I want you to be happy, but this, this," she responded, obviously struggling for words, "this whole thing is wrong. You have a husband," she cajoled, her eyes burning into me.

High from the production of the play, I could only answer her loving and formidable concern with, "Mama, I love you too."

At this point, Dominic approached to say hello. Mama took a step back before she whispered angrily to me, "I can't speak to him!" and left the theater. I felt confused for a moment – this lack of support from my best fan left me feeling odd, displaced for a moment. My mother could bitch and moan a ton, but she never really left me. This was a first. I was treading in new territory. But I didn't have time to reflect, as Dominic squeezed my elbow and whispered into my ear: "Let's get out of here and celebrate our success!"

....

I went out with Dominic after the show instead of going home to my husband. I fully intended for this to be our goodbye dinner.

Dominic ordered us a bottle of wine. He held up a glass: "In celebration of the beginning of our artistic relationship!" he toasted. "And I have a very special gift for a very special person."

Dominic handed me a purple book. It was a book of love letters between a fictional couple. I was taken aback. Did he expect me to take this book home? What if Cliff found it? I thought the gift was too indiscreet, and disrespectful of my situation. A book about lovers... from my lover. I felt the urge to run out of the restaurant, to escape him, us, and the crazy charade we were playing. "Dominic, I can't accept this," I protested.

I wanted to say that this should be our goodbye. But I didn't say that. For some reason, I was stuck in the momentum, stuck in Dominic's expectations of me, lost in the sea of complications I had created. I was now paralyzed in the intensity of it all, a deer stuck still in the headlights of an approaching car.

"Mila, I would be extremely hurt if you didn't take this small token of my affection," Dominic replied with a mean set to his lips.

I didn't want him to disapprove of me. Cliff was so busy with work and withdrawn into his own world that I had ended up letting Dominic occupy a large space in my mind. His disapproval would make me feel almost worthless.

Perhaps if he had reacted less strongly, I would have felt justified in my decision. If he had cried or looked sad, then I may have found the space to escape. But his confidence, his dismissal of my reality, hypnotized me all over again.

I took the book home and hid it in my dresser.

....

The next week, I told of the affair to two girlfriends.

"Mila, this is terrible!" said Jessica, who had been my best friend since we attended Hebrew school in New Jersey. "You and Cliff are so good together! You've been inseparable for years. Can't whatever is going on be fixed?"

"But Jessica, you don't know everything."

And this was true: Jessica did not know that Cliff and I did not have sex for almost as long as we had been married. People never know what goes on behind closed doors – this most trite of comments made the world go round.

"Cliff loves you too much, Mila," said my Brazilian friend Lara. "You must not tell him of the affair. He will never forgive you." Lara was more practical – do what you need, but don't let your husband know. Lara knew men – she was adorable, and had hordes of suitors when we were in law school together at Columbia.

"He and I have always told each other the truth," I proclaimed proudly. *Except for the last month, of course,* I thought to myself.

"The truth is overrated," advised Lara. "Be smart; keep quiet!"

I told my mother. She cried. "Mila, an affair! I knew it. I knew it when I met him at the play." Even though my mother had anticipated the truth, she still had questions – valid questions, questions that kept me up at night. "But why? I don't recognize you! How can this be?" she asked. "You are my daughter! You are not a liar!"

This much was true: in ordinary circumstances, I was not. There was no explanation I could offer; my mother was right. We were honest people.

Were. I had let everyone down.

"I am sorry, Mama," I responded quietly.

My mother looked at me, looked into my eyes, and tried to bring me down to earth. "But you and Cliff love each other," she reasoned with me. "Remember how you waited for years to be married to him?"

My mother soon discovered I was not open to reason when it came to Dominic. And since I did not respond to the perspective she offered, she tried to scare me: "You are heading for a divorce. Nobody will ever love you like Cliff does – you two grew up together," she reminded me. "As a divorced woman, you'll take a big fall in status. And you'll be sitting home alone."

"Mama, that attitude is so old-fashioned!" I laughed. Although I had been afraid with Dominic, I dug in now, feeling pressed to defend myself. Yet my argument was almost academic: I didn't truly want to get divorced. I didn't even know any divorced people. Besides, I had been spoiled by Cliff's devotion. When it came to Cliff, I felt invincible – like he would be there when I came out of this fun exercise in free-thinking. "And anyway, who cares about invitations to parties? That's no reason to stay in a marriage," I continued flippantly. I always had to push back at Mama, even when, somewhere deep inside of me, I agreed with her. She just had so many strong opinions, especially about my life.

"I know that, Milochka! I am just warning you that if you and Cliff split up, your life will be very different. You have no idea. I've lived longer, and I have seen some things," she warned me. "Stop this... this craziness and whatever you do, do not tell Cliff anything. Ever. What he won't know will not hurt him."

I looked at my mama, at this woman who had left all she had known to forge a new life in a new country with her husband and daughter. Mama has been married to Papa for over thirty-five years now.

"We're in America; this isn't Russia," I responded cheekily and dismissively. "It's the new century, you know."

....

A few weeks passed with more clandestine lunches, brainstorming sessions, and emails about the theater and plays.

Cliff and I went to a wedding. His eyes were teary when we danced. "What's wrong, baby?" I asked this man of mine who rarely got emotional.

"I want to remember this night," Cliff proclaimed.

I pressed against him; I felt slightly afraid, but shook this feeling away.

My intuition was right: The next day, Cliff looked through my texts when my phone was charging in the kitchen. One text from Dominic said "See u soon my manatus." This endearment had been meant as a joke; Dominic and I had gone to the Manatus diner in the West Village on the closing night of our collaboration.

When Cliff saw the text, he demanded to know the truth. "Only the truth will serve us, Mila," he pleaded. "If you love me, you must tell me," he insisted.

I hesitated. I heard my mother's and Lara's advice to keep quiet; I heard Jessica's words about fixing things with Cliff.

But I did not want to cover up the affair. I knew I could have said the text was nothing – just a silly exchange. I could have blamed it on Dominic; said he was crazy to write something like that. And Cliff might have thought so; there was no real evidence of anything improper at all. But I wanted for Cliff – for years my best friend, my soul mate – to know me fully, even if what I were to show him was ugly. That part of me wasn't all of me, anyway; just a terrible singular transgression I had done. We would overcome this, and be that much closer. Cliff had always said I could tell him anything. We were special.

I told him.

The rest of that night passed in a blur. We ended up in bed, clutching each other. We kissed fervently and Cliff pulled off first my tank top, then my thong. He entered me tentatively, but then pressed into me with all his body weight until I could hardly breathe. We had sex. Cliff was more passionate than he had ever been before. His open eyes met mine. This is what I had wanted for so long.

Cliff cried then, and he held onto me so hard I was afraid he'd hurt me. "How can you do this, Mila, how?" he asked, searching for an answer.

I had no answers; I didn't know the "how" myself. I did not realize I was capable of this – of any of this. Nothing had been planned; it had just happened and taken me along. It felt like inside, I wasn't in control. But I couldn't explain this to Cliff.

"Why? All I ever wanted was to take care of you!" he wailed as his tears landed on my face. "Why? Why didn't you want that?" he howled as he collapsed on top of me.

"I did want that, Cliff, I did! I am so, so sorry," I howled back. "I love you!"

And I did – despite the affair, despite the infidelity, and despite our lackluster, sometimes animalistic and impersonal, sex life.

....

I swore to Cliff the affair would end. I even called Dominic to tell him it was over. And I stopped seeing Dominic completely – going cold turkey.

But weeks after, even though we no longer saw each other, I could not stop calling Dominic. That's when I realized – it wasn't the man I wanted; it was his world.

God knows why I was so intent on belonging to a poseur theater scene. But I was, and my life with Cliff, with all the couples we knew, with my parents, and with all our plans and goals, seemed stifling. My Upper East Side apartment felt sterile and suffocating. My brain spun and my head pounded. The only thing that made me calmer was dialing Dominic's number, even if I did not speak with him.

And I didn't. I dialed Dominic's number over and over, only to hang up repeatedly before there was an answer. I tried to explain my new revelation to Cliff; I pleaded with him to understand that I could not control my actions. I even thought of going to Brazil to stay there a while with my friend Lara; I needed the allure of a new land to physically tear me away from the quicksand that was now New York.

December came, and Cliff told me he needed some time to think. He was planning on going to California over Christmas break to visit his family by himself. If he did, this would be the first time in years that I didn't go.

When I told my mother of his intentions, she screamed. She told me I had to fly out there, even if he said he did not want me to, even if it meant I went out there on a different flight. "What does he need to think about out there without you, Milochka? You must fight for your marriage! Go find him! If you're not together on New Year's Eve, it will be the end of your marriage," she said ominously.

Then my father got involved. I don't think my father knew of the affair exactly, but he was aware that something was very wrong between Cliff and me. And when he heard Cliff and I would be apart some of the winter break, he pleaded with me, "Milochka, please do the right thing! Cliff is a good man!" That's when his voice broke, and his eyes welled up. "Do it for Mama and for me; for our family."

"Papa, don't be so dramatic!" I interrupted, cutting him off.

That night, I found I couldn't sleep. I was devastated to see so much pain around me, and confused by the pain I was experiencing inside myself as well. I was so worried that something strange was happening to me, signaling something I didn't fully comprehend.

So the very next morning, with my mother's fatalistic words and my father's plea ringing in my ears, I told Cliff I wanted to go with him to see his family.

He said that if I did, we would be over.

I didn't let up though, and after enduring much of my begging, Cliff finally agreed to my coming out for the last two days he would be there. Secretly, I was happy to go for only two days. Having Cliff on the other coast meant I could spend a few last days with Dominic in wintry New York City. The affair was technically over, so that meant I couldn't be friends with Dominic any longer; Cliff would never stand for that. But I longed to be a part of Dominic's theater scene again. And like an alcoholic who has gone cold turkey but who yearns for a few swigs from a vodka bottle for a few minutes – I wanted a momentary relapse. I wanted to be up, not down. Without Dominic about whom to obsess, there was only the sad truth of my very damaged relationship with Cliff and all the hard work of getting my marriage back to speed. I wanted – no, *needed* – a small fix of fantasy. Dominic would be that escape.

And then, symbolically, Cliff and I would resume our marriage in Los Angeles on New Year's Eve.

That's what I wanted to believe.

....

On the thirtieth of December, I stood on the steps of the Brooklyn Library. Dominic was inside renewing some library books as I spoke to Cliff on my cell. I told him, "Baby, I think you're right; it makes no sense to fly back and forth for just forty-eight hours."

"Why, Mila?"

"Well – it's as you were saying, the tickets are so expensive, and we will have time together next weekend when you get back."

Cliff was silent for a few minutes. "Where are you, Mila?"

"Just returning some books." I wasn't lying. But I knew Cliff would imagine I was at the Barnes & Noble on the Upper East Side, not at the Brooklyn library waiting for my former lover.

"Okay, don't come," he said, but so quietly I could barely hear him. As I hung up, I heard my mother's voice: "Fight for your man!"

Some fight I was putting up... Why couldn't I just do the right thing?

I needed to run away from Dominic right now, leaving him to search for me out here on the steps of the library when he came out with his pile of books. After all, I no longer found his frequenting of the library so exotic – why didn't he just go to Barnes & Noble like everyone else! He would be angry if I just left, but soon, he'd find someone new anyway; someone more simple; someone who had less to give up. Then he'd tell her stories of his "married girlfriend" whilst he complained of husbands always getting in the way of "true love."

But I stayed put on the steps of the Brooklyn Library until Dominic came out.

....

Cliff called on New Year's Eve: "Happy New Year's, babe," he said. He was still trying. Maybe that's what he had decided to do after consulting with his family? I reminded him I was staying home that evening, and would be awaiting his return on the 2nd.

And that is what I had planned: I would stay home on New Year's Eve. I would read a book, take a shower, write in my journal.

But at 10:00 p.m., Dominic called. He insisted I should not be alone on New Year's Eve. I responded by telling him I needed to be alone, to think.

A half hour later, he called again. "Are you sure, my darling Manatus?"

I was no longer sure. As if hypnotized, I got up, put my journal down, got dressed, and met my old lover at a party. We drank punch out of paper cups and stood under fluorescent lighting with strangers. I felt completely empty. At 11:55 p.m., we got stuck in an elevator going up to the roof for a midnight toast.

Another bad omen.

....

New Year's Eve was the last time I ever slept with Dominic. There was no more magic; I felt too crazy about the situation to be present. Each thrust seemed to be a dagger stabbing me into the ground. My eyes were red with tears, but in the scented candlelit room, Dominic didn't notice.

Cliff never found out I spent New Year's Eve with Dominic. And so, New Year's was not the last straw. Although things with Cliff were tense when he came home on January 2nd, we tried. During the month of January, I did not see Dominic at all.

But I or he or we – I'm not sure who – couldn't stop the calls. I contemplated throwing out my cell phone, but I thought this would be too drastic.

I guess I did not want to admit I had so little self-control.

When the actual last straw came, it was as mundane as it could be. My parents had come over to our apartment for brunch on the last Saturday of January. As the four of us ate bagels and lox, I was distracted, but tried to focus on the conversation. My father and Cliff were talking politics.

"You're completely out of toilet paper," my mother yelled out from the bathroom.

"I'll go get some!" I hollered quickly, and jumped up. I grabbed my coat.

Outside, it was cold, but the chill felt good. I walked the few blocks to our local CVS. When I went inside, my phone rang; I saw that it was Dominic. I let it ring.

I walked up and down the aisles of CVS, lost in my thoughts. The phone rang again. This time, I picked it up.

"Dominic, we can't talk anymore. I am sorry," I said quickly before I hung up. But then I felt bad about my abruptness, and I called back. I explained that this was a difficult choice for me, but Cliff and I were really going to try hard to make it work.

"As you wish, my Manatus," Dominic replied, his tone stoic. And that was that.

I returned to the apartment. Once inside, I looked about; all the people dearest to me were right here in this dining room. I was safe with them.

I did not know then that this would be the last time the four of us would ever be together.

"Mila, where is the toilet paper?" my mother asked.

I felt confused; where, indeed, was it? I had completely forgotten to even get the paper. But that explanation wouldn't cut it. "Oh, gosh! I left it at the store," I replied, shrugging my shoulders dismissively.

Cliff and my mother looked at me strangely. My father was reading the paper, clueless as to what had just transpired. I looked away.

"I'll go get it," Cliff said quietly. He sounded weary. "You stay in; it's freezing outside." And off he went.

He did not make eye contact with me. This frightened me. My unusual absentmindedness had affected Cliff. My actions had been unlike me, and for the rest of the day, he was contemplative as he did ordinary things: read the *Times*, drafted a contract. I asked if he wanted to watch a Woody Allen film, something he loved, but he just shook his head and said he had a deadline.

The next morning, Cliff was already up when I awoke. "Cliff?" I called out. He entered the bedroom. He looked tired and rumpled, as if he had had a bad night's sleep. "How was your sleep, baby?" I asked.

"I didn't sleep, Mila," he said, shaking his head slightly at me, and making me feel as if I were a child who didn't get the lesson. This Cliff was not familiar to me. "I waited until you slept. Then I checked your phone. You texted him. You called him. You talked to him. Isn't that why you forgot to bring the toilet paper back, Mila?"

I gave no answer, and he was quiet for what seemed like an eternity. And then, "Mila, you have to leave. All you can think about is him." He sounded matter-of-fact now, no question in his voice, no slight quiver that would indicate he was hurting.

I spent the rest of the day crying and explaining and begging and yelling. I don't think Cliff cried; he just held me through most of my tears, still in the habit of caring about my feelings.

That night, the Superbowl was on. I never liked this very American celebration, and Cliff never insisted that we go to Superbowl parties. But tonight, he said he was going to a party, and by himself.

I pleaded with Cliff to stay home to talk.

He didn't want to.

"I love the Superbowl, Mila," he proclaimed, shutting the front door closed behind him as I sobbed in the bedroom.

Chapter 5 — Home Again

Cliff insisted I had to move out; "temporarily," was how he characterized it. I told him that it was impossible: Not only did I have nowhere to go, but I wanted to stay married, and I didn't want to work on our marriage from some other place! He said I owed him at least this, and vaguely hinted that things would be much worse if I didn't leave. I caved; I told him I would move out for one month. He said he couldn't promise it would only be one month, but I didn't hear that. I heard, "One month, and we will be back to where we had been before Dominic."

Moving meant I would lose my office space, since I tutored kids out of our apartment. Too, I would become dependent on Cliff financially for rent, and behind the eight-ball in terms of the limited work I did. I had no savings account, and no separate checking account. Cliff took care of all things financial, and we had never gotten around to organizing things properly. Things would get harder fast. Still, *my suffering would be a means of making it up to Cliff*, I thought. *Perhaps if I suffered enough, he would realize I was hurting as much as he was. That this mess we found ourselves in was not created cold-heartedly; that it was a colossal, crazy upheaval wreaked by a woman who was temporarily lost — his wife.*

I still loved Cliff, and I was sadder than I had ever been in my life.

....

The weekend before I was to move out, we went to look at an apartment on the West Side. Cliff's coworker Ronald was moving out to Connecticut because he and his wife were having a second child, and they needed a larger place to live; he had offered us the chance to rent their apartment at a bargain price.

Cliff and I had been considering moving into their space for several months. B.D., that is: Before Dominic. And although Cliff said it made no sense to go see the place now given our upcoming separation, I urged him to stick with the plan: "Honey, this separation stuff is all just temporary, right? The apartment will be great for later, after we work everything out," I declared.

So Cliff called Ronald and made an arrangement for us to view the space. It was a cold but sunny Sunday afternoon when we went. Ronald and his wife Laura were a nice couple; they had been to our wedding, and were happy to offer to pass their great New-York-City deal on to a couple whom they liked.

We moved about the space, ooh-ing and aah-ing.

"Cliff has said you will be expanding your family soon too," Laura said at one point with a sparkle in her eye.

I smiled at her, although inside I felt broken and sad. "Yes, we will be," was my response.

Laura then said, "Let me show you where we set up our little one; it's a wonderful place for the baby to sleep." She led us to an alcove next to the couple's bedroom; a crib stood inside it.

"We keep all of our little boy's toys inside one of our closets too. I never thought I'd voluntarily give up closet space in this city!" Laura laughed pleasantly.

"It's a wonderful space for a baby, darling!" I exclaimed to Cliff. He just nodded, keeping completely silent.

Ronald and Laura looked at Cliff, then at me. Did they sense something was amiss?

No, no, they probably are just wondering if Cliff and I are going to make an announcement about the expansion of our family, I thought.

After the tour, Cliff and I went out to dinner near Lincoln Center. I only poked at my chicken Milanese; our time together now felt awkward.

"Honey, I don't want to move out. This is all crazy. I want to work things out, and move to Ronald and Laura's apartment together," I said.

"Mila, there will be no more discussion of this now," Cliff said.

I forced a piece of chicken down my throat. That willpower I had always admired in Cliff was working against me now.

....

The next evening, the movers came. There wasn't much for them to cart; I was only taking a few things and one suitcase. Cliff was not there to say goodbye. Coincidentally, he had been invited to a boys'-night-out dinner at Peter Luger Steak House to celebrate the finalizing of a friend's divorce. In our old life, Cliff may have not gone – or invited me along, despite the fact it was boys only. But he was now on the other side.

It felt as if he were exiling me. I was being thrust outside of the walls of our city, into the wilderness. From Manhattan to Brooklyn.

....

I waited until after the move to tell my mother of it.

"What! Mila, are you crazy?" she screamed, her tone one of complete horror.

"Mama, it is not open for discussion," I said succinctly. Not that my mama was trying to discuss anything with me right now; she was sobbing on the other end of the phone.

I put on a confident front: "A month apart is the ideal solution. I need time to get my head together, and calm down. And I will be closer to the new job I got with the judge. Let's see how that goes. Cliff and I can get back together when I'm feeling settled."

Wanting to secure a steadier income, I had applied for a law clerk job with a federal judge in Brooklyn. Surprisingly, the judge had offered me this position. At the interview, he told me he loved the theatre, and was happy to help an actress who wanted to get back to the law. That was my story – and by virtue of that lucky coincidence, it worked. Of course, the timing of my trial separation was not great – starting a new job from a place of bizarre limbo was hardly sensible.

My show of confidence didn't inspire a similar confidence in my mother about the decision.

"Milochka, a separation is not how you work on a marriage!" she said once she was able to quell her sobbing. "I know this is America and you are the younger generation, but things don't change all that much when it comes to keeping a marriage together. How do you know the separation will be for only one month?" she probed.

"Well, Cliff said that it would be for one month or two," I responded with conviction.

"What about your evening tutoring business? What will you tell the children?"

"I'll tell them I'll just tutor them at their houses. Since it's only for a few weeks, I'll say we're doing a renovation."

"And what about the job with the judge? You will work all day in Brooklyn, and then travel to their homes in Manhattan at night, and then go back to Brooklyn? All those subways!"

"Subway" was a four-letter word to my mother, who preferred to go everywhere in her newly leased Lexus.

"Milochka, you need to take better care of yourself than that; it'll be too much for you."

"Mama, it will be good for me to work hard, and to become more independent! You'll see; it will be okay," I stressed.

Together, though, my mother and I decided it was best not to tell my father what was going on. Since I would be back in my apartment in just a few weeks, there was no reason to worry him about my temporary situation.

Still, when I hung up the phone, I knew I had not fully convinced my mother about the timeframe.

....

The room I had found was in Brooklyn. It was close to where Dominic lived, so this neighborhood was one I knew. When I called Dominic to tell him about my decision to move out from Cliff's and my apartment, he was cautious in his support. "Are you sure this is what you want, Mila," he said. I didn't tell him that this choice was hardly mine. I was too embarrassed at the mess I'd created and mortified that Cliff was essentially making me leave. As for the fact that I would now be so near to Dominic, well, Dominic didn't try to discourage me. I convinced myself that the location of my temporarily home was just a coincidence, but even I wasn't sure. Did I want to be near Dominic in some very small way that I didn't even understand? I didn't want to look so deeply inside my exhausted mind and heart.

I didn't think for even a moment of how this scenario might appear to anyone looking in: as if I was the one who wanted to leave Cliff so that I could live closer to my lover. Only later, when my mother pointed this out, did I realize that I had made yet another stupid move in a series of unplanned and increasingly bizarre acts.

I rented the room from Don, an African-American activist I had found online. I would be paying him $900 a month (rather than $1,200) because we agreed I would walk his dog Marvin G. twice a day. I told Don at the start of our arrangement that I would be there for one month at the most.

On my first night in Brooklyn, Dominic came over with a bottle of wine. In his hand was a card: "Welcome to your new life, Manatus!" he had written on it. "I know you will discover yourself – the butterfly will emerge out of her cocoon!"

Still a bit shaky over the sudden expulsion out of my apartment, I was not excited to host Dominic. My whole situation, and this very night, felt a little surreal. Previously I may have wished to spend a whole night with Dominic instead of having only an hour before my dinnertime with Cliff, but that had been just a fantasy.

Be careful what you wish for, I thought to myself a thousand times that night.

I told Dominic I did not want him to stay over: I needed time to myself.

....

Two days after I moved out, I'd had enough. Suddenly, the intoxication and rush and anxiety of Dominic fell away, and reality returned. It was like I had been on vacation, and now longed for home. Or, I had been an actor in a movie, and just been playing a part or role that was not the real me.

Now that I had returned from the Dominic trip I had been on, I was learning that my actual life had disappeared. This feeling was terrifying.

I looked around the room that was now my home. The ceiling was peeling, and there were some pee stains on the carpet where Marvin G. had relieved himself. I felt almost confused: How did someone manage to extricate me entirely from everything that was familiar, that was mine? And had that someone... been me?

When Dominic came over on the third night, I felt irritated. Suddenly, with the gauze of make-believe gone, with the excitement of the affair lifted, I felt a slight dislike for this stranger who just keep chattering on about the issues he was having at Chase. I looked at closely at this man who had been my lover: Everything about him now bothered me. His long hairstyle was too unkempt, his platform shoes revealed an annoying sign of vanity, and his fired-up eyes signaled some emotional imbalance. *Why couldn't he stop droning on about how shitty everything was!*

And why did he never spend more than ten dollars on me at one time! I was sick of receiving all these little trinkets, cards, and glass butterflies from him. Why had he never treated me to even one cheap dinner? Too, I was bored of repeatedly looking at his headshots to help him choose the "best one;" tired of reading his crappy poems; and fed up with his incessant critiques of avant-garde theatre.

That night when he tried to kiss me, the revulsion I felt had an almost physical component to it. "No, Dominic, please, this is so wrong!" I protested as I squirmed away from him on the couch.

"What is so wrong?"

"This. Brooklyn. This room. You. Me. You and me. I have no idea how the fuck this all happened!" I practically shouted, wanting to hurt him.

"Manatus!" he objected as he tried to tickle me.

The use of this nickname startled me; didn't he realize I was upset, and my words serious?

"Can you please stop calling me that stupid name!" I hollered at him.

He looked momentarily confused, as if he didn't recognize me. "Mila, you wanted independence. This is good for you," he said weakly.

"How do *you* know what's good for me?" I pointed out in a snide manner so this... this *acquaintance* would get *gone*. Who was this crazy-looking artist, and how had he disrupted my life so?

Dominic finally sensed something of my attitude. "I refuse to talk to you when you are in this mood," he said in a high, strained tone. He walked toward the door. "I am sorry about your change of heart. But don't blame me for your mess, Mila," he said shakily, his eyes glistening with both tears and fury.

A little compassion came over me as he moved to leave. "Dominic, I am sorry. I just... It's just. It's too much," I called after him.

Then I lay down on the mattress in my new room. I tried to go to sleep, but I couldn't. I was in a panic. I needed to go back to my apartment, my life. This room, this old mattress – it all made me feel like I was crazy. Or actually, it felt like I was not crazy, for the first time in several months. There had been some crazy person who had wrought havoc on my entire life, and now I was back to me, and I was someone who realized what I wanted was Cliff and our old life together.

I called Cliff, but he would not answer the phone. So I called again. And again. Repeatedly. Finally, after what seemed like an eternity, he called back.

"Cliff, baby, I am so incredibly sorry. Please, I want us to try again. I would like to come home. Tonight."

"Mila, it's been only two days. That is not enough of a break."

"But how long is enough, Cliff?" I asked.

He answered with, "...at least one month."

"I can't do that, Cliff," I protested.

"Mila, it is the only way we have a chance," he insisted.

With tears in my eyes and a shaking body, I hung up the phone.

....

Over the next two days, I called Cliff over and over for forty hours straight. I was in a completely panic over our separation and what was going on.

But his phone just rang and rang. I left about ten messages total, each one more desperate-sounding than the last. And as I waited for him to call back, I lay in bed, running scenes of the affair in my mind like a movie.

It's our anniversary, and Cliff and I are to meet his mother and her friend for a Cezanne exhibit at the Met. The summer rain is pouring down, and Cliff is already there. But I am still at home, engrossed in reading Dominic's poems, when Cliff calls to ask me if I'm on my way. "Honey, I'm just feeling a little tired. Can I call you in twenty minutes?" I say when

I realize I've lost track of time. But even after we hang up, I can't get the energy to leave my bed, and the poems. It's like I'm paralyzed. I end up never making it to the museum.

Flash-forward.

It's September. Cliff and I are away for a weekend in upstate New York. We are staying at a small hotel right near an aerodrome. We go to dinner that night, and we feel close. But I know that in my bag is a phone full of messages from Dominic, telling me how he can't wait to taste the soft skin of my shoulders, that he needs to see me, feel me, and smell me every day.

Flash-forward.

It is November, and I remain full of illusion. I tell Cliff that I need to find myself, to exist apart from the unit that we are. I tell him I want to live in Rome or London or Rio for a year. "Is it Dominic?" he asks. I say no, that it's just that I have never been on my own, so I have never understood who I was. I am grasping at straws, testing Cliff's patience, his love.

My mind went on and on like this, flashing onto hundreds of little scenes — a minute here, a moment there, a dinner with Cliff, a drink with Dominic, a fight, a kiss. The images were flashing inside my brain faster and faster, and I could barely keep up. And over and over, the scene of Cliff pinning me down and shaking me on the night I told him of the affair replayed in my mind; his hot tears kept falling on me, over and over.

I could not sleep. I felt great empathy for Cliff, and I imagined how scared he was as a little boy when his parents told him they were going to divorce.

My crying turned into shrieking. I could not contain my sadness; it was riding over me, and it was larger than me, commanding my muscles and my nerves. The experience was exhausting. I left more messages for Cliff, each one begging him to meet me in person.

Finally, on day four after our separation, at one in the morning, Cliff called back. He agreed to a ten-minute meeting.

I left the Brooklyn room right away in my pajamas, too scared that if I took any time to change, Cliff would change his mind. It was too late for the subway, so I caught a taxi to the Upper East Side.

When Cliff opened the door to our apartment, I burst in and fell to the floor. Overwhelmed with emotion, I grabbed onto his ankles and sobbed on the floor.

"Get up," Cliff commanded, showing not a scrap of feeling on his face. His voice was strong and even. He shook his head as if in disbelief. "You're pathetic." His lips curled around the "p" in "pathetic" as if he would spit at me.

Even in my distraught state, I could tell Cliff was relishing this. *Payback time.*

I was pathetic, but I did not care. I was acting on instinct.

"I love you. I'll always love you! I am so, so sorry, Cliff! I don't get it; I just don't get what happened to me. I just... I couldn't stop," I wailed.

The man who used to love me stood there and said simply nothing. Nothing.

"Won't you say anything?" I implored.

He wouldn't.

"Please, say something to me!" I shrieked, acutely aware that I was now a rejected, groveling lover.

"I don't love you anymore," Cliff responded flatly and steadily, standing straight and tall. He was in stark contrast to me, a prostrate, quivering mess on the floor.

I clutched onto his pants leg as I sobbed even more. He shook me off, a grimace of annoyance washing over his face.

Annoyance, I thought, *that's bad. He doesn't respect me. He is done feeling anything for me. That means as a couple, we have no hope.*

"For God's sake, Mila, stop being such a baby. Stop humiliating yourself; it's unattractive. Get up and go," he spat out in a voice full of contempt.

I pushed myself to my feet and wiped at my eyes. Then I looked around at my apartment. I noticed all the pictures of us together were off the walls and lying face-down on some tables. My favorite image – of the two of us sitting on the piazza in Sienna – been replaced by a picture of Cliff and his sister. I felt hot; my chest got tight. I grabbed onto the dining room table for support.

"Time to go," he said crisply, looking at his watch. "Ten minutes are up."

I looked down at the dinner table. Just a few weeks ago, we had sat together at this table, eating Thai takeout from across the street. We'd had shrimp curry and green papaya salad.

"But Cliff, this is my apartment, too," I reminded him. After all, I had left for the Brooklyn room with just some clothes and a few books. A lot of my things were still around me – I saw the pink-framed picture of entwined lovers we had found at a Turkish bazaar, the art deco ashtray sculpture from the nearby junk shop, the soft plaid wool blanket from my uncle which we used when we watched all those Hitchcock movies. My new laptop had finally arrived too – it sat on the dining table in its packing case.

"The sooner you treat this separation seriously, the sooner we'll resolve everything. So you need to go now," he replied.

Somehow, these words sounded a little promising to me. I thought his use of the word "resolve" meant we'd solve things – figure them out. I left without taking more than a week's worth of stuff – I even left the laptop. *I'll be back*, I promised myself. *We will be back together soon.*

Cliff had something else in mind, though. And little by little he carried out his plan.

....

A week after our face-to-face, Cliff texted me for my set of the apartment keys. He said his friend was visiting from San Diego for a week, but he was too busy right now to make a set for him. I agreed to drop off my only keys to our apartment, glad to show Cliff he could rely on me.

When I got to our place, Cliff was not home. Our doorman avoided my eyes – a good thing, as they were full of tears.

I went back to our apartment one week later to ask the doorman if he had anything for me. But there were no keys. I waited to hear from Cliff for a few more days. Nothing. I was slightly afraid to ask Cliff outright for the keys. When I called, I found he had disconnected our apartment phone. And he wouldn't answer his cell phone. The wall was up: Cliff was now unreachable to me.

I was devastated. I stayed put on the mattress for several days, getting up only to go to the bathroom and walk Marvin G. I drifted in and out of sleep, although mostly, I was awake. I felt as if I had just come off a red-eye flight, except that there was no rest arriving for me.

I had just a little bit of reasoning left – enough to call the judge's chambers where I was to report for work next week. Even though it was only my first week of work, I told the judge I was sick. Although I had never smoked – except for a brief bad spell in college – I went out and bought a pack of cigarettes. I chain-smoked the entire pack before I went out to buy another.

I wrote old-fashioned letters to Cliff in my journal. Hundreds of pages of letters. The letter-writing made the time pass. I was entering a time warp where morning and night merged into one long sad day. In part the letters said:

"Please Cliff, there was no malice on my part, no bad intentions, I meant no harm."

"My dearest darling Cliff, words cannot express how I love you and how ashamed I am..."

"My love. It's 6:22 a.m. now, and I'm still awake. I think I'll stay home today from work – sick days are for heartache too."

"Cliff. Why, why, why? I hate myself for being so ugly to someone who trusted me and loved me and gave me their world!

"Cliff, my darling, I beg you for a chance to redeem myself. Let's not AMPUTATE our past."

"Cliff, this is the worst nightmare in the world – please God, don't let this be true, please. My dearest, please accept me back."

I never sent these letters, just let them pile up in a mountain in the corner of this strange Brooklyn room where I found myself. I knew I would not send them – I was more talking to myself, or to God.

I still dialed Cliff's cell phone out of habit but he never answered it. I sent pitiful texts. I left voicemail messages at his work begging him for redemption. I wrote more letters – though none of these long treatises on the sad demise of our great love and friendship ever made it to the mailbox. Cliff's impenetrable silence broke me: I became disoriented from lack of food and sleep, and I let my cell phone battery die. After I did not answer my phone for a day or two, my mother took action. She told my father about the separation, and the two of them came to see me. The bell rang, but I couldn't will myself to get out of bed to go downstairs. I heard my landlord Don let them in.

They found me lying on my mattress. The window was open, and about twenty cigarettes were on the ground immediately outside of my window.

"*This* is where she is living? Where is the *schwartze's* room?" my enraged and horrified father asked as he turned to my mother.

Even in my disarray, I cringed at the word "schwartze" — a word that means "black" in Yiddish but is often used as a derogatory Russian-Jewish term for black people. Over the years, I had tried to convince my father that *schwartze* was not an appropriate term to use, even while aware his use of such a pejorative term was not personal: it was representative of many Russian immigrants who had not encountered black people living in their homeland and so were unfamiliar with them.

"Papa! Don't say that, please!" I objected, emerging out of my fog briefly.

"Since when does she smoke? Filth, only filth, smokes! I quit smoking so I could live longer for her, and she smokes now?" my father said, almost crying.

"Anton, let's talk about it later; it's okay," my mother said to calm him down. Then she turned to me. "Milochka, you have to get dressed and brush your hair. It's already 3:00 in the afternoon," she instructed.

"What day is it, Mama?" I asked weakly.

"Friday," she said. "Let's go."

Friday. I shook my head weakly — so much time had disappeared. The letters on the floor showed where the week had gone, though — the mass of smelly cigarette butts outside the window too.

I got up and off the mattress.

"She is so skinny!" my mother exclaimed in true fear as she spied my figure. Then she looked at the papers crumpled all over the floor. "What is this?" She picked up one of my discarded letters to Cliff.

"Mama!" I cried out. "Give it to me!"

My mother saw the "Dear Cliff" salutation, to be sure, but she just handed the letter back to me. She looked tired.

We went to a restaurant, but even though I had not eaten for days, I was not hungry. I sat tearing my napkin up into smaller and smaller pieces until my mother grabbed the pieces away from me.

"Mila, you haven't eaten a thing!" my mother chided me. "And what do you keep on mumbling?"

I said what I had been saying over and over again out loud: "We love it! It will be great for the baby."

"What baby? And love what?" Mama asked, genuinely perplexed.

"The apartment; the one on the Upper West Side we could get at a bargain price. We were just checking out a new apartment a few weeks ago. Oh, Mama, I fucked up!"

"But I don't understand, Milochka. There is no baby – right?"

"Well, Cliff and I were *trying* to have a baby! And I screwed it all up. I know now that he knew when we were in that apartment that I would never set foot there with him and a baby. But he still said, 'We'll think about it,' to the owners. Mama, he knew then I wouldn't be back. He *knew!*"

"Shhhhh. Milochka, have some tea," my mother advised as she looked at my father with renewed concern. That was when she decided it – just like that.

"Mila, you are not staying in Brooklyn another minute," my mother declared.

I didn't even argue. I was happy to be wanted.

My parents took me to their home in New Jersey. They yelled at each other during the entire drive home – about stupid things, like my father taking the wrong exit when leaving Brooklyn, and about the fact that my father did not want to take a sick day to spend a day at home with me. He never took sick days – and had about a thousand of them left at his job. This infuriated my mother: She felt he was giving away too much to his American bosses. And she let him know it.

This was how my parents were: they yelled instead of talking. Normally, I would keep quiet until I could not stand the noise anymore, and then I would yell at my parents to stop yelling. It was like a vaudeville routine, and we had been practicing it since I was about five.

This time though, I just let the yelling go on. I didn't have enough energy to break it up. I was playing a new part in a new play: the messed-up adult child coming home in a truly pitiful state in the back of her parents' luxury sedan.

It was a glorious suburban homecoming.

CHAPTER 6 – AWASH IN MISERY

My first few days in Fair Lawn passed in a fog. I cried from the moment I awoke each morning until I crawled into bed at night.

I slept in my parents' bed. For the first few weeks, I slept with my mother; my father slept on a couch. I don't know why we decided on this arrangement, but it did help me fall asleep. I was now a hurt, bawling baby, with no sense of how to soothe myself.

During the daytime, I chain-smoked in the backyard. I walked around the house like a zombie, picking things up and putting them down. I kept on seeing Cliff in every room: *Here is where we would sit when we read the paper. There is the hammock where he loved to nap.* Everything looked the same. But nothing was. There was a ghost in the house now. Cliff's dining room chair remained empty.

Periodically, I would scream out something like, "How could I do this! I stabbed my best friend! I am a monster!"

This would cause my parents to exchange more alarmed glances.

"Milochka! Please!" my mother would cry as she ran to hug me and calm me down.

Almost every night, I would have night terrors. I'd sit straight up in the bed, yelling at the top of my lungs, with my heart beating a million times a minute. At first I would think there was a strange man in bed with me. It always took several minutes to realize that I was okay, and that there was nobody in bed with me except my mother.

Other times, I'd wake up shrieking about the baby dream Cliff and I had shared. For that's what it would remain – a dream. "It will never be! I ruined it. I ruined our baby! And for what?" I would cry into the night. I would turn to my mother, who would be awake by now. "I don't deserve to live; I've killed my love. I don't want to live without Cliff."

"Your whole life is ahead, Mila! Don't tempt the gods," my mother would respond. "Try to sleep, *solnyshko*; life is long."

Hearing that familiar endearment made me feel momentarily happy. It was a glimmer of light fighting through the dark fog that enveloped my mind and made my body feel like lead.

"But I don't want to live without him, I don't!" I would insist.

"Well, he wants to live without you. He's living without you right now."

Mama was right: Cliff was living very well without me. He still refused to answer his cell when I called, and seeing him was out of the question. He had unfriended me on Facebook. My texts landed nowhere.

Nor would Cliff answer my parents' calls. So my father began composing a letter to Cliff in which he implored him to give all of us – the family – a chance to survive this storm. But he never got very far when it came to the writing; his English was too poor. And truthfully, he didn't seem to want to write that letter. After all, he was also a man, and he had some pride. He was in a tough position – having to beg his son-in-law to forgive his wayward daughter.

My father, mother, and I all felt like Cliff was the king and we were the peasants begging for a royal pardon. But despite his previously close relationship with my parents, Cliff did not want to grant them an audience.

One time my mother did manage to get him on the phone. When she tried to explain my regret to him, he cut her off to say, "I cannot tell you the details of what your daughter did to me, Raisa, but if you knew, you would understand that what she did is unforgiveable."

End of story. Cliff had moved on.

"Milochka," my mother questioned me, "were you really so horrible that there is no erasing of the past?"

"I guess so, Mama," I called back over my shoulder as I headed for a pack of cigarettes.

....

Mama kept my coming home a secret from most of her friends and neighbors.

My arrival had not been easy on her; in ordinary circumstances, she would spend hours on the phone discussing a horde of daily minutiae with her Russian friends. But she was embarrassed about my situation, and hoped the separation and the *meshugas* – craziness, in Yiddish – would end.

But word got around. With my finally starting the new job at the judge's in Brooklyn, I took the commuter bus to Manhattan every day. So I ran into people I knew on the bus. Others learned the news when I called them to beg them to intervene with Cliff on my behalf.

One person I spoke to was my law school friend Sarah, a stay-at-home mother whose husband Thomas was friends with Cliff. She went into shock over my news: Despite the fact that affairs seemed so common in literature and the newspapers, they were not a part of our world, and I may have well been the antichrist. Everyone adored Cliff, and could not imagine why I would do anything to hurt him and our relationship. It didn't help that I couldn't adequately explain the reasons, the events, and the energy that had pulled me in and made me part of something outside of me. I didn't get it fully myself, so it was hard to convey the lack of control I felt to a perfectly content woman who made dinner for her husband and tucked her children into sleep each night.

I knew that Sarah was thinking the same thing as many of my friends when she first heard the news and about my separation: "Thank God it's not me!" And when our conversation ended, she wasn't ready to tell me if she would talk to Cliff on my behalf.

The next day, I called Sarah again to see if she would intervene.

"I am sorry, Mila," she said in quiet, steady tone. "But Thomas and I do not think..."

"Thomas? What do you mean, Thomas?" I asked in total shock.

"Well, of course I spoke to Thomas," she confirmed.

"Sarah! But this is such private information, and Thomas is a man and knows Cliff, and besides, I haven't even told you one-tenth of the story! It is very complicated!" I objected, although it was after-the-fact, and already too late.

"Oh, but I tell Thomas everything, Mila. He is my husband," she responded, her voice sounding a touch smug.

I could tell she loved saying the word "husband." But then again, so had I. And I guess that's what made hearing it from someone else even more painful.

Besides, Sarah's use of it at this particular moment had meant even more – like she was indicating she had been smart enough to hang on to her safety net. I knew why, too: Sarah had always been afraid of everything, especially the possibility of being poor and single.

"And we just don't think it is right to interfere," she confirmed as we finished our call. "I am sorry, Mila, I really am."

After we hung up, I simply sat staring at my cell phone. My casting out from Manhattan had begun.

....

My mother, ever my staunch supporter, decided to travel down a new avenue for me: She called Cliff's mother. She explained my sorrow and regrets to Barbara, and reminded her about the sacred bonds of marriage. I listened to the call right next to Mama, straining to hear.

"I am sorry, Raisa," Cliff's mother responded sweetly in that fake California way she had. "But if my son doesn't want to pursue this relationship further, then that's what I have to support."

"Yes, Barbara, I understand you must be there for your son. But we all love Cliff as if he were our son, too; he's lived here close to us for many years! So it's not about just the couple's relationship. We are a family; our children are our family. If we all insist that they should stay together, maybe they can work things out. We don't want Cliff to be unhappy, but life is long, and this is their first real test," my mother reasoned to Barbara.

Barbara wouldn't budge, and eventually my mom hung up, exasperated.

Doors were closing before me, fast. We did not bother even trying with Cliff's father, as he lived in his own world.

I attempted to reach Dean, Cliff's best friend at work. Dean was a Jewish guy from New Jersey who worked in entertainment, so I thought he might feel some kinship with me. I left a crying voice message on his answering machine: "Please, Dean! Please have some pity. Please, would you call and just listen to me?"

He would not return my calls. But I know that he let Cliff know I was trying to reach him, because I received a text from Cliff stating,

"Leave my friends alone!" However, I was happy to have some contact from Cliff, no matter how negative.

One day I ran out of chambers into a private conference room down the hall to call Cliff; I simply had to hear his voice. Using a 'private caller' number, I got through, and when he realized it was me, he screamed: "You are a bitch, Mila, and you got what you wanted. Can't you see that I deserve some rest from all this shit!"

"Please!" I screamed back at the top of my lungs, right before I broke into body-heaving sobs.

Another judge's secretary walked into the room. "Is something wrong? I was walking by, and I heard…"

She didn't finish the sentence. I certainly must have looked scary, standing there wild-eyed with mascara running down my face.

"No, no, I'm okay," I responded. But I couldn't meet her eyes, and I looked down at my feet. "Please, I just need a minute."

She respectfully left the room.

Another time, I called Cliff on his cell for three hours straight on a Saturday night until he finally answered.

"Cliff, darling, I am so, so sorry. I have letters I have written… I want to give them to you!" I begged, in the hope that my written words could do something my verbal utterances could not.

"Do not call me anymore," he said as he cut me off.

In the background, I could hear people laughing. A woman's voice said something. It sounded like one of his law school friends, Kayla. I'd always been threatened by her – a gorgeous, thin brunette who did public interest law. I heard more laughter before the line cut off.

In utter dismay, I sunk down to the kitchen floor. My mother came into the kitchen to make a cup of tea when she found me there.

"Mila, what are you doing! Get up!" my mother hollered before she reached down and physically lifted me off the floor.

....

I still could not eat. I would sit at my parents' table for breakfast, but the sight and smell of the food always made me sick to my stomach. My weight continued to plummet. I called in sick again to the judge – said I had a stomach virus and needed a few days off.

My parents were at a loss. They had no idea how to help me. And I needed help. A doctor friend of theirs told them to take me to a psychiatrist; that I needed some help climbing out of the blackness. My parents drove me to see a Russian shrink.

Misha Krasnov, an attractive fifty-year-old man, lived in a new luxury condo on the ocean in Brighton Beach. At our first appointment, we sipped Turkish coffee and smoked Dunhills on his balcony. I told him I had had an affair. I told him I had lost the one thing that gave my life meaning – Cliff. And I cried. Oh, how I cried. I said I had no idea how it happened, and that the past few months had passed in a blur.

Misha prescribed Lexapro, an antidepressant. He said it would work in a few days. He also gave me a sedative for nighttime – this would make the screaming go away.

After a few days on this new regimen, I slowly began to feel some relief from the depth of my sadness, and I returned to work. But when I went in, I guess I looked so emaciated that my stomach virus excuse seemed plausible to everyone who looked at me.

I don't remember getting much done those first few days back at work. Mostly, I sat at my desk, rereading the emails I'd composed to Cliff over the past month. At lunch, I would run out and go to the park outside of chambers and smoke cigarettes. I'd eat a chocolate bar and drink a coffee for lunch, and then count the days down to my trek to Brighton Beach for my twice-weekly appointments with Misha.

The subway to Brighton Beach would take an hour and a half, but I enjoyed the ritual: The subway was full of people different from the ones I'd known and seen in Manhattan the past few years. There were many Russian immigrants on board; these were my people! So in many ways, the ride made me feel like I was coming home.

When the train would arrive at the beach, I would feel a lightness surrounding me. I received a rush of energy from people going home to their families or doing pre-dinner grocery shopping. There were groups of teenagers who stood joking around, and old people sitting at their stoops to pass the time.

As I walked to Misha's place, the ocean was on my right. Catching glimpses of it in between the streets gave me a sense of hope. This was something big and beautiful and fresh and blue, and it was so much bigger than me, and the maelstrom of emotions I had swirling inside of me. The sight of the water made me feel that this, too, will pass. And the chemical assistance provided by Misha didn't hurt.

Misha's twenty-eight-year-old girlfriend Lena, a computer programmer with great hair, fantastic breasts, and remarkable culinary skills, would cook in the kitchen during my evening appointments with Misha. Always, it seemed, a fabulous smell of lamb shish kebobs and borscht would waft over to my nose as I wept about my life. With a broken relationship, no place to live, and a weak nervous system, I already felt like a colossal failure, but Lena's overall excellence at what seemed like *everything* made me feel even worse. *Things will improve*, I reassured myself each night as I waved goodbye to the uber-productive Lena as she set the dinner table. I then crawled away from my session to take the R train to Port Authority.

Misha felt no sympathy for my predicament, and his advice to get past my heartbreak could pretty much be summarized as: do well at your job, get in shape, swim, do yoga, and have sex without any emotional attachment.

"But Misha," I would protest, "I don't think I can do that — have sex indiscriminately, like many men can."

To my objection, Misha would simply shrug his shoulders before he told me I should think of myself as a shipping port — and that when I became a "good port," a great and perfect ship would come in! And in the meantime, I could get ready for that great ship by hosting a few "inconsequential" ships (or something to that effect).

....

After several weeks on the Lexapro, I felt calmer. I also felt less sad. I still cried for Cliff every night, but I decided to try Misha's healing advice. I decided I was ready to try some male therapy, and apply the "Be A Great Port" theory. I began to feel excited about the possibility of finding a new man.

Hyped-up and sped-up, half-weepy and half-ecstatic, hyper-sexual and realizing no men were rushing to my parents' backyard, I decided to give online dating a try.

Chapter 7 – Sportsguy

I created a very basic profile for myself on JDate, a dating site mostly for Jewish singles or for singles who wanted to date Jewish singles. I didn't post a picture at first, and chose the name "Rose17" to honor my grandmother on my father's side who had lived with us in Riga. I admired her – she had raised three children on her own after losing her husband in World War II – and I thought using her name would inspire confidence in me. I chose the number 17 as it was my birthday day, and I was hoping I would meet someone soon, before the day arrived when I turned thirty-two. I included a brief physical description, and a few words about my being newly "separated" and needing some new "friends." I also wrote that I came to the United States from Latvia when I was eight, and that I spoke Russian.

As I did not have a picture, few men wrote to me, and so I picked a few random profiles and wrote to them. I even picked a few men who also had no pictures up. Only later did I learn that profiles without pictures were without pictures for a reason: either the men were cheating, fat, or bald – or cheating, fat, *and* bald men.

The first guy I wrote to was Sportsguy – a weird choice for me, because I had never particularly cared for sports. His profile also boasted no picture. I thought, *Well, Larson, my college boyfriend, was an athlete, so why not try this guy?* And so we exchanged a few emails and then our numbers, and he called to chat one evening.

In that first call, we exchanged the basics – schools (mine was Columbia; his, a small college in Florida), and jobs. As for living in New Jersey with my parents, I tried to hide that embarrassing fact.

Sportsguy was from Long Island. He had a low, interesting voice, and he told me he was "built" and loved to work out. Really, I hardly cared; I was just so happy to hear a male voice at night after work! Did it truly matter that he knew nothing about Kundera or Chopin or Fiesole or Ephesus or Epistemic Implication or the Heidelberg Uncertainty Principle? It was hot, it was the summer, and talking to him was better than hearing my parents' weeping in their bedroom about the loss of their son.

During our second or third call, it was late, and my parents were sleeping. I was talking to Sportsguy and getting ready to go to sleep in my old bedroom alone (progress!) when it started.

"So, what are you doing?" Sportsguy asked me casually.

"I'm in bed," I answered, thinking nothing of it.

I soon thought something.

"In bed," he repeated.

"Un-hunh," I confirmed.

"Do you like it?"

I wasn't sure what to make of that question exactly. "It's okay." I didn't really like it. It was my old teenage bed, for God's sake! He didn't know that, of course, and would not know that. That was the beauty of late night phone calls with strangers one met online.

"Just okay?"

"Yeah." I thought for a second; I now had an idea of where this was heading. So maybe I should be more flirtatious? "Could be better."

"Oh yeah, how?" he said suggestively.

"Don't know," I responded, naïve but still curious.

"Would it be better if I were there?"

"Maybe..."

I wanted to add, "Although my parents probably wouldn't like it," but held off on apprising him about my pathetic living situation.

"Would it be better if I were touching you?"

"Maybe..." I answered, playing a little hard-to-get.

"What if I were touching you reaaaallllly gently?"

He was now going beyond friendly phone chit-chat. But I was dying for a little excitement, so I continued our conversation.

"Maybe...."

"If I was touching your breasts, caressing them?"

His voice was husky and deep now. I gulped. But it was nice to be caressed, even if only with his voice.

"I'd have to think about it," I teased back. *Well, that wasn't so hard.*

"If I was touching your stomach, tickling it?"

He was almost purring in a slightly menacing way now. Like he was a large cat playing with a small mouse.

"Sounds promising..." It was a feeble attempt at encouraging him, as I was, in fact, beginning to like this.

"If I put my hand on your ass?"

Wow, he got right to the ass!! I didn't expect that. Silence on my part.

"And what if I put a finger in your ass?" Okay, this was it; I could choose to cut him off. But I didn't.

"Hmmm...," I said now in a sexier way. I was letting myself go. But quietly, lest I wake up anyone in the house. I put my hand under my gown. I may as well go for it and have some fun.

"Would you like that?" he pressed on.

"Hmmm...yes." I said with more assurance now. "Yes."

So, here I was, a thirty-something-year-old woman getting off to some stranger's voice on the phone in the dark of her parents' house! In her – my – old bed. How illicit and creepy and kinky!

What I wasn't picturing, of course, is that somewhere in Long Island, some strange man was also getting off by imagining his finger in my ass... Well, blame it on the Lexapro.

Nightly calls and texts like this soon became par for the course. At his urging, I even texted a picture of me in my red lacy underwear. I felt a pang of regret the minute I pressed send. After all, I had no idea who he was, really. "Wow!" he texted back. "U R So Hot!" This gave me a small – about ten seconds long – ego boost. Yes, ours was no epistolary exchange of deep thoughts. And on the morning after, I still would wake up and get ready for work. My parents would do the same for their engineering jobs.

At sixty-five years of age, my father still woke up at 6:30 every morning for his job. My mother woke up at seven, and then drove to her engineering firm in New Jersey. I had forgotten during my time away from home – when I was away from my parents' daily lives – how hard they had worked all these years, and how hard they continued to work.

In the mornings, my mother prepared Irish oatmeal with berries and instant coffee, and made sure I took my pills. I must admit, I enjoyed being waited on hand-and-foot like this. But I still found riding the bus to Port Authority in New York City a bit embarrassing, as I had sworn once to never set foot in New Jersey on a permanent basis again. But now here I was, taking the New York City bus with all the other Russians and various suburban commuters at whom my Manhattanite-self had previously scoffed. And then, once I reached the city, I had to take a subway all the way to the judge's chambers, located in Brooklyn Heights.

I found the responsibilities at my job somewhat overwhelming. My job was to act as a senior law clerk, and at this point my legal skills were seriously rusty. As a law clerk, I would read the parties' papers, research the law, and write a bench memo to the judge recommending a ruling on the motion. I then would have to turn the bench memo into a written opinion. I also had to take care of small personal administrative matters for the judge.

Still, the first thing I would do upon sitting down at my desk was to log onto JDate or Facebook. And so far, the only connection I'd made was with Sportsguy.

....

There came a time when Sportsguy asked if I would like to meet him.

"I guess so," I replied over the phone, sounding very uncertain.

"I have an idea. My friends have this beautiful house in Quogue. They will be having a weekend party, and we can have our own room there," he proposed.

Hmmm... going to Quogue seemed cool. It was a summer resort located on Long Island, and I'd been there once already – to a fabulous house owned by one of Cliff's bosses. If I went with Sportsguy, it would mean a weekend away at the beach.

"Maybe; the idea sounds cool," I admitted.

"Yeah, think about it," Sportsguy encouraged. "We can relax, swim, or do whatever when we're there."

"Well, why not?" I decided.

Only after I hung up the phone did I think of several reasons "why not." For one thing, there could be rape by a stranger! Abduction! Murder! I could see the news headline now: "Internet fiend lures unsuspecting, newly separated Lexapro-ed woman to Long Island and she is never heard from again."

....

When I told my mother about my weekend invitation, she thought it would be "terrific" for me to get away for a free weekend in the beautiful Hamptons – especially after all the crying and smoking I had been doing all summer on her porch. And so I would go – with the male involved Sight Unseen!

Yes, that's right: I still knew next to nothing about Sportsguy, except that he was good at talking dirty. But none of that mattered right now; I would be meeting Sportsguy the following weekend in the small New York hamlet of Hicksville. He would pick me up there on Friday evening from the train station in an SUV, and we would drive to his friend's house together. On Sunday, he would drive me back to the city. We had a plan.

Even more importantly – I had a date.

Chapter 8 – The Ring

To celebrate my upcoming weekend away from the backyard, my mom and I did what any self-respecting mother-and-daughter team would do: We went shopping for a summer weekend escape wardrobe. As I was skinny now from months of non-eating, trying on bikinis would be especially fun!

I felt exhilarated. Shopping for bikinis represented some sort of normalcy, when nothing had been normal in our house for several months. Plus, it no longer seemed as if the future was a complete and horrifying mystery. Why think of how the last ten years of my life had been erased when there were Brazilian bathing suits and wraps to try on?

At Neiman Marcus, I picked out two suits: A black halter-top one with white shells that wrapped around my neck, and a brown string-bikini with pink appliqué flowers and gold beads. Each came with a small matching wrap skirt.

I stepped out of the dressing room in the brown one first. My mother beamed as if she was at my law school graduation again, and the sales girl clapped her hands in delight – "A perfect fit!"

I'm sure she was excited to sell $600 worth of *shmatas* (rags) in ten minutes right as the store was closing.

So, when *the* Friday in June arrived, I packed my suitcase in the morning, abuzz with anticipation. I didn't have to go in to work; I had told the judge I would be taking the day off – and he didn't mind, because he never came in on Fridays anyway.

When I was ready, I took the commuter bus to the city and went directly to get my eyebrows done. Just because I had been cut off from all our money by Cliff and currently slumming it in New Jersey did not mean I would give up my perfect arches. I also went for my monthly facial.

Once I was waxed and squeezed, I sweated in my new Theory t-shirt and black mini as I dragged my suitcase to Penn Station. There I bought a ticket to Hicksville, and I hopped on the train. I began to imagine a weekend of frolicking in a posh beach house with my sporty mystery man: Would he have curly black hair? Be wearing a polo shirt? Have a nice smile?

When the train pulled in at my stop, I hopped off, dragging my suitcase behind me as I scanned the parking lot. And there it was: The black SUV, just as he'd mentioned. I bounded toward the vehicle, licking my lips and flipping my hair. The door opened and ... wow, Sportsguy was nothing like I had imagined. He was of medium height, above average weight, and completely bald. He was wearing enormous black New Balance sneakers and a black running suit.

"Hey, sexy, what's up?" he said as he gave a wave.

I was speechless. Hearing that smooth night voice come out of the puffy man in front of me was disturbing.

"Hi ...," I greeted as I struggled to recall his name. "Jake – I mean, Jack."

"How was the train?"

"Fine," I uttered, although I no longer felt fine.

He was standing right near me now. *Oh no, he wouldn't try to kiss me, would he?* He leaned in toward me. *He might!* I turned my face, and he got me on my cheek.

"Great! Let's put your stuff in the back; hey, wait a sec, just gotta move the beer first."

As Sportsguy opened the trunk, I saw several six-packs of Coors Light.

"I made sure to get lots of beer; we just have to pick up the steaks," he told me.

"Great," I answered, thinking, *I hate beer.* I found this guy so, so... American! Yes, that's what it was! He was a typical American frat boy. Now, that wouldn't have been a big deal had we just agreed to meet for a drink or even dinner in the city, but I had agreed to spend two nights – the entire weekend – with this guy!

I climbed into the front seat and looked straight ahead; I couldn't face him. I suddenly felt silly and ashamed of how I had acted with him over the phone. *This guy must think I'm a sex-starved lunatic!*

Out of the corner of my eye, I saw his hands on the steering wheel. And then I saw it: The class ring. The very oversized class ring on one of his fat fingers.

I despised class rings. In my mind, this utter lack of taste and sophistication signified a moral depravity. Cliff would have never worn a class ring. Instantly, all the tension I was holding back exploded, and I let out a huge sob.

"What's wrong?"

"Nothing!"

But I was wailing like a banshee.

"What's up?" he pressed, his face turning a little white.

"I... I... I don't know, it's this whole... I don't know."

But I did know. It was that... he was so unattractive and foreign to me, and he had talked about sticking his finger in my ass with my own permission. I felt so cheated – and so cheap – at the same time.

I didn't want to hurt him – he hadn't done anything wrong – and so I blamed my sudden despair all on me: "I am," I sniffed, "...just not ready to date yet. It's too soon; I miss my husband!" I bleated, my nose running and my tears flowing down my face. "I'm so sorry; I was looking forward to this, but... but... I have to leave."

"You what?" he asked, his face turning an unattractive shade of red.

"I'm sorry, but I have to go," I said.

"Are you sure?" he pressed.

I nodded. Quietly. Miserably. And with conviction.

"We can grab a cup of coffee," he urged, trying to keep me with him. But I had already scrambled out of the car.

Outside the car, I heard his normal nightly tune reverberate in my head: *"How would you like it if I touched your....?"*

Oh, God, I couldn't even think it. I grabbed my bag and sprinted towards the station. I turned around once, when I was already on the platform, to wave goodbye. But he was gone.

Sportsguy must have been pissed off. His weekend lay was going back to the city.

....

I took the next train back to the city, crying most of the way. When I reached my buddy Jessica, she said, "Oh, Mila, I'm so sorry!" And she was. She was such a great friend. But the reality of her sympathy sucked too: I was sick of having her feel sorry for me. And just like everyone else, she was only human – so I'm sure inside she couldn't help but be grateful that it wasn't her life that was so derailed.

You also come to learn that when you hit bottom, your friends sympathize and mean well, but they all are busy on the weekend with their errands and plans and family. That's just life. I once had been busy like that too.

Meeting Sportsguy had been such a stupid idea in the first place: I had gotten into a car with a stranger I had met online only. Completely demoralized, I took the subway train to work.

Milton, the judge's deputy, and Ragani, another law clerk, looked at me with surprise when I came in at nearly five -o'clock on a Friday night, lugging my suitcase.

"Don't ask," I said, and flopped down into my chair. I was happy to have some mindless paperwork to do until my parents could pick me up.

So this was the inauspicious beginning for me: I was now on the runaway dating train.

Chapter 9 – Sleeping Over

After Sportsguy, I decided I needed to be more selective about potential boyfriends. Honestly, the thought of *not* dating did not even occur to me: the possibility of romance was the only thing that made the pain of Cliff recede into the background, if only for an hour or two. Besides, Misha the Russian shrink had suggested some casual dating as a way of forgetting. I was happy to try and put his port theory into practice. While the port was being prepared for a grand yacht, why not welcome some less important ships?

One Monday at work, Damian, a comedy teacher who ran the stand-up comedy shows in which I had performed occasionally, friended me on Facebook. From his status update, I learned that he was headlining at The Comic Strip. I decided to check it out.

After the show, Damian and I chatted. I told him that Cliff and I broke up. Damian was a guy who had flirted with me when I was with Cliff, but it had always been just pretend-flirting. Now that he learned I was available, he wasted no time: "Hey Mila, you want to come to my birthday party next weekend?"

"Sure," I agreed readily; I had no social life to speak of, now that all of the wives of Cliff's friends decided I was persona non grata, and our mutual couple friends were keeping low profiles. Sarah now no longer called after I had filled her in on my affair: She was too moral, and had had a life that had progressed too easily to allow her to sympathize with the mess that my life had become. To worsen matters, several of my good girlfriends had moved during the past few years, meaning Jessica was in Connecticut, Carla was back in her homeland of Chile, and Lara – my Brazilian girlfriend – had followed her doctor-husband to Oklahoma.

Damian's birthday celebration was at a friend's house in Astoria. Four actors shared the run-down house; it was one of these places where people came in and out at all hours.

At the party, I hung out with Damian and his friend Nelson, a sweet black guy with dreadlocks who danced in musicals on cruise ships and had recently performed on Broadway in *The Lion King*. Nelson's girlfriend was a skinny Hispanic girl who looked as if she were twelve. She had tattoos all over her arms, and wore pink leather shorts. We drank a vile red punch as we watched Nelson's video of *The Lion King* over and over. I only had one glass, but it was strong stuff, and pretty soon, the room was blurry.

It was already 11:30 when I realized that I had no way to go home: It was too late to catch a bus to New Jersey. Although my dad would have picked me up, it was a Tuesday night, and I felt bad about asking him to come out to get me so late on a weeknight.

When I asked Damian if I could crash, he was only too happy to volunteer an empty bed in one of the bedrooms. I called my mom to let her know.

"You're staying over in Astoria, Milochka?" she asked. "Is it a nice house?"

"Mama, it's not a big deal; it's just a house a friend of a friend rents. Remember the comedian-teacher Damian?" I prompted.

"Is he good-looking, this Damian?" Mama wondered aloud.

At this, I had to smile; Damian had always joked that he and Cliff were twins. And they did look alike: They were both thin, were six-feet-two-inches tall, and had heads full of jet-black hair. Out loud, though, I objected to the question: "Mama! I'm not sleeping with him; I'm just sleeping *over!* There is a difference!" I responded.

But there wasn't much difference, really. I laid down in the bedroom alone, at two a.m. Only a few minutes later, Damian got in with me. Soon, he was kissing my neck and pawing my breasts.

"Damian!" I squirmed as I shooed him away. "I'm trying to sleep."

But I didn't really mean it. I hadn't gotten used to sleeping alone yet. And even though Cliff and I had not had sex in years, I still had loved sleeping next to a warm body at night.

I found it was nice to touch someone, and Damian and I ended up making out that night. At some point, he took off his pants. I didn't sleep with him, but there are always permutations on fucking around.

I stumbled into work late the next morning, with only one earring and matted hair.

· · · · · · · · · · · · · · · · · · · ·

A few days later, Damian messaged me on Facebook to go to one of his shows again. I agreed: He was my only suitor at the moment, and something was better than nothing.

Onstage, he was good. He had one especially funny joke about Valtrex, the Herpes medicine. The audience loved him, and I felt happy being the date of such a talented guy.

After the show, we went out for a hamburger with some of his comedian friends. Everyone was bitching about the audience and breaking down jokes – analyzing what worked and what didn't. It was dull, being with these performers after the fact, but I listened and tried to nod appreciatively.

When we finished at the diner, it was almost two a.m. I was exhausted, but Damian said he needed to stop by his comedy office near Penn Station. He said it would only take a minute, and he wanted to get some headshots for a mailing.

At three a.m., we were still there. It turned out that Damian planned to package and mail his new headshots and resumes to a few comedy clubs.

"Damian, I'm tired," I explained politely. "Can't you do this tomorrow?"

Apparently, he couldn't. It was an acting emergency. I lay down on the couch in the office, and tried to rest.

At four a.m., Damian woke me up and said we could now go to his apartment in Forest Hills. We fell asleep as soon as we got there.

In the morning, I woke up and went to take a shower. A woman's robe hung on a hook. On the bathroom cabinet stood a box of tampons. When I saw the living room in the daylight, I realized there were pictures of Damian with a pretty brunette all over the room.

"Damian," I said, nudging him awake. "What's going on? Does a woman live here?"

"No, no," he mumbled.

I looked around; I saw now that women's clothes were strewn all around the bedroom.

"What's all this stuff then?"

"It's nothing," he answered as tried to pull me back into bed. But I demanded an explanation first. "Okay, okay! My girlfriend just left me to go back to Canada. She got on a TV show there."

Oh, I hadn't even known Damian had a girlfriend.

"Ahh...doesn't she...want her clothes?" I asked.

"Oh, they're hooking her up big-time with this show. Costumes and everything."

"But, are you still together, then?"

"Oh, no. The long-distance thing is not gonna work. I'm just holding on to her things until she makes some arrangements. She'll come back for them soon. It's the least I owe her; we were together for five years," he said, now looking a bit sad.

Whatever the truth was, it seemed dicey. I thanked Damian for the evening and left.

I boarded the R train back to Manhattan; it was bustling with excitement. Most folks were off for the weekend, and the happiness of others going about their ordinary tasks together with their partners and families made me feel sad. Encountering the energy of life, and witnessing others living large, made me feel hopeless, as I had nothing to be excited about except for my parents' backyard and some cigarettes.

I found I couldn't even read the newspaper or a magazine! I preferred to stay inside my bubble and ruminate endlessly on the loss of Cliff, reflect upon the extent of my badness, and contemplate whether I deserved anything positive to ever happen to me.

The Lexapro was helping in that I no longer cried when I thought about these things. But I still hadn't made it over the hump of leaving these thoughts behind altogether.

CHAPTER 10 – FOLLOWING DOCTOR'S ORDERS

I met Eric at a party given by some actor friends. We had little in common, other than our Russian roots.

Eric was tall and bald and into music. He lived with two roommates in a grungy apartment in the East Village, with the floor completely covered in dirty laundry. His obsession was mixing music, and he had a top-of-the-line sound-editing station set up in his living room.

Every weekend, Eric hung out at a club called the Crow Bar with a bunch of Russian guys and their young girlfriends. The guys looked like pimps. The girls, all professional career women during the day, wore five-inch heels and teeny halter-tops. Everyone else did ecstasy and drank bottles of premium vodka all night long.

One Saturday I went to the Crow Bar with Eric. After, I slept at his place, and suggested to my mother that she tell my father that I was staying with "a friend."

"Milochka, you have to respect your father and me!" my mother scolded me. "This is not good. Your father is an old-fashioned man, and he's been through a lot."

But I couldn't be sensitive to my parents at this time; I was too desperate for some male interaction. So, my only response was, "Mama, I'm a woman, not a girl! And I was married!"

So yes, Eric and I had sex. I was tired and drunk after having a few vodkas at the club. I didn't particularly want to have sex with Eric, but it happened. *Maybe I should have had more to drink with Cliff,* I thought to myself. *Maybe then we would have had some sex.*

My father came to pick me up in the morning. Even though I knew my mother had told him I stayed over at a friend's, I felt terrible seeing my father.

"How was the party, *dochenka*?" he asked quietly.

I looked away, out the car window. "It was okay, Papa, just okay."

We drove home in silence. My moods were more even now, and my crying jags less frequent. But my speed was up: I was working full-time, running around to parties, and sleeping out.

It was, after all, what the doctor had ordered. The ships were coming, and I had to be a good port.

Or something like that.

Chapter 11 – Daddy's Girl

Typically, I bolted out of chambers as soon as the judge said his good nights to his staff. *Five-o'clock was a wonderful ending time,* I thought. Still, it was a bitch to take the train to Port Authority and then the bus to Jersey: Even leaving at five on the dot left barely any time for anything.

Not that I needed more free time right now; as it was, I was spending a good deal of my workday drafting pathetic emails to Cliff. About how horrible I was. How sad. How sorry. How selfish. How stupid. How insane. How ashamed. How devastated. How confused. How horrible and sad. How sad and horrible. And countless variations on the same.

Somewhere inside the blank space that was my mind, I understood that I could probably get away with not working too hard for a few months. Milton the court deputy picked up a lot of the slack for me; all I had to do in return was listen to his monotonous movie reviews.

Thank God for Milton. Yes, I was fortunate, as I had all sorts of support – especially when it came to my parents. My father was back to picking me up from either the bus stop in New Jersey or from the city when I needed. Picking me up like he had when I was younger.

Years back, in Riga, my father would pick me up from nursery school: I'd run to him, my handsome daddy in his elegant hat and black coat, and he would hold my hand as we walked to the tram together. Sometimes, we would stop in at the ice cream parlor in the center of town. My parents and I always ate at home, so this was extremely special for the two of us. I loved the cold metal sundae cups, filled with one perfect vanilla ice-cream ball and topped with strawberry jam. Although my father didn't enjoy sweets, we both loved ice cream. My mother didn't, so this was a treat we snuck in before our family's evening meal at home.

Over the years in America as I grew up, my father would always pick me up or drive me – to junior high school, to cheesy dance clubs when I was a teenager, and to Columbia University. Now he drove me to and from the bus stop, and also from my tutoring jobs in Manhattan a few nights a week. He would work a full day, and then drive in and wait for me in the car on Park Avenue or Central Park West. Tonight, though, he was picking me up from the bus stop in Fair Lawn.

"How was your day, Milochka?" my father asked tentatively when I got into the car. I could tell he was worried that an innocuous inquiry could set off a crying jag, though I had been doing okay now for weeks. Still, some days were better than others, depending on the judge's mood or on whether there were any promising new dating leads on JDate.

"Fine," I responded shortly. Today, I was not in a mood to talk. The judge had yelled at me. He had disagreed with my recommendation on a class action case, and was angry that I had forgotten to follow up with the insurance company on one of his medical bills.

"How is the judge?" he asked then to fill the silence.

"Papa! You know how much I hate this whole thing – the law is boring. It is terrible!" My voice suddenly became loud and harsh. "Why do you even ask?"

I loved my father, but I simply could not spare showing him my misery. I realized I was displacing my anger. The law was not truly terrible. It was just not as fun as being on stage. And worse, I knew that I never spoke this way to anyone but my parents – the two people who loved me the most and treated me the best.

"Milochka, speak softer," he counseled me. "I ask, *milaya*, because we are very proud of you," he said.

I smiled through tears. My father was so kind. "Papa, what is there to be proud of?" I asked, needing to hear his response.

"You are a lawyer again!"

"Papa, everyone is a lawyer here in New York! It is a completely unremarkable thing," I said, hating myself so much right now that I wanted to convince my father that I sucked. My dreams – of marriage; of children; of great creative success – were shot. It was becoming upsetting to see him supporting me when I wanted to disappear.

I looked at my father closely: He had aged in the last few years. His blue eyes were faded, almost translucent. His hair, once dark and wavy, was thin and white. Yes, my father looked tired.

And he had reason to be: His life had not been easy. He never knew his father, an officer who had been killed in the fighting during World War II when Papa was only four. Papa hated to talk about it, so I just knew the basic facts. After transporting his wife and their three children to Siberia, my grandfather had been called for duty in the Soviet army and was killed shortly thereafter. After the war, my Baba Rosa turned her house into a boarding house to support herself and her three children, but often, they all went to bed hungry. Some nights, Papa ate grass patties — a sort of hamburger made of grass and stale bread. To this day, my father hated salad because it reminded him of eating grass.

In Belarus, my father had been a star student. Upon graduating from school, he received the highest Soviet honor — a gold medal. He had also been a fabulous dancer. In Belarus, he would even sometimes spend his few extra kopeks on new dancing shoes.

This innate joy for dancing would sometimes bubble up at birthday parties in Brighton Beach nightclubs, when my father, with the help of some vodka, would dance too energetically for the stout wives in my parents' circle. Too bad that my mother was an awkward dancer; they could never glide together on the dance floor. But as for me, I loved to dance; I had inherited my father's sense of rhythm. My father and I would often dance together, him with his dated but smooth moves, fingers snapping, feet clacking, and me, shimmying along with a modern groove. We both felt the music. And when he danced, he became light and radiant.

Dancing lifted all my father's sadness, his profound daily state since we'd come to America. I guessed something had eluded him, but I never knew exactly what it was. Was it that he never found a place to practice his passion? He had wanted to study medicine, but since his mother did not have the right connections, he had become an engineer here, like many of his Jewish peers.

Also, the English language that came so easily to my mother and me tortured my father. In Riga, he had been the head of a department, an important man. Here, at every job, he struggled to fit in. He was a tireless mentor though, teaching everything he knew to younger engineers, only to see them rise up in the company to positions he himself could not hold because of his language skills. "My boss, he doesn't understand me," my father would complain to me as he drove me to junior high school. "This country eats you alive," he would lament, looking so very broken.

I didn't understand this then; I loved it here. And I wanted him to be happy. "Papa, you should focus on your English," was the best advice I could give him. Oh, and, "It will get better."

Maybe my father was just too honorable and proud to fight for survival the way many successful men do in this capitalist system. He never lied, and he always was deeply empathetic. Whenever I'd criticize someone, he'd remind me that people were human; they made mistakes.

But maybe it wasn't any single external circumstance that brought Papa down though; more likely, depression was his natural mindset. A few years ago, I had wanted him to go to a psychiatrist and get evaluated. But he refused to talk about his moods with anyone, including my mother and me. "What, you want some crazy American doctor to tell me I'm crazy?" he would scream back at us.

This summer, I was sorry to add stress to his already stressful life. Sorry that here he was, picking me up once again, propping me up, when it should be the other way around.

CHAPTER 12 – MY PRINCE?

The seriousness of my new job hadn't sunk in. I knew I should appreciate the fact that I had a full-time job as a senior law clerk for a judge. But no job I'd ever had seemed particularly real or important to me. Whether I was waitressing at California Pizza Kitchen in New Jersey, sitting at the reception desk at Columbia's Butler Library, tutoring on the Upper East Side, or recommending a judgment in a RICO case in a federal court in Brooklyn, it was all somehow the same: There was a veil between me and my life at work. The American grind that ate up my parents was just something I flitted, flirted, and flew my way in and out of. I found work dull, and craved romance to feel alive. Romance was my oxygen.

This night though, I was staying late for me, finishing up the judge's weekly medical form insurance submissions. I didn't mind doing the work; the calm of making photocopies and sticking stamps on envelopes allowed my brain to focus on pursuing online romance. So after I finished filling out the insurance forms, I logged onto my online dating profile on JDate. Since Sportsguy, I had added a few more details to "Rose17," including a picture.

"Hi Rose."

A chat screen opened up on my computer; I quickly looked at the profile to determine whether to respond. Dr. Jordan was tall, dark, and "geographically challenged," according to his greeting. In his photo, he stood in front of an award in a white coat and stethoscope. It was really time for me to catch the last express bus to Fair Lawn. But this seemed fun, and would probably take only five minutes.

"Hi, Dr. Jordan," I typed back.

"How are you, Rose?"

"Great. How are you?"

I was, of course, far from great. I was pretty damn low. Ah, the beauty of the Internet...

"Great now that I am chatting with u, darling. ;)"

"Thanks. So what makes you 'geographically challenged' if you're from New York?"

"I'm now doing a residency visit in Cooperstown."

"Where is that?"

"Near Rochester. It's beautiful here."

"Cool. What residency?"

"Surgery."

"Wow, impressive. So how long have you been in Cooperstown?"

"A few months. I will be back at NYU in January."

"Great. I went to school in New York. Columbia – for college and law school,"

"Cool! Beautiful AND smart ☐" he wrote.

I smiled at the compliment – trite, but I'd take it.

"Thx. Oh, so you want to meet women from New York because you'll be here in six months?"

"Not women, a woman. I don't have time to date around."

"Yeah, of course, residents are so busy!" I wrote back, happy to read that this guy wanted to be a one-woman man.

"Yes. Plus, there are no interesting local women, as you can imagine."

"Sure."

I guess he thought I was "interesting." Based on what, I wondered.

We continued to flirt, until I noticed the time. If I didn't leave now, it would be too late to catch the last fast bus to Jersey. I was not now technically a woman from New York, but this was a minor detail.

"I have to run, Jordan. It was nice to meet you!"

"Same here. Hey, can I call you later?"

Oh, so this is how it worked. Now I had a new friend to talk to at night. Well, at least I knew what this one looked like, unlike Sportsguy.

"Yes, looking forward!" I wrote back, and I gave him my number. "Btw, my name is Mila," I added.

Jordan called later that night. "Hi, Mila darling," he lilted with a slight Southern accent.

I didn't even find his use of "darling" cheesy, given that he was a smart, hard-working medical resident. Yes, I was being shallow, giving him extra points for his professional success, but dating brought out the shallow in many, myself included. Besides, I'd had enough depth to last me for a while — a long while!

Jordan and I soon discovered that we had a friend in common. He had gone to summer camp with Sarah's brother; they all hailed from Virginia originally. I seized onto this connection — it made Jordan safe, like he was someone I knew. He was a nice Southern Jewish boy, a somewhat exotic type for the East Coast therefore, and nothing at all like Sportsguy, the random, faceless, sports marketer from Long Island.

Jordan sent me a picture of himself in a bathing suit, on the deck of his parents' summer house. He had a perfect tan and wore light blue swim shorts. His white teeth and dark brown eyes stared invitingly at me from the screen. He asked if I had any more revealing pictures than the one I had posted. I laughed, and replied that since I was new to this online dating thing, the face picture was all I had. But I told Jordan not to worry; I was skinny. And I was: My misery had been good for my figure. Smoking a pack a day and not eating had worked way better for me than any diet ever had.

I soon found I liked Jordan way better than Sportsguy. Jordan seemed caring, and he did not mind that I was living at home with my parents; he even told me he had lived with his parents during medical school. We talked about all kinds of things: relationships, law, medicine, and acting.

I also told him I loved the way he said, "Darling." At the end of each conversation, I would ask, "Can you say it now?"

"Good night, darling, sleep well."

"I'll think of you," I would murmur before I drifted off to sleep. But I couldn't think of him that much; I'd never even met him.

During one of our nightly conversations, I spontaneously told him that how much I had wanted to have a baby, and how stressful it had been for my marriage that it didn't happen right away. Jordan was very sympathetic: "Oh darling," he drawled, "I know how sad that must have been for you."

So why had I told this guy I barely knew about something so private and frankly, so unattractive? Fertility — or a lack thereof — was a thoroughly unappealing topic for a casual flirtation! This guy would think I had babies on the brain! *Oh goodness, Mila, what the heck! You are totally stupid,* I thought.

At this point in my musings, my mother came out on the porch to get me to come inside. "When are you going to sleep, *solnyshko?*" she prodded, concerned as always for my health.

"Soon, Mama."

"Who is that you are speaking to? That doctor?"

"Oh, we're done talking; I was just thinking," I replied, lighting a cigarette.

My mother looked at me as I lit it up, but did not say anything. I had promised her I would quit soon, but that smoking was helping me keep it together mentally right now.

"I told him about the baby-making problems," I eventually confided.

She looked at me in disbelief. "Why?"

"I don't know," I replied. It was the truth.

"Milochka, doing that is very stupid! How many times can I teach you men do not need to know everything about you! My mama had told me this a thousand times, but obviously I was a poor student at the Russian school of womanly wiles. "What kind of woman tells all her secrets?" my mother continued, flabbergasted and disappointed in me. "Especially anything that has to do with your body making babies! I know a woman who had no ovaries when she got married. Her husband found out only years later that they couldn't have children. The two of them are happy together still; they live in a big house, and have a cute dog."

"Mama, I couldn't help it," I replied, looking down. Mama was right, and I was ashamed of my lack of self-control. Lack of cleverness. I hated that she was right – but she was.

"How is it that you couldn't *help it?* You're just talking on the phone! Did you tell him why Cliff left you too? Why leave anything unsaid?" she scolded me in a harsh tone that her voice seemed to go to automatically when she thought I, or more often, my father, was acting stupidly.

Mama threw up her arms in frustration, looking at me in horror as if I were a silly child who had made a beeline for a busy road.

I found her criticism too harsh. "Stop it!" I screamed.

My mother started at the scream. I did too; I didn't want to yell, but it's just that she knew exactly how to push on my weak spots.

"Mila, shhhh, the neighbors will hear you," my mother cautioned.

"Why do you care what everyone thinks!" I retorted, still angry and upset.

"Mila, hush, it's almost midnight!" My mother, as usual, was concerned with appearances. She didn't want to make the neighbors think we were the wrong kind of people: people with messy lives.

"I don't care!" I shrieked, my voice going up an octave on purpose.

"You are so irritable! Who screams like that so late at night?"

I knew I had completely confused my mother, but I didn't care. "Mama, stop telling me what to do all the time. I am an *adult*."

"This is our house, and if you don't like how we live here, you don't have to stay."

I knew she didn't mean it; Mama was always there for me. She always forgave and forgave. I wanted to hug her and say I was sorry, but I couldn't. The intensity of my pain made me selfish. So I went back inside, leaving my mother on the porch sadly looking at some cigarette butts.

....

Inside, I climbed into my old bed, in my old bedroom, where during my unpopular months as the new nerdy Russian immigrant girl in class, I had fallen asleep every night with the same fantasy: that the cutest, most popular boy in our third grade class – Ryan, an athletic Irish boy – dared anger the rest of the girls in our classroom by asking me to be his date for a school dance. Every night in my bed and in my head, Ryan and I waltzed through the school-gym-turned-ballroom in my heavy silk ballet dress, a costume I had used to wear in Riga for New Year's Eve.

Now, as a thirty-plus woman, I was still in my childhood bed, and still dreaming of a finding a prince.

Pretty sad, Mila.

CHAPTER 13 – DRAMA QUEEN

Jordan was supposed to come down to New York City for our first in-person meeting. It was late June, and we'd been talking for a few weeks. He was going to stay at his cousin's apartment on the Upper East Side. But he called last minute, saying he had to be on call; some surgeon has gotten sick, and he had to pick up the slack now. I was disappointed – his next weekend off was over a month away. So I offered to take a train up to Rochester. I had seen Jordan's picture, he had an excellent career, and he knew my friend's brother from camp. It was a relatively lower-risk situation than the Sportsguy meeting.

Jordan seemed a little hesitant about taking me up on my offer. "Are you sure you want to make the trip, Mila? I can get to New York in a few weeks."

"It's no trouble, really," I insisted. "I know you're busy."

In truth, would be great to get away from Fair Lawn and my parents' backyard for a few days. This was my first summer in some years without a vacation: Cliff and I usually went somewhere – to Italy or Spain or Cape Cod or Maine. Sure, Rochester was not the most exotic destination, but it was the best I could do right now.

I told the judge's deputy, Milton, that I was seeing a new guy, and needed a day off for a visit. (Yes, I'd never actually "seen" Jordan, but that was a technicality.) I got his approval before I boarded the train to Rochester, where I read *Glamour* and sipped an iced coffee. I wore a bright-blue Banana Republic sweater (size extra small), a white linen skirt (size zero), and four-inch heels. The shoes were a little high for a summertime lunch meeting, but they were sexy, and I wanted to impress Dr. Jordan. *I look great,* I thought for the hundredth time that day. I was allowing myself this tiny bit of vanity: My appearance was the only positive outcome of the horrid breakup.

When the train arrived in Rochester, panic ripped through me: *What if Jordan were obese and wore a class ring, like Sportsguy? No, no, that couldn't be,* I reminded myself. *I have seen the picture of him shirtless; he was bronze-colored and ripped!*

I looked around. There was a bunch of ordinary-looking people everywhere.

"Mila?" a guy questioned as he approached.

I focused in on the man; he wasn't six feet two, but probably just under six feet. He wore white sneakers and white socks, khaki shorts, and a faded green polo shirt. His hair wasn't black, like in the photograph, but salt and pepper. This guy was pale, not bronzed, and he looked tired. *Ah, the picture must have been a few years old, and now the residency, with all those sleepless nights, was wearing him out,* I thought to myself. He had a red pimple on his chin, and held a baseball cap with "Baseball Hall of Fame" written on it.

"I'm Jordan," he offered, as if I hadn't figured his identity out.

"Hi, Jordan, I'm Mila," I giggled nervously.

"How was the train ride?" he asked, his voice smooth and lilting and just as sexy in real life as on the phone. But he was nervous too; he kept on twisting the baseball cap in his hands.

"Fine; nothing unusual."

We kissed on both cheeks. He took my bag, and we walked over to his car. I felt a little ridiculous being on four-inch heels right now: It was noontime in Rochester, and I looked as if I were going dancing in Manhattan on a Saturday night.

"Are you hungry?" he asked.

I was. We went to a Mexican restaurant. It was empty, and in the daylight, the room looked scuffed and dull. *Mexican restaurants should just be open at night,* I thought, *when tequila goes down more smoothly and the greasy tortilla chips look more appealing.*

I never would have chosen this dive for our first date. This was far from the intimate meeting I had expected. I had imagined something more along the lines of him sweeping me up in his arms and whispering in my ear, "My darling! I am so very happy to finally hold you close."

The margaritas we ordered were killer, however. And I was a lightweight. After just one, I hopped onto Jordan's lap. "So, Dr. Jordan, are you happy to meet me?" I whispered in his ear.

Jordan looked somewhat confused — after all, he didn't have to work very hard at all to seduce me. Turns out I was going to be the perfect houseguest.

We drove to his place. He lived in the residents' housing, right next door to the hospital. Jordan shared the house with a first-year intern.

Inside, it looked as if nobody had cleaned it in months. In the downstairs kitchen, dirty dishes were piled up in the sink. But we did not linger downstairs. We went straight upstairs to Jordan's bedroom.

"You are so hot, darling," he whispered in my ear as we fell into his bed.

One minute later, we were done. *Wow, that was quick. I didn't even have a chance to take off my Banana Republic size-zero skirt.*

Jordan looked a little embarrassed: "Sorry... ehh, it's been a long time... I'm so tired, I just let it all go right away."

"It's fine, Jordan, really." And it was fine; I wasn't here for the sex. I was happy to spend the day with *him*, even if I had to eat greasy Mexican food and console him regarding his sexual prowess. Why be so concerned about stamina? Did he think I was some marathon sex fiend?

Later, we went out to dinner at Chef Amore's, a nice suburban Italian restaurant. Some doctors Jordan knew were dining there, too. He introduced me: "This is my friend Mila from New York."

Just a friend? When I heard those words, a feeling of displacement came over me. *Why was I in this hick town with a tired doctor in a baseball cap?* Just a few months ago, on a Friday night like this one, Cliff and I would have been eating dinner in our apartment on 74th Street and sharing an easy intimacy. I had belonged to someone, and to some place.

I felt incredibly empty — hollow. *How silly it was to be excited by the stupid size-zero skirt, Mila.* But, I shook the sadness away, pinching myself back into the moment. The moment, —this moment, no matter how sort of pathetic — was what I had now.

"So, the garlic bread they have here is killer," Jordan enthused as he read over the menu. Of course, he hadn't even noticed the flash of storm that had blown over me. *He doesn't know me at all.* I shook that thought away too.

When we got back to Jordan's house, he asked me if I wanted to watch *Grease*; he had the movie lying around. I loved *Grease*, and so we put it on.

It was 10:30 at night, and during Sandy and Danny's laments about lost love at the very beginning of the movie, Jordan fell asleep. I sat completely awake in some resident housing in Cooperstown, my excitement over Penn Station, my outfit, the margaritas, and my romantic fantasy vanishing, just like that.

Jordan woke up briefly during the amusement park scene – when Sandy has transformed into a hot chick and takes charge of bad-boy Danny.

"Sorry, I'm so tired. So, so, tired," he mumbled.

"It's okay, the movie is good," I reassured him.

"Hey, I'll go down on you, okay?" he offered.

If I didn't feel like crying, I would have laughed at how stupid this – our – scene - was.

I shrugged, not caring one way or the other. "Sure."

And as he did, I felt empty. *This is what I deserve*, I thought. *My penance for the Dominic saga is sex with strangers.*

....

In the morning, Jordan and I went for breakfast. We bumped into more doctors from the hospital, but Jordan didn't want to linger and talk with them. Later, he took me to the train, saying he had to be in the hospital by four p.m. He said he'd call me to see that I got home safely, but he didn't.

"So, tell me all about the doctor, Milochka!" my mother greeted me when I got home.

"There's nothing much, Mama. He's handsome. He works a lot." I didn't want to tell my mom that our rendezvous had felt off. Let her be happy there were possibilities for me.

....

Jordan and I spoke a few times over the next several weeks. He told me he had taken his profile off the dating site, and this made me happy.

I didn't take my profile off, but I mostly stayed offline. Once in a while I checked my inbox to see if anyone interesting had written, but I did not reply to any mails.

One day I saw he was online. I called him, confused. He explained it away, saying, "I'm just checking some girls out for my friend from Chicago. He's using my profile to meet women in New York." I didn't exactly get why Jordan's friend could not just have his own profile, but it seemed plausible enough.

I wanted to see him again, but he was very stressed, and picking up extra shifts at the hospital. "I will come to New York at the end of July, I promise," he said. Since he'd be back in New York for good in September when he would resume his residency at NYU, I was willing to keep on talking to him; our relationship would soon not be a long-distance one! Still, I told him I needed to see him sooner, and I was willing to come to him a second time because I realized how sleep-deprived he was.

And so I took the train to Rochester again. I had the same routine – coffee, magazine, high heels. Jordan met me. He was in his uniform too – shorts, sneakers, polo shirt, baseball cap. He seemed a little sheepish when he grabbed my bag – *did he feel guilty that I had to come up to see him again?*

We kissed, but I could tell he was preoccupied. "What's wrong, Jordan?" I asked.

"Just tired," he said, looking away. This seemed a bit unconvincing even to me; yes, of course he was tired, but he also seemed preoccupied.

"Really?" I prodded. But before he could answer, I gave him a big hug. "I am so happy to see you!"

I guess I didn't really want a downer at that moment; I had just arrived.

We went back to his house. This time, he had to go back to the hospital for a few hours.

When Jordan came home, we went over to another resident's house for dinner. Jordan's friend was hosting a guys' steak night since his wife was out of town, so I would be the only female there. The surgeons told stories of body parts wrongly removed, of surgical instruments left in bodies, and of nurses screwed in empty patient rooms. The stories got cruder with each round of beer – hardly the romantic evening I had imagined.

At 11:00, we finally left. At his house, we had sex for three minutes. At 11:20, Jordan fell dead asleep.

The next day, Jordan gave me a tour of the hospital. Then, he had to go fill in for a sick resident for a few hours. I stayed at his house and read his favorite book — it was titled, *House of God*. This book was about the hardships and adventures of a group of medical interns. The young doctors in the book screwed everyone — their wives and girlfriends, the nurses, and the patients. I wondered if Jordan was trying to tell me something.

I put the book down, and decided to make a to-do list for my upcoming week at work. I went over to Jordan's desk to grab some paper and a pen. Lying on top of the notepad was Jordan's American Express bill. I couldn't help but look closer. I saw an entry for last Friday, the night he had told me he had to cover yet another emergency shift. He had gone to a restaurant— Dino's in Rochester. So he had lied. He had gone out on that night — and not even in Cooperstown. He must have had a date. *Well, what had I been thinking? Jordan and I had no formal commitment. This was only our second in-person meeting, and just because we talked all those nights on the phone did not mean he was seeing only me.*

I put down the bill. I next noticed a framed picture on the desk, of Jordan and a girls' soccer team. *That's great that he volunteers*, I thought. And then I noticed what it said on the plaque held by one of the girls: *Cooperstown Girls' League, June 2004*. My breath caught. June 2004? That was a few years ago! But Jordan had told me he was only in Cooperstown temporarily, on loan from NYU for just one semester.

My chest constricted, and my cheeks felt hot. Jordan had deceived me. I only decided to meet him because I thought he would be in New York in September. Why else would I invest in a man who lived so far away and had zero free time!

The phone calls were a lure, because as a resident, he did not have enough time or energy to go trolling for women in bars. But he had just enough time to convince me to travel to him for dinner and sex via the Internet. What an idiot I was. I had not even made him travel to me! I was like a call girl he had ordered up.

I decided to gather my things and leave. I would call a cab to take me from Cooperstown to Rochester and get on the next New York train.

I was just packing my bag when I heard the front door open. "Hello," someone said. It was Jordan. What was he doing here? He said he wouldn't be back until much later!

"I'm up here," I called down, my heart racing. Should I confront him about his lie?

Jordan came upstairs. He was wearing his scrubs, which were splattered with blood.

"Stomach work," he explained when he noticed me looking at the blood. "It was dirty. I came home to take a shower."

"Wow, that's a lot of blood," I said nervously.

As he looked at me, he noticed I was holding my bag. "What are you doing?"

"I... I just decided to get ready."

"Ready for what?"

"Well, for t-t-t-tomorrow," I stammered, sweat beginning to pop out on my forehead. And then I blurted it out. "Jordan, you lied to me."

"What?" He cocked his head slightly to the side. His left eye twitched slightly.

"You lied to me. I saw the picture."

"What picture?" he said with a smile. But he was not smiling with his eyes, just his mouth.

"The soccer picture." I paused. "From 2004. You were here in Cooperstown in 2004!"

"Oh," he said, processing the information. He blinked a few times.

"You said you were in New York until this January. So what's going on?"

I narrowed my eyes in a challenge. My breathing felt shallow, and I crossed the fingers on my right hand behind my back – my secret wish gesture. I did this when I was either willing something to happen or willing something not to happen. I wasn't sure what I wanted to happen here; I was just nervous.

The bedroom suddenly felt very small. I was near the window, and he was blocking the door.

Jordan seemed very tall now, way taller than six feet. He still looked pale and worn-out, but he also looked pissed. He was scowling, and it looked like he almost hated me. The blood on his scrubs made him appear almost deranged. I looked straight at him, clutching my bag in front of me in case he lunged at me or something. I realized that if he did, I couldn't even go anywhere safe; I was near the window, and he was blocking the door.

Damn! What the hell was I doing here? I imagined my parents' frantic search for me when I would fail to return on the Sunday train. Actually, they would realize it even sooner, when all of my mother's many calls and texts went unanswered. It would be a horrible ending to my family's American Dream — more horrible even than a divorce and a nervous breakdown. After all, nothing's worse than murder.

Then I told myself, *Relax, Mila, he's a Jewish doctor who went to camp with the brother of a friend. Don't be such a drama queen.*

"I'm going to take a shower," Jordan said, breaking the silence, and turned away from me. "This blood is gross."

"Fine," I replied. I guess he wasn't planning to murder me after all. When I realized I was still holding my breath, I released it to take in some air.

When Jordan came out, he looked a little less angry — even almost pleasant. *Had I truly witnessed a naked hatred of me? I must have imagined it,* I thought.

"So, Mila, the truth is that it is very hard to meet women here, and women from New York do not want to date men from Cooperstown, even if I'm a great guy. It's as simple as that," he said.

I don't remember whether he apologized. But the dream of us together had been burst. We were not going to be a couple. Jordan was only looking for some sex — very little sex, actually. About five minutes worth, because then he fell asleep because of his general state of complete exhaustion.

I asked him to take me to the train. We barely talked on the way.

I called my mom from the train and told her I was coming home a day early. She was upset to hear this news.

"So, you and Jordan broke up? Why, Milochka?"

"We were never even going out, Mama," I said before I hung up.

My romantic dreams gone, I no longer found the train buzzing with a happy energy. It was just a shitty Amtrak train ride from Rochester to New York, hauling tired, disappointed people to their realities.

CHAPTER 14 – THE SHOW MUST GO ON

With the dreams of being a doctor's wife going bust, I continued to smoke. I hated to make my father so upset; he practically cried every time he saw me smoking in the yard, and claimed, "Only vulgar women smoke!"

I needed the cigarette hits though as I pondered why Cliff hadn't wanted to fight for the sake of remaining a family. *Romantic love was ultimately its own genre, with its own rules. So it was almost as if the more you loved someone – the more you could hate them. Love and hate connected on the circle of emotion; was that what had gone on with Cliff? His strong love had turned into a strong hate....?*

I attempted, for my own sake, to shake away Cliff's ghost: After four months of begging and hundreds of imploring but unsent letters, I needed to accept the situation and move on. But it was hard, and when distraction came in the form of my acting agent Sheila one day in July, I said yes. What she had offered was: "Mila, I have a great opportunity for you! And if you do the play, it'll mean a weekend in the Hamptons!"

The play was called *Couple in the Hall* and it was about the disintegration of a marriage; ironic, right? The part Sheila had in mind for me was not of the wife, however, but of the husband's lover, a Russian escort named Lana. The husband accidentally strangles Lana during rough sex. That Sheila thought the part of a Russian whore was perfect for me was no surprise – I had auditioned for many such parts during my days as an actress.

I was poring over the audition side – a short monologue – at my desk at the judge's chambers when Dominic texted me.

"How's my dishy Manatus? Cheerio!" he wrote.

I was surprised at the text, but then realized Dominic must have just returned from his summer teaching trip to London. "Hi. Please don't call me that anymore," I texted back.

"Lunch?" he wrote. I did not reply.

The next day about lunchtime, the chambers' phone rang. "Judge's Chambers," I answered.

"Manatus, I'm right downstairs!" responded Dominic's chipper voice.

I hesitated; though I wanted to blow him off, I felt bad. The situation wasn't entirely his fault; after all, the crazy turn-of-events was just as much my responsibility as his. So I decided that I would try to explain to Dominic over lunch that we could not really be friends. He was the instrument of my downfall, and I was in mourning over the loss of Cliff, my wounds still raw. Our romance had been too destructive for me.

We met in the park right outside chambers, where we sat on the stone steps of the memorial there and I looked closely at the face of the man who had ripped apart my world. He was so ordinary. So plain. Close-set brown eyes, a slightly hooked nose, and a thin upper lip. True, his hair was still beautiful; the thick brown ringlets fell to his shoulders. He was wearing cheap plastic sunglasses, a black oxford shirt, and as always, his Doc Marten platforms. He carried a messenger bag, and, at the ripe age of thirty-four, looked like a graduate student.

At first we exchanged some pleasantries about his time in London and my new job. Then I said, "Hey, Dominic, I have an audition for this kooky Russian prostitute part; want to give me some tips?"

Dominic and I analyzed the part together. We laughed a little as we read through the parts of Lana and her client, the cheating husband.

"Do you vanna faack first, or shop first?" I said as Lana.

"Let's fuck," Dominic said as the client, and he leaned in closer and I could smell his musty New York City post-subway-on-a-hot-summer-day scent.

I shook my head; it seemed there was no getting away from sex, and that was both absurd and depressing. I decided to say nothing to Dominic about my change of heart about continuing our friendship; undoubtedly we would just get busy, grow apart, and there would be little need for me to have to spell anything out.

As we hugged goodbye – a little stiffly – Dominic gave me a miniature can of Earl Grey tea. "Souvenir for you, my sweet," he said.

I looked away. *People just repeat themselves,* I thought. *They do what they do, no matter that there has been a seismic shift in landscape.*

....

I nailed the audition. There were seven in the cast; five of us were professional/aspiring actors from New York, and two were the director's star local pupils from the Hamptons.

The other New York actresses were Connie and Serena: Connie, a fifty-year-old former dancer, now waitressed most of the time. Serena was a gorgeous blonde model, and a successful actress in commercials. The two New York actors were Chris, a cute musician and indie film actor, and Harrison, a chain-smoking Shakespearean theater actor who had just separated from his wife.

A few times a week, we'd have a rehearsal in the playwright's well-appointed New York City apartment. We pretty much had the run of the place. Everyone, except for Serena, smoked; she said she spent too much money on her skin care to undo the benefits with cigarette smoke. As for me, it was clear to everyone – including myself – that I was smoking too much. When I had first started, my doctors had told me to worry about ceasing my smoking later, after I stopped being depressed. But now that my depression had been pretty much replaced by hyperactivity, I found myself with a new habit. I promised myself I would stop as soon as my life got more settled.

And hyperactive I was now! I could accomplish a lot in one short day: commute to Brooklyn, write legal memos, work on my lines, meet a new guy for coffee, take a bus back to New Jersey where, in the evening, I would check Facebook, chat on JDate, and exchange dating stories with Serena. Then sleep, and in the morning, I would do it all again, with enthusiasm. Some mornings I would even feel hugely optimistic about my future. I was happy to be so energetic and grateful that my crying jags seemed to be a distant memory.

I loved acting in the play – it made me happy to meet new people who knew nothing about Cliff, nothing about who I was before this summer. Serena and I especially hit it off. She was like a savvy older sister – and she was single and approaching forty. I was excited to have a confidante, someone whom I could ply for dating advice. But Serena told me she did not like online dating, so she did not have much advice about this way of dating. Her general take on men was, never let them see you feel – an outlook about as opposite to my dating philosophy as one could get.

....

The weekend of the play arrived, and Serena had offered to drive me up to the Hamptons. I left work early, and took the subway uptown to the garage where she had her car. I had a few extra minutes, so I decided to get a coffee at Oren's Daily Roast. As I sipped my coffee, I remembered when Cliff and I had sat at this same counter together: We had stopped in for a break before heading to Chinatown to meet up with friends for a Sunday brunch.

I shook my head as I realized, New York was now a city of memories for me: Almost no place here was clear of Cliff! Ten years would do that. It was the city in which we had met, the city we had explored together as students, the city in which we had our first apartment together, and the city in which we had gotten married.

Nobody understood the full extent of my pain. I felt as if Cliff had died, yet once everyone learned we had split up, they thought that I should be doing fine. Our friends whispered that I must have left him; he'd never have broken up with me, as he was "too in love." Even my closest friends somehow believed I got what I wanted, what I deserved, because of the affair I had. I felt desperately alone in my mourning.

The phone rang. I felt a surge of hope when I saw it was Cliff. But he only wanted to talk about the sleeper couch I had just charged. I had bought it because I was tired of sleeping on my old twin-size bed. Too, I was beginning to consider moving back into Manhattan and would need a couch for my new place. The couch had been expensive, true, but it was almost the same couch that Cliff and I had had in our apartment – and Cliff had kept that one. I told him that: I said that I only wanted to have a couch like the one we had had together.

He was furious. He said that even though the credit card was in my name, he was still legally responsible for helping me pay the bill. And given that I had no money in the bank, I needed his help. Therefore, I was not to make any big purchases without asking him.

"But, Cliff," I pleaded, "don't you care about me at all? Why wouldn't you want me to have a good couch? And if things work out between us in the future, it'll become your couch too."

"Mila, I told you that things are not going to work out," he said, his tone angry and harsh.

"That's not what you said!" I begged, becoming increasingly desperate. "You said that we needed time apart, and that you didn't 'think' that things would work out, but that of course they could. You just didn't know."

"Fine. But I've been meaning to talk with you. Mila, they won't work out. I want us to sign a separation agreement," he said crisply.

I could barely speak. "An agreement? Why?" I whispered, feeling a sinking feeling in my stomach.

"Mila, we are *not* together. We *will not be* together. I want a divorce; that's all there is to it."

"Cliff, I don't understand!" I yelped. My cheeks felt hot and my breathing became short. I blinked back tears.

I did understand. But, I didn't want to. There were no surprises here, only my hope against hope that this strange life I had been living all summer was a fake life and that my real life would one day resume. I was living one of those Russian fairytales where the heroine must make her way through a forest of thorns and terrors before getting back to her village and to safety. New York this hot summer was my forest of thorns – the epitome of the Russian character Baba Yaga's lair.

"What part don't you understand?" Cliff's voice roused me from my Russian fairy tale reverie. "*I want a divorce.* I want us to sign a separation agreement. I've wanted this all along, but I was waiting to tell you because you weren't feeling well," he answered me.

"You mean because I got depressed, and you wouldn't even let me into my apartment for a minute, and you wouldn't allow me to even see you in person since March?" I shot out, completely furious.

His response was totally unexpected: "Mila, my friends already think I have been overly indulgent of you in this breakup."

"Are you fucking kidding me?" I screamed at the top of my lungs even though I had just moved outside the coffee shop onto a sidewalk bustling with pedestrians.

I felt weak at hearing his news. My head felt light, and I dropped my coffee, spilling it all over my black miniskirt, which was part of my costume I had to wear for the play. "Fuck!" I screamed. "Fuck! Fuck! Fuck!"

"Excuse me!" some lady said. "You are blocking the door to the store!" When I didn't immediately move out of the way, the lady's friend added, "So rude!"

I stepped to the right, and sunk down on the sidewalk. "Cliff, wait! I just want *us* to wait. Maybe we can try therapy or something," I suggested in a last-ditch attempt to stay a part of his world.

"Mila, I've thought this all out. We can talk about the details later, but there is nothing you can do. I'll call you later to talk about the agreement. You will need a lawyer, but that won't be a big deal. And you will not spend any more money on things like couches without checking with me first, understand?"

I couldn't answer. I just held the phone in my hand as I cried, my sobs overtaking me. Finally, I whimpered, "Cliff, it's just a couch. A fucking couch. Don't be such a jerk."

"And you don't be such a bitch," Cliff said in a quiet tone. "You made your choices. There are consequences to them."

"Cliff, how could you not care about me?!" I finally screamed at the top of my lungs, not caring if the whole world heard. "I need a couch too. Why should you keep everything – the couch, the apartment, the friends! I made a mistake. A *mistake*. One fucking mistake! It was not a cold blooded-crime that I committed."

"Yeah, it was," Cliff said quietly as he hung up.

I sank down to the ground in hysterics.

A man walked over to me and said, "Do you need some help?" He helped me up to my feet.

"Thanks," I said quietly. His act of kindness restored some sanity to my brain. I had to go meet Serena – and the show must go on.

....

The drive out to the Hamptons was fun, despite the phone call and news I had just endured. Serena and I shared some stories of dating, especially as I was now beginning to have my own arsenal of entertaining "doesn't dating suck?" tales: Sportsguy, Damian, Dr. Jordan.

Serena told me that she'd just broken up with an older man. He lived in Italy with his daughter, and came to New York for business every month. Serena dated high-powered men only: hedge fund managers, entrepreneurs, and producers. She'd never been married, never had children. I didn't ask her how she felt about this; we kept our talk light and full of laughter.

The play turned out beautifully, and the audience loved it. After the show, the whole cast went for drinks in their costumes. Serena and I flirted with some men at the bar. That's when we overheard some women there saying Serena and I were "sluts."

That's funny, I thought, *I've never considered myself a slut.* But, of course, I had forgotten I was wearing a micro-miniskirt, thigh-high black boots, and a bathing suit top – and that I had played a prostitute in our show. And if I thought about it, I was guilty now of some pretty slutty behavior in my new life. It was a turn-of-events that made me want to cry – a common emotional landscape for me now. But I smiled instead, and proposed a toast to Serena: "Here's to the sluts!" We clinked our cosmos.

After the cast party, the lead actor, Harrison, and I made out on the porch of the house where we were staying. He showed me a picture of his little daughter, and said that he missed her.

"Why did you and your wife separate?" I asked.

He didn't say. "Why did you and your husband separate?" he asked back.

I understood then that this had been a stupid question.

CHAPTER 15 – HATING SUNDAYS

After I returned from the Hamptons, I called my psychiatrist Misha. I told him I wanted to stop taking Lexapro; that it was making me too hyperactive. I told him I was thinking too fast, talking too fast, working too fast, and dating too fast! I was now in constant motion, and I hadn't felt tired in weeks. Misha agreed that I did sound a little fast, even on the phone. He promised to lower my dose gradually, and I promised in return that if I felt myself becoming too down once again, I would call him immediately. I just didn't like taking drugs, illegal or legal.

But before I slowed down too much, I looked for, and found, a new apartment in which to live. Since Cliff and I were not getting back together, there was no need to save money to show him how responsible I was with our funds. The apartment was in Tribeca, in a luxury building with an enclosed swimming pool on the 40th floor. I hadn't swum in years, but thought that swimming laps would be a good way to reduce the pain I still felt – and pain that I knew would feel overwhelming again at times now that I would soon be completely off the magic happy pill Lexapro.

Cliff had rented a new place too; he had left our apartment when the lease was up. When Cliff had sent me a list of our mutual furnishings he wanted to keep, I didn't make any changes. I wanted him to keep the things we'd shared, so that he might feel my energy, and live surrounded by some reminders of me.

Cliff asked if I wanted to stop by his new place to see about the little things he still had there – things that he wasn't particularly attached to. I agreed, but asked my mother to come with me; I felt scared of seeing Cliff by myself. It had been six months now since I'd seen him, with the pajama-clad middle-of-the-night visit being the last time.

In the lobby of my husband's new apartment building, the doorman sent my mother and me up. How strange it was for me to be a guest in my husband's place! I felt foolish. How could I have gone from such a position of power and privilege – unimpeded access and free reign to a wonderful man who was my husband – to such a lowly place where my entrance had to be approved, and I was a visitor, one who would be in and out in thirty minutes?

I could almost hear my mother think to herself, "What a guileless fool my daughter is! How could I have raised such an un-conniving woman!" It was almost as if I rejected the entire culture of man-control refined over many years by smart Russian women in their quest for survival. The manipulation of men was my cultural birthright, and yet my command of this legacy left so much to be desired.

Cliff let me in at the door. When I saw him, my reaction was automatic: I flew into his arms, hugging him hard. He hugged me back, but stiffly; clearly, this is not what he had expected.

"How are you?" I asked, looking deep into his eyes. I was searching for an opening, some glimpse of familiarity, care, and recognition of our status as soul mates over ten years' time. There was nothing. He was reserved. Not mean or rude, but just polite.

My eyes welled up: How was this possible? Didn't he remember anything good from our time together?

"Mila, I have a meeting later, so we should get to work," were the words he spoke to me.

I understood. My mother did also, because she pinched me. "Mila, *davai* (let's go). *Vozmi sebia v ruki!*" she said in a low voice. "Get a hold of yourself!"

I nodded. And so the next thirty minutes passed quickly. Cliff and I and my mother walked among the things Cliff and I had shared, and decided who got what. I would take the vase we brought back from Riga; he would take the travel books about Italy. I would take the little brass fertility-god paperweight from Ephesus, Turkey; he would take the juicer. I would take the vegetarian cookbook from the little restaurant we went to in London; he would take the spa towels we brought back from Turkey. This and that, this and that; "You take that, and I take this," and, "You never liked this anyway," or, "Here, you always liked this more." Funny how once the "us" had disappeared, it could all be so clear and mathematical: Everything could be reduced, or subtracted, into "his" and "mine."

Soon, we were done. As I prepared myself to leave, I saw that Cliff had been using our blender to make smoothies; half a banana and some strawberries lay on the counter. He had never made a smoothie when we were together. And that's how it goes: A man and wife are an organism. And when they split, neither ever knows what the other person will do, how they will evolve, and what parts of them didn't show up earlier because you were around for me. When it came to me, I did not know where I would go without Cliff, or who I would become. I was a blank slate right now, with much to be written on.

"I guess this is it," I said as I readied myself to walk out the door and leave my husband behind.

"Yes, I think we got it all," Cliff said.

I blinked back tears; he'd seen me cry enough. I looked into his eyes again, once so kind and warm. But now, there was nothing behind the blue of them. I wanted to hit Cliff hard, to jar him into recognition of the darkness of life, and how unbearably sad our situation was. *Didn't he get it? We had been run over by a train.* We didn't know what had hit us, but here we were, a bloody carcass thrown off the track. I longed to shake him too, and say something real: "Cliff, don't you remember *me*? I was your best friend! I am still here! It was all a huge, crazy event, and I don't understand it, but I am here; it's me!"

I wanted to say all this. But I said nothing. I looked at my mom for support; she was my rock, now and for always.

Mama squeezed my hand. "It's okay, Milochka," she said, not looking at Cliff.

"Okay, Cliff. I think that's it, then," I said.

My mother went to the door. I followed her. At the doorstep, I turned around. I rushed back to Cliff and looked him in the eyes.

"Cliff, it is still me. And I love you."

I hugged him. He hugged me back a little, then held me at an arm's length.

"Okay, I know that, Mila." His blue eyes showed a brief flicker of his old warmth. Or maybe I imagined this.

"Do you really know that?" I questioned in a trembling voice.

He didn't answer my question. "I am sorry," was all he said as he swung the door open for me.

....

Once we got outside the building, I burst into tears. "Mama! Why did this have to happen to us! Why! Everyone is leading a normal life, and yet we fell off the normal path. Why?"

My mother looked at me kindly. "Milochka, there are worse things in the world. Believe me. This is sad, but you are not an old woman. Be strong." My mother was not going to let me fall into self-pity this time. "Do you want to get a pastry?" she asked.

"Mama! No!" I almost shrieked. She was so wise, and yet, why did everything have to end in a pastry? A half-smile lit up my face; obviously my mother didn't get that I was now single in the dog-eat-dog world of Manhattan. Pastries would have to wait. I had to have a figure!

Mama and I hugged goodbye, and she went back to New Jersey as I walked by myself to Union Square. I looked at the people in the street, searching deep into their faces. Were they happy with their identities? Were any of them heartbroken too? Nobody was so unique as to be protected from suffering.

Today, I realized, was a Sunday. When Dominic and I had been starting up, he had told me he hated Sundays; he said he always felt so alone on this day, because it seemed everyone other than him was with their lovers or children. Once I heard this, I had always made a point of calling Dominic on Sundays to tell him he was in my thoughts.

Now, on this Sunday, I was alone. Just like Dominic. Just like all the other lonely people.

Now I hated Sundays too.

Chapter 16 – Go Brazilian!

The permanence of the separation became even more real: In December, Cliff and I signed a separation agreement. My lawyer did not endorse the terms. She said that she "...could not in good faith recommend such a poor settlement."

She knew some of the details, and thought that after several years of marriage, I should be better provided for, especially as my husband was an investment banker at a top investment bank. She felt I was getting screwed.

But as for me, I just wanted to get on with my life and not be mired in a divorce proceeding. So I signed a release stating that I was going against my lawyer's advice. Cliff was happy with the outcome, and wired some money into my banking account. I paid off credit card bills with it. Whew: I had made it through the crunch.

Now, however, I had to figure out a better "money job." A *money job* is what actors and artists call the activity that produces their income stream. So I submitted my resume to a few large law firms. At the resulting interviews, I spoke earnestly about the law being my "secret passion" all these years, and that I had just been temporarily distracted by the arts.

At one office, I interviewed with a junior partner. He was tall and dark-haired, like Cliff. On his desk stood pictures of his wife and two children. I swallowed hard and looked away, out the window. It was so sad. I wanted to tell him that I was married to a man who was about to be partner, and that he had kept a picture of me on his desk; that we were going to add pictures of our children to his desk one day, but then our lives had veered off in a different direction.

The lawyer smiled at me and asked something.

"Oh, I am not married," I replied. I saw that he looked confused, and I realized he had asked me something else entirely. "Gosh, I am sorry," I said, "I thought you had asked me about... I must have misheard you."

"Of course," he said. "I was just asking about the time you took off from law." Sure he was; that made much more sense. Lawyers knew better than to pry into your personal life. *Damn, now I won't get an offer*, I thought.

But the law firm called the very next day – with an offer! *Yes! My money woes were not to be long-lived. Take that, Cliff! I can make it without you.*

My parents were in heaven. Finally, something was going to go right for us again. I would receive a big advance for my clerkship, and a fat paycheck as soon as I started.

When I told the judge I was leaving to work at a law firm, he said he was happy for me – although he had expected that his medical billing would be more organized by now than, in fact, it was. He then asked for a few months to find a replacement.

I agreed to this readily; I was set. All I had before me were a few months of easy paperwork during April and May, and some time off to relax – before, voila, I would be back to big business in June, when I started my new job as a lawyer. Things were starting to happen for me, and it seemed to me that I was now ready to date – full-speed ahead.

My Russian shrink Misha gave me his blessings, telling me only to use condoms.

Obviously he still did not get that I was looking for love, not sex.

....

I had not logged on to any dating sites since Dr. Jordan the summer before. I decided to give online dating another go, and thought I might expand my horizons when it came to my choices in men. This time, I tried Match.com. I tried different search parameters to get older men, even older divorced men, in my filter. I clicked on many to show my interest.

My strategy worked. A few hours after rejoining, I began receiving emails from scores of older men – lawyers, accountants, and podiatrists. All of them seemed to be 5'6" with brown hair. But I didn't find podiatry terribly exciting, and after reading too many profiles, I felt dizzy. No one man stood out.

Under the description of the perfect match for me, I added the words "SEXY and EDGY." Then I giggled: Likely, anyone attracted to this wording would not be husband material. But it was fun to play around with the preferences.

The very next morning, I had this email in my in-box: "Hey, I think you're very cute. My name is Zoran." Zoran had longish black hair, a straight nose, and full lips. In his picture, he pouted into the camera. He looked like a rock star.

Zoran's profile stated that he wanted a woman who was passionate and a free thinker; someone able to carry a baby on her back while navigating both the Amazon and Soho. I thought this was clever and insightful. And possibly, that this guy was thinking of having babies.

I wrote him back. He sent me some more pictures, and asked me to do the same. His pictures were some beach shots from an exotic location; *wow, what a good idea to send along some bathing suit shots in the guise of 'travel' photos*, I thought. And I could see that the man really was gorgeous.

In return, I sent him a picture from some long-ago cast party for *Platonikov*, a rave-style production of the early Chekhov play *Platonov*. In the photo, I was standing on a table in a miniskirt and stilettos.

A few minutes later, Zoran replied. "Hi, Mila, I will be very direct with you. Your picture is hot! My 'edge' is something I am well known for, let me assure you."

On Saturday, Zoran wrote me again. "Hi, sexy, any big plans for the evening?"

"Staying in," I wrote, wondering if that made me seem too available but shrugging this thought off.

"Me too. Doing some writing tonight."

"What kind of stuff do you write?" I inquired; maybe we had something in common here.

"I write magic. If you're lucky, I will let you read some."

"Really? Do tell more," I was intrigued.

He wrote a longer email, explaining that he had wanted to be a writer, but that a family business had required his help. He was now the CEO of a modern lighting import company. He was definitely NOT a podiatrist.

We exchanged emails for a few hours. It was now close to five p.m. He asked for my number so he could call me. But at six p.m., I got a text instead.

"This is Zoran. So, hottie, where do u live?"

"Tribeca," I wrote back.

"Me 2!"

It took few more texts before we figured out we lived across the street from one another. Moreover, that our buildings faced one another. And, that we both lived on the seventh floor of our buildings.

"Wow! So u can see me from your window?" I wrote. This was almost romantic.

"Yes!" Zoran wrote. "What are the odds?! I'll put a candle in the window 4 u".

"K. I c u!!" I texted.

"Will call u now?" he asked. I felt my heart race a little bit on reading this. This was first-rate excitement, like in a movie.

"Sure," I replied, still trying to seem casual. My phone rang, and I was afraid to answer for a moment. Shaking that away, I mustered a nonchalant: "Hey." He had a low voice with a soft cadence, and just a hint of a foreign accent, Spanish. He suggested we meet for a drink.

"Tonight?" I asked. I had planned to take a bath and read some fashion magazines. And I did read somewhere that you should always make men wait for a date.

"Sure, why not go with the flow? The universe is smiling," he observed. I could only agree.

He came to get me in my lobby. The man was gorgeous: tall, tan, and muscular, with that thick black hair I saw in the picture and perfect white teeth. Zoran was the very picture of health and virility. He wore a fitted black t-shirt, black pants, a black blazer, and green Puma sneakers. Stylish, too – downtown, definitely.

We went to a local bar. Zoran ordered a bottle of wine. He told me he moved here from Spain as a teenager. His father was an art dealer before he founded the family lighting business. We spoke about poetry before he told me he exercised two hours a day, every day. "Why so much?" I asked. He explained he'd been fat as a child, and wasn't found attractive by girls during high school. Then, in college, he had lost the weight, and boom! The women wouldn't leave him alone; that's why he worked out so much.

He didn't ask me too many questions about myself. So I didn't tell him about my childhood in Latvia, going to Columbia, or anything about acting or my marriage.

I thought maybe we'd order dinner, but Zoran didn't suggest it. He smoked a few cigarettes as we chatted, a surprising habit for an exercise fanatic. I began to feel lightheaded from the wine. "Well, I should really get home now," I said.

"I'll walk you."

We walked out of the bar. As we got ready to go to our separate apartments, he said, "Hey, Mila, my place is right here. I have a great bottle of wine up there. Don't you want to continue our night?"

It was still early, and he was my neighbor. He didn't seem particularly dangerous. I agreed. He took me up to his loft. The apartment was lightly furnished, with just several furniture pieces. Zoran had the entire floor of the building for his apartment. Even better, his apartment's eastern windows faced my western windows. I couldn't help exclaiming, "Wow, this is nice."

He shrugged. "It's OK." *False modesty*, likely, I thought, but I didn't feeling like analyzing the situation too closely. *In fact, coming up here is stupid, Mila*, my voice persisted. *He is a total stranger.*

The stranger put his soft hand on my arm and ushered me into the living area, toward a low coffee table full of books—Shakespeare, Joyce, Artaud. Several packs of cigarettes lay on the kitchen counter. A hammock hung in the Southeastern corner. "A hammock!"

"Yeah, I like to chill. The city gets to you, you know?" Zoran purred. I knew, certainly. He said all the right things. He lit candles and put on music.

"Rachmaninoff, in honor of your Russian roots," he said. "Do you want to play a game of Scrabble?"

Scrabble? I didn't expect that. "Sure, would love to." We played. It turned out he loved Scrabble; his score notepad revealed many, many games.

"How often do you play?" I asked.

"Whenever I can get someone up here," he smiled. *Hmm*. That sounded almost dangerous. He was hardly hiding the fact that this was his lair.

"Do you mind if I change into something more comfortable?" he asked.

"Sure, that's fine," I said, wondering only for a slight moment why he would need something more comfortable than shorts and a t-shirt.

He went into his bedroom and emerged in just pajama pants. I giggled like I was fifteen. *This guy gets right to the point,* my inner voice said. *But, so what, Mila, you are choosing to be here, right?*

We continued to play, but soon, he leaned over to pour me more wine. His lips found mine and we fell on the couch, forgetting the Scrabble game. "Roarrr," he joked, biting my neck.

"Grandma, what big teeth you have," I joked.

"The better to lick you with, my darling," Zoran whispered, making me blush.

"I should really get home now," I said as I managed to get free of his arms. But he grabbed me again, and this time we sank back on the couch. "OK, but let's set a timer for ten minutes, Zoran," I said, "I need to go soon." He laughed. We kissed more, but I finally got up more definitively and made my way to the door. "Hey, you can walk me home, if you like," I offered.

We went across the street to my apartment, which now seemed like it was a stuffy closet compared to Zoran's spacious loft. I showed him around. He said my space needed better Feng Shui: the "love corner" of my bedroom was too crowded. "You should put a picture of a couple here instead of the clothes hamper," he advised before we kissed good night. It was almost morning.

....

The next day, I felt on top of the world. I did think for a few seconds that Zoran talked much more than he listened, smoked too many cigarettes, and had zero interest in having dinner together. I wondered if he had eating issues because he had been fat. Not to mention he wore pajamas on our first date.

The whole thing felt a little surreal, especially with our windows facing each other's across the street. We'd always be able to know when the other was home.

In the evening, he called me. "I saw you prancing in front of your window! I had to call."

His observation was true; I was spending more time in front of my window than usual because I wanted to see him again.

"Zoran, I'd love to come over to continue our Scrabble game!" I suggested, instead of waiting for him to suggest a proper date. It was 9:30 on a Sunday evening.

"Sure," he agreed.

I practically ran across the street. When the elevator stopped at his loft, he was waiting. In his pajamas. "I wanted to be comfortable," he explained when my eyes moved over his body.

"Of course," I uttered, as if this was perfectly courteous date behavior. He took out the Scrabble board. "Wanna smoke a joint?" he asked.

"I don't smoke pot," I replied. "But you can." He went over to the kitchen and filled a pipe.

"I am reading the poet Antonin Artaud right now. Do you know him?"

"Vaguely."

"It has not been definitively proved that the language of words is the best possible language," Zoran quoted, massaging my neck.

"That's ironic, then," I quipped, "that we are playing Scrabble."

"He had a fascinating life," Zoran said. "He was institutionalized."

Hmm, I thought, *is that what qualifies as fascinating for Zoran?*

We sat down to play the game. A few minutes later, Zoran leaned in to kiss me. "Let's go to the bedroom," he said.

I hesitated. Sundays were always lonely days for me now, and I really wanted some company. But I did not mean to invite myself over so that we can go directly to the bedroom.

"Why, because Artaud says so," I joked. "The language of the bedroom is preferable?"

"Aha," Zoran said, his eyes smoldering, his pajamas showing a distinct bulge. "Fine, but I only have a few minutes," I said. "I have to get up early for work tomorrow."

We managed to keep it relatively mild. There was no sex. A short while later, I left. Zoran walked me home again, but just across the street. He wanted to smoke a cigarette in the park, he said, as he waved goodbye.

The next morning, he texted. A note about his obsession with making his bed every morning until there were no wrinkles, only perfectly pulled, perfectly white sheets. But today, there was a black bra in the pristine bed.

I felt happy that he revealed something intimate about himself to me, even if I thought he had too many issues to be boyfriend material. He smoked non-stop. He exercised too much, had insomnia and OCD, and seemed never to eat.

I wrote back a gushing email about his great writing talent.

It was early, only six a.m., but I didn't feel tired. I cleaned my apartment, then went for a Brazilian bikini wax appointment before work.

After the appointment, I went to work full of energy. Even though I was not taking the Lexapro any longer, I discovered the potential for romance was keeping me excited and lively. I nodded distantly at Milton as he told me about yet another dinner he had at Chez Something or other. And that is when it hit me: I would throw a "Go Brazilian!" party for Zoran. We would drink traditional Brazilian *caipirinhas*, and listen to the Brazilian singer Camille. I would show Zoran my new bikini wax —it would be a perfect third date!

I spent the afternoon composing a text: "How about a "Go Brazilian" evening at my place?" I texted him. I thought this at once clever and intriguing.

Zoran wrote back immediately: "Mila!!!!!! I don't know what 2 say! Thx, will b there in 10."

Our evening was infinitely less exciting than the actual composing of the invite and the preparing of the party. We did exactly what I had planned: caipirinhas, music, dancing, and making out. Naturally, our embraces and kisses got hotter. Then Zoran asked me if I had condoms.

"Condoms? No. I wasn't planning on having sex, Zoran," I responded.

"Why not?" he asked, sounding a bit mean and whiny, like a petulant child who expected to get candy after dinner and was not.

"I don't think we know each other well enough yet," I elaborated.

"But *you* invited *me* to this Brazilian bikini party, Mila. What did you mean by that?" he urged as he pressed against me more assertively.

"I don't know, Zoran! I thought it would be fun, but we don't have to do everything tonight," I answered, my tone a little shrill.

He kissed me harder, almost hurting me. "You're so sexy, Mila. So incredibly sexy."

"Thanks, Zoran," I responded, although I was feeling uncomfortable. "There is plenty of time."

"Mila, you make me so hard!," he whispered, pressing his crotch insistently into me. "You know that, don't you? You know how sexy you are," he murmured, his dark eyes gazing into mine.

I began to feel ambivalent about my decision to keep it PG-rated. Well, if I were to be honest, R-rated. But I stuck to my resolve; I did not want to have sex just yet.

After another half hour of back-and-forth, Zoran said he was going home.

I felt strange, like I was being weird. "I am sorry, Zoran."

"It's fine. It's not a big deal," he said.

I wondered if I was making an arbitrary distinction. What was the big deal about having sex anyway? I wasn't a virgin. But I was a novice when it came to dating – and I felt put off by Zoran's pushiness. After all, I barely knew him.

Single life was harsh, I thought. *It involves an endless parade of strangers.* I opened the door for Zoran and we stiffly kissed goodbye.

The next day, he did not call. At work, I was anxious, and I called my mother a few times to calm me down. As the day progressed, my mood became blacker and blacker. I tried to reason with myself: *But, Mila, you and he are not a couple. He knows nothing about you. Why do you care if you never hear from him again? You've lost nothing.* But the loss felt bigger and bigger as the hours went by and no email from him arrived.

By evening, I was unable to concentrate on anything other than the thought of Zoran. This situation was exacerbated by the fact that I could see that the lights were on in his window. He was home, and not calling me. What was he doing? Was he trolling JDate? I had to see.

I logged on. Sure enough, there he was. He was online, his chat signal blinking. That asshole! The taunting chat indicator made me livid. I paced around my living room in full view of the window, hoping he would see me and call or email.

Nothing. No text. No candle in the window. I wished that I could fall asleep, but I felt too wired. I called Jessica. She listened sympathetically, as always. "Mila, maybe you should take a walk," she suggested. "This guy's a jerk."

I went outside, feeling trapped by my anxiety about Zoran. I bought a pack of cigarettes and smoked a few outside. So much for quitting. I went back in and got in bed. Zoran's light was still on. This was sheer torture. I dialed Cliff's number. It had been a few months since we last spoke.

"What is it, Mila?" he said as he answered the phone.

"Cliff?" I asked, surprised. I didn't expect him to answer.

"Yes, you called me, remember?"

"Of course, I did, right. Cliff, I am not doing well," I said. "I wanted to hear your voice."

"I am busy," was his crisp response. He obviously picked up only to find out if I had something to say that would have legal consequences.

"Cliff, please, let's just talk for a bit," I begged.

"Mila, for God's sake, grow up! I am not your husband anymore."

The phone went dead. I lay down in my bed and closed my eyes. Eventually, I fell asleep.

The next day, my anxiety only increased. I waited for a text from Zoran the whole day, but nothing came. At 8:00 that night, I spied Zoran's lights on. I dialed his number, without even bothering to text first.

"Hi, Mila, what's up?" He sounded utterly not excited to hear from me.

"Nothing much, Zoran." I wanted to ask him why he had been blowing me off. Instead, I heard myself saying, "Zoran, I would love to see you right now."

"Really?"

"Yes."

"Well, I have to be up early."

"I know; me too. I was thinking just for a short visit.."

"Hmmm. I still have to do my exercises. But I guess it's okay."

I wasn't sure why I wanted to see him so badly; I think I wanted to feel that everything was okay, that he wasn't blowing me off, and that there was a connection like I had thought. I almost ran across the street in my hurry to get to him.

When I got there, Zoran was in his pajamas. He met me in front of the elevator doors, as usual. This time, we did not talk. He took me right into the bedroom where we pounced on each other.

I knew we wanted different things: I wanted to connect. I wanted some intimacy, a male touch, and a male body next to mine. I didn't care about the sex. But the sex was what he wanted.

An hour later, it was time to go home. Zoran did not bother to walk me across the street this time, and this made me feel like a call girl. I had come to his apartment, satisfied him, and left on my own. In and out. I asked for nothing from him.

I felt slightly ashamed. How is it that I was so ready to please this random guy, a self-centered jerk who could not even call me? *I didn't understand myself these days,* I thought to myself. *This was the universe paying me back for walking out on Cliff.*

Of course, Zoran did not call on the next day, Friday. I went to a movie with my married friends Oliver and Salma, but I could barely concentrate.

After the movie, we went out for drinks. I asked Oliver what he thought of the situation.

"Did you sleep with him?" asked Oliver. I looked down into my drink. "It's the dead deer phenomenon," Oliver assessed, shaking his head.

"What's that?" I asked.

"You got rid of the thrill of the chase. He got you. He was a player, and he doesn't want dead meat." Oliver then did an imitation of a sweet deer lying belly up and batting its eyelashes.

We all laughed, although I felt my head throbbing: The romance with Zoran was over, and so quickly! It hadn't even lasted a week. Maybe Misha the shrink had been right. Zoran was a young, rich, and great-looking guy; perhaps he was out of my league. *Boy, seeing Misha had certainly not helped out my self-esteem!*

I got up abruptly. "I have to go home, guys; I don't feel well." I dropped some money on the table and ran out to get a cab.

At home, I collapsed into bed. My mood turned pitch-black. So did my energy. I thought of Cliff as I fell asleep. How I longed to be back in my other steady, predictable life, one warmed by love.

The next day, I wrote a one-page email to Zoran: "Zoran, I was hoping to hear from you after Thursday. Everything went so quickly. We connected instantly, and I think we let the excitement take over. Is it possible to rewind? To start over?" The email went into all sorts of detail: the poetry we spoke about, the Scrabble words we made, the travelling overseas we had discussed. "Please write me to let me know we can start over and be friends as we are neighbors after all."

He wrote me back later that night. "Mila! Don't worry about such stuff. I am very ill, and that is why I have been out of touch. Food poisoning, most likely. Then I am going to Milan on business. We can be friends, of course. I will email you when I return."

I sat looking at this response a little while before I logged on to Match.com. I discovered Zoran's chat sign was on.

I recalled a recent issue of *Glamour* I had read at the nail salon. There was an article about creating the life you want. Step one was to keep a daily journal of intentions.

As my first entry, I wrote this email to myself: "Dating Lesson: Nobody wants a dead deer."

Chapter 17 — The Naked Island

I went back to JDate. It seemed more familiar. The very same day, a new love prospect emailed me.

Jake was not the typical East Coast JDater. In his "about me" statement, he wrote that he intended "to soar." His idol, he wrote, was the anthropologist Carlos Castaneda. Under his hobbies, he indicated, "lucid dreaming." His occupation was motivational speaking. He wrote that he had recently moved to New York from Chicago where he motivated at-risk youth to engage in community sports. Hmm. I was intrigued. I agreed to meet him.

I hoped Jake would be my first good JDate – no class ring à la Sportsguy, no lying about living in the city like Jordan the Cooperstown surgeon, and no manipulative poetic musings à la Zoran the neighbor.

Our first date was dinner at Gigino Trattoria, an Italian restaurant in Tribeca, and then dancing at a funky Euro bar in Soho. Throughout the evening, I tried to learn what I could about him, without telling him much about myself. I did not feel comfortable talking about the divorce or the time I spent in my parents' yard the summer before.

Jake, in contrast, was forthcoming. He'd gone to college in Madison, Wisconsin, and lived in a commune for a few years after. He had a Masters in psychology, and had studied both Jung and the archetype work of Joseph Campbell – work which organized life and all good stories around the story of the hero's journey.

At dinner, when I took an early bathroom break, I Googled, "Hero's Journey" so I could sound knowledgeable on this topic during the main course.

I found out Jake had had a concussion when he was seventeen; he claimed that this accident changed his life, making it impossible for him to pursue investment banking – an occupation for which he was actually genetically suited. (He was, after all, a jock who stood six-feet-two-inches tall, and was good with numbers.) However, he said the crack in his skull made him now too "off-center" to pursue such a straight-laced existence.

Jake's passion? NLP – or Neuro-Linguistic Programming. The basic idea, Jake told me, was one could exert control over oneself and over others through the targeted use of language. Jake applied NLP principles to his own life: On our first date, he said my name almost every thirty seconds. He later explained that a person's favorite word in the English language is his or her name.

"And so, Jake, were you manipulating me on that night so that I would like you better?" I asked later.

He winked at me. "Sure, baby. Life is all a manipulation."

Talking about NLP turned Jake on. "Come here, sugar, I want to get me some fine tail!" he would say as he slapped my ass. "I like to pleasure my honey," he'd drawl, and I would giggle. In bed, he was intense, present, in the moment. It was almost impersonal though; his total involvement was more with himself and the experience than with me. But I didn't complain. I was on my own trip – as Jake seemed sensitive, romantic, and into me. The romance of it made me feel safer about the relationship and our intimacy. Jake's apparent concern for my pleasure and wellbeing – banal questions such as "Are you too cold, darling?" – was enough to get past my defenses, which had been up with Zoran. And, I was now more comfortable with the idea that there was a definite *quid pro quo* to dating in New York: After several dates, it was important to put out a bit.

Jake had a perfect physique – tall, creamy golden skin, and long hard muscles. He wore tank tops to show off his arms. I teased him that he was born a few centuries too late for his calling, which would have been modeling for Michelangelo. He exercised several hours a day, doing a martial arts workout he had discovered on QVC.

He liked walking around naked in my apartment, sometimes spontaneously jumping down to do one hundred naked push-ups or twenty naked military squats. One day, he pulled me over, and said in a serious tone, "You know, it just hit me that you may find it offensive that I like to walk around nude in your place."

I assured him it was all good. I wanted to try to be more of a free spirit, like Jake.

....

We were lying in bed one night when Jake told me he dreamt of applying to work for the CIA.

"You know, Mila, we all have a mission," he elaborated when I expressed my surprise.

"Really?"

"Sure, we're all living out personal mythologies. And I am a Warrior."

"Warrior?" I murmured lazily.

"Yes, the Warrior archetype. A man who accesses this Warrior energy will have unlimited power. This man will use this energy, his aggression, decisiveness, mindfulness, purpose in the service of others – to fight for good and protect the weak."

"Aha – Is this why you've told me you want to be a soldier? Is that some primal need you think every man has but ignores? Are you sure you are a Warrior?" I teased – intelligently, in my opinion.

"Yes! I want to do what all men have an instinct to do: fight for what's right."

But I was too tired to really listen. Besides, I had never quite read the *Warrior* book series Jake carried around and pored over daily.

Jake's current plan was to start a local "NLP-based warrior program" in which he would take fat, stressed-out executives into the wilds of Maine and teach them martial arts and hunting. He would then write a book, put out a *Warrior in Maine* video, and star in an infomercial on QVC, making bazillions while fulfilling his life's mission.

In the meantime, as Jake wrote up a business plan for this, he would have to settle for a less glamorous self-empowerment mission. He took a job counseling a dyslexic and socially phobic man named Sampson from Hackensack, N.J., whom he'd met at a Starbucks on Route 4. And so the only program Jake was actually running was this one.

Jake tried to tell me there was no future for us – and not so indirectly: "Mila, I don't think there's a future for us," he said one day.

"Oh, Jake," I purred, kissing his beautiful biceps, "you have to give these things some time..."

"I don't know. I don't want to waste your time, Mila."

"Let's talk about this another time, Jake, OK? Why don't we just enjoy the moment!" I responded.

Nothing could touch me in my Jake-induced euphoria – not his cautionary words, nor the need to attend to routine, everyday things. In my now-again hyper state, I found taking care of details to be boring. Phone calls, bills – all these tasks felt too slow for my romance-induced high. I preferred to spend my time buying flowers for my apartment and getting my hair blow-dried for dates with Jake.

....

A few weeks later, Jake and I went to the Museum of Modern Art. I'd been raving about the art on display, and wanted to share the experience with him. At the museum, I chattered away: "Come here, Jake, you have to see this Chagall... this Picasso... the cat by Klee."

Jake looked at me critically, with his psychologist eye. "Mila, I'm right here, Mila. Relax and let me look at it myself. I don't need a tour guide."

"Oh, I am sorry," I answered quietly. I was hurt. Cliff had loved how I got very excited about things; he had said I made him less cerebral and more passionate. But it seemed that instead of enjoying my excitement, Jake became annoyed by it.

Later on that night, Jake told me he didn't want to go out for the evening. He said he needed to detox from the day's stimuli by doing a deep meditation, something he did daily. I heard him, but was in a silly, frantic mood, and still wanted to discuss our day.

"So, Jake, wasn't it as amazing as I told you? We live in such a tremendous city and hardly take advantage. You know, another museum I love is the Guggenheim; have you been recently? I saw this amazing exhibit there; it was just projections on the walls, in red, green, and yellow. So minimalist. Well, really, I didn't get what was so amazing about it, come to think of it..."

"Mila!" he interrupted me.
"What?"
"You seem manic," he analyzed.
"What do you mean?" I asked, pressing against him. I wanted to kiss, and kiss again, but he had something else on his mind.
"Your energy — it's too much. Aren't you tired? We had a very long day."
I shrugged as I answered, "No, not really." But come to think of it, I hadn't been tired since our first date. These days I barely slept.
"I need some quiet, Mila," he said before he closed his eyes and started making an S sound with his out-breaths to get into a meditative mood. "Sssssssssssssssssssssssss."
I moved away to make some tea, feeling like an intruder in my own apartment. His meditation was a boring way to end our date. And why was it that something was off with *me*? Was I truly the one who had too much energy? After all, Jake had a tremendous amount of energy too. He always got so excited talking about his Warrior seminars and workouts. It never occurred to me that I was in a romance-ignited manic phase, and that Jake's own excessive energy was simply feeding mine. But Jake knew how to come down from things, whereas I reveled in riding this high — it took me far away from the disaster of last summer in the backyard when the world was blacker than black.
I soon was to discover there was something that excited him even more than the Warrior stuff though: One day Jake confided that his ultimate fantasy was to retire to an island in the Caribbean and to live *au naturel*. "You mean *naked*?" I asked him. "You want to go to live at a nudist colony?"
"An island with no people is not a colony. But I would like to eat coconuts naked. You know, get back to nature."
"Hmmm." This vision of Eden was not exactly what I would paint as my ultimate fantasy: I would prefer wearing a fabulous outfit from Barneys while sailing on the French Riviera with a staff of ten.
This difference in our dreams would ultimately be one of the reasons for our split.

....

For the Fourth of July weekend, Jake and I decided to visit my friend Scott, one of the actors from the play the summer before. He was a general contractor by day, and he and his wife Alice, a sweet and likable social worker, were going to host us in their gorgeous Hamptons home.

As we drove through the Hamptons, Jake told me he didn't like all the snootiness about the Hamptons, so he would prefer to stay at the house the whole weekend rather than go out in the town. And he did: He spent many hours drafting his business plan and swimming laps in the home's cold pool.

I watched him as I read through the mammoth binders I had received from my new job, which I had started a few weeks before. I found big firm law even duller than my job at the judge's. But the paycheck made it palatable – quite. Oh, and the fact that I was now a legitimate Manhattan professional. Not quite as good as being a corporate wife – in my opinion – but at least respectable.

I could tell that Scott and Alice were not as enamored with Jake as I was. Unlike me, they did not stare at him with great enthusiasm as he did hundreds of sit-ups by their pool. Their eyes glazed over when he spoke about the Warrior trips he longed to lead. And they found it odd that he constantly repeated their first names: "Thanks, Alice, that's a really delicious steak, Alice. So Alice, where did you learn how to barbecue like that?" Jake would say as he ate.

When I had the chance, I asked Alice, "So, what do you think? Isn't he fascinating?"

After a slight pause, she smiled kindly and said, "He is a nice guy."

Perhaps what they found even odder was my promotion of him: "Alice, Jake just got back from Florida; he'll tell you all about the crazy heat," or, "Jake, you should tell about the NLP stuff that you do." Alice prompted me to speak a few times, asking me what I thought about things. But I was happy to defer to Jake. It was as if I had nothing interesting to offer to Alice and Scott.

I could tell I was too excited – I saw the sidelong glances Alice and Scott would exchange when I went on yet another rave about Jake – but I couldn't slow down. And I didn't want to: The infatuation was like a shot of adrenaline, washing all the nuances of my life in a bright pink hue.

The next weekend, I invited Jake to spend some time with me in New Jersey. I was excited to show him off to my parents' friends, to prove that I was doing well just one short year after Cliff. "Good-looking guy," they murmured. I took that comment for a rousing endorsement.

On Saturday night, we attended an anniversary party at a Russian nightclub. I had a wonderful time. But when I looked at Jake, I saw he was uncomfortable. The glitz and excess of my Russian culture was hardly similar to what it must be like to live naked on a desert island. I moved closer to Jake so that he would feel more at ease. At this gesture, his body stiffened slightly in response.

On Sunday morning, we went to an outdoor jungle gym in a park. Jake did pull-ups and ate a Zone bar as I watched admiringly from afar. After, we went to a birthday party for a family friend, Tatiana. Tatiana's mother and my mother had been friends since Latvia.

Tatiana had married very well: Her husband Sam, a sweet, funny guy who doted on her, had just sold his business, making millions of dollars.

"What do you think of him?" I whispered to Sam when Jake left for a moment to go to the bathroom.

"He seems young," Sam said.

"Only a year younger than me," I said with a dismissive shrug.

"I mean, not the settling type," Sam said, not one to mince words.

My mother told me later that all our friends thought Jake was too into his body, and that I was not seeing things clearly because I was still reeling from the breakup with Cliff.

After the party, Jake drove me home to Manhattan. We did not talk much in the car, but he did have two questions for me: "So this is what you aspire to?" he asked. "All this glitz?"

"What glitz do you mean?" I shrugged.

"The party on Saturday, the jewelry the women were wearing, the tables with all that food, Tatiana's house, all that art, the pool, the caviar," he responded, looking increasingly disgusted.

"No, silly," I trilled, "but you must admit, the caviar was quite wonderful!"

Jake did not respond. He nodded his head as if he understood, but he didn't try to hide his utter lack of interest in continuing our discussion.

I felt a bit bad I didn't stand up for my culture more. In fact, I thought the Russian restaurant had been fun, and I wanted to tell Jake that Russians liked to celebrate life by indulging in a bit of excess. I liked Tatiana and Sam, and I thought they were generous and deserved to enjoy all they had earned – especially the caviar. But I didn't say any of that.

At my doorstep that night, Jake handed me the last two pieces from his pack of green tea gum. "Here, you love this gum. See you soon," he said.

But that was the last time I ever saw him. The following night, I got a phone call in which he explained that our relationship was "all wrong" for him, and that now was the time for him to build a Warrior weekend-getaway business. Besides, he had realized that actually I was not the woman of his dreams; did I really want to live naked on an island? I would never be able to get a weekly manicure with such island living.

"But Jake," I protested, "I just got these manicures to look nice for our dates! I did not realize you were so... so anti-grooming!"

Of course, somewhere deep inside, a small voice told me that Jake was right – we did not belong together. But this weak voice of reason was buried deep inside the mess of infatuated feelings that resided closer to the surface.

"Mila, no, look, it's very simple, Mila. We are not meant to be, Mila. It's been fun, and you are a wonderful woman, Mila. I've been caught up in your energy and exuberance. But you, Mila, and this relationship – it's not what I want."

And indeed, I understood: Jake had a mission, and I was not a part of it. His plans to inspire the world did not include me. I tried to plead with him, saying, "But honey, I know you care for me!"

I got no answer – just a click, and he was gone.

In the morning, I woke up obsessed with the idea of convincing Jake he was terribly wrong. Jake had his Warrior mission, and I had mine – my Romance mission.

I called Jake at six a.m. and tried to reason with him. He let me speak for a moment before he responded, politely but firmly, as if he were talking to a child: "Mila, you are speaking emotionally; take a step back. I am sorry, but I'm just not interested in you like that. You are great, Mila, but I am on a path."

"Yeah, all of us dumpees are so *great!* And that's why you're dumping me, because I'm too great for your shitty little self!" I hollered after he had already hung up.

I called Jake several times throughout the day, he wouldn't pick up. So I emailed him: "Dearest Jake, I think you misunderstood me. I could easily live on a desert island; would love to, in fact. I get so tired of all the mad energy here in Manhattan, and the rat race! And if I just wore a high-SPF sunscreen, it would be fabulous...."

There was no response.

....

I fell into a deep depression. Suddenly, it was as if a year had not passed. In my mind, I was back on my parents' porch, and bereft of the love of my life, inconsolable and empty. At my new apartment, I couldn't shower or eat. I chain-smoked in the beautiful garden outside, throwing ugly butts all over the pristine grounds.

I still went to work, but I would cry at my computer and run out for frequent smoke breaks. Several times each hour I called my mom and dad; I needed their assurance that I would get through this.

I felt like I was a huge gaping wound, one completely open for insult and abuse. Luckily, I had no deadlines at work, and so I did not screw anything up that badly. But personally, it was down the black rabbit hole once again. In my mind, I went back over my behavior a thousand times to figure out what I had done wrong this time.

"It's all my fault," I would howl over and over to my concerned friends and family. "I should have insisted we go out less! I bet he thought he couldn't afford me!"

My behavior terrified my parents. It was easier to understand the erratic nature of my behavior the summer before, as it was due to the breakup of a ten-year relationship. But this time? They had met Jake, and just did not get it. They knew Jake was just a random man passing through – so why the intensity? Why such grieving?

My mother asked me these questions, hoping to jar me into a place of sense. She was tireless in her attempts: "Milochka, *solnyshko*, you have much to live for and this Jake, he is just a passing thing – a flirtation. You don't need him. A woman must be a survivor. *You* are what you need."

But I couldn't escape the bleak place I was in. All I wanted was to figure out what had turned Jake off, and to talk about it for twenty-four hours a day. And so I did, stopping only to light a cigarette.

My friend Jessica listened patiently as her boys screamed in the background.

"Mila, I just don't think you are ready to date yet," she finally said when I paused in my outpouring of words to light the next cigarette.

"I think you're wrong, Jessica! It is only dating that makes me forget Cliff. You have no idea what it feels like, to be alone night after night after night. You've been married for years, and so you are never alone. *Ever*," I stressed.

"Yes, I know, it's true. But Mila, I think you've been through so much in this past year; don't you want a rest from the stress of relationships?" she questioned.

"I just want to forget Cliff," I admitted honestly. "And I can't forget him when I am home crying about him all by myself. Jake made me have fun, and he kept me distracted from the pain of my breakup!"

Jessica still insisted that dating was not a good idea for me at this time. "You're not seeing these guys you date for who they are, Mila," she pointed out. "Jake sounded like a total flake! All that stuff about the NLP, warriors, and joining the CIA? He was on his own trip!"

At these words of wisdom, I thanked Jessica and hung up the phone. Then I looked at my cellphone's contacts list to see if there was another ear I could bend. I chose to call Tatiana, who had hosted us the weekend before for her birthday.

"Tatiana, what did I do wrong? Was I too demanding? Did he not like the way I wanted him to try all the food? Was I pushing the *blini* pancakes too much? Is it possible someone could get offended by me offering them caviar?"

Tatiana counseled me that caviar-pushing was the norm. She pointed out, "Mila – your Jake was not a serious man. He certainly was not marriage material... assuming that's what you want, of course," she said, tactful as always. "He wasn't good enough for you," she added.

"Yes, I hear you, but then, why would *he* break up with *me*?" I asked, struggling to understand. But Tatiana didn't have anything illuminating to offer about why Jake dumped me first.

Not hearing what I wanted, I called Alice, who had hosted the two of us in the Hamptons that weekend.

"Alice, what did I do wrong? Didn't you think he was so interested in me that weekend?"

Alice paused for a few seconds before she said in a quiet tone, "Mila, do you want to know the truth?"

"Of course, Alice, that is exactly what I want to know! Don't be afraid of hurting my feelings," I begged, desperate for a solution to the mystery of our breakup.

"Mila, I thought you were out of his league. He did not get you. It was all about him, his body, and his theories. You need someone less self-absorbed, and more dynamic. Mila, you need to know your value."

I started crying at these words; a part of me knew she was right, so my complete lack of perspective on the relationship was scary. I had never had a problem knowing my value before. I had had confidence before Cliff – a lot of confidence. But it was difficult to call up that confidence now, to have it join me in my new single life.

The old me was out of focus, a beautiful but blurry movie. The new me was a stark, raw, weeping mess.

....

When I found myself staring into space, yet again, at work, it began to dawn on me that I needed some help.

I hadn't been to see my therapist Misha for a few months; with my new job, I found it pretty impossible to travel all the way to his office in Brighton Beach.

And today I was realizing I desperately needed to talk to someone – a professional – before my distraction and my emotional despair cost me my job. On impulse, I called the psychologist help line cited in the binder the Human Resources department provided to all of my firm's employees.

CHAPTER 18 - EMERGENCY

The help-line operator took my name and number. A few hours later, Lynn Sternberg called. She was a psychologist, and the evaluator who would refer me to an appropriate psychologist.

Lynn and I spoke on the phone. Or, I cried on the phone as she spoke to me. She asked me if I was going to hurt myself. I said no, that I was already hurt because I had a broken heart.

I don't think Lynn got my joke. She asked again whether I had thoughts of ending my life. Honestly, I didn't, and I told her that. She said she would see me the next day then.

....

Lynn's office was on Wall Street in one of these rent-stabilized buildings full of old people. This comforted me a bit: Even though I felt weak and down, at least I wasn't old. I could get places, and I didn't have to hobble around in a walker, assisted by an indifferent home aide. If I could only fix my sadness, I would come to appreciate living once again.

Lynn was in her forties. She was attractive and thin, with large sympathetic eyes. She even looked like a therapist: She wore loose black pants, a black sweater, and very little makeup. When I asked her about her background, she said she had two Ph.D.'s – one from Stanford and another from University of Chicago – and had been in private practice for more than fifteen years.

Lynn asked me why my marriage did not work out, and so I told her about Cliff and Dominic – in detail. I hoped she could make more sense of my life than I could. But how do you tell the story of ten years in ten minutes?

She also asked whether I had gotten some help after my breakup. So I told her about Misha, and that he had prescribed some Lexapro during that black summer. It had helped me, I said, but after a few months, I decided I did not want to take it anymore, and that I had been fine ever since. That is, fine for a year – right up until I had met Jake.

"And did you call Misha this week?" she probed.

"Yes, I did, to ask for some advice about Jake. He prescribed me some Lexapro over the phone, and I have taken it since Monday. It's helping a bit, but I do not intend to stay with it; I hate having to take drugs!"

Talking to Lynn made me feel a little optimistic; she seemed so solid and capable. She asked me to come back a few days later to continue the evaluation process. I agreed, and returned to work, where I reviewed some deposition materials. The case was convoluted – a contract dispute over a merger gone bad.

I looked out my window. The sky was blue, and it was a summer Friday. Many of the partners were leaving early, heading to their summer homes.

I wished I were going somewhere – perhaps a weekend in London or Paris. My mother called, and asked me if I wanted to come to New Jersey.

It was not exactly what I had in mind.

I logged on to JDate.

CHAPTER 19 – FIFTEEN MINUTES

I opened the unread message from MosesLES waiting for me in my inbox. MosesLES, the CEO of an ebook publishing company, said he loved family and Israel and picnics in the park. He wrote that he lived on the Lower East Side – the LES in his handle – was happy with where he was in his life, and was ready to find someone with whom to share his happiness. This sounded promising, so I wrote back. Before the day was over, we had a plan to have a picnic in Battery Park the next day.

I went to New Jersey for the night first. There my parents looked at me with sad faces as I spent most of the night crying in the backyard. I thought of Cliff. I missed him more than ever, but I was also a little angry at him: He had released me into the wilderness of New-York-City dating! What had I really had in common with Jake, a self-absorbed pretty boy? But although I recognized objectively that the loss of Jake was inconsequential to my life, sadness still ripped through me. It came in waves – a slight wave, and then a huge overwhelming wave that made me gasp.

As evening turned into night, my mother came out on the porch with a plate of raspberries.

"Milochka, please eat something."

Mama looked at me kindly. She was suffering right along with me; this was clear. And food was, of course, love – an offering of food was an offering of love and support.

"The berries are fresh, from the organic market," my mother said softly. Mama wasn't always articulate during those quiet moments, but she could always offer.

"Mama, I'm not hungry," I refused. I couldn't let anyone into my fortress of sadness. My despair made me selfish.

"Mila, this boy was nothing. Your father and I thought he was not right for you at all. Not interesting enough, like you."

"Mama, I know. It still is sad."

"Why should it be sad, Mila?" my mother responded simply.

Her words caught my attention, and I realized I wasn't sure my sadness was about Jake at all. "I wish Cliff were here tonight. We could watch a movie together in my old bedroom."

My mother looked angry. "Do not talk about Cliff! We have forgotten him."

"I don't believe you," I said. I knew how much the relationship with Cliff had meant to my parents, how it had been like they finally had a son of their own.

"In the end, he wasn't good, Mila," my mother pointed out, in a strident tone now.

"It wasn't his fault, Mama," I suggested quietly. *It had been mine. Our marriage had broken up ultimately because of my affair, and my lies.*

"Milochka, you must stop thinking about Cliff. He is not thinking about you. He is gone."

"Mama, how can you say that!" I screamed, suddenly enraged. But my emotions were all over the place. The next second, I was once again sobbing hysterically.

My mother came over and hugged me. This felt good. She was so solid. And she reminded me that someone very important loved me – my Mama.

I wiped away my tears with my hands and took a raspberry.

....

The next morning, my father drove me back to Manhattan. We went for a swim in the pool in my new building.

It was quiet in the pool; my father and I were the only ones there. With each stroke I made, I felt more and more calm. I kept the same pace as my father. We did not talk very much, but once in a while, my father would smile at me at the end of a lap.

"You will show them all," he said as we climbed out. "But you must be stronger. A woman must be strong in our world, Milochka. Life is not for weak women."

I felt bad I had exposed the weakness of my temperament to my father. It hurt him very much to see me suffer, especially at the hands of men. I nodded yes, then kissed my father goodbye.

Upstairs, I dressed for the picnic with MosesLES – whose real name was Ezra. I put on short shorts, a pink t-shirt, pink high heels, and pink jewelry, as if I were a giant pink candy to dangle in front of a potential beau. I smiled at the silliness of this dating dance in which I was such a willing participant. At least I could look sexy, even as my heart was breaking.

....

Ezra rode up to the corner where we had agreed to meet on a bicycle. He was balding, with very white teeth, large green eyes, big unruly eyebrows, and a slight paunch. He was tan, and wore a white button-down shirt and khaki shorts. He looked pretty good.

We walked over to some grass. He took a purple cotton blanket out of his backpack and spread it out before we sat down. It seemed like magic when he pulled an entire banquet out of his bag: French bread, hummus, olives, tomatoes, several types of cheese, and a bottle of wine. He uncorked the wine and poured some into two plastic wine glasses. "To a beautiful Saturday!" he toasted. I lifted my glass, flashing him a quick smile.

If he only knew. If I weren't sitting here with him on this date, I would be lying in bed. I might be thinking about Jake. Or reminiscing about Cliff. Or more likely, both of them.

I looked at Ezra to come back to the moment. I focused in on his lips. They were full and sensual. He was growing on me.

We covered the basics before he complimented my pink ensemble: "Such a pretty girl in pink!"

Ezra ate the cheese and hummus, dipping his fingers directly into the jar and licking his fingers. He grabbed a tomato and took a bite, squirting tomato juice into the air. I leaned back so that the juice would not get on my pink sweater. He ate as if he were in a hurry, like there was someone nearby would put away the food any minute. *At least he has a zest for life,* I thought.

"Here, eat the hummus," he said, moving the jar toward me.

I looked at the outline of his finger in the jar. "Maybe later," I said as I smiled back. I took an olive instead.

Before long, it was almost seven, and I had dinner plans with my friends Oliver and Salma. Ezra asked if I wanted to ride to Chelsea on the front of his bike. I had never done that in Manhattan before. "Sure, sounds fun," I said. I was beginning to feel a little more upbeat. It was really a very nice day, and Ezra was not so bad.

We biked up Hudson Street and then Eighth Avenue. I enjoyed the fact that he was so strong and athletic.

When we arrived at Oliver and Salma's, I asked Ezra if he wanted to come up to say hello. He did. He came up to their loft carrying his bicycle. Oliver let us in.

We sat on the sleek pale blue couches in Oliver's spacious living room, sipped some champagne, and exchanged a few pleasantries about the summer heat and weekends in the city. Oliver and Ezra talked about their businesses.

Ezra then excused himself. I walked him to the door. He looked me right in the eyes. "I will see you very soon," he promised. I nodded, and shut the door behind him.

Not one second later, my eyes welled up with tears.

"What's wrong, Mila," Salma asked, spotting the change in my mood instantly.

"I am sorry," I whimpered as I tried to hold it together.

"He seems like a pretty solid guy," said Oliver.

"Yeah," I sniffed.

"Here, take a tissue," Oliver offered as he handed me a box.

I took one, and dried my eyes before we went downstairs for dinner at a French bistro. Oliver and Salma had just returned from Japan, and had pictures to show and stories to tell. I listened, but it was hard to concentrate: I found it impossible not to think back to my own trips with Cliff. Too, I was also envious of their easy couple's camaraderie; it was Oliver and Salma against the world.

The night passed in a blur. When they finally asked me what was new with me, a fresh wave of tears came up. I mentioned Jake. I told them that I had met a very cool guy who was into NLP – did they know NLP? – and that he and I had spent some time together in the Hamptons and that he liked to meditate and was trying to start a Warrior workshop.

"Jake?" questioned Oliver. "But I thought his name was Ezra."

"No, Jake and I were going out last week," I reminded them.

Salma joked, "I can't keep up with your boyfriends!"

When she said that, I started bawling into my entrée. "The very last night, Jake gave me some gum, and then I never saw him again. He even met my parents." I knew I seemed scattered to my friends. "And worst of all, I just still miss Cliff," I choked out. "Cliff was my only love."

We did not stay for dessert.

....

On Monday, I went to see Lynn to complete the evaluation. I told her about going out with Ezra.

"My initial prescription for you, Mila," Lynn said firmly, "is no dating."

"What do you mean?" I asked her. "Why would I sit out these next few years? I am not getting younger. I want to marry again, and have children!"

She looked at me. "Mila, dating is a very, very bad idea for you right now. I've seen these situations play out before. Trust me. You are not ready, Mila. Men will only create more problems for you right now. You need some time to recover from your breakup. Once you heal, you may be ready for something."

I stared at her blankly. Was she *serious?* Cliff and I had already been apart for more than one year, and I did not want to take time off from looking for the love of my life. What if he was on JDate just during these next few months? "That is really impossible," I objected. "I need to meet men now! I can't wait until I'm too old to bear children!"

Lynn said our time for today was up, and that she would be able to make time for me in her schedule, should I wish to continue with her as my psychologist. If so, then she would consider whether I needed to see one of the psychiatrists with whom she usually worked.

"Sure," I replied. I liked her enough. And I had survived this past weekend.

At our third meeting, Lynn asked if I would go for a consultation with a psychiatrist other than Misha.

I agreed, and went to see Dr. Hauser. He wore glasses and sat behind a laptop during our entire session.

"Hi. I'm Dr. Hauser. Do you mind if I take notes while you speak?"

I didn't. I told him the story of my past year, starting with the affair and ending with Jake. As I spoke, he typed fast, and never looked up. I wondered if he took typing in high school, as I had.

When I was done, he diagnosed me in two words: "Bipolar disorder."

"What's that?" I inquired.

"Extreme highs and lows," he said. "You get really fast and manic before you crash, and get slow and sad."

"Well, when I was with Cliff, Dr. Hauser, I was really quite even in terms of my moods. I didn't crash so much. Or ever, actually."

"This kind of disorder doesn't always come out until a patient is older. A trigger event, like a divorce, can set it off. I can prescribe some medicines for you to keep your moods more even," he replied.

I sat for a moment as I took in the information. True, I had a big emotional range right now, and I did get depressed at times. But I was a woman, and many of my women friends were sometimes down too. My feeling low was often related to some event – usually my weight. When I felt fat, I was depressed. When I felt skinny, I was happy. And the difference between fat and thin was often only five pounds.

"Dr. Hauser, I am not so sure I want to take medicine. I just feel like I was really okay and even for so long, until Cliff and I broke up, really. And so it doesn't totally make sense to me that I am biologically this way. Besides, I don't like to take drugs."

At this, Dr. Hauser actually stopped typing for a minute to look at me with genuine surprise. "Then, why are you here?"

That wasn't a bad point. I suppose many people wanted drugs, and health insurance would cover all sorts of uppers if a doctor prescribed them. Before I could form a response, the doctor went on. "Mila, our time is about over; we only have a minute left. Would you like to try some Lamictal?"

"What's that?" I asked. I had never heard of it before.

"It's a mood stabilizer. Off-label use. It will help you get even for now. You don't have to stay on it forever."

"Well, I'm not that keen to take more meds…" I said, hesitating for a moment. "But how about you give me the prescription? I can hold on to it for the next month while I see how I feel, and then decide."

"Great; here you go." He quickly wrote out a prescription, made an entry in his laptop and smiled feebly, still looking somewhere over my shoulder rather than right at me.

I was in and out – in fifteen minutes. Had this man really listened to the best story of my life that I could cobble together in fifteen minutes and labeled me already with a disorder? It put me off; his analysis seemed too surface and superficial. Obviously this doctor was being paid for the volume of patients he could shuttle through his office.

As I went home to my apartment, I noticed the city around me seemed empty. It was the third week of July; the summer was half over. People were leaving to go on vacation or coming back from places where they were spending time with loved ones. At least I no longer was able to say, "Last year at this time, I was with Cliff and happy." No, last year, at this time, I was already in my parents' yard and miserable.

I looked at the prescription. What the hell was this disorder? An online Google search of bipolar disorder revealed many artists and writers had had it: Virginia Woolf, Peter Tchaikovsky (possibly), and Sylvia Plath. Many had committed suicide. *That's interesting,* I thought, *because I haven't really ever contemplated suicide.*

Even when I was practically a member of the walking dead, during the summer after my breakup with Cliff, I still knew deep inside that I would pull through. *Otherwise, my mother would kill me,* I remember joking to myself.

I did not trust Dr. Hauser, with his intake interview that had lasted all of fifteen minutes. But, did I truly care if he was right or wrong? Maybe taking this medicine would make me feel better about Jake. No doubt it would act upon me like the Lexapro had the summer before.

So when I saw Lynn the following week and she asked me if I wanted to try the medicine, I told her I was ambivalent about it. I told her what I thought about Dr. Hauser, and asked her what she thought of Hauser's diagnosis. Lynn said she would need more time to come to an opinion. She realized I was completely stable for many years, and that I had gone through a very rough time for the past year. She thought this history of mine was relevant to my present state. It could be that I never got over the breakup, or that the stress of the breakup had made me emotionally vulnerable. Each of my romantic encounters now were mini-triggers, hitting my weak spot and making me more unstable and sad.

"My recommendation is an immediate moratorium on dating," she pronounced.

CHAPTER 20 — YOU, YOU, YOU

Unlike Lynn, I didn't think it was a particularly good time to stop dating: I had already made plans for a second date with Ezra. He invited me to a show with his friend Denny and Denny's wife.

The show was a very downtown event, a sixty-minute performance of all of the world's major philosophers' works. It had been a hit at the Edinburgh Fringe Festival, and was now in New York on a limited engagement. I was impressed that Ezra knew about this relatively edgy theater performance. Sure, it was a bit pretentious, as many of these shows often were. But, it was still nice to be invited to the party.

Ezra looked good. He wore a white shirt that set off his tan. His teeth practically sparkled, and he had arranged his hair to cover the bald spot. We sat in the second row. After the first hour, he put his arm around me. He was confident, and I liked that he seemed so certain of what he said and did. He was growing on me, and as the doldrums induced by Jake's leaving receded, I became open to filling the hole in my heart once again.

After the show we went to a dimly lit Thai restaurant in the East Village. Ezra ordered for the table: Pad Thai, but make it spicy. Chicken Massaman curry. Thai iced tea. He asked if I liked his choices, but looked away to the waiter before I had a chance to nod. I didn't care; I liked the way he took control.

At one point during our meal, the talk at the table turned to Israel.

"Has Ezra told you his army stories?" asked Denny.

"No, not yet," I answered as I looked over at Ezra. "What stories?"

"It's nothing, really," said Ezra. But he was smiling broadly and didn't seem to mind too much that the topic had been brought up. His chest puffed out and his arm flexed around me, and he squeezed my shoulder. I pressed myself against him a bit more tightly.

"It's really something!" exclaimed Marisol. "He is so humble."

I was intrigued. "What?" I said insistently, pulling at Ezra's shirt sleeve. "Tell me! I want to know!"

"Ezra was in Israel's elite commando unit. All secret. He was a commander," said Denny. "A super soldier."

"Wow, really?" I looked at Ezra closely. The reason for the air of supreme confidence surrounding him became clear: He was the epitome of a man's man, a man chosen by other men to lead because of his psychological strength, quick thinking, and physical attributes. He was a Jewish king – no wonder he had chosen the name Moses for his JDate profile!

How ironic that Jake had only dreamed of being in the CIA, whereas Ezra here had done the real thing! Now, I was getting somewhere: *Poof! Jake now was completely gone from even the recesses of my brain.*

Afterwards, Ezra took me home. He leaned in for a goodnight kiss outside of my building.

He was a pretty good kisser. I didn't see fireworks or anything like that, but that would be a lot to expect at this stage in my dating career.

"Hey, sweetheart, want to go on a day trip next Saturday?" he asked before he left. "I want to scout locations for my company picnic."

"Sure; that sounds great," I responded.

Hmmm... not bad. Only two weeks after breaking up with Jake, I was dating someone new, and going to fun places. Life was looking up.

....

The morning of the picnic, Ezra was an hour late. He said he had some emergency project to troubleshoot in the morning, and that the Zip car he had rented had been in a faraway garage. I wasn't too upset by this; I had sipped my coffee and ate a croissant while I waited.

I felt good too: I was wearing tan short shorts, a white button-down shirt, and sneakers. I was extra-skinny because of the mini-breakdown I'd had due to Jake. A few days of not eating was a perfect way to get in shape! At least there was one positive to my romantic lows. Oh, and another positive right now was this: As of last Friday night, thoughts of

Jake had been completely exorcised from my mind. Ezra had been my perfect cure.

On the drive out, we talked. Actually, he talked, and I listened. Ezra simply loved to talk. But I didn't mind. He was interesting. He had a way of making everything about his life sound like a tale – more grand, more meaningful, more of a legend. His grandmother had been a great, great woman who spoke eight languages. His stint in the army had afforded many opportunities for intense experiences. His film career had been full of dramatic meetings. Ezra was a person who found true meaning and joy in life's banal events. This made for a fun day trip.

At one point Ezra told me. "I made a movie that showed at the Tribeca Film Festival."

"Cool! What was your film about?"

"A boy who learns his father has a secret family only when the father leaves to live with the other family."

"That's interesting. Why did you choose that topic?" I asked.

"It was a true story. My father left my mother and me when I was eight to live with his girlfriend and children."

He looked very serious as he said this – his easy smile gone from his face. At the same time, he spoke smoothly, and it seemed like he had said this many times before.

We drove in silence for a while as I digested this new information.

"For a long time, I thought I was not loveable at all, that my father left us because he was tired of my tantrums. You see, I was a difficult child. It took me a while to get over this," Ezra said as he extended his arm toward me.

"That's heavy," I said, patting his hand. *Especially for a second date,* I wanted to add, but didn't.

....

We hiked to the waterfall site. I was in expert hands: Ezra carried both our backpacks, undoubtedly used to carrying much more during his army days in Israel. The waterfall was lovely, reaching high into the blue sky. The treetops obscured some of the mountain peaks surrounding the water. Ezra laid out the same purple blanket he'd used on our first date and got out the provisions: tomatoes, several types of cheese, and croissants from the Moroccan place next to his house.

There was a raw sensuality to the way he handled food. He put a huge hunk of cheese on a croissant as he offered, "Here, gorgeous, I'll make a sandwich for you." He then took a bite first, with flakes from the croissant going all over his mouth. He didn't bother to brush these off. "Open up!" he commanded, and put the sandwich up to my mouth. I took a small bite, but the flakes got all over my face too.

When we finished eating, Ezra got out his camera and snapped some pictures of me. "I'll make you a character in one of our books," he said.

"A character?" I asked.

"In a graphic novel. You'll see. I'll have one of my illustrators do it."

"That's great, Ezra!" I exclaimed. "You must love running your own company."

"It does feed some people," Ezra said proudly but not too boastfully. "I have thirty employees. It's nice to make a career out of doing what you love."

He spoke from the heart now, and I found this very charming. "It sure is," I agreed.

We got up to take a walk to the heart of the waterfall. The rocks were slippery, and I lost my balance, falling with a yelp. Ezra swooped down and lifted me up into his arms. "Are you okay?" he asked, saying the right thing although not in a terribly concerned way.

"Yes." My thigh was throbbing from the impact with the rocks, but I didn't want to be a baby about it as I was sure Ezra had seen much worse.

We returned to the blanket, and Ezra moved in for a kiss. Again, it wasn't so bad. I wondered how many men I had kissed since this time last summer, and how many of them had kisses which I thought were just like that – "not so bad...?"

....

When we returned to Manhattan, it was already dark.

"I'm starving. Want to grab dinner? I know an amazing place, and it's run by a friend," asked Ezra.

We went to an Italian restaurant near his apartment on the Lower East Side. Ezra's friend brought out a bottle of red and many courses – grilled calamari, sea bass, linguine. Ezra ordered for both of us, assuring me he knew "exactly what I wanted." And he did. Everything was delicious, and I loved that he had ordered the perfect things. Ezra was more than growing on me now – I was definitely having fun with him. We talked about his business. He didn't ask too much about me, and as usual, I was happy about that. I had too much of what I considered drama in my personal life, as well as a mostly boring job and overprotective Russian parents. What would there be to talk about?

The wine made me tipsy, and I let Ezra kiss me in the restaurant. His kisses were better when I was a little drunk. He then asked if I wanted to watch a movie at his place. I thought about it. It was late, and I didn't want to sleep with him. Officially, it was our third date. This meant that he probably thought it was time for the 'big deed.' I still didn't fully buy into a random three-date rule that so many men in New York appeared to live by. It really was quite agonizing to negotiate this dating battle of sex-versus-commitment.

"I live right around the corner," he urged.

Sure, they all did – right near the restaurant, the bar, the theater.

"I don't know, Ezra, I'm tired," I hedged.

"Oh, sure. If you're tired, I can take you home," he said graciously as his hands pawed my breast. Fortunately it was dark in the restaurant.

"Really? You won't mind?" I asked, somewhat surprised at his response.

"No, I want to respect the lady," he said.

But then I found Ezra wasn't budging. Instead, he moved closer to me and put his hand on my neck under my hair. He leaned in closer to my ear. "Let's watch the movie; it's one of my favorites. It's a Russian love story. What do you say?"

His mention of the movie's setting intrigued me. "It's a Russian movie?" I inquired.

"Yes, a superb film I discovered in film school."

This reminder that Ezra had gone to film school impressed me – especially now that I knew how talented Ezra was in so many different ways. He was an intellectual, a "gentleman soldier;" is that what they say? His wasn't a totally inept attempt at seduction.

"Well, okay. And will you take me home after?"

"Yes, sweetheart. I certainly will."

He smiled a large smile full of his brilliant teeth, leaned in and brushed his lips lightly against my ear. This was hardly convincing, but I was feeling like the choice had already been made for me. Ezra's setup had been too smooth – the apartment was, of course, right there – and it was simply too difficult to continue to say no.

His place was one of the most interesting apartments I'd ever been in in Manhattan. From the street, the space didn't look so special; it was just another Lower East Side tenement building. But, inside, it was huge. There was an immense living area, a sitting room, a kitchen, several bedrooms, and a cavernous downstairs with a two-floors-in-height theater space. "Friends sometimes do shows here," said Ezra. We sat on the leather couch in the theater.

The film, *Prisoner of the Mountains*, was heartbreaking. In it, two Russians were taken prisoner by two Czechnians, and two Czechnians were taken prisoner by some Russians. The movie focused on the mother of one of the Russian soldiers and her struggle to free her son, as well as the unconsummated love between one of the captive Russian soldiers and the Czechnian daughter of the man who had imprisoned him.

Tears rolled down my face when I watched the story of the doomed fighters and the suffering of their loved ones. Ezra watched it only out of the corner of his eye. Every ten or fifteen minutes or so, he had to go into the other room to email someone about some project. He was a hard worker – working on a Saturday night.

I assessed our day together, and how being with Ezra made me feel. I now admired Ezra even more: He was capable and good at so many things. He was a great businessman, and yet a fun guy, a man who liked picnics and romantic Russian movies and knew what to order at the restaurant. Still, my admiration did not make up for the fact that I found his humor a little old-man-like and that he was a bit aggressive physically. And, more importantly, I didn't really get the feeling that he was into me. I felt like he was going through the motions of being aggressive, whereas inside, he really would have preferred to email his clients and make ebooks.

Ezra started kissing me, and we began making out. Before long, it was too late for me to go home. I was simply too exhausted, and I felt like passing out right on Ezra's theater room couch. *Good job, Mila,* I said to myself as Ezra pawed me, trying to get under my short shorts.

"Ezra, can we just take it slow?" I asked him.

But soon enough he slipped off my shorts – and the rest, as they say, was history.

Score: Ezra: Home run. Mila: zero.

That's how low my acquiescence made me feel.

....

On Monday, I saw Lynn. I told her about the picnic at the waterfall, Ezra's movie on the topic of sexual abuse of minors, our restaurant date, and Ezra's suggestion to watch *Prisoner of the Mountains.*

Lynn was not impressed: "Sounds like a player to me, Mila."

What does this mellow Upper-West-Side Eileen-Fisher-wearing therapist know about players? I wondered to myself.

Lynn must have read my mind, because her next comment was, "In case you are wondering how I might know this, people tell me stuff. It's part and parcel of my job. Besides, I've been around the block a few times too, Mila."

"Lynn, how can you say that he's a player? What about the stories about his father and his commando career?" I objected.

"I understand that he has been through some trauma, but, Mila, there are a lot of signs that indicate he's a player. Besides, you know my recommendation: total abstinence from all dating. I know I may be boring you with the repetition of this message, but I'm okay with having you think I'm boring."

Near the end of the session, Lynn said she needed to discuss some scheduling with me: She would be gone a few weeks for her vacation in August, and then for a whole six weeks starting with the second half of December. I felt slightly anxious. *Gone for all of January?* I was beginning to enjoy checking in with her about things, even if I did totally ignore her downer advice to quit dating cold turkey. "The thing is, I will be on maternity leave through the end of January," she clarified.

"Maternity leave?" I asked in disbelief.

"Yes, I am pregnant," she said in a confident tone

I looked at Lynn. *Of course she was!* I could see a definite bump now, but as she normally wore such loose shirts, I hadn't really looked closely at her figure. It was July, so she must have been more than four months pregnant by now.

"Congratulations!" I said.

"Thank you, Mila," she said, looking happy. Judging from her appearance, she'd be one of these older mothers in Manhattan. Well, better an older mother than an older single – at least, in my opinion.

When I got back to work, an email from Ezra awaited. The reference line was, "You, You, You..." The inside of the message continued with the words, "...are a bombshell!" Ezra had used the picture of me from our picnic to make me the main character in a short graphic novel about a sexy lawyer named Mila who defends New York City from violent green thugs.

I decided I looked pretty good as a cartoon character – as Ezra had exaggerated a few of my features. My normally full lips were huge and red, and the breasts were certainly DD's inside a tight pink jumpsuit.

....

For the rest of the summer, Ezra and I dated. He never called me to just talk though; it was always to ask me out for our next date. The dates were his usual repertoire of picnics, dinners, and karaoke nights.

But still, I never really became his girl. There was a distance between us, and I just couldn't figure out what it was. My inner voice whispered, *Maybe it's the fact that he has zero interest in any of the details that make up 'you, you, you.'* Ezra didn't ever notice if I was paying attention to a conversation or thinking about something else entirely. He often had his arm around me, but we weren't really a couple.

One weekend, he invited me to a dinner party at his house that would be attended by his publishing and movie industry friends. I wanted to bring flowers to the dinner, and went to the green market near Duane Street in Tribeca. It was a bright summer day, and I was happy to have plans. I walked around the market, checking out the peonies and daisies. I saw one stand with pretty purple and pink wildflower bouquets.

I leaned in to smell one just as the sales lady lifted the bouquet up toward my face so that I could see it better. The head of a flower poked me exactly in the center of my eye. "Ouch!" I cried out.

But even though my eye started throbbing and tearing, I did not want to miss the dinner party at Ezra's.

When my mother called, I told her about the accident. "Milochka! You can't go to the party!" she screamed in horror.

"Mama, I am totally fine; it's just tearing," I reassured my mother. "It's not exactly comfortable, but I can deal. I don't want to cancel."

I should have, though. The dinner was a bust. Ezra's artsy friends were nice, but they preferred to speak in Hebrew. And everyone smoked non-stop. Tears poured out of my injured eye the entire night. The smoke made it sting even more. I had to sit with a towel, and wipe away the tears every few minutes. After a few hours, Ezra asked if I was okay. But he never offered to stop his friends from smoking, or, actually, to even stop smoking himself.

I said nothing. I was not one to tell Ezra that he was a jerk. Or that he had no manners. Or that he didn't give a crap about me. Instead, when he asked me if I wanted to have a quick Sunday lunch picnic near my house the next day, I said it was a great idea.

At the park, Ezra spread out the purple blanket, and got the usual assortment of cheese, tomatoes, and hummus out of his bag. We sat in silence for a while. Ezra didn't have much to say to me, and for once, I didn't want to make small talk about his avatar business. My eye was throbbing and red. After about twenty minutes, Ezra looked at an email on his phone and told me, "Shit, Mila, I am sorry; I have an emergency call I have to go do."

"Oh, okay," I replied, and started to get up off his blanket.

"No! No! You stay here and finish the picnic. You look like you are really enjoying it."

With that, Ezra kissed me goodbye and fled, leaving me the wine glasses, the rest of the cheese, and the purple blanket.

I lay back on the blanket. It was still early, the day was just beginning, and I wasn't sure what I would do later. Still, it felt silly to be here on the blanket by myself, with two wine glasses and a hunk of Havarti cheese. After a while, I gathered up my things and left.

....

The next weekend was the one before Labor Day. I expected that Ezra would call me on Friday to make plans for that Saturday, as he usually did. But by Friday evening, there was no word from Ezra. He also hadn't emailed me even once during the week to ask me if my eye was okay.

When my cell phone rang, it was my mother. At first I was annoyed that she wasn't Ezra. But when she greeted me with, "Milochka, how are you," I had a change of heart; I heard the love she had for me in her voice, and it made me tear up. I told her I was waiting for a call from Ezra, but it was already getting late, and there had been no word.

"Milochka, he is not serious about you!" my mother exclaimed, sounding exasperated

"I know, Mama. I don't understand what I do wrong," I said dejectedly, shaking my head in disgust.

"Nothing, Mila," my mother responded with certainty. "You did nothing wrong. It's not you; it's him." She was speaking slowly, very slowly, as if to make sure that I understood each word.

"I must have done something wrong! Why is he leaving me like this? It's just like it was with Jake; maybe I was too nice or too eager! What is wrong with me?" I derided myself.

"Milochka, stop this craziness! Not again," said my strong Russian mother, sounding angry. "Ezra was a jerk, and he is not worth one more minute of your time! He has never asked you about your eye!"

I heard her, and I knew she was right. But it was too late; I was already sad. I pulled out a pack of cigarettes, and went outside to light one up. As usual, my mother somehow knew. "Mila, do not smoke a cigarette!" my mother cried out over the phone. "Are you smoking?"

I couldn't even answer. The sadness was enveloping me, the huge dark hood that came over me every time the excitement of the new guy would recede and I was being dumped. It didn't matter that I really didn't like Ezra very much, and that he was basically a jerk when it came to me.

I wished I could say to him, "You know, when you told me about your father's deceit, I was taken aback. I thought you had been so hurt, and I wanted to be nice to you. I thought you must be so sensitive because you made a film about your experience. But actually, Ezra, you've been completely callous during our entire time together. You call or text me just once a week, and it's only to make a plan to get together. You order all the food for us every time we eat out, always assuming you know exactly what I want. And even if you do know, I would like to be asked once in a while! You've not asked me one question about my past or my job or my family. You work constantly when I am around, always texting or taking a call. Everything with you is really about 'You, You, You,' Ezra!"

But I had no strength to say anything to Ezra. Sadness was suffocating me. I was in Manhattan, but it may as well have been the Siberian gulag: My mind made it so. Inside the prison of my mind was a place of great suffering and hardship.

My mother called again, but I couldn't reach to pick up the phone. And that's when I knew I was in a danger zone: When doing small things like that seemed overwhelmingly difficult, it signaled I was emotionally out of whack. I felt like a boulder was pinning my chest down and my arms were made out of lead.

I was grateful that my mom kept on ringing my phone, however. Even though I couldn't pick it up, the rings were like shrill "I love yous" reaching into my foggy state and making sure I felt tethered to something somewhere.

Once again – Mama was my anchor.

CHAPTER 21 – THE LONG WEEKEND

Ezra texted me on Monday morning: "Hey bb. Spent w/e entertaining radio folk from Europe. Dinner Thurs.?"

The Thursday in question was later this week – and the Thursday of Labor Day weekend. After reading the text, I immediately called my actress friend Serena, my go-to expert on dating assholes.

"Tell him you're busy," said Serena. "He'll want you more."

I sighed. These dating games were hardly intuitive to me.

I labored over a reply to Ezra's text for an hour: "TY. Sorry – busy Thurs. but would love to see u another time."

The last phrase was the part about which I was most unsure. Should I have suggested an alternative date? Or acted more casual? I had opted for casual.

The response was silence. No counteroffer. The days passed. By Thursday night – nothing. Friday morning – still nothing. As I pored over some legal documents at work on Friday afternoon, my anxiety increased. His lack of prompt interest was not good. Clearly, I was low priority to Ezra.

"Why did you not just agree to go on Thursday, Milochka?" my mother chided. "Then you would know his plans for Labor Day, and you wouldn't have to wonder. He is probably going somewhere for the weekend."

"Mama, if he actually was interested, he would have asked me to join him in whatever it is he is doing. By asking me out on Thursday, he was downgrading me to just a date just before the last long weekend of summer," I pointed out.

"Milochka, you knew this Ezra is not serious about you! You knew that last weekend when he was too busy to see you," my mother reminded me. "So it is actually fine that you won't see him Thursday or this Labor Day weekend. Best to forget him now before you are too involved."

I heard Mama, and knew what she said made sense – but still I had a hard time staying blasé about his lack of interest in me.

What added to my nerves was that even my parents were going to be out of town for the holiday weekend. They were leaving later on Friday to visit friends in Florida, and the very fact that I was worried about their absence embarrassed me. Was I really so emotionally fragile that I couldn't handle a few days by myself during this long weekend of being sort of blown off by a guy I only sort-of liked? Ezra wasn't my even boyfriend! We had just dated for a few weeks – six, to be exact.

All my attempts at logic and control failed, though. As I realized that the long weekend had begun, my mood darkened even more. Ezra would never just do *nothing* on a holiday weekend! Maybe the European radio people were still in town? And maybe they were not people, but women? I imagined Ezra with two bikini-clad French girls playing Twenty Questions, a game Ezra loved, on a beach.

On the Saturday of Labor Day weekend, I woke up feeling desperately alone. I went into the little garden by my building and smoked a cigarette before even having a coffee.

I took a walk toward the Hudson River and sat on a bench. The sun was up. It was a stunning, windless day, the start to a perfect holiday weekend.

I watched a young woman walk a very small white dog along the river. She texted away on her Blackberry as the dog, a Maltese or Pomeranian, yapped at her feet. I desperately wanted to speak to someone, but everyone was away: Jessica had gone to Cape Cod with her husband and kids; Serena was in Europe visiting yet another married boyfriend; and my therapist Lynn was on her August break.

I looked at my cell phone, scrolling through the contacts for someone I could call at 7:30 a.m. on a Saturday morning. No one. I called my mom.

"Milochka?" she answered, sounding sleepy. "What time is it?"

"Almost eight o'clock."

I thought that sounded a little better than 7:35 a.m.

"Milochka, is everything okay?"

"Yes." But clearly, it was not. Why else would I call her in Florida on the Saturday morning of Labor Day weekend.

"Why are you up?" my mother asked.

"I couldn't sleep," I answered crisply. "Mama, I was just thinking, why would Ezra leave me his purple blanket, and then disappear?"

"Who?"

"Ezra! You know, the Israeli guy," I prompted.

"Oh, him. What blanket?" she then asked.

"Mama! Don't you remember anything?" I snapped. I could hear the emotion exploding inappropriately out of me. "The purple picnic blanket! He left it for me, that day of our picnic. I think he must have intended to see me again. It's his favorite blanket. What do you think?"

"Milochka, are you okay?" my mother asked again. "Where are you?"

"In the little park by my building. Stop changing the subject! What do you think about the blanket!" I demanded a bit harshly.

"I don't know, Mila!" she shot back, sounding upset. "Are you smoking?"

"No," I answered as I put out my cigarette. *How did my mother always know when I was smoking?* My eyes felt itchy, and I knew I was about to cry. Again. For the God-knows-what- number-time this crazy fucking summer. "Mama, I'll call you later. Tell your friends Lydia and David I said hello."

I hung up the phone and broke up all the cigarettes from my pack into little pieces as tears streamed down my face. Was Cliff away for the weekend? It had been almost a year since the last time I had seen him. Was he dating someone? Probably: He was relatively young, handsome, and successful. Not a total asshole, so he was more or less a prize in Manhattan.

I looked over at the water. I imagined disappearing under its surface, and floating away from my life. *No! I wouldn't become a tragedy like that.* In fact, I found even the momentary thought of not breathing terrifying.

I walked along Battery Park; it was emptied of all the locals. Tourists were beginning to walk around, snapping photos and chatting happily with each other. An Italian family sat near the Marina eating croissants.

The world was made of happy families. *And unhappy families too,* I reminded myself. *Thank God for Tolstoy.* The famous first line of *Anna*

Karenina came to mind: *Happy families are all alike; every unhappy family is unhappy in its own way.* But the reality was, I didn't need the famous Russian novelist to tell me about the unique nature of unhappiness.

God, it sucked to be alone on a long weekend.

My cell rang. It was my mom. "Milochka, Lydia here wants to talk to you."

"Lydia? Why? What did you tell her?" I asked quickly. But Mama never answered, for Lydia was already on the phone.

Lydia, an immigrant friend of my mother's from way back, was soulful and kind, and had the gift of storytelling. Lydia spoke in a low, hypnotically rhythmic voice, of love and men and boys, and said that I would know it when it was love that came into my life again. As for now, I had to be strong. She said that Russian women were always strong, because they had to be: "No woman can rely on a man. What if he takes to drinking? What then?" She said that as a Russian woman, I had to know how to suffer, and also how to persevere — that this was my cultural imperative.

As Lydia spoke to me, I stared at the water rocking gently back and forth in the beautiful Hudson River, and I felt calmer.

"We all have suffered, Milochka," Lydia concluded. "You must have faith."

"Thank you, Lydia," I said quietly, as I recognized my mother's friend was wise — and right. All the women in my parents' circle were strong: They worked, and they took care of children and parents and husbands in this new land. How brave they all had been to even get here! They had left their friends, family, jobs, language, and culture to come to this new land for the opportunities it afforded them, so that they could enjoy their religion and afford the fruits of capitalism today.

I remembered how back in the U.S.S.R. my father had lost his job once his management had learned of my family's request to leave the country on the grounds of our religion, and the religious discrimination we faced. That day he had come home with a completely white face and spoken with my mother in a hushed voice, taking care that Tonya and Vova, the young Russian couple who shared the kitchen and bathroom of our communal apartment, could not overhear. He was very worried about his future livelihood, as our leaving could have easily gone the other way for us: If some random bureaucrat had had a stomachache on the day our application was being reviewed, no doubt we would have been *refuseniks*.

We were lucky to be able to immigrate here, and my family drank to America every January 10th, the day of our landing in JFK. A picture of my mother and me by the baggage claim on that day still rested on my parents' bedroom dresser.

In that picture, my mom wears a big orange fox hat and a striped turtleneck from Italy; I have on my own new Italian wardrobe — a white rabbit hat and scarf set, and a red plaid skirt with a gold pin. We had sold the Russian *matreshkas* (nesting dolls) and other trinkets that we'd brought with us so that we would have some lire to spend as we waited in Italy for America to grant us refugee visas.

America was my home; where was my gratitude? If I could bother to emerge out of my own mind for two seconds, I would see reminders all about that life was relatively good for me — even a life without Cliff. Just yesterday, I'd read in the newspaper about a suicide bomber in Israel, and the snatching of a little girl from her Florida bedroom. Lydia was right: In the scheme of things, I had nothing to cry about. *Screw Ezra and his stupid purple blanket!*

I rose up off the bench as the prison of my mood let up for a moment, and I saw some light on the horizon. It was, at least, a little bit of perspective.

....

A very little bit — as it turned out. It took just another moment before I sunk back onto the bench. Damn; how easily did sadness over one's personal disasters trump the elation from not having to experience many of the world's other problems! My tears started once again.

It was almost four o'clock on the longest Labor Day Saturday ever. I was so lost in my feelings, I wasn't even sure where the time was going. *Was there anyone else I could call or text?* I couldn't call Mama again: She deserved a small holiday from my sadness.

I thought of Cliff: *No. Terrible idea. He would just laugh inside if I got in touch.* I didn't need to offer him more evidence of my inability to thrive without him. He'd had plenty of it already.

I scrolled through my contacts, from A to Z, landing on Oliver. Nope, he and his wife Salma were on a sailing trip in Croatia. Ahh – Lara. No, she was in Brazil with her kids for the summer.

I scrolled back up to the A's. Ezra. *Fuck! I thought I had erased him.* A pang of hurt ripped through me. Quickly I moved on. Zoran. Zoran! Oh, sure! Why didn't I think of him before? *Because he wasn't a good idea.* He was a user, an insomniac with OCD. And he'd probably be out of town like everyone else.

I looked at Zoran's number. I knew I shouldn't, but my thumbs were already moving.

"Hi Zoran – r u around?"

Not even a minute passed, when my phone beeped: "Gr8 2 hear from u – yes. Just chilling."

My heart beat a little faster. "Cool. I'm here too."

"Not away w/ new boyfriend? :-)"

"No." There was not much more to say. It was that stark – I was either away or I wasn't and clearly I wasn't. There was no boyfriend.

The next beep came immediately: "Scrabble?"

Don't do it, I thought, but I'd already pressed send: "Could be cool."

I felt the dark hood lift a little. Somebody was actually around.

I knew Scrabble was only a pretext. I knew what he wanted. Sex.

I, in contrast, just wanted to talk to someone, to pretend there was some possibility of romance. But I agreed and went over to his penthouse.

He greeted me in his usual attire –pajama pants. "Hey, stranger!" he said, hugging me for a few long seconds. "I've already set up the board. Can I get you some rosé?"

I nodded, overwhelmingly relieved to be with another human being – even if he was really a wolf in grandma's clothing. Or was he just a wolf in wolf's clothing? After all, he wore pajamas... *Hmmm.* I contemplated all this as he poured me the glass of wine.

"Mind if I smoke?" he asked as he lit up a joint and motioned me over to the sleek brown leather couch. Italian, of course.

Through the three windows that faced south, north, and west, I saw the Statue of Liberty, and Ellis Island, where I had paid to have my parents' names inscribed in the immigrant wall of honor. Some American Dream this was! I was glad my parents were far away.

So much for being a strong Russian woman! Or a strong woman, period. The sense of pride Lydia had tried to instill in me earlier had vanished. *Sorry, Lydia, sorry, Mama, sorry, Jessica, sorry, Lynn, and sorry, Mila,* I thought as I smiled at Zoran.

I knew my presence turned him on; he was breathing slowly and looking at me with hooded eyes.

And so, Mila, my inner monologue progressed as Zoran rubbed my shoulders, *you're at another new low.* Or was it one, really? Zoran and I had been together before. Anyway, how many lows could there be? And besides, no one needed to know of this low; everyone was away. I didn't have to tell anybody, not even my therapist Lynn.

As Zoran put his hand on the bulge in his pajama pants, I hated myself.

As Zoran touched the top of my t-shirt and whispered "May I?" into my ear, I thought of Cliff on some Greek beach with his new girlfriend.

As Zoran undid my bra, I looked out at the sun setting over the river. Saturday was coming to a close. *Good. Only two more days of this long holiday weekend were left.*

CHAPTER 22 – THE IMPASSE

"So, what do you think happened?" Lynn asked during our Monday session. I had told her of my plunge into darkness over Labor Day weekend, and confessed that I had called Zoran.

"I think that purple blanket was not so important to Ezra," I joked.

"Yeah, sure," she responded readily, "but what do you make of your hanging out in the park for so long? And why did you want to see Zoran?"

"I don't know." And truth was, I didn't: My black mood had passed. Now that the holiday was over, my parents were back, work awaited, and my sessions with Lynn had resumed, I felt more upbeat. The sad post-Ezra holiday weekend was receding in my mind. It almost felt as if someone else had sat in the park crying for all that time – someone dull and listless and sad. It was like I had been hypnotized. And as for Zoran? Well, I preferred to just forget that sad Scrabble game entirely.

"Well, do you agree with me now that Ezra was no big prize?"

"I do. You were right," I answered somewhat reluctantly, shrugging my shoulders in an attempt to minimize this conclusion. I was ashamed – even here, with my therapist, to whom I was supposed to show myself, warts and all.

Lynn looked at me calmly and smiled in encouragement. I recognized that she wasn't trying to make me feel bad, but she was anyway.

"Mila, I'm not saying that because I love to be right. Really, I would be happy to be wrong! But it seems to me that your judgment when it comes to men these days is off, and you're not getting that. Why do you think you did not see the truth about Ezra when you first met?" she prodded.

"Because, Lynn, I am still feeling so sad about Cliff," I suggested. "Besides, I never would have stayed with Ezra long-term. I know he wasn't right for me. He was way too full of himself. And too tan. I hate tanning."

Lynn did not smile at this, my attempt at humor, but pressed on mercilessly. "So why date the guy at all, Mila?"

"I was happy to meet someone," I explained.

"It does not sound to me like you have any problems meeting someone," Lynn pointed out. "In fact, you've been meeting 'someones' nonstop since last summer."

I sighed. All this psychology stuff was so depressing. I could barely stand to listen to my own story, and I wondered how Lynn could sit for hours on end listening to one patient after another complain about the inane details of their lives.

Lynn did not let up. "There is something else going on. These men are making you get too excited. You are missing the details, or the truth, about them in your excitement."

I nodded. I did agree with her.

"If you are going to continue dating against my advice, I strongly counsel you to not drink at all on these dates. Drinking clouds your judgment."

"I suppose you're right," I conceded. "I probably wouldn't have gone back to watch *Prisoner of the Mountains* with Ezra if I hadn't been a little – really, more than a little – drunk. But I never realized that drinking was such an important part of dating in New York!"

"Can you give it up?" Lynn questioned.

"Well, the guys all seem to want to ply you with drinks," I said thoughtfully, "and I already don't drink a lot, Lynn; a glass and a half, or two at the most. How much less can I drink?"

"There is always zero," she said with a knowing smile.

It was kind of irritating that Lynn always had an answer for everything.

"Okay, zero," I said a bit too brightly. "Whenever possible," I quickly amended.

"Great!" Lynn responded, seeming pleased. *Good. I did want her to approve of me.* "And, Mila, I would get off that – what is that online site; Jewish Dates?"

I smiled. Lynn was so unhip. "JDate," I corrected.

"Yes, JDate."

I thought about her suggestion. "Lynn, how can I just put an end to dating when I am in the prime of my life?"

I looked straight at my very pregnant therapist, who was patting her growing belly. Lynn was in no danger of being dried up and childless.

I thought for a second of the baby Cliff and I had never conceived. If things stayed on track, the baby would be a person by now. I waved away thoughts of Caterina or Caleb – the "C" baby names Cliff and I had discussed. "Can't you help me as I date instead?" I asked Lynn. "I mean – this is urgent!"

Lynn shook her head. "Mila, you are paying me a lot of money for advice. But you aren't taking any of it! I would not be doing my job if I helped you out with the dating. You are emotionally spent, and you need a break from the emotional rise-and-fall you experience as you date."

Lynn and I were at an impasse. And our session was over.

Chapter 23 – Family

It was fall. The leaves were turning. People were still happy, invigorated by the freshness in the air, not yet beaten down by winter's onslaught of rain and snow, and not yet resentful of the seemingly unending gray of a New York winter.

I sat in the park a few blocks from my office. It was lunchtime. A single yellow leaf broke free from a tree and twirled in the wind. I followed it with my eyes as it fell on the dirty sidewalk. Now another leaf followed. Then another. In a few weeks, all the trees would be bare.

Fall meant the Jewish holidays. Celebration. Food. Family, or in my small family's case, friends. Another Thanksgiving was fast approaching.

I wondered when I would stop thinking of every holiday in terms of Cliff. The first Thanksgiving without Cliff. The second Rosh Hashanah. The third New Year's Eve. And yet there was something reassuring about the unending repetition of events: The outside world was letting people know that life went on after loss, cyclically and steadily. The future had an inexorable pull, and time passed. So long as you woke up every day and went to sleep every night, you would move forward in the stream of time, and be caught up in this most basic truth of physics and history. Only the daily details were up to you.

I thought about the details of my single life in New York: work, men, therapy. My own personal never-ending New York winter, it seemed. It had been almost a year and a half, since the day Cliff said it was over for us, and still my new life still felt foreign to me.

"Milochka," my mother said when she called later that day, "I am thinking of having Boris and Tamara over for Rosh Hashanah. We'll just do something small this year. What do you think?"

"Fine." It didn't matter much to me. These days – the smaller, the better.

....

Boris, my mother's younger and only brother, had been "Boris the bachelor" for years, as he was the only bachelor in my parents' large circle of married friends and family members. When I was a little girl, I told him I wanted to marry him when I grew up.

But when I was seven and he was thirty, Uncle Boris left us to go to America. He was the first of all of us to go; it was a brave move for a mild-mannered man.

My parents thought he could only "do better" in America. They figured in Riga, he'd never get married. He was a quality engineer in a brewery, and so he always smelled like beer – hardly a way to find a good Jewish wife, my parents had thought.

Uncle Boris had indeed married in America. His new wife, Tamara, was in her early thirties – old by everyone's standards at that time.

I was twelve when Uncle Boris married, and I wasn't happy about it: after all, I was losing my future husband! My uncle and aunt moved deep into Brooklyn, and spent most holidays with my aunt's family. So my mother's dream of a big family gathering in America over Rosh Hashanah did not materialize. Rather, over the years, we saw Boris less and less, and my mother spent many nights crying about the realities of American work demands and car distances. A casual visit was all but impossible, and Mama missed seeing her little brother terribly

Yet Mama remained grateful she had any family at all in America. "We have a lot to be thankful for, Milochka," she said every year around this time, even though the American relatives who had been so eager to invite us to their split-levels with pools on Long Island had long since moved to Florida.

When I met Cliff, our family of three became four for the holidays. This was a solid core of people: Cliff rounded us out, and he made me feel more whole. I felt four was better than three when it came to gatherings. But now, it was back to three, and I found it hard to look forward to the holiday dinner. It still felt raw to look at Cliff's empty chair, and to remember how he would always eat triple portions of my mother's lamb with prunes.

I told Mama I would come for dinner in the evening; that during the day, a friend had invited me to go to Rosh Hashanah services at a new synagogue in Lower Manhattan.

The Downtown Synagogue had been formed after 9/11 by a young couple from Brooklyn, Benji and Rivka. Benji was a rock-and roll-rabbi who wore all black and sported a crew cut. Rivka wore long skirts and Jimmy Choos.

I found the services short on content and long on style. The crowd was young and hip: It was a glorified singles scene here. It was another total miss on my part, a place where I felt like an outsider. I sat in the synagogue, put up for the occasion in a raw loft space in Tribeca, feeling like I belonged less than ever.

Perfectly groomed Jewish girls dressed in their Barneys' best and self-important New York Jewish men filled the seats. One after another, there were speeches praising Benji's and Rivka's efforts to revitalize the downtown Jewish scene. Benji introduced each as a dear friend in such-and-such industry who has given time and money to the synagogue. A filmmaker with a goatee, a banker, and a real-estate managing director spoke of the joy of being a part of the New York downtown Jewish scene.

The room was full of labels and nose jobs – and people from JDate. I kept seeing familiar faces: the guy who liked long walks in the West Village on a Sunday afternoon; the restaurant owner who collected art; the knee doctor from uptown.

Cliff and I would have surely bonded in our feeling of being outsiders here. Maybe it was due to his parents' divorce and my immigration to America, but for whatever reason, we both always felt like we did not fully belong in such a status-driven scene (not that I had something in particular against a Barneys' wardrobe). As I leafed through the prayer book, I thought of how much I missed laughing with Cliff, and after services, when it was time to mingle, I fled.

I went to Port Authority to get the bus to New Jersey for our dinner. Back to Fair Lawn, back to my parents and Uncle Boris and Aunt Tamara, back to where I once had belonged.

At Rosh Hashanah this year, I found my Aunt Tamara was supportive now, when it counted. I didn't feel that I needed to pretend to be perfectly happy around her. I knew too my mother appreciated her, and how she called often to check in.

I guess I had quite gotten over my girlish jealousies over my uncle's devotion to his wife. As Mama loved to say: Family is family.

Chapter 24 – The Birthday Watch

Saturday was my birthday. The arrival of my birthday, just like the arrival of the holidays, meant another year without Cliff had gone by. This was now my second birthday alone.

My parents came in the morning for a birthday brunch. I was happy to see them. They were the one constant in my life, the way parents should be. I was lucky to have them. They kept me grounded, tethered to some sort of structure in the midst of all the turbulence of the past few years. We went to Bubby's, a trendy Tribeca diner packed with both families and hipsters.

My mother was glowing: She loved birthdays and festive brunches.

"We are so proud of you, Milochka!" my father proclaimed as we sat waiting for our omelets and French toast.

"Proud? Why? What is there to be proud of?" I asked.

"Milochka!" my mother exclaimed. "You have been through so much. And you're a lawyer at a big firm now. You have a very nice job."

My parents were especially proud of my re-entry into the corporate world of New York City. I had my own office and an assistant, and they, as hardworking immigrants, had never had the luxury of closing their office door to have private conversations whenever they liked. In their eyes, I was a part of Manhattan society.

"I do," I confirmed quietly. But that's all I said. I didn't want to burst their bubble at this minute. I hated the whole big law thing, and they knew I hated it, but this was my birthday. And it was true that I had essentially found an entrée into the world that I had been a part of prior to my breakup. My parents loved that America was full of second chances – even for divorcees. It was an old-fashioned calculus, but there was some truth in it all.

"Mila, what is wrong!" my mother screeched, looking at me more closely. "What are you thinking about?"

Mama was good. She could tell I was distracted; that I was smiling a bit too vacantly.

I knew I should have been enjoying this nice brunch with my wonderful parents. Nobody else in the entire world would do as much for me, and would ever love me as much as they did. At one time, I thought Cliff would always be there with his love. But I had been wrong.

So, I, of all people, knew I should have been full of gratitude to my parents, and by extension, to the universe. I had just heard a lecture about gratitude at the Soho synagogue. But I couldn't shake my desire for more in my life than my job. I hated being alone, being part of a threesome of two parents and me.

"I'm okay, Mama. Really, I am," I said, a little too brightly.

"You don't look fine." My mother looked worried for a second, and then waved it away. "Here, Milochka," my mother said as she handed me a beautifully wrapped box and a card.

I tore open the card. It said: "On your special day, go for your dreams!" My mother had written underneath: "To our wonderful daughter. We know you will achieve your dreams. We love you always and support you in all your choices! Love, Mama and Papa."

I felt a heavy feeling in my heart. What was I going for exactly, on this special day? My job sucked the life out of me, and the men I had been dating were losers. Everyone knew that – most of all, me.

"Oh, Mama, Papa, I love you too," I said, hoping to push down the despair my emotions brought. But, suddenly, I burst into tears.

"Milochka, what's wrong?" my father asked, a look of concern on his weathered face..

"Nothing's wrong, Papa. It's all okay," I sniffed.

The truth was, I couldn't explain it. Seeing how much my parents cared for me made me sad. I wanted them to be happy. I wanted them to have less to worry about. But most of all, I wanted to thank them: I owed them my life. They constantly nursed me back to sanity!

But I could not manage to tell them that. As much as we talked when we were together, the real deep stuff often went unsaid. I promised myself I'd write my mother a card for New Year's that said what was so often left uncommunicated.

"Look at the gift," my father prompted.

I unwrapped the box. Inside was a stainless steel, diamond, and pearl watch with a black lizard band.

The watch was shiny and elegant.

"Wow!" I exclaimed in true delight.

"For our lawyer," my father said, his face beaming. "Lawyers have nice watches."

I nodded in agreement before I put it on. It was important to my parents that I look the part of an American success.

....

For my birthday evening, I had plans for dinner with my friends Oliver and Salma. But as I began to dress and looked out the window, I saw it was beginning to rain. I contemplated canceling the birthday plan: with this weather, it was a perfect night for a movie and takeout, and Oliver and Salma would probably be grateful to stay home. But it felt like another one of these nights where I was on automatic. My body went through the planned agenda while my soul hid somewhere deep inside of myself.

The three of us took a cab to a restaurant in Far West Chelsea. Over dinner, Oliver spoke of ice climbing equipment and the difficulty of transporting it on an airplane. In return, I reviewed for Oliver and Salma the personal quirks and hobbies of the inconsequential men I had dated this year: Southern surgery resident. Midwestern seminar salesman. The Israeli ebook entrepreneur they had briefly met.

By the time we finished dinner, it was cold and pouring. As we stood outside the restaurant waiting for a cab, I looked up and down the empty street. Dark silhouettes of apartment buildings surrounded us. Some apartment lights were on, and some off. As I often did, I imagined the life that went on behind the windows here: families reading by a lamp; couples lovemaking or perhaps fighting.

New York, with its sometimes-empty streets, was the kind of place that could suddenly make you feel terribly lonely, even as you were in the middle of a birthday evening with friends.

....

As I went to bed on my birthday night, I thought of Cliff. Was he watching a movie with his new girlfriend on our old couch? Did he have his arms around her right now? Fortunately the ring of the phone distracted me from these going-nowhere thoughts. The caller turned out to be Serena.

"How are you?" I asked, happy to focus on someone else and their problems for a change.

"The asshole won't pick up the phone," she shrieked into my ear.

"Who?"

"Richard! That ass!"

Richard was Serena's new – and – married boyfriend. Although he had told Serena he was now separated from his wife, and no longer living with her and their three children.

"Oh. Him," I said softly.

"The nerve. After everything he promised me! How could he just disappear like this, after getting me to go to London for a weekend with him!"

I grimaced. I knew full well Serena had just spent the weekend with Richard in a hotel, and that he had told her he would buy a new apartment for the two of them once his divorce was over.

I heard crying on the other end of the phone. My eyes widened: Serena never cried. This man must have been something to her.

"Oh my God, Serena, I am so sorry," I said with true feeling. I knew how she felt. I had thought Cliff would be there for me too – and then he wasn't.

"Mila, he was lying! He never meant it. He'll never leave her. He won't, because he wants to see his kids, and he's scared he'll lose them if he splits with his wife. It's so unfair. He said they never even have sex anymore, that he's been in a totally loveless marriage."

I stayed on the phone with Serena for another hour as she vented. One of the things she spat out was, "I hate that stupid astrologer!"

You see, Serena recently turned forty, and so she had just gone for a special consultation with a celebrity fortune-teller/astrology guru. The guru had told her this was the year she needed to invite love back into her life. To do this, the guru claimed, Serena had to put away her defenses, and soften. And so, after years of being a tough, city-savvy man-eater, Serena did soften – with Richard. I didn't think the guru had specifically suggested that Serena be open to a married man who was already in a relationship. But this was a small detail I could not point out to Serena without risking our friendship.

"Men suck," I offered up instead, although I didn't want to think this – despite all the crap I had just been through. And I didn't really think this one hundred percent. I knew that some men sucked and some didn't, and that some people sucked and some didn't. And that some people who ordinarily did not suck may suck in some circumstances. And that it also could be your fault for allowing someone to suck. But right now, what Serena needed was for someone to understand her pain, and so it was best to keep things simple. As I commiserated with her about men and dating in New York, I realized our talk was essentially the same conversation we'd been having since last summer.

"My forties will not be about men," Serena finally swore through her sobbing.

"What will they be about?" I asked.

"About me, about my art, about my business," she promised.

"Sounds great!" I said, being quite her cheerleader. And frankly, it did sound like a good idea. Not necessarily a practical one for a woman dying to have a baby, like Serena was, but perhaps the only way for her to get through her fortieth birthday.

We hung up, and my parents called soon thereafter to say goodnight. "How was your night?" my mother asked. "Did you wear your watch?"

"What? Oh, the watch; no, not yet."

"Mila! Wear the watch! You have to be proud of yourself and your accomplishments," my mother counseled me.

"Sure, Mama, sure. I will."

I didn't tell my mom how I was really feeling after the evening out with my friends, or about my conversation with Serena. I did not want my mom to think I was lonely and sad on my birthday. There was plenty of time for loneliness the other 364 days of the year.

Chapter 25 – Dr. Gold

As I thought about Serena's experience and her decision to focus on herself for a while, I decided I would stop dating for a few weeks. This minor epiphany came suddenly. I finally truly understood that I needed a break. I couldn't wait to tell Lynn.

At our appointment, Lynn asked me when I was going back to Dr. Hauser for a follow-up. I told her I did not want to see him again, as I did not think he paid attention to anything I said. Besides, when I had taken the Lamictal, it had given me a rash, and so I hadn't continued with it and did not need him to prescribe anything more.

After hearing my complaints, Lynn suggested that I go for an evaluation with another psychiatrist, Dr. Gold, whom she had not suggested initially because he was more expensive.

"Is he someone who may actually listen to me?" I asked her a bit eagerly.

She nodded. "I think you will like him. He is a very good doctor."

....

Dr. Gold's office was uptown on Madison Avenue, in a pre-war apartment building with an elevator attendant. I did not like going to the Upper East Side, as it was my old neighborhood. The doctor's office was above a Mayle cashmere store where I had once bought Cliff a scarf for his birthday.

I took the elevator up to Dr. Gold's floor, thinking all the while about life having so my turns. As people from my former milieu built their families, I was building relationships with paid professionals. I was being drawn into therapy land. Fabulous.

Dr. Gold's office door was open, so I walked right in.

"Hello, I'm Mila."

"Hello. I am Dan. Come on in to my office," greeted a short, thin man with large brown eyes.

I followed him into an office full of antiques. He showed me to an elegant thirties-style sofa covered in red silk pillows with art deco geometric motifs.

Dr. Gold had dark brown hair with a small bald spot, and he wore a very dark suit. His Harvard med school degree hung opposite the couch. I giggled at this: At least all my therapists were Ivy League grads.

"I've heard a lot about you from Lynn," he said.

"Is that good?" I joked back.

"It's helpful," he assured me, smiling. His big, open smile and quiet, confident voice made him that much more attractive. He was one of the short, successful, and very smart men who populated this city. *He's the kind of man I should be dating*, I thought.

Dr. Gold asked me to tell him my story. I tried, but found myself rambling after only a few minutes: "And then Cliff said we needed some time apart. The two of us really loved each other. But although Cliff and I had been trying to have a baby, our sex life... well, we didn't really have sex a lot. Or sex that I liked. So that was a problem."

I started crying. Dr. Gold handed me a tissue.

"Thanks," I sniffed as I dried my tears. "And then I had a bad breakup with a guy I was dating in July, and that's why I found Lynn."

It was difficult to figure out what was important enough to share with someone whom I had never met before. Besides, by now, I was bored of telling my own saga. But Dr. Gold listened carefully, taking notes in a small pad, and at the end of the hour, said he wanted me to come back. He told me that he although he normally evaluated patients in one session, he preferred to hear more about me before making a recommendation. He wanted to schedule two or three more meetings.

"Okay," I agreed, happy he hadn't offered me a slam-dunk diagnosis of some fashionable malady.

Chapter 26 – The Do-Over

As I took a break from dating, I, like Serena, began to focus on work. My new boss, Erin, was a mousy woman in her early forties. She had frizzy brown hair and a wide pale face. Erin dressed in red reindeer sweaters for three months on either side of Christmas, and she wore no makeup. Her most salient feature was her half-smile: She had a strange paralysis of the lips – she could only smile with one side of her mouth. So her smile always looked like a sneer.

I was helping Erin with a protracted contract dispute – some Ponzi scheme in which our client, a bank, had bought a bad loan from another bank, and been duped out of almost a million dollars as a result. The main issue was whether the selling bank was aware it had sold our client a doozy.

Erin liked to talk about herself, and after a few meetings with her, I knew enough about my boss to write her biography. She told me she came from a huge Irish family, and had paid her way through college and law school. She had "...worked her ass off at school," as she put it. I could tell she was proud that she rose up to an of-counsel position at a major law firm.

Erin was a plain talker and a tough litigator. I'd often stand outside her office while she threatened the other side: "Mr. Horowitz, pardon my French, but are you fucking kidding about this discovery production? Zilch, you have given us zilch. If you don't produce, I assure you, things will get much worse. Quickly."

She'd hang up and look at me. "Imbecile! We'll show him."

"Yes," I would say, nodding in agreement. I actually had little to add: I could care less about "getting" the other side. This, I knew, was a problem for a litigator. I didn't have that go-for-the-jugular instinct that Erin and other successful lawyers at my firm had; I found getting down and dirty with the other side to be unpleasant. I would be much happier talking about the philosophy of the dispute with the other side over coffee. But the firm was paying my rent, and therefore, I was happy to pretend I enjoyed being Erin's sounding board for her strategies of ripping apart the other side.

Erin's husband was a partner at another big firm. He was Dutch, she explained, and this therefore was the reason for her difficult last name with its many consonants. She loved saying her name and lingering on those impossible consonants: "This is Erin Rotmensen," she would answer her phone. "That's R-o-t-m-e-n-s-e-n; a Dutch name, my husband's."

Erin always talked of needing to get her work done so she could go home to the husband and their two daughters. Because I was so junior at the firm, Erin thought I was a bushy-tailed young innocent: "You have no idea, Mila, how hard it is to leave your kids at home," she would say, her eyes misting over as she held up a picture of two bucktoothed mousy little girls.

"I'm sure, Erin, it must be very tough," I'd say in return, yearning to explain that I, too, had been somebody's wife and had already paid some life dues. That I was supposed to be going home to my babies now too – but things had gotten fucked up. So here I was now, for round two of my life. Ten years had been erased. I was a do-over, and Erin simply had no idea.

Chapter 27 – The Dating Prescription

I saw Dr. Gold two more times. At the end of our third session, I asked what he thought about me. He said it was hard to make a definite diagnosis.

"Do you agree with this bipolar stuff that Dr. Hauser said?" I asked him softly.

"I really cannot say that I agree," responded Dr. Gold. "The case with you – it is not so clear. I think there is a tendency now for you to have mood swings."

This I got. But then he went on to say some stuff I didn't.

"You have had some stressor events, fertility troubles, career issues, a busy husband, perhaps a low-grade depression. Then you met Dominic, and perhaps what is a natural hypomanic state in you got a revving up. Hypomania is a state characterized by high energy, decreased need for sleep, and creativity. So, a hypomanic person talks easily to strangers, takes pleasure in small things, has an increased sex drive, but is often fully functioning. Some therapists argue hypomania leads to productivity and creativity and so is a positive thing for our society. Well – as this all pertains to you – you welcomed the excitement of this new romance. It could very well be that the Dominic period, and your inability to find the energy to break free, was due to a hypomanic state. This was followed by a sharp fall into depression, which might never have happened if Cliff hadn't broken up with you. Now, hypomania followed by depression is quite problematic. Taking the Lexapro got you out of the depression, but it created a mania in you, which led to things like restlessness, your desire to smoke, and perhaps your engagement in reckless behaviors. "

He looked at me to see if I was following.

I nodded, although he was saying something so involved and clinical-sounding, I couldn't truly get a handle on it.

"Actually, I am certain of one thing," Dr. Gold continued.

"What's that?" I asked with some trepidation.

"I agree with Lynn about her recommendation for no dating. The men are inducing too much excitement in you, and given your recent history, put you in danger of mini-highs and mini-lows."

"Okay. I see. Well – That's a lot of information," I said to Dr. Gold. "So what do you suggest for me?"

"No dating," he nodded, and wrote in his pad.

Ah, did he mean this no-dating thing as some sort of prescription?.

"Did Lynn pay you to say that?" I said with a smile, although I didn't feel like smiling, and I had a million questions about what he was saying: *Did I have some kind of condition now? And if so, is it temporary, or permanent?*

"What else?" I pressed. "I don't feel that not dating is a good long-term option for me."

"No drinking, eight hours of sleep, and exercise," he replied.

"But I already do all of that. I was never a big drinker, and now I'm not even drinking a sip, since I'm temporarily not dating."

"Mila, you need a stable situation – the more stability your life has, the better you can control your current mood state."

"What's with this mood thing, Dr. Gold? It's new to me. I can tell you I didn't really have 'moods' before Cliff locked me out of our apartment," I emphasized.

"Well, it may all be temporary, but right now, the men are triggering mood swings in you. We need to stabilize your brain chemistry, and then we can figure out what to do long-term. It is quite likely that you just need some medication in the short term, and then, in the long term, you will be fine. Of course, with some people, if they can't remove the stressors, then the condition gets worse."

"What?" I questioned in some confusion.

"There is an importance to you having a calm environment. You need little or low stress. Dating is too stressful. Romance is a trigger for your moodiness right now."

"Thanks, Dr. Gold. I will consider your advice," I promised. I wanted to be somewhat receptive: At least this doctor had listened to me, and looked at me during our sessions!

"Additionally, Mila, I would like you to take some medicine for a few months to get you to a more stable place as soon as possible. We will figure out some combination of drugs that works – I would like to give you an anti-depressant like Wellbutrin, but I am afraid that this might make you even more manic. So maybe we'll try a mood stabilizer with an anti-depressant first, and also an anti-anxiety drug."

"Dr. Gold, that is a lot of medicine!" I said in horror.

"I will write out a prescription for these drugs, and then you can think about it first, okay? We will need to talk about possible side effects too, once you decide what to do. As I mentioned, it is likely that you are not going to be taking medicine like this forever. But you do need some help now, while things are so acute."

We said goodbye and I left, clutching the prescription and wondering if things were really that "acute."

It was dusk outside as I walked to the Lexington Avenue subway. It felt like winter was on its way. The air was colder, and winter coats were being worn. I thought of how nice it would be to go to my old apartment right now; it was just a few blocks away.

This time of year – November – had always been a time for me to go inside, and focus inward. I realized too that right now was the time of day when Cliff would be coming home from work. I'd read the paper as I waited for him. I'd run to greet him at the door, and we'd set the table for dinner together. We'd eat something warm, maybe the chicken cutlets my mother had taught me how to make. If it started raining, all the better. We were safe inside, and together.

Before long, ten o'clock would arrive. My mother would call around this time to say goodnight, and I'd always tell her I'd call her tomorrow; that I was busy spending time with my husband right now.

Now, when my mother called, I didn't have a good reason not to answer.

CHAPTER 28 – NO DATING

I didn't take long – two weeks, actually – before I was itching to date again. I joined The Right Stuff, an Ivy League dating service. This way, I could follow one piece of Lynn's advice: get off JDate.

I just couldn't quit dating completely – this would be too radical a change, and remove the main thing that gave me a sense of purpose in my life right now. My job was dull, and most of my friends were focused on their families, so I derived my main source of excitement and inspiration from dating. I still did not totally agree with Lynn and Dr. G that excitement was my enemy – although of course, their combined efforts were creating some doubts in my mind.

I was still deciding about trying the medicine cocktail – Depakote, Wellbutrin, Klonopin – Dr. G had recommended, and would look at the script in my purse once in a while. I was frightened, feeling like Alice in front of the rabbit hole of "crazy meds."

I had learned the slang term "crazy meds" from Googling the pills Dr. G prescribed. Depakote was extra-scary, with all sorts of uses, both approved – epilepsy – and off-label, and having potential side effects such as hearing loss and weight gain. Klonopin was used for epilepsy, panic attacks, anxiety, and mania. The seemingly "super pill" Wellbutrin had a bunch of funny uses for what was a kitchen-sink of ills – off-label uses for weight loss, pathological gambling, ADD, and sexual dysfunction. *Sexual dysfunction*, I giggled. *Not my problem, not now,* I thought. *Why don't they just make a No-Dating pill for me instead?*

After much contemplation, I decided I would compromise. I would try the meds and take the dating down a few notches. This way, I reasoned, I would be working on finding more stability but would still enjoy some entertainment and nights out. This did not seem totally contradictory to me – rather, I was pleased to find such a reasonable – in my opinion – middle ground. The meds would actually help me date better and perhaps even meet someone for a serious relationship. At least the pool of men in The Right Stuff seemed less scary – there were a lot of older professor-types. The profile I created was along the same lines as my JDate profile: "Doing Right Stuff just for fun, nothing serious, blah blah blah. Did JDate for a while and wanted to see what the snooty set was up to." A few guys emailed me. At least I knew they were smart.

My single girlfriends and I discussed what types of things we were looking for in men, but we also complained about the fact that there were so many trade-offs. My Russian debutante friend Roxanna said she was willing to forego sex appeal for stability, hair, and height. Ana, an overachieving Japanese-American banker, said as she was just too complicated for an average American man, she was willing to settle for a man who did not understand her, and who was not her equal in intellect and talents. My actress friend Serena said she could never do bald, although she could do fat. And she could handle him smoking so long as the guy did not sport a ring on his wedding finger. And my Chilean friend Carla, who was now an economist, said she did not care at all if a man was fat or even ugly. She just wanted someone brilliant who did not believe in God.

I wanted Cliff. Or rather, resigned now to the fact that Cliff was gone from my life, I wanted my soul mate. I wanted him to be intelligent, cool, funny and tall, dark, and handsome, like Cliff was. I wanted a prince to rescue me from my crappy current life and whisk me into a shiny new one.

My father laughed at me when I told him about my desires. "Mila, a man is not a pretty face. A man is what's on the inside. A man is his character."

"A good-looking man also has eyes for more than just one woman!" my mother would always add.

I ignored the first note I received on The Right Stuff; it was from a man named Albert, who lived in Hawaii and was sixty-six! My friend Roxanna, who was ever-so-practical, had counseled me against dating anyone over forty-four: "Too close to impotence!" she had said. Neither was I ready for excessive eyebrow hair.

I also deleted the note from a forty-year-old hedge fund manager who stated outright that he did not want children. This seemed to be a strange way to attract a woman in his age range. But when this man, Randall, persisted in emailing me, I finally wrote him back.

"What in the world do you have to offer when you don't want a family, say you have no free time on Sundays, and write that you never take vacations?" I asked in my message.

"Wait and see," he responded.

After another barrage of emails, I agreed to meet Randall for lunch. The day of the lunch, he called me to make a plan, and the very sound of his voice turned me off. It was high and pinched-sounding.

When I saw him, I realized what it was immediately: The man was gay. He was a thin and effeminate marathon runner who carried *The New York Times* in one hand and wore unfashionable old-person jeans. Upon a closer look, I realized that he wore eyebrow gel and mascara! He'd just come from a singing lesson uptown, so perhaps the gel was some theatrical make-up, but still, the overall package was suspect. Most likely, this guy was oblivious to his own gayness. I made sure our lunch was short, and wrote that I was too busy when he asked for another date.

The next email I opened on the Right Stuff was from a guy named Henry. His note was humble and self-deprecating. He wrote that he was sure I was being bombarded by emails, but he would be very happy if I responded to him. And he casually referred to a URL for an article in *New York* magazine, "if you need to check references." I bit: I found the article, which discussed the most promising young scientists of the year. Henry was the featured star because of his work with stem cells.

I was excited. Henry was a pioneer! A real-life explorer of uncharted terrain! A scientist! A stem cell wonder! A Big Brain! He had worked with Michael J. Fox on Parkinson's Disease, and been part of a fundraiser with Alec Baldwin!

In the article, there was a picture of him. He was standing in a lab, behind some test tubes and jars. I could barely make out his face, although I could tell he had curly hair. "He has hair! He has hair! Tra la la! He has hair!" I sang to myself. *One less thing for me to give up!*

Finally, my entrée into the world of academia, with all of its cutting-edge thinking, fundraisers, and summer cruises to give lectures on! Of course, Henry would be the one giving the lectures, but that was almost as good as, if not better than, me giving lectures: There would be no preparation or deadline anxiety. I envisioned a trip to the Galapagos with Henry reading some obscure science tome while I did yoga on the deck of the ship. In the evening, I would listen proudly as he held court at a dinner table captivating various intellectual senior citizen alumni of the Ivy Leagues.

I thought of the old cliché I knew: bachelor professor = zero sex appeal and huge ego. But I was tired of all the self-absorbed business-men playboys I had been meeting online and around town. So I wrote back to Henry, and he promptly replied. We made a plan to talk on the phone.

When we spoke, we seemed to have some things in common: He was born in another country as well (Germany), and had moved to America when he was young. We both liked literature, restaurants, and new music. We decided to meet for dinner at the Michelin-starred "gastro pub," The Spotted Pig.

Work flew by, and in the afternoon, I ran home to change into my first-date costume: a black-and-white DKNY wrap dress that showed off my cleavage, and high-heeled gold cowboy boots. I got a mani/pedi, and treated myself to a deep-conditioning oil treatment at the salon. On the subway, I smiled back at the men glancing at me. Male attention never failed to give me a buzz.

When I got to the restaurant, Henry was already there, standing in front. "Hi, hi, you're Mila?" he greeted me, his words coming out in a nervous rush.

"Hi, yes. Sorry I'm a few minutes late; the subway!"

We air-kissed. There were no sparks. Henry definitely looked more pasty in person than in the picture I had seen. And now I could discern that he had fishy eyes. His hair was brown and curly, but poorly cut – it rested around his head like a big furry hat. Henry's skin, however, was smooth, and his lips surprisingly sensual – full and pink. It was like the top half of his face belonged to a fish scientist, and the bottom half to a sensual cherub.

He seemed younger than the age he had cited of forty. Like Cliff would, he wore a blue Oxford shirt with dark wash jeans and Ferragamo shoes. It was the conservative Barneys look.

Henry carried a backpack. Cliff had too; he had only recently switched to a briefcase.

"I write on the subway," Henry explained when he saw me checking out his bag. "So, are you starving? I am!"

He was excited to eat, and after we sat down inside the restaurant, we ordered way too much food. When the appetizers came, Henry stuffed a few herrings in his mouth and even licked his fingers. Normally, I wouldn't have minded as this meant the man had an appetite for life. But Henry was the second brilliant man I had dated who licked his fingers. On Ezra, I had found this habit sexy. But even with the finger-licking, Henry wasn't so sexy. He was... awkward. I felt a slight tinge of annoyance.

I looked over at the table next to us, where a hot movie-actor type and his glamorous blonde date were flirting heavily. I felt darkness seeping into my mood, and I reminded myself it wasn't Henry's fault I did not find him attractive. It was due to pheromones, and as a scientist, Henry would be the first person to understand that.

After dinner, Henry saw me to a taxi and asked me if I wanted to see a movie the following weekend. I smiled sweetly and agreed. *Second date planned. Easy.*

Maybe this was the secret: To date someone I was not attracted to too much. When there was zero chemistry, I didn't feel inclined to drink — and that meant I could keep my promise to Lynn. Plus, as I felt no anxiety about whether Henry would call again, I felt confident and in control. I was eager to tell Lynn about how easy and smooth the date had been. Yes, no attraction was much better. Though I also wondered if Dr. Gold's meds were kicking in and helping me stay more even.

Lynn was not so impressed: "I don't think dating someone you are not attracted to is the answer, Mila."

"Why not, Lynn?" I questioned. "Isn't it almost like not dating?"

"No, it is very different. What will you do when Henry wants to kiss you?"

"I don't know. He seems so nice, I am sure he would wait before trying," I responded.

"You think nice men don't want sex?" Lynn asked.

As she subconsciously patted her big stomach, full with a baby-to-be, I wondered who the father of her baby was. It was strange to know so little about her when I was exposing so much of myself to her.

"I'll think about it when it comes up, Lynn," I responded, my tone a bit smug. I was flattered that all these men wanted to have sex with me, and just imagining myself turning Henry down when the time came made me feel more in control. I would definitely not be guilty of another third-date capitulation.

Lynn shook her head like a disapproving teacher. "I would like you to think ahead, Mila. Remember, thinking ahead is something we are working on."

Lynn then reminded me she was going on her maternity leave in December, just a few weeks away, and we spoke about the drug cocktail I was now taking. I told Lynn I didn't think my mood was particularly unstable – just that the stress of dating was creating some ups and downs. We were all on the same page on this issue, but it's just that I wanted to continue to try dating.

"So, are you feeling OK with the medicine, Mila?" Lynn questioned.

"I think so," I said. "Dr. Gold said that there may be side effects, like hair loss or weight loss or gain. Weight loss would be preferable, of course," I joked.

Lynn smiled slightly. "Yes, I know there could be, but not everyone has those."

I told her I was feeling more confident now about the course of treatment. And I did: After all, I liked Dr. Gold, and I thought he was very smart. I thought about his promising me that he and Lynn would work together to help me make a recovery from the turbulence of the last year. They said they could help me get stable. Still, I was skeptical about this "recovery:" As far as I could see, my doctors couldn't help me with my main illness – a terrible heartache.

CHAPTER 29 – FRIGID

After three weeks of taking the medicine, I did not feel a large shift in my mood or energy. Actually, I felt the same as I had for the whole summer – which was average. Unless, that is, I was dating someone – then I would be happy, until we broke up, at which point I'd be sad.

I told this all to Dr. Gold finally, who said he wanted me to continue with the Depakote and Wellbutrin combination for another few months anyway.

After this conversation, I asked my mother, "Mama, what do *you* think? I don't feel any different, so maybe I should quit the medicine

Mama too hated the idea of drugs. But this time she advised me, "Milochka, you can try what Dr. Gold suggests. Take the medicine for a few months. He is an expensive doctor." To my mother, "expensive" always meant "good." She was a bourgeois Russian immigrant, after all.

"Okay, I'll stick with it, Mama," I responded, "but I don't think I need it." I knew how worried my parents, Lynn, and even Dr. G. were that I would have another crash, like the one I had after Cliff. Oh, and then, after Jake. After all, didn't everything always come in threes?

At first, there was no turbulence in my new dating life, for Henry was a diligent suitor. He called me every few days to check in, and listened while I complained about my boss Erin. I loved telling Henry about the case I was working on too: He was so smart we were even able to intelligently discuss some of the more complex legal issues!

I also liked knowing where he was every evening. He was in one place: his lab. He told me he was working furiously on some major experiment, and needed to publish a paper with the results before another leading research scientist did. His calls, always originating from the lab, did a world of good for my ego: I did not have to imagine him pursuing other women. So far, so good – minus the sexual attraction, of course. My brain really felt unencumbered for the first time in a while, unshackled from the chains of anxiety over date etiquette and phone calls and texts. Dating Henry was proving a vacation for my nerves.

Our third date was at a jazz concert. It was frigid in New York – that kind of cold that makes you curse you ever left your apartment – so I wore my mink Russian hat and long black coat. *An elegant look, one absolutely perfect for a jazz concert,* I thought. In the taxi, I imagined for a moment that I was meeting Cliff, but soon waved the thought away.

When I got to the venue, Henry kissed me awkwardly as I sat down next to him. "Hi, hi, hi, hope these seats are all right! I bought them late, and I couldn't get much else," he said.

I looked about to check out the view: We were all the way to the left, and even below the stage. We had a perfect eye-level view of all the performers' shoes and ankles.

"It's fine," I said quietly, looking straight ahead at the lead singer's stiletto.

"Is everything okay?" he questioned as I didn't meet his eyes.

"Yes." But even I knew something was off. I was stiff during the show, and a little angry when Henry put a clammy palm over my hand. I knew I had no reason to be angry at Henry; he'd only done everything by the book, but there was something about his energy that needled me. I tried to focus on the concert instead of the man next to me.

After the concert, I watched as Henry put on a fur hat. "It goes with your hair," I joked.

"Oh, what do you mean?" he questioned with a puzzled look on his face.

"Oh, it was a poor joke; nothing, really," I responded, as I had made sort of a mean joke; after all, I had meant that his bushy hair looked like a furry hat already. I wasn't sure where this nastiness had come from: I'd never been mean to anyone on a date with me in the whole past year of dating all sorts of guys.

We went outside, and Henry stood in the middle of the street for a while attempting to catch a cab. He wasn't aggressive enough though, and I ended up being the one to successfully flag a taxi down. I felt even angrier at him: *Why the fuck couldn't this dude even catch a cab?* Cliff had been so *agile and assertive; he was always able to hail a cab!* I could feel blackness seeping into my mindset: I suddenly hated myself. And I hated Henry for being so inept.

We settled into the cab, and I gave the driver the address for my apartment. Talk turned to movies, and I mentioned that one of my favorite movies to watch at home was *Vanya on 42nd Street* by Louis Malle.

"I've never seen it!" exclaimed Henry.

"Oh, it's wonderful," I breathed, happy to focus on something other than my mood. "Chekhov is really misunderstood by Americans, you know, but this movie is based on a Mamet translation, and Mamet gets the humor. The comedy is dark, but Chekhov really embraced humanity, you know," I prattled on, happy to show off my own my knowledge to this brain.

"Let's see it!" Henry interrupted.

"Sure, that would be cool. I'll look at my schedule and we'll figure out a night."

"No, I mean now."

"Now?" I asked in surprise.

"Sure, why not?"

"But... it's late. I have to be up early to meet my friend Carla. She's visiting right now from Chile."

"That's fine; we can just watch some of it," Henry suggested.

"Well, I don't know..."

"Let's! Let's!" Henry interrupted, practically jumping up and down a little in the seat of the cab, full of enthusiasm for his own idea.

"I guess we could," I responded, wavering a bit.

"Yes! Great!" he said. I noticed he was already putting on his coat.

"But do you really want to come to my place for less than an hour?"

"Yeah, yeah, yeah, of course!"

As the cab pulled up to the curb outside my building, Henry wrenched the door open and practically fell out in his hurry to depart the cab. I guess he didn't want me to change my mind.

His eagerness made me tired and even sad: I had found it hard to say no to him. He was nice and polite, and despite his big brain, he was still a man. It was the third date, and he deserved something more than a casual peck on the cheek. At least, that's what the dating books said. And so, I let Henry come home with me.

In the lobby, I waved to the night doorman as I rushed Henry through to the elevator; I didn't want him to notice that Henry was a new guy. Not Ezra. Not Jake. Sure, since I was single, it was acceptable to have company once in a while. Still, I didn't like the way the doorman seemed to wink at me on this night.

I opened the door to my apartment, took Henry's coat, and told him to have a seat on the couch. "I'll put on the movie," I said, and I did so. Then I sat back down next to Henry.

As we sat down on the couch to watch the start of the movie, I felt nothing. This guy just didn't do it for me. Worse, he again looked so eager.

"Do you want to turn down the lights?" he asked softly.

"Why?" I said.

"So we can see the movie better."

"Oh, actually, I prefer to watch it with the lights on. And you're only staying for an hour, remember, it's so late already."

We sat stiffly next to each other as the credits rolled by.

"I acted in this play once," I said to break the cool temperature in the room. "I had wanted to play Elena, but then I was cast as Sonia. Elena is the beautiful bitchy one."

"And who is Sonia?" Henry questioned.

"She is the heartbroken one. She's in love with the doctor. The doctor is really Chekhov's alter ego. The doctor is in love with Elena, but Elena is married – to a pompous professor." I grinned a little at this: Henry was a pompous professor.

"I'm a professor," Henry said. "But I am also a doctor," he added with a strained smile.

"Yes, that's right," I said. I knew there was a joke in there somewhere.

Henry leaned in toward me, putting his hand on my lap, and I could tell Henry was barely listening to the movie. He began trying to put his arm around me, and I understood this was what Lynn was talking about: He was a nice man, but that did not mean he wouldn't want some action.

"Henry, are you watching the movie?" I asked, even though I knew that he wasn't.

"Actually," he said as he clamped a hand onto my shoulder and forcefully pulled me close to him, "I don't really want to see this movie right now."

"But you told me you did. We are here to watch the movie, Henry," I reminded, wriggling out of his grasp. "You agreed. And we only have a short time."

Henry looked at me with those fishy eyes. "I thought you weren't serious about that. It is so freezing outside, it would be awful to have to leave in the middle of the night."

"Oh, Henry, I, ahh....I don't know what to say. I thought you understood," I said, my voice sounding like it was pleading.

I looked at him. He looked back at me intently and leaned in for a kiss.

I sighed. And kissed him back. His lips were soft, but it still felt like I was kissing a relative.

Henry put his hand on my breast, squeezing it a little bit. He closed his eyes and let out a moan. The lights were still on, and the movie was playing. I stared at the TV screen as Henry's tongue darted in and out of my mouth.

It was absolutely ridiculous. I should have thought through dating Mr.-Nice-Guy-Big-Brain, which is what Lynn had suggested. Because somehow, Henry's poor attempt at seduction had taken me by surprise, even though it was our third date and I had invited him over. *Poor planning, Mila, very poor planning,* I thought to myself as Henry groped me.

He was now unbuttoning his shirt with one free hand. Next, he put this hand on his belt.

"Henry, stop, please."

I pulled back and sat upright. Henry opened his eyes.

"Stop?" he asked.

"Yes, I am sorry. It's time to go. You have to go."

"Now?" he asked in disbelief.

"*Now.* It's already been almost an hour, and I have to be up early. I'm meeting my friend Carla tomorrow morning," I reminded him crisply.

Henry got up and buttoned his shirt. He still looked shell-shocked as I handed him his coat and hat.

"There are cabs right downstairs," I said. "I'll walk you to the elevator." And I opened the door to my apartment and walked out with him into the hallway. The fluorescent lights in the hallway made Henry look even paler than usual.

Henry put on his fur hat. "Bye," he said.

"I am sorry. I know it's really cold out right now," I said.

"It's frigid," he clarified.

We stood waiting for the elevator in silence.

"New York winters; you just have to power through them," I said to fill the silence.

We both knew we were speaking in code.

Henry stared at the hallway carpet as he got on the elevator. "Bye," he said, not making any eye contact.

"Bye," I said, giving a short wave as the elevator doors closed on him.

I went back inside, turn off the TV, and climbed into bed. I felt more alone than ever.

....

I woke up feeling awful. Had it been mean of me to send Henry home? I wasn't sure. I decided to call him later and invite him over today to watch the rest of *Vanya*.

I met Carla, my law school roommate who had been around when Cliff and I first got together, at Bubby's. She was tall and striking, with waist-length black hair and almond-shaped brown eyes. Carla had lived in New York for several years after law school, and that was a time in which she had been "Crazy Carla." She'd had many boyfriends, many of them jerks. But she had been after experiences.

Since then, Carla had gotten her life together in an entirely new way. She went abroad for a while, and then went to Chile where she pursued a Ph.D. in economics. Now, she had confidence, a prestigious position at a university, and a new apartment. Oh – and a boyfriend.

I caught Carla up on my own experience-filled year. I told her how much I still missed Cliff, but that I knew I needed to find someone new, and soon.

"Mila, *bambina*, your focus is wrong," said Carla. "I was in the same place you were until I learned that men will not be the answer."

"Carla, I am not saying that at all! I don't think men in general are the answer. I just want a man like Cliff. I *miss* Cliff! I wish we were still together."

"I think that you should put your energy into something more for *you*," Carla advised. "When I started my Ph.D. program, I found I was much happier during that whole time than I had been when I was going to parties in New York. And then, only after I was alone for two years and working hard on my dissertation, did I meet Pedro."

I listened closely. I was happy my friend had found her way. But I also felt jealous of how together she was right now.

....

I texted Henry later in the day to invite him over. I expected him to text back yes, and to jump on the next subway downtown. But he wrote he had some work to do in his lab tonight, so getting together wouldn't work. Since I still felt bad about tossing him out of my apartment the previous night, I called him. Perhaps if he heard how sorry I was, he, and I as well, would feel better.

"So, what are you doing tomorrow?" I asked.

"Laundry," he said.

"You mean you have to wash that one shirt?" I giggled.

"What one shirt?"

"The shirt you always wear!"

Henry stayed silent after hearing my witty (or so I thought) comment.

"Henry, are you still there? Hello?"

"I don't always wear the same shirt, you know," he said, his voice shaky, like he was about to cry.

"Hey, I was only joking, because you always wear a blue shirt on our dates. I think it's cute," I said hurriedly.

"Oh, I didn't understand the joke," he said, stating the obvious.

"Forget it. It was another stupid joke. I know they are different shirts, but they do look the same. You're very conservative in your style, you know," I pointed out.

"Okay," Henry said briskly.

That was as much as he would say. Henry didn't ask me anything about my lunch with Carla, or about my plans for the next day. This made me feel anxious: I didn't want to lose him just yet. And yet, I also realized I hardly liked him. So panicking like this about him was strange; it was coming about without having anything to do with the actual facts! I really did not want to see Henry again, and yet now, because he was indifferent to our getting together, I felt extremely sad.

"Ummm, Mila, I have to go now," he finally said next.

"So, Henry, do you want to make a plan for Tuesday instead? You can come over to my place, and we can have dinner?"

"Okay, that works, let's do that," he said, with the same level of enthusiasm he would have when making a dentist appointment.

"Fine, it's a plan. I'll see you on Tuesday," I said as I hung up the phone.

But he never called to arrange the time. I waited until six p.m. Tuesday, at which point I texted him. "Hey H – time for tonite?" No response. I called him. The call went straight into his voicemail.

I called a few more times. No answer. The professor was standing me up. I was furious. Why couldn't he have at least called to cancel? I didn't think I did something so terrible to deserve being stood up.

Again, a voice in my head reminded me that I did not even like him. Worse, I found him sexually repulsive. But, still, I felt a terrible sadness. I noticed myself sinking in blackness – a reaction that felt completely involuntary.

I wrote Henry four texts, each one more desperate than the last. I implored him to make some sense of the situation for me. I told him I had been replaying the scenes in my head, and nothing made sense. I asked if somehow I had insulted him. I apologized for sending him home into the frigid New York winter. I raved about his brain, and I wrote that I felt terrible that I had joked about his blue shirt; that I did not mean it, as the one man whom I had loved had also worn what looked like the same blue shirt every time we went out. The texts went something like this:

6:11 PM: Where r u? Beach in Thailand? Please call or text ASAP.

6:13 PM: Wish I could be relaxing near u while u work on saving the world from the twin enemies of Alzheimer's and Parkinson's!

6:25 PM: Sorry if I was defensive w/u. I was recovering from a few recent hurts caused by my openness and optimism.

7:00 PM Please keep all this to yourself. Your friend, Mila.

Henry did not reply. Even though I didn't really like him, I felt unbearably sad.

Chapter 30 – No Substitutes

Thirty-six hours after being stood up by Henry, I saw Dr. Gold, who gave me some extra anti-depressants for my meds cocktail; he did not want me to fall into a funk while Lynn was off in the hospital having her baby. Lynn had also given me the number of a substitute therapist to call, in case of an emergency.

I decided I would go to see the therapist Lynn had recommended. I found Roslyn was well-groomed, with a glossy bob and a brown Chanel jacket. She looked like a wealthy housewife who had gone back to school to get her Ph.D. She spoke with a slight New Jersey accent. She had an office in Manhattan and also in Short Hills, N.J., an upscale suburb, where she likely lived with her husband, children, and pets.

I gave her some background – or rather, I rambled on about love. Marriage. Babies. Affair. Depression. The backyard in New Jersey. Acting. Law. Men. Cliff. Dominic. Zoran. Jake. Ezra. Henry. After fifty minutes, I couldn't tell if she even understood why I was here.

I started crying, saying between my tears, "If I only had been nicer to Henry, he wouldn't have disappeared!"

"Henry?" she asked. "Which one was he?"

I became hysterical. "I miss him; I miss him so much! It was all my fault, completely my fault. He loved me. And I loved him."

"Henry?" she asked, seeking clarity.

"No, not Henry! Cliff." My nose started running as I convulsed in sobs. "I hate men, I just hate them," I went on, my thought patterns indiscernible. "And it was so stupid for me to make fun of his fashion sense."

"Cliff?" she asked.

"No, no. Henry."

Roslyn offered me a tissue. "I'm sorry, Mila, your story is hard to follow. Lynn told me you were working through the breakup of your marriage, and that you have been depressed. Also, she said that you cannot stop dating."

"I CAN stop dating!" I whimpered. "I can! Of course I can. But, why should I? Everyone my age is dating."

"Not everyone should be dating at every point," Roslyn interjected. "If you had a broken leg, I would say you need to let it heal before you go running again. I have the same advice in the area of love and relationships for you at this moment: You need to heal and get strong again before you allow yourself to be vulnerable. Right now, you are not seeing things clearly, and neither are you seeing men clearly. You said yourself that Henry was not someone you could ever be in love with. So why be sad that he's gone?"

Roslyn was very nice. And what she said was smart enough. But I was angry that she wasn't Lynn. How could Roslyn from Short Hills possibly understand me? It had taken me months to reveal myself to Lynn.

"Thanks, Roslyn," I said as I got up. "I will call for another appointment."

But I didn't think I would.

CHAPTER 31 – THE EYES HAVE IT

My overachieving single friend Ana emailed me with an invite me to an eye-gazing party. *An eye-gazing party?* I had to call her up.

"What is that?" I asked curiously.

"Just something new; a kind of dating game. You go to this lounge. Music plays, and you stare into the eyes of complete strangers. It's supposed to encourage connection. Empathy. That kind of thing. It is a change of pace from the usual superficial bar scene."

"Is it like speed-dating?" I wondered.

"No, not at all. It's more spiritual," Ana pointed out. "Good for networking too, as you never know whom you can you meet in New York. And it's so very time efficient, because then you are multi-tasking."

I smiled. That was so New York, to combine dating and business. Ana was one of these super-networked people. She was a person who knew everyone, and loved to recommend someone for something. You're looking to buy an apartment? She knew a broker. Need knee surgery? She knew a surgeon. Want to write a book? She knew an editor.

"Sounds a little forced," I replied. I wasn't convinced.

"Oh, Mila-kins, it would be fun to see you!" she encouraged.

Ana was right: It would be fun to hang out. And I needed more good girlfriends in New York right now.

. . . .

I met Ana at the lounge in the East Village. Dark red curtains split off an alcove of the bar, where romantic Spanish music played in the background. An energetic party promoter named Marco was running around, making sure everyone in the alcove had enough wine. Clearly, eye-gazing required quite a bit of social lubricant. Most of the guests looked sheepish – like they too thought this was some crazy dating game only lonely New York City singles would dare try.

Or maybe I was projecting.

We played the game. All the women were given permanent stations, and the twenty men were told to rotate their positions in the alcove. A man passed by my station every two minutes. At one point a tall guy with short brown hair and brown eyes sat across from me. He seemed nice enough. When he smiled, he showed a row of straight white teeth. As we listened to the song, we stared into each other's eyes. I felt a blush spreading over my face, and then my neck. This is what had been missing from my connection with Henry – a pure physical attraction.

At the end of the song, I got up and went over to Ana. The guy followed me.

"I'm Adam," he said.

"I'm Mila."

"That was fun," he said as he motioned toward the bar: "Hey, want to grab a drink?"

We sat down and he ordered a glass of wine for me, and a whiskey for himself. My plan was to have a few sips – this was more social than saying I didn't drink.

I found out Adam was almost five years younger than I was. I decided I wouldn't tell him my age just yet. What was the point? This was just a fun flirtation.

He was a talker. Within the next fifteen minutes, I knew that he was a real estate lawyer from Westchester who worked with his uncle and had just broken up with his girlfriend of seven years. That the ex didn't realize how good she had had it because now she had to lose ten pounds to get a date. That he had spent a year in Italy studying architecture. That he loved karate. And that a friend had registered for this eye-gazing party, but she needed to cancel at the last minute and suggested Adam go in her place.

Adam motioned to the bartender for another whiskey. "I see you're not really a drinker," he said, looking at my full glass of wine. I smiled – meaning to look enigmatic. "Anyways, she did something awful," he said, talking about the ex-girlfriend again. I wondered what could be so awful. *An affair?* I kept quiet and nodded empathetically.

"I don't want to get into it, but let's just say she regrets what she did. But there is no turning back," he proclaimed as he picked up his second whiskey and downed it. "Another, please," he said to the bartender.

"Sorry about the breakup," I commiserated.

"Her fucking loss, you know?" Adam said, anger quickly moving over his face.

The vulgarity was a bit surprising, but I gathered his hurt was still quite fresh. I wondered whether Cliff still felt angry when he thought of me, after all this time.

I was not planning on divulging too much about myself at this stage as I was practicing some of the dating tips from the dating books I had been reading: *Be mysterious. Smile graciously, but don't stare at him too much. Don't mention past relationships or weight issues or therapy.* This all turned out to be easy to do, because Adam liked to talk. There was no great danger of me saying too much about some inappropriate topic.

At one point Adam leaned in. "You have to give me your number before the night is through. Please," he begged.

"Do I?" I questioned with a smile. I had the upper hand here: This guy was clearly interested, and I was surprised he seemed so worried about getting my number. *Didn't he realize I thought he was really cute?*

In any event, it seemed I was getting stronger by the second; I could feel it. *And, abracadabra! It was as if a magic wand had waved over me, making Henry and his test tubes now just a vague memory. There was no more sadness within me. Something much more exciting was in the air — some physical chemistry!*

I felt a surge of energy. Adam was cute. He loved his job as a real estate lawyer – he loved closing deals. Moreover, he was smart, and funny, and spoke fluent Italian.

I left in a cab at two a.m., and it wasn't long after my departure that Adam texted me. "This was awesome! Most fun I had in a while. Let's do it again!"

He called on a Sunday to ask me out for the following Friday. Even after I agreed, Adam asked, "Are you sure you want to go out with me?"

"I'd love to," I confirmed. I really liked his combination of confidence and shyness. Of course I wanted to go out with him!

....

We met at a new Vietnamese restaurant in the Meatpacking District. Adam told me his sister had recommended it as a good first-date place. That was a good sign: He cared enough to do some research, and had wanted to impress me. After, we went to a private club nearby. We got in because Adam had handled some leases for the owner.

Adam and I sat on a couch in a dark area drinking chocolate martinis. Soon, he leaned over for the kiss. It was the nicest kiss I'd had all year. There was a huge flow of electricity between us. Sure, we'd been drinking, but just a little.

"Do you want to go out again next week?" Adam asked.

"Yes! I'd love to!" I responded, feeling warm and light inside. This was how it was supposed to be. Nice and easy. Next date arranged while on current date. It was going right by the book.

"What day works for you?"

"Friday or Saturday is good," I offered.

"Saturday? You mean on...New Year's Eve?" he questioned.

"Oh, gosh, I just forgot that Saturday was New Year's Eve!"

But I hadn't forgotten. The truth was, I didn't have any great plans, so indeed I was free. But perhaps I should look more busy than that to Adam? Should I claim I was going to some cool party? Or in the process of fending off my other suitors? I guess I shouldn't look like I had zero going on. Reluctantly I replied, "I suppose Friday may be a better date night."

"Oh, yes, that's great. I still have to figure out New Year's. I'm going to some parties with a few friends, and my sister invited me to something that one of her fashion-editor friends is throwing. Should be fun."

"That sounds great!" I enthused, putting out a cool-girl-with-plans-too vibe, while wondering inside why it wasn't okay to just be direct and tell him I would love to go out to those parties with him.

"Friday is great, Mila," Adam confirmed. "I'll plan something fun for us."

He took me home in a cab, making sure to tell the driver there would be two stops. The man was a gentleman.

"I'll call you next week," he said when I got out, "and we can make a plan." And by the time I got upstairs, there was already a text from him thanking me for our date.

. . . .

It was now the day before Christmas Eve. My parents were leaving the next day to go to a wedding in Israel. A cousin was getting married, and there was going to be a big family reunion. My parents would be seeing my father's only brother, Arkadi.

My parents wanted me to go too, but although I longed to feel more connected to our overseas family, I was ashamed of my divorce. I didn't want that to be the big news that I had to share! I didn't want other people to feel sorry for me, to wonder whether I would ever have a husband and children.

"Milochka, it will be the holidays; are you sure you want to be alone in New York?" my mother asked me over the phone again today.

I knew she was thinking back to Labor Day weekend, which I had spent weeping and smoking on the bench outside of my building while my parents were enjoying a vacation in Florida. I told her that it would be fine, and that I had a lot of work to do. But this wasn't true, really. I always spent the holidays with my parents, from when I was a baby to now. There was rarely a time when I wouldn't see them for at least part of a holiday weekend. Even when I was in college or happily married to Cliff on the Upper East Side, my parents would drive from New Jersey for our ritual meal or outing together. Or, I would come home to eat my mother's delicious borscht and baked cinnamon apples. So there was a strong connection between holiday time and family for me – and my immediate family was now only Mama and Papa. It was back to the three of us against the world.

"What about New Year's Eve?" Mama pressed.

"Something will come up," I answered, trying to sound as upbeat as possible. "It's still early, not even Christmas. Don't worry, Mama," I said.

But my mother was worried. New Year's Eve was a big deal to the Russians. It was a night of exchanging gifts, drinking vodka, and eating too much. Since there had been no Christmas in the Soviet era, New Year's Eve had become the focus. There were New Year's trees, and even a Soviet version of Santa Claus – *Ded Moroz*, or Grandpa Frost.

In Riga, my parents had often hosted a huge New Year's Eve party. We would first watch the Communist party leader, Leonid Brezhnev, do his annual greeting, and then the party would start – presents under the tree for all the children, vodka and potato salad and borscht for the adults. At midnight, my dad would lift me into the air, and my mom would kiss me. The adults would then dance to Abba hits late into the night, as this candy-pop music had been allowed on our side of the Iron Curtain.

New Year's always was the most magical night of the entire year. And, though I put on a brave front for Mama's sake — I did not want to ruin her much-deserved vacation to Israel — I had, in fact, been full of trepidation about the impending date — at least, before Adam arrived on the scene. Now, at least, there was at a small possibility of New Year's magic in the forecast for me.

CHAPTER 32 – HOME FOR THE HOLIDAYS

Lara, my Brazilian friend from my old law school days, was coming to visit me in New York with her two children on the same day my parents were leaving for Israel.

Lara and I were pretty tight. Back after we had just graduated from law school, Lara had had all sorts of odd jobs in New York, and when she was between jobs, she would crash with Cliff and me so that she wouldn't have to ask her parents for rent money. I had loved those days: Cliff would go off to work or basketball on a Saturday or Sunday, and Lara and I would drink strong Brazilian coffee in our pajamas and then watch Truffaut movies until it was time to go out to a party.

Now Lara was married to a doctor whom she had followed to a small town near Tulsa, Oklahoma. Her husband had become the town's baby doctor for a stint that was supposed to last for just three years. In Oklahoma Lara had one baby, then another, as Oklahoma became more than just a three-year commitment for her husband.

Lara often called to complain about how much she hated life in Oklahoma – how terrible the other women were in her small town; how much they didn't like her. As much as Lara hated the state though, she loved having the money and time to go to Brazil for two months every summer, and to take the kids to Europe for vacations.

Lara was one of these super-cute women. Everything about her was adorable: Her tiny stature, her shiny chin-length black hair, her bright white teeth and full red lips, her huge brown eyes and lashes, her Brazilian accent, and her belly perfectly tanned and taut, even after having two kids.

The day Lara arrived – Christmas Eve – started out as an absolutely miserable day. It was cold, and sleet rained down on the New

York sidewalks. I went to the office to work on a case, but had a hard time concentrating.

I thought of my parents on their way to Israel, where it would be hot and sunny. I really should have gone with them: I hadn't been to Israel to see our family in almost ten years! So what that I was divorced? What was so shameful about that, anyway? Why had I stayed here in New York alone, where I was suffering from a terrible bout of holiday depression?

Lara, always on Brazilian time, finally called a few hours after she had said she would: "Mila! What a crazy time we had coming from the airport! Zack got a stomach virus, and we went to Ilan's sister's to pick up some mail – thank God she wasn't there – and Zack was just too tired to go out right away. So, he took a nap, and now Sofia is feeling sick too, and is it okay if we are not coming today? The children need time to rest, and now we are already settled here at my sister-in-law's."

"Oh," I replied, feeling disappointed. I had expected we would meet up for a nice dinner together, during which we would laugh about the old times. I was even looking forward to hearing the chatter of the children's voices in my single-girl apartment afterwards! "That's fine, Lara. Whatever is best for you."

I left work, walking through the dark downtown streets. They were now empty: People were home wrapping gifts or lighting the Hanukkah candles. Yes, it was also Hanukkah.

I entered my apartment building. Most of the doormen were off. The lone Jewish one nodded at me, and said, "Happy Holidays!" I smiled back, struggling to keep myself from breaking into tears.

Once upstairs, I suddenly felt hungry, and I darted over to the refrigerator. I had stocked my fridge with kid-friendly things for Lara's children: yogurt, apples, and bread for toast. My parents had also filled it with some stuff from a Russian store before they left for Israel. I pulled out some *sirochki*, little raisin-filled farmer cheese balls hidden inside pink- and purple-foil wrappers.

Holding these, I misted up: My mother was so thoughtful, remembering always what I had enjoyed eating as a child. I used to love to have these for dessert, after I had feasted on Mama's chicken soup and *kotleti* (mini-hamburgers) with fried potatoes.

Touching one of the small cheese desserts made me nostalgic, and reminded of how grateful I should be for my mother's unconditional and fierce love. And now, she was often responsible for pulling, pushing, and cajoling me out of despair. It made me sad that she loved me so much even when I disappointed her so.

I took three of the foil-wrapped *sirochki* my mother had gotten and ate them.

....

Lara called the next day, and we made a plan to get dinner and dessert with the kids. We met in the village. I found her children beautiful: they sported sandy hair and large blue eyes.

We walked around the West Village, where we passed a homeless man who asked us for money. I keep silent and looked to see what Lara would do, as her decision would set an example for the children.

"I am sorry," she said simply to the man before walking on forward.

"Mama, why is he asking us for money?" questioned her daughter Sofia.

"Because he needs money to get a home, my love," answered Lara.

"He doesn't have one?" asked Lara's son Zack.

"No," Lara replied.

"Why?" asked this boy from Oklahoma who was not used to seeing homeless people.

"Because some people don't have a house," Lara explained patiently.

"Why is that, Mama?" questioned Sofia.

"Because they can be lazy, or not have a job, or be sick," Lara answered.

"Sick in what way?" Zack asked.

"Sick because their body doesn't work, or sometimes because they are sick in the head. In this man's case, he's probably homeless because he doesn't work. Everyone has to work, darling."

We then walked into Café Dante for some gelato. But it seemed the line of questioning from the kids was far from over.

"But Mama, you don't work!" Sofia burst out. "So why do we have a nice house? Why do you have so many nice things?"

"Because Daddy works, darling," Lara smiled. "He works hard so that we can have the house, and this trip to New York, and this ice cream."

"And Mila; do you not work either?" asked Sofia.

"I do work," I answered quietly. "You see, I don't have a husband."

It felt odd to say it, and right then I was jealous of Lara. At this minute, I was dying to switch places with her: I wanted to be tan and adorable and speak in a charming, animated way that left people smiling. I wanted to have her kids be my kids, and to be able to laugh casually as I explained to my daughter that there was no need for me to work because I had gotten someone else to work for me.

I shook away the fantasy; it wasn't the right one for me anyway. Wasn't my goal now independence? Self-reliance? Self-esteem? The true kind of self-esteem that did not arise from the fact that one was desired by a man?

But as much as I might fantasize about thriving without a man, I often found it hard. At times, it seemed to be impossible.

....

Adam called midweek to reconfirm our Friday night date: "I'll plan something cool," he promised. "I can't wait to see you!"

"That sounds great," I said. But when my mother called from Israel, and I told her I would be seeing Adam on Friday night, she had a somewhat different response.

"What? You will go out with him the night *before* New Year's? BEFORE? Did I understand you correctly?" Mama shot out.

"Yes, before, Mama," I answered very quietly.

"Milochka, that is stupid!" my mother hollered. "Any smart Russian woman would make sure that she was going out with a potential boyfriend on New Year's Eve itself, and not the night before the holiday! The night before, you should be getting a pedicure and reading, so that you look gorgeous on the big night!"

I winced, pulling back from the phone a bit. My mother was screaming. She always did that when we spoke long distance, even though I could hear her perfectly when she spoke in a normal tone.

"Mama, stop yelling. I can hear you," I reminded her. "Anyway, it's fine. I know what you think. We don't need to discuss it anymore."

"Milochka, you should call him and say you changed your mind; that you will go out with him on New Year's Eve instead!"

"Mama, I can't do that. He didn't exactly ask me out for New Year's Eve night."

"No matter!" my fierce and sometimes overbearing mother retorted. "You must do it," she urged. "I don't want to worry about you alone on New Year's Eve when I am all the way over here in Israel and at a wedding. Here, talk to your father about it for a minute. Hold on!"

I could heard Mama whispering to my father, "Tell her!" before he got on the line.

"Milochka, *dochenka,* my little daughter," my father greeted me when he got on the phone.

"Papa! I am fine. Don't listen to Mama. Just enjoy yourselves," I begged.

"Mama tells me that you have no plan for New Year's Eve?"

"It's okay, Papa! I will find something!" I promised, and I said goodbye quickly before my mother prodded my father to speak with me about my lack of strength and confidence.

In my mama's mind, any woman worth something had a date on New Year's Eve. She might have to cajole a date for herself. Or even demand a date. But a strong, confident woman would make sure she had a New Year's Eve date, period. Case closed.

I bet my mother would be praying at the Western Wall tomorrow for a miracle.

Chapter 33 – The Eve Before

With New Year's Eve looming and no good plans on the horizon for me, I kept hearing my mother's voice from across the ocean chanted a warning in the back of my mind: *Before, before, who goes out the night BEFORE!*
 No, I would not dwell on the negative: I would allow myself to be excited about having a date with a very cute guy – even though he was young and somewhat naïve. I would give him a chance. Everyone else was out of town, and I felt grateful to have something to be excited about. I put on tight jeans (good, no weight gain since the Henry breakup) and a pink long-sleeved t-shirt, then went to get my hair and nails done.

....

 We met at the wine bar downstairs from Peasant, a candle-lit Tuscan-style Italian restaurant. Adam was wearing faded jeans, a red Polo sweater, a pea coat, and cowboy boots. He bent down to kiss me. He had a clean soapy-musky smell. Our kiss lingered.
 "You smell great," I said, my arms around his neck.
 "It's so good to see you," he said as he helped me take off my coat.
 "How's the case?"
 "Oh, it's going fine," I said dismissively. I didn't really want to talk about the law.
 We sat down at the bar and ordered red wine and some small plates of food. During our small talk it came up that he'd taken a comedy course at the Comic Strip on Second Avenue.
 "So have I!" I exclaimed in delight.

"No way! So you're funny?" he asked me.

"Yes! Of course I'm funny, Adam; don't you know that by now?" I teased, batting my eyelashes at him. I found him so cute and sweet that my cheeks were practically hurting from smiling so much. But maybe he didn't know I was funny: I had done my best to stay quiet and mysterious when we were together. I still hadn't told him how old I was, or that I had been married. These days I was adhering to both my mother's advice of not revealing too much, and to the dating advice gleaned from *Cosmopolitan* magazine during my weekly manicures. Some *Cosmo* dating experts touted 'active listening'— which meant something like asking your date questions while strategically batting one's eyelashes at critical moments.

According to my mother, Russian women did much of the *Cosmo* advice instinctively: They never needed to learn them from a magazine, the way American women — many of whom were naturally honest and real and casual in terms of their lifestyle — did. For example, a Russian woman would never leave her house in anything other than a full knock-'em-dead getup and a face of makeup. And, during a date, she would speak little not because she was so entranced in her date's every thought, but because she was quietly scheming, "How will I get him to buy me a new car?" (It's impossible to both talk and scheme at the same time.) My mother's view of what it meant to be a Russian woman on a date was clearly outdated, in my opinion. But, still, I could aspire to maintain some of the control over myself and the evening that my mother was attempting to teach me.

All in all, the night with Adam went very well — and very long. We stayed for a while at Peasant, and then went to a dance club near NYU. As we walked on lower Broadway on this cold, empty night, he hugged me in the street and kissed me passionately. "Don't ever stop kissing me, Mila," he whispered as our lips finally separated.

At his words, I felt a surge of excitement, an incredible lightness. It felt like I was floating.

It was four a.m. when he took me home in a cab. We kissed upstairs in my apartment, but he was a gentleman, leaving as we had agreed he would.

....

On New Year's Eve day, I woke up late; it was well after noon. I grabbed up my phone, expecting to see a text from Adam. After our other few dates, he'd texted me after we saw each other. But there was no text. *He's probably still sleeping,* I thought. I stayed in bed resting for a few hours, and then got up to make some coffee. By now, I was feeling just a little bit nervous that there was no text or call from Adam. No social media updates either as far as I could tell – I couldn't resist some light social stalking.

He must be up and preparing for the night, I thought. *Would he be going to the party with his sister, as he had said he would? If so, shouldn't he be inviting me too by about now? I would love to continue hanging out. And, since he had begged, "Don't ever stop kissing me!" shouldn't we be starting on that soon?*

But it was my mother who called: It was already New Year's Eve in Israel. "Happy New Year's, *solnyshko!* I love you, my little sun. I wish you a wonderful New Year, one both healthy and happy!"

"Happy New Year's too, Mama. Tell Papa I love him too."

"You tell him, *Milochka,*" she said before she put my father on the phone.

"*Dochenka,* we love you," my father told me.

"I love you very much, Papa."

There was so much more I wanted to say to him, but I didn't. Sentiments like: *Thank you. Thank you for rescuing me, thank you for helping me, and thank you for driving me everywhere. Thank you for your love, because it is saving me still.*

My parents and I didn't say what we were all really thinking: *Let this year bring some quiet. Let this year bring some stability. Let Mila become herself once again, and let her parents have some peace.*

My mother took up the phone again. "So, Milochka, how was last night?"

"It was good, Mama." I know she was dying to ask for more details, to ask how I felt, but I didn't say any more.

"He is too young for you, Milochka," my mother said in a cajoling tone. "Papa and I agree. You shouldn't waste your time. I am glad you had fun, but next year means a new start for you."

"Mama! Why are you talking like that! We will be seeing each other in the new year!" I protested passionately. "Adam is a great guy!"

"Fine, Mila, fine." Switching gears, my mother said next, "What are you doing tonight?"

"Not much, Mama. One of my friends emailed me about a party in New Jersey, but that's too far. I don't know. I may just stay home."

"Mila, you shouldn't stay home alone tonight. Why don't you go to that party?"

"I'll think about it, Mama, okay?"

"Fine. We are going to sleep soon here. I'll call one more time to see what your plans are."

"You don't have to, Mama. But it's fine if you do," I replied, and ended our conversation. Once I did, I got back into bed.

The truth was that I wanted to hear from Adam, and I did not feel like doing much until I did. I was in a strange state; it was like a partial paralysis. My mind kept replaying our last date in excruciating detail. What he had said, when he had said it, and how he had said it. Then how I had responded. And what he had done next. And on and on it went. I knew I wouldn't be freed of thinking of about last night until I got some sign from Adam, a sign that he had had a nice time like I did. I needed some indication from him that we would see each other again. I recognized too that my therapist Lynn had called this kind of fixation on some thought or thoughts, "perseverating."

I stared at my phone. Nothing. No ping, no sound sweetly announcing the arrival of an all-important text that would save the day for me. Adam wasn't reaching out, and when a text did come, it was from Eddie, a friend from high school. He was a local rock musician. He was sexy and women liked him, though he was always broke. "Big Comedy Central party tonight with Ben and Mimi; wanna join?" he wrote.

Ben, another one of my high school friends, was now a cardiologist. He was divorced, but everyone who knew him thought he was still pining for his ex-wife. Eddie's friend Mimi was a big-time publicist with clients like Natalie Portman. Mimi had a crush on Eddie, and so she invited him to many hip parties. I texted Eddie back, asking for more details. "11 at Suba in the East Village," Eddie responded.

I stared at his reply, wondering whether going to this would be better than spending New Year's alone. *Damn, why wouldn't Adam call me and ask me out! It was almost seven o'clock on New Year's Eve! I would not call him. I refused to call him. I must not call him.*

At 7:15 p.m., I called him. Miraculously, he picked up the phone! "Adam, hey, it's Mila."

"Mila! I was about to call you!" he replied, sounding happy to hear from me.

"Oh, good!" I breathed a sigh of relief. *He had been about to call me.* "I wanted to thank you for last night. I had fun."

"Yes, it was great, definitely. We should do it again."

"I'd love to," I said. "Adam..." I began, then stopped. I was dying to ask him to join me at the Comedy Central party, but I didn't want to seem desperate.

"Yes?"

"I just thought...okay, well, hope you have a good night," I mumbled instead.

As we hung up, I felt a shudder of sadness rip through me. And then an even darker wave of despair followed. *What had just happened?* Adam had to have known I was interested because I had called him, so he should have asked me to get together with him tonight. But he didn't, so maybe he wasn't that interested. The sadness I was feeling now was too big a reaction to a guy I had only gone on two dates with – it was not justifiable or rational. "Not a justifiable sadness," I said out loud to remind myself to put some boundary or constraint on my feelings. But the plunge into blackness kept on happening. I could feel it, and I couldn't let it happen while everyone was out of town. So I jumped out of bed: *Shower, makeup, taxi, night out,* I recited in my head over and over again. *Hanging onto this plan should keep me from falling even further.*

I forced myself under the warm water and into one of my going-out uniforms: jeans, tall gold cowboy boots, gold halter-top, and brown cashmere sweater. I brushed my hair, staring into the mirror. I could feel energy draining away from me. My face became less animated; my body, heavier. I could see pronounced lines around my eyes and lips. I couldn't look at myself in the mirror anymore, so I darted out the door of my apartment.

"Happy New Year, Ms. Mila," Raj the doorman said on my way out.

"Happy New Year, Raj!" I tossed back. As I smiled a big smile, I wondered if I looked happy.

Soon enough I was at the dark lounge in the East Village. Eddie waved at me from a red leather banquette in the far end. The dance floor was packed with hipster twenty-somethings. There were skinny guys with sideburns, and girls with streaked hair and butterfly tattoos. It was an Eighties-themed party, and Tainted Love was blasting. I pushed my way through to the banquette. It was hot and loud and dark, and I was sweating by the time I reached Eddie.

Eddie was wearing his trademark outfit: black turtleneck, jeans, and sneakers. He had large blue eyes and a head full of black hair. Eddie was aging well; he was doing what he loved, and he was a vegetarian. He didn't drink much either. Eddie was single right now; his girlfriend of many years, a pretty speech pathologist, had broken up with him a few months ago. She had finally realized music would always come first with him.

Mimi and Ben were in the booth too. They were drinking champagne. Mimi was average-looking except for her pretty thick black hair. She wore a pink Chanel-style jacket over a camisole, and stilettos. By Manhattan standards, she needed to lose twenty pounds. Mimi sat right next to Eddie, hanging on his every word.

Ben was balding and somewhat abrasive. But, being a divorced cardiologist in a top Park Avenue practice and holding joint custody of his son, he was in his mind a ladies' man extraordinaire. And he did, in fact, seem to have a new woman around every time I saw him. Not tonight, though; I guess I was technically his date.

"Hi, guys. Happy New Year! Well, almost," I said, glancing at my watch and seeing it was still a few minutes before twelve.

"Happy New Year!" said Mimi.

"What happened; no hot date?" joked Ben. Eddie laughed, and Mimi rolled her eyes.

"No. No hot date, Ben," I retorted. "Just you." I smiled at my joke; it made everyone else laugh. "And you, Ben; where's your hot date?"

"She's right here," he grinned, and pulled me into the booth. "Have some champagne."

I sat down and we raised our glasses. "To a happy and healthy New Year! To many great gigs for all of us!" Eddie said. We drank and Mimi leaned in closer to Eddie. I saw him slightly stiffen.

"So, Eddie, what's new?" I asked.

"Just got back from our gig in L.A."

I barely listened to the banter at the table, tuning out as much as I could. I was wondering if Adam was already at his sister's friend's party. I checked my cell a few times. Nothing. No texts.

"Expecting something?" Ben asked.

"No," I said shortly. I didn't want to talk about it.

"Come on, Mila, what's up?" asked Eddie. "Expecting a message?"

"No," I said.

"Spill the beans! Who is it? A boy?" Eddie said.

"Oh, a boy!" Ben said. "Do tell!"

I caved. "Just someone I went out with last night. We had a great date. He's really nice."

"Cool," said Mimi.

"Did you speak to him today?" asked Eddie.

"Yes! Of course!" I deliberately neglected to explain who had called whom, and steered the conversation in a different direction.

At a few minutes to midnight, we all got up. The music got louder. The countdown began. 10. 9. 8. 7. 6. 5. 4. 3. 2. 1!!!! Everyone screamed, and the music went up another notch. A kid in a Clash T-shirt hugged me. "Love your boots, girl," he said. "Can I have a kiss now?"

"No, sorry." I didn't feel like kissing anyone. I was thinking about Adam: Was he kissing someone? Maybe some gorgeous French girl, or a Midwestern tourist who had been invited to a New York party? Or worse, perhaps some skinny tan girl from Westchester? She'd be his type for sure. I checked my phone. No text. Not yet. I glanced about, and saw Eddie and Mimi kissing. She must be on Cloud Nine.

Ben came over to me looking for a kiss. I gave him a hug. No free New Year's Eve kiss for him. I felt like a grump, and I moved away into the crowd so I could check my phone.

No peace for me, though; Eddie found me in a moment. "What are you looking for?" Eddie inquired.

"I'm waiting for the guy from last night to text me Happy New Year," I admitted. "He should do that, right?"

"Did you sleep with him?" Eddie asked matter-of-factly. He was gathering information so he could help me figure out the real deal.

"No! And Eddie, that's not the point. I like him, and in fact, we had a great date. He told me, 'Don't ever stop kissing me!' Doesn't that mean something? He said that just last night," I emphasized. "Who says that if they don't mean it?"

"He should be texting you, Mila, yes. It's pretty simple." Eddie said kindly. He was a good guy.

My phone remained silent as I went to the bar in search of a drink. No texts, no calls, zilch. It was now almost 1:30 in the morning. Was Adam so absorbed in some conversation with another woman that he had totally forgotten his words to me the night before? I wanted to text him the words, "'Don't ever stop kissing me.' What did you mean by that?" Instead I drafted a text that read, "Happy New Year's, Adam!" Before I sent it, I reconsidered; it was a pretty boring text, and I probably should write something more flirtatious, like "Missing your hot New Year's kiss!"

Eddie moved up next to me at the bar. "Did he text you?" Eddie asked, when he saw my phone out.

"No, I was going to text him," I answered honestly.

Eddie didn't say anything. He just shook his head.

"I shouldn't?" I asked a bit timidly.

"If you have to ask, the answer is no," he responded.

"Fine, I won't. Anyway, he's probably drunk right now; he loves to drink. He'll call tomorrow," I said as I closed my phone and put it away into my purse. "It's New Year's Day."

I watched Mimi order another vodka martini and lead in toward Eddie. I saw Ben and a hip Asian woman slow-dancing. My sadness tightened its hold on me.

Mama was right; I should not have gone out with Adam on the night before New Year's. If he didn't want to go out with me on the big night itself, he was telling me he didn't really like me all that much.

Chapter 34 – Heavy

Depression: I felt it approaching when I went to sleep. And then it was here, with the new day, the new year. It was as if I was pinned under something: My limbs and head felt heavy; my blood like it had turned into gritty sand. It was that hard to move.

I had forgotten that such utter blackness could come. When I was up, it always made me forget the true depth of the down. Only when I was in it, when I was sad again, did I recognize it. And then, it was so unbearably familiar, I wondered how I had ever managed to forget it. The depression was like a terrible toothache, which pounds and grinds and whips you and then, once the gnawing and soreness is gone, you forget the exact quality of it until the next time it hurts. You only remember the fact that it was there, but that's all. You don't recall what it was like when you were in the grip of it.

In this depression, my brain swirled around a repetitive thought: "He didn't text." Just three small words: He. Didn't. Text. That's the silly part of it: An ordinary dating event – innocuous, really – became poison during a period of depression. Diving into romance was the drug; leaving the romance behind was the withdrawal.

The depression brought a haze with it, too; it was like I'd been awake for forty-eight hours. A lucid dream state. What day was it? Sunday. Or was it Monday? It was New Year's Day, so it had to be Sunday. "Sunday," I said out loud, to block the poisonous *he-didn't-text* thought. "It is the first day of the New Year. A Sunday, Mila, a Sunday." I realized I wanted a cigarette – not a great way to start a healthy new year.

Surely, surely, everything would be fine soon. Adam would call today. For sure. He had to. He said, 'Don't ever stop kissing me,' and today was New Year's Day.

Wouldn't you think of the person you wanted to keep on kissing forever on New Year's Day? Of all the days of the year, this was a day to do that. And he would. Adam would.
I drafted an email to him. And another. And another. I didn't send them, of course. No, I would wait until tomorrow. I had to give him until the end of the day to get in touch.

To distract myself from the emails, I picked up the phone to call my mother in Israel. No dial tone. That was odd. I wondered if there was a cable outage. Damn. A disconnected phone was not good. I grabbed my cell. I needed to call someone. Now! I was sinking. But I shouldn't call my mother yet; she had said she would call when she and my dad were in for the night. My parents deserved to have some peace.

I put down the phone, and again I thought of having a cigarette. I hadn't smoked in a while now. Ever since Henry had stood me up, and then I had only smoked one or two cigarettes. I knew why, too: Because I had met Adam, and so my need to smoke had evaporated. I was too busy having fun and fantasizing about the possibility of a new boyfriend.

Moving slowly and heavily, I mustered up just enough energy to walk to the corner deli and buy a pack of cigarettes. I headed to the little park by my building and smoked two sticks in a row. They smelled foul. They tasted foul. They made *me* feel foul.

I started crying. My sadness was bigger than me. It was suffocating. It was so many things. It was heavy, slow, dark, blurry, and agonizing, dull but with a razor-sharp focus on the offending trigger: "No text. No text. No text. Don't-ever-stop-kissing-me. Don't-ever-stop-kissing-me. Don't-ever-stop-kissing-me." The words cut just like a razor too, and repeating them was like emotional cutting. Each time I said the words, I slid further down the bottomless hole.

I dialed my mother in Israel. There was no other choice: I needed help.

"Milochka, I was just thinking of you! How are things? Did you have a good New Year's Eve?" my mother asked.

"Mama, he didn't text."

"What, Milochka?" my mother asked in a puzzled tone.

"He didn't text. Adam has disappeared."

I hear my mother sigh on the other end of the phone.

"Milochka, he is nothing," Mama said. "He is not the important thing. You are. Where are you?"

"Nowhere." I took a drag of a cigarette, not even bothering to hide the sound of the inhale from my mother.

"Mila, are you in the park?"

"Yes, Mama."

"Smoking?"

"Yes."

"Mila, go inside. Please! I can't talk now; everyone is still here. We are having our dinner. Milochka, please, you have to stop the smoking. I can't tell your father you started again! This is why he didn't want to go to Israel and leave you by yourself over the holidays."

"Mama, I feel so sad. I am so, so, sad. I can't describe it. I feel sick."

"Milochka, my dear, can you call Lynn your therapist?" my mother asked.

"No, she's still out on her maternity leave," I replied.

"But, she already had the baby, right? And this is an emergency."

"It's New Year's Day, Mama! I am not calling Lynn," I said defiantly.

"What about that psychiatrist, Dr. G.? Why don't you call him?"

"Mama, I don't want to. I can't call a shrink every time I am disappointed by some guy. I can get on with things myself, I know I can. And, Dr. G. is on Christmas break." I became quiet for a minute, then I started crying. "Why didn't Adam text me?"

"Mila, be smart! Why do you care about some young, silly boy from Great Neck with whom you had two dates? Milochka, please, don't you see how strange that is for you to care? You're a grown woman, not a lovesick teenager."

Silly. I grabbed onto that word. *Silly. This whole thing was silly,* I said to myself. *I had said so myself earlier! The word "silly" even had a fun sound to it; wasn't this silly in a fun way!*

But depression had its own logic – and the happy word "silly" just floated away. Instead, the gray dullness took its place. It was the combination of the cutting voice in my head, and the heaviness of my body, and the foul smell of the cigarettes, and the lack of food, and the complete inability to formulate even a small thought about the future.

There was only *now*. Only *today*. Only this heaviness, and it would go on forever. My feet were glued to the earth, stuck in cement. And I could not breathe.

That is how depression grabs you.

....

I didn't listen to my mother. Somehow, I mustered up the energy to get off the park bench. On instinct, I walked to the subway. I had a vague idea of going uptown, back to my old neighborhood where I had lived with Cliff.

I walked through streets that had that abandoned early-Sunday-morning look, even more so because it was January 1st, the day after a city celebration. Purple and gold party hats swirled in the gusts of wind, and noisemakers lay limp in the gray slush. Confetti peppered gutters. Lost in my thoughts, I moved slowly through this post-party cityscape as if pushing through Jell-O. I kicked a pair of those silly glasses with the numbers announcing that a new year was here, and nearly tripped on an empty beer bottle. The bone-chilling wind at my neck was welcome. The biting cold made my body feel real, like I, Mila, was not just a loud voice stuck in my brain.

Down in the empty station, I hung on to my phone, tapping it mindlessly, as there was no reception below ground. A couple in their twenties, still in party clothes, sat entwined in each other on a bench. Suddenly, a huge disheveled man I had noticed earlier let out a loud bellow, and surprised, I dropped my phone. As it tumbled toward the platform edge, I heard the sound of the train screeching in, and, for a brief moment – it seemed totally clear to me the way this could all go down. It would be so simple. I could just jump. Like Anna K. Then, there would be no more downs. But, the thought didn't stick. Instead, I saw my Mama's face down inside the tracks screaming in her shrill voice and rolling her r's like she always did: *"Mila! What arrrrre you; crrrrrazy? Life is for the living – You arrre lucky to be one of the living! Davai* (let's go).*"* Yes, I was not a heroine in a book, but a person. Anna K didn't have my Mama.

I shook my head, and the momentary trance was over. My phone did not go into the tracks but landed right at the yellow line at the edge. The train pulled into the station. As I stood paralyzed, not daring to even take a step toward the yellow line, a skinny guy with a skateboard picked up my phone. "Hey, you OK?" I nodded. *Yes. I would be. Hopefully sooner rather than later.* The train left the station. I turned around and went back out through the turnstile.

....

Back in my apartment, with the brief burst of energy that had propelled me outside now used up, I sank back down to the floor, weak and purposeless once again. Rain pounded on the window and time passed. Then, daylight was nearly over and the cars on the highway below screeched and slid on the slippery road. The sidewalks were empty, or perhaps they just stayed that way all day. The space inside my room felt suffocating – like the walls created a soundproof booth with just my blaring black thoughts *(You are all alone, Mila!)* reverberating throughout.

My survival instinct kicked in. For me, survival required connecting to someone. And that I could try to do through my cell phone. I needed to talk – not email, not text, not post status updates and like photos of friends' babies on Facebook, but talk. Connect.

For the next forty-eight hours I hung onto my cell phone for life, talking and talking and talking to anyone who would listen to me. I called my friend Jessica on vacation in Miami. I called my parents in Israel over and over again, not caring that all my relatives would wonder what the hell was up with me in New York. I called my mother's friends. And, admitting to myself that I desperately needed help from the professionals, I finally called them too. As I knew, they weren't in the office, and I simply left messages for Lynn on her maternity leave and for Dr. Gold. My cell phone ran out of power, and I talked even while charging it, hanging onto my lifeline for every second it was there.

What did I talk about to anyone who gave me one minute of attention? Adam, Adam, and more Adam. Adam 24/7. All Adam, all of the time.

Time. I had no sense of it. Time got warped. I don't know how many hours I didn't sleep, didn't eat, and didn't do anything other than cry, smoke, and write.

It was now emails and texts I drafted, not letters. I addressed them to myself so I didn't send them off by accident, and then I saved them. It was as if I was back to that summer after separating from Cliff, and I was in the Brooklyn room where I got lost in delirium for a few days. I recognized what was happening, but there was nothing I could do. I was powerless; I was paralyzed.

Accounting for time at this moment seemed impossible. I was lost in something elastic. Time flowed around me, but it was slow. Gooey. I was like a fly stuck in honey on a windowsill. Like the flies that were on the windowsill when we made jam in my father's great-aunt's house near Minsk. We licked jam from wooden spoons, the smell of strawberries filling the kitchen, and bees circling the stove.

Adam. Why did he say, "Don't ever stop kissing me?" The text that never came.

I picked up my cell. *I must talk to someone right now. Ask what day it is. When are my parents coming back. Damn. Low battery. I should charge it. Coffee would be good. Or a cigarette.* My brain was a swirling circle of words: *"Where is the text where is the cigarette where is the text where is the cigarette where is the text where is the cigarette?."*

The phone rang. *Thank God!*

"Mila?" an unfamiliar male voice asked.

"Yes?" I breathed out.

"It's Doctor G."

"Oh, hi, Doctor G. How are you?" I asked politely.

"How are *you*?" he asked.

This doctor was not beating around the bush.

"I'm okay, Dr. G," I said. "What is it?"

"You called me, Mila," he prompted, a questioning note in his voice

"I did? Oh, gosh, I did! I am sorry; I totally forgot!" I gushed.

"Yes, you called, and said you needed to speak to me A.S.A.P."

"When did I call?" I asked, confused.

"This morning."

"Ah, okay. Dr. G., I am having a bad day. Or maybe it's been two days. What day is it exactly?"

"It's Wednesday, Mila."

"Oh. Wednesday. Wow. Okay." I lit a cigarette and opened the window. I saw some butts on the windowsill.

"Mila, what is happening with you?" he questioned.

"I am feeling sad, Dr. G.," I finally admitted. "I went out with this guy on Friday. It was the day before New Year's, you see, and my mother said you should never go out with anyone on the day before New Year. But I didn't listen. That's so stupid, 'cause she's always right."

"Yes, Mila, and then?" the doctor asked.

"Then, he didn't call and...!" I started crying. "I am sorry, Dr. G. I thought I was doing so much better. But I can't stop crying. I want to. I realize it's nothing to cry about, really. 'Silly;' my mom said it was 'silly,' and I agree. But I can't stop it! I just can't stop the blackness! He said, 'Never stop kissing me,' and why would anyone in their right mind say that to a woman and then never text her again? Isn't that totally fucked up? Men are so fucked up, Dr. G. Sorry; I don't mean to swear. It's just that I am so sad."

The battery indicator on my cell turned red. The phone started flashing.

"Damn, Dr. G, I hate this phone! I need to recharge it; can you call back in a few minutes?" I asked, and when he agreed, I hung up, and plugged the phone into an outlet.

My crying got louder. In a few minutes more, as I waited for my phone to reboot, I started howling – literally gripping my phone and howling.

....

After some passage of time – I don't know how long – the phone rang. Dr. G again. He said he spoke with Lynn, and since she was not coming back from maternity leave until February, she wanted me to go see him as soon as it was possible. Which was not so soon, he said, as he was on vacation for the rest of the week. In the meantime, Dr. G said I needed more anti-depressants, and he would prescribe some.

"You think that will help?" I managed to ask. Dr. G's confidence gave me some hope – for a moment, I even felt a flash of lightness as I struggled to emerge from under the ton of bricks pinning me down. Then, the numbness overwhelmed once again. *More medication, Mila? That's not a real solution. Just a fix.*

"It's just a temporary fix," Dr. G was saying to me, always a step ahead. "And we do of course have to be careful not to overmedicate, as you're already on some meds for your regular treatment program. But I want you to have some extra support during the holiday while everyone is away. Let's see how you do."

We agreed to meet on Monday. I put down the phone, realizing I could not go into work; I was a mess still. I quickly sent off an email to my secretary about needing a day off to go to the doctor. Dr. G. had said it was Wednesday, so I wouldn't be seeing him for five days. Maybe a session with the emergency therapist Roslyn from Westchester could help me? But when I called, her message revealed she was also out of town this week. *Who else could I call?*

Mama. I called my mother. I wondered what time it was in Israel. But I was having a hard time remembering what time it was in New York, and Israel was ahead, six, seven hours or so I recalled. Was it the middle of the night? I hoped not.

"Mila, how are you today? Have you eaten?" my mother asked immediately, her tone full of worry.

"Yes, I have," I said. But it was a lie. I couldn't really remember.

"What did you eat?" she drilled down.

"Something."

"*What*, Mila," my mother repeated.

"I don't know, Mama! And who cares; that's not what's important. You know, I've been thinking of those words Adam said: 'Don't ever stop...'"

"Mila, stop it!" my mother said harshly, trying to break through and save me from the morass. "You are stuck on one thought. You've told this line to me fifty times – *every time we speak*. The cousins here are all asking me what is wrong with you! Papa and I will be home in four days. Sunday. You have to get a hold of yourself, Mila, while we are not there."

'*Get a hold of yourself, Mila,*' I repeated to myself. *What did it mean?*

"Mama, I can't! I am so sad," I wailed. I shakily lit a cigarette and took a long drag.

"Are you smoking? Inside the apartment?" my mother asked.

"Yes," I replied, too engulfed by sadness again to lie.

"Mila, darling, *why?* You are young and beautiful and smart! What do you have to be sad about? There are many people who have things to be sad about! What about my good friend Marina – her son is so ill he cannot walk, so she has reasons to be, and yet she remains positive; life goes on. Please put out the cigarette! How could you even think of smoking! Please stop hurting your father and me." Long pause during which I doodled abstract star patterns around Adam's name on the cigarette pack. "We are tired," my mother's voice startled me back into the room. I scrunched the cigarette pack in disgust at my own weakness.

Yes, for once, my mother sounded tired. She wasn't even shouting as she usually did.

"I know you're tired," I sobbed back. "I'm so tired too, Mama! I am exhausted." I laid down the phone and let my tears come.

The phone must have changed hands, because my father's voice came over next: "Mila! Stop crying! That is no way for a grown woman to behave. Why are you full of this... this... male sickness? It is shameful!" he chided.

"I know," I sobbed, unable to disagree. It was all true — true, and even boring and predictable by now. Adam was not what was relevant here; my upsetness was bigger than something caused by him.

My mother got back on the phone. "Milochka, *dorogaia* (dear), let us all have some moments of peace. And please stop smoking. Isn't there someone else to call?"

"No, there is no one, no one, no one. I am completely alone," I wept.

"Mila, you are not alone," my mother corrected. "We are here in Israel, and we love you. Just promise me you won't smoke another cigarette. That's a good enough beginning."

"Okay, fine, I won't smoke," I said, knowing I wouldn't be keeping my word. *How could I promise to do something so impossible? The only thing that would help me now would be a call from Adam — as stupid as that was.*

When I hung up the phone, I lit another cigarette. The phone rang again after a few minutes. It was my mother.

"Mila, I am calling your Uncle Boris. Someone has to check up on you, to get you some food and to get those cigarettes away. He's around."

"Fine, Mama." Spent, I hung up the phone and lay down on the floor in my coat. I closed my eyes, clutching the phone, my lifeline. I connected it into the charger: I would take a nap right on the floor next to my charging phone.

．．．．．．．．．．．．．．．．．．．．

  I woke up in this same spot some time later, my head right next to the outlet. I tried to get up, but sank back down, feeling dazed and dizzy, and, as if that were not enough, sick to my stomach. The phone said 6 PM, but I couldn't at all remember what time it was that I first lay down next to it. I guess it was still Wednesday, and I had, in fact, stayed home from work. A few hours later the doorman rang up: Uncle Boris, the same uncle who lived with us in Riga and whom I wanted to marry when I was a little girl, was downstairs. I let him in.
  "Milochka! *Privet (Hi)!*" he said as I opened the door and showed him in.
  "I am sorry, Boris; it's a mess. And so am I." I shook my head helplessly as tears flooded my eyes.
  The ugliness I was feeling was splayed out for him to witness. My hair was matted; there were tear stains on my face; and I was dirty because I hadn't showered probably since New Year's Eve. The apartment was smoky, and I knew Uncle Boris had had no idea that I had ever smoked one cigarette. I looked at the bag of groceries Boris held.
  "Milochka," he said in an awkward and soft tone. "Here is some food." He unpacked the bag. It held a loaf of fresh brown Lithuanian rye bread, cheese, kielbasa, meat-filled *piroshki,* farmer cheese, grapes, pomegranate juice, and Russian chocolate candies.
  Boris put on some water for tea and walked over to the window. He cleaned up the cigarette butts on the sill and closed the window to keep out the cold. I sat down on my couch, feeling embarrassed. I was beginning to grasp I had disappeared into a rabbit hole for a day or two. Or had it been three?
  Uncle Boris took me to his house in Brooklyn for a hot dinner. I was still feeling catatonic, but able to raise a New Year's toast with Boris and his wife Tamara. "S Novim Godom! (Happy New Year!)" we clinked, even though the New Year had arrived with a big black bang.

．．．．．．．．．．．．．．．．．．．．

  Boris drove me back to Manhattan. I rested, and the next morning I felt well enough to take a shower and call my secretary to tell her I would be out for the rest of the week. I continued to rest. On Friday, I erased a few of the draft emails and texts I had written to Adam. A small victory.

On Saturday, my friend Jessica came down from Connecticut to spend a day with me. She had groceries with her. "Your mom called me," she explained as she unpacked the bag. There were crackers, cashews, and Ben & Jerry's chocolate ice cream. "For later," she smiled. "Here, let me make you a bath; you need to wash and relax."

She drew a bath for me, and I got in. I sat there, the warm water washing over my naked body. Tears streamed down my face. "I miss Cliff, Jessica," I said, "I miss him so much." I cried harder and louder until I was sobbing. It felt good to release all my sadness into the tub, to feel the warm water support me as I rinsed out my misery.

"Shhh. It's okay, Mila, it's okay." Jessica came in and sat next to the bathtub so she could hold my hand. "Shhh. It will be better."

I closed my eyes and repeated her words to myself. *It will be better.*

....

Sunday arrived, and with it, the return of my parents from Israel. I didn't pretend I was okay; it was too hard.

"You look so pale, Milochka, but it's nothing some blush won't cover," Mama said matter-of-factly. She firmly faced forward – wiping my counters and straightening the closet as she talked of the wedding, showed pictures of my cousins, unpacked souvenirs. When my father asked how work was, she looked at him sharply and shook her head. After my parents left, I cried as I clutched the red coral earrings they had brought me from their stopover in Prague.

I had let them down, and I continued to let them down. *It will be better,* I reminded myself.

When, and how, though, remained to be seen.

Chapter 35 — Swimming with Papa

One week and a day after New Year's Eve, my father and I went for a swim in the pool in my building. The pool was always empty, and today, only a teenage lifeguard was there, reading his chemistry book.

I always loved the time I spent swimming with my father. On Saturdays in Riga, when I was eight years old, my father took me for swimming lessons at the city pool. In the summers of my childhood, he and I would swim in the Baltic Sea at the seaside resort of Jurmala. My mother would watch us from the shore, proud her daughter knew how to swim. It was a sign of success: she was able to give me something she didn't have a chance to achieve herself. Once back on the shore, Papa and I would change out of our wet swimsuits behind some trees, and then eat the creamy vanilla ice cream cones for which Latvia was famous.

When I swam with Papa this Sunday, it reminded me of who I used to be: an optimistic, happy, confident girl. Underwater, time was suspended, and my life above water seemed less real, almost like a story that was happening to someone else. Inside the water, I connected to the tiny strong part of me that could take on whatever it was that had happened to me. And each time I came up for air, I imagined some life force was flowing into me from the vast anonymous city outside. It gave me the energy to get me through another difficult night, and I felt stronger.

"Milochka, *dochenka*, I believe in you," my father said at the end of our swim. "Mama and I believe in you."

"I love you, Papa," I replied.

....

On Monday, Dr. Gold increased my Wellbutrin dose yet again. He said it was a temporary solution so I could get back to work. I agreed to it, for the extra Wellbutrin was helping: I could get out of bed more easily. And for every cigarette I smoked, I broke one and threw it out in the bush behind my smoking bench in the garden. This was progress. Besides, a week out of work was all I could afford.

At the office, Erin asked me to review ten boxes of bank loan documents for our case. I could barely concentrate though, and was nervous that if I didn't do so, this time, I would actually lose this job. My mind felt hazy, like I had just emerged out of a time warp. I stared at the first box of documents. I picked up a few pages and attempted to read them. But by the time the week had passed, I still had nine boxes – and thousands of contracts – to review. These contracts were in addition to all the online documents in the case.

"Mila, how are you doing at work?" my mother asked on Friday night. I told her I was worried about the review. "We'll come tomorrow," she reassured me. "You'll get it done. You always do."

"I always *did*, Mama. I don't know if I can now," I corrected her.

On Saturday, my father accompanied me to the office so I could make up the work I hadn't accomplished during the week. It was my mother's idea: She thought my father's presence would help me concentrate, and it did help to have him with me in my beautiful Wall Street tomb. I knew Papa found the dark wood finishes and the brown suede couches impressive. He sat on the guest chair in my office, happily reading a Russian newspaper.

I sat at my stately desk across from him, forcing myself to read the bank papers. *I will concentrate!* I commanded myself. *I will read the documents for my father, if not for me. He's worked too hard to give me the opportunities I had in America. He gave too much. He gave up too much too.*

I read the documents until my eyes hurt. When I glanced over from time to time at my father, I noticed he looked smaller than he had just a few years ago. His hair was whiter, his frame thinner, and his eyes a more faded blue. My dear Papa, so patient, so generous, was now sixty-seven. And my repetitive post-romance collapses were taking a toll on him.

I knew that when his phone rang, he answered in the hope it was not another anguished phone call from me. I called him whenever my mother couldn't talk, to tell him about this guy or that guy. He always answered the same way: "Milochka! How is your day?" He always sounded so happy to hear from me, and I could hear a smile in his voice when he said hello. But I knew Papa's smile evaporated as I told him, the man who thought I deserved the moon and stars, yet another saga about the jerk who didn't call. I tried to hold back, but there were times where I felt unless I talked with someone, my mind would explode from sadness.

Today, I managed to keep some of my anxiety about dating in check. Papa's presence motivated me to make it through this day: I could review title documents and loan syndication agreements *for him*. I knew too this law firm job provided me with some much-needed stability.

As I finished reviewing the last contract, I looked over at my devoted father. I felt an expansive warm feeling – a desire to make Papa feel secure. I felt a love for the boy inside the man – the four-year-old boy who had lost his father to the front of World War II. I realized that one day we would have to switch places – I would have to be there for my father, rather than him being there for me. But not yet. Today, being a child was still my best role.

Pretty sad.

....

On Monday, I went into Erin's office to give her my summaries. She nodded at me when I walked up to her desk. She was putting another picture of her daughters into a frame. The girls smiled in their bright red dresses as they stood in front of a Christmas tree.

"Is that from this December?" I inquired politely.

"Yes, it was at my in-laws' this year," she said. She put the frame on a shelf, next to a wedding picture. "My first wedding," she said, when she noticed my looking. "My first husband died from a brain tumor."

"Oh. I didn't know. I'm sorry, Erin," I responded sincerely.

"It's okay; it was a long time ago," she elaborated. "That was a rough year for me. My father had a stroke and died just before our wedding. Then, within the year, my husband died too. It was a really tough time."

I nodded again, not sure of what to say, but reminded of how many people had their own private heartaches. Erin was a survivor, a strong

Irish Catholic woman who had put herself through law school and clawed her way into partnership at a top firm. She was as strong as the strong Russian women I knew, and even though I still didn't quite like her, I respected her more now.

Erin hadn't folded. I wished I had some of her resilience myself.

CHAPTER 36 – HYPER AND ANXIOUS

One Friday, my single girlfriend Roxanna called me in the morning: "Milochka, darling, do you want to go to a Shabbat service with me tonight? It will be relaxing, darling. And so good for your soul. Today's lecture topic is 'Modern Transformation Through Ancient Wisdom.'"

Roxanna often went to lectures and dinners at a synagogue on the East Side. She then posted pictures on Facebook of her looking glamorous at these events – one week Roxanna glowed in a midnight blue gown getting a book signed by a famous rabbi, the next week she earnestly delivered lunches in a smart red suit to homebound senior citizens.

The transformation event was clever marketing on the part of a synagogue looking to recruit new members. Who going to these singles dinners/religious gatherings couldn't use a transformation grounded in some tested wisdom? I decided to give it a try.

The synagogue was in a townhouse at the corner of 62nd and Central Park West. I walked there after taking the subway on Lexington Avenue, all the while shivering in my coat. February was here, so soon, it would be spring again. Spring was the traditional time of transformation when stark, seemingly barren trees erupted with buds and then leaves. I wondered what ancient lessons I would pick up tonight.

Inside the synagogue's basement, Roxanna was already seated at a table; she waved for me to join her. Felix, her podiatrist boyfriend of a few months, sat next to her, his big black unibrow now groomed into two. He was slimmer as well than he had been the last time we all went out together, and his pinstripe suit looked snazzy. Roxanna's tutoring was certainly paying off: He looked attractive. She believed in working with raw material, she had confided in me once. A man with a good job and heart and a generous spirit – i.e., ready cash, of course, could always be made over to be more stylish and handsome.

"Shabbat Shalom, Milochka," Roxanna said as she air-kissed me. Despite Roxanna's friendly greeting, I now had an urge to run. I felt like a third wheel; I hadn't realized Felix would be here. "I'm going to make a phone call," I said to Roxanna, and went upstairs.

Upstairs, I stood outside the coat room. Maybe I would grab my coat and leave, and then text Roxanna that I realized I had to get home to finish a work project. As I stood deliberating, a tall, dark-haired guy in a yarmulke approached me. And that's how I met Alexander.

We talked briefly: He told me he was with his friends and wanted to be more active in the synagogue. He was born in London and had lived in Paris until recently. He was a sales executive for a pharmaceutical company. He expressed interest in contacting me, and we exchanged numbers. I saved him as "Alexander Paris" in my contacts list.

"R u ok?" Roxanna texted me as I stood with Alexander.

"Fine – sorry – just chatting w/ a guy."

"Oooh, is he cute? :-)" she replied.

I went downstairs in my coat to say goodbye to Roxanna and Felix. My spiritual growth would have to wait for another Shabbat. I felt a slight glimmer of hope. Perhaps the holy place energy was making me optimistic about my future in this city and in the world. Or maybe it was just that there was another cute guy on the horizon. I hoped it was the former.

....

A week later, Alexander called me and asked me out for dinner. We went to Bottino, an Italian restaurant in Chelsea's gallery district. There, it soon became clear we had no deep connection; we came from different cultures, and had different likes and dislikes.

Alexander loved soccer and hated dancing. I loved dancing, and was indifferent to soccer. He preferred movies to reading or theater, and had never heard of Chekhov. He loved martinis and surfing. When he was out, he snuck out of gatherings to sneak a cigarette. On Friday nights, he prayed with friends at various Shabbat dinners around town.

Still, due to inertia perhaps, we dated for a few months. Alexander took me to parties where we stayed until dawn while techno blared. He communicated with me via texts: "Hey, pussycat, how r u?," or, "Bonjour, gorgeous, where r u?" or "Am out 4 drinks with clients, *ma cherie.*" Because he was in sales and traveled every week, we saw each other only on the weekends. He wasn't much of a boyfriend, but I took myself off JDate. I was happy a new guy was around, and still a bit numb after my recent dive into blackness. I found I was not anxious about whether Alexander would call: Since I knew we were not a love match, our limited contact suited me.

....

Lynn returned from maternity break. She showed me pictures of her and her baby. There were no pictures of the baby with her father, and I realized Lynn was a single mother. Somehow, I hadn't even considered that, even though Lynn had never mentioned a husband and wore no ring.

Lynn said she was sorry I had fallen off around Thanksgiving and New Year's, when she wasn't there to help me. I told her I was doing much better now, and that I was so happy she was back: I felt much less accountable without her available to me.

Toward the end of February, I finally finished a few important briefs at work. I did notice I didn't need much sleep, though. I was still taking the high dose of Wellbutrin Dr. Gold had prescribed in January, after my holiday blues. I realized I would probably be okay without such a high dose, but I liked that it suppressed my appetite and alleviated my desire to smoke.

I was just so grateful to not feel too depressed that I didn't tell Dr. G that my thoughts were racing, and that I was beginning to feel hyper and anxious.

CHAPTER 37 – THE FOREST

On a Tuesday in March, a friend invited me to the Met to see *Mazeppa*, an opera by Tchaikovsky. Ian was an investment banker who meditated and practiced reiki. We had dated for a few weeks ten years ago, and now had a comfortable familiarity with each other that replaced any past chemistry.

Going to the Metropolitan made me happy to be in New York. I loved the excited chatter of the crowd, the magnificent Chagall canvases at the entrance, and the shimmering crystal chandeliers. This beauty lifted me out of the state of controlled anxiety of the past few weeks.

Mazeppa was a marathon-length opera with glorious costuming for the dancing kossacks. By the Third Act, it was getting late, and I was sleepy. On stage, Maria, the heroine, was learning of the murder of her father by her husband. I closed my eyes, lids heavy, and opened them to find Maria in a state of anguish. She sang a heart-piercing aria as she wandered, wild-haired and mad-eyed in the forest, grabbing at the trees and pushed over the brink by her heartbreak.

My breath suspended and my stomach dropped. My heart went out to Maria, a lost, crazy soul. Her desperate wail filled my ears. My tears were sudden, unexpected. Shivering, I pulled my wrap up over me. "Ian, I don't feel so well," I whispered over to my companion. "I must go."

I got up and climbed over the people to our right. I ran outside to the hall, then down the grand staircase. Ian followed. Outside, I apologized profusely, and said I had to get home, go to bed. Ian waved for a taxi.

In the taxi, I wept. My thoughts raced. Suddenly my future was terrifying me; I was overwhelmed by the vastness of the world, and the possibilities of a life's trajectory. Had Maria ever imagined she would wind up in the forest of madness?

My mind was full of flashes: *Flashes of the opera scene, Maria weeping and tearing at her hair; flashes of Dominic and me in the Chase closet; flashes of me at Cliff's feet begging for mercy; flashes of the string of men I had dated this year, face after face, pick-up line after pick-up line. Damian, Zoran, Jake, Henry, Adam. Adam, the-Night-Before-New-Year's-Eve. His kiss. "Don't ever stop kissing me," he said, and then he stopped kissing me. He. Didn't. Text. Those three words had driven me to the edge in January. Or had it been over the edge? Like Maria? Heartbreak pushes people over...*

The phone rang during the cab ride; it was my mom. "How was the opera, Milochka?" she inquired, as cheerful as ever, and anticipating that my life was slowly getting back on track.

"Mama, I'm so scared," I howled, even as the taxi driver glanced back at me through the rearview mirror. "What if I can't recover? What if I can't find my way back? Maria lost it, Mama! She was so lost she couldn't even recognize her husband. He searched for her in the forest, but she was so lost in her own world. Her world was wrong, confused; the forest is a symbol of that." I rushed from thought to thought, intent on conveying the enormity of the world's bad luck heaped on random suffering souls.

"Maria who? Who is this Maria?" my mother questioned, utterly bewildered.

"Maria, in the opera; she was the heroine. Why do people always go mad in a forest in the opera?" I wept.

"Milka, darling, calm down," Mama said. "You are fine, and you're not this — who??"

"Maria, Mama."

"Yes, Milochka, you must realize it's just a story. It isn't real. With you, all will be fine."

"But how do you know, Mama?" I cried in despair at the opera my own life had become.

"Mila, it's an opera!"

"Mama, how do you know I'll be fine? I asked you how you know, so tell me!" I yelled.

"I just know," she said calmly.

And indeed, my mother always "just knew." Whenever I turned to her in fear or uncertainty, she always reassured me. Despite the fact that I often resisted her advice and insisted on doing things my own way, I knew my general sense of wellbeing and optimism about my fate in the world came from her. And now, I wanted her to promise me with divine confidence I would survive. I wanted her to say I could beat my racing brain and dark sadness into submission.

"How do you just know, Mama?" I insisted yet again, all the while knowing I sounded like a child. I felt like a child too. How I yearned to be a strong woman like all the Russian women I knew: my mother, my grandmother, and all my mother's friends who carried their immigrant families spiritually, and often financially. But these past two years, I had been a woman-child, always asking about the unknowable, always searching for strength. I had been weak, crying over breakups with faceless men, and forgetting in my anguish what mattered. My mind had felt broken these past months, and so was my spirit. I needed Mama's faith to buttress me, to stand in for my own lack of center.

"I just do, Milochka," she said.

"But you don't, do you, Mama?" I pressed. "Nobody knows. It's all random. I got sick, Mama. And he didn't know it."

"Who didn't know it?"

"Cliff, Mama, Cliff. Why did he..."

"Mila, stop it!" she shrieked, cutting me off, and speaking suddenly in an even firmer voice. "Cliff is *gone*. It is *two years later*. You must save yourself."

"I'm scared, Mama. I feel like I'm losing my mind. How many ups and downs before I break forever? The forest is not so far away for me, is it?" I cried softly, weakened by my fearful thoughts.

The taxi stopped, and even though I got out, I did not hang up the phone; it had become my lifeline once again. I needed to hear Mama tell me it would all be okay again and again until I fell asleep. And that's just what she did.

"Everything will be okay, Mila," Mama reassured me as I climbed into bed.

In my bed, I wiped at my tears, my hands black from the mascara that had run. "But Mama, there is so much tragedy in the world!" I pointed out.

"Yes, darling, that's true," my mother responded, sounding tired now. "Nobody knows what life brings. We can just hope, have faith.

And if you have your health, Milochka, that is all you can ask for. Life is for the living, and so we live."

So Mama didn't know everything would be fine; nobody could know for sure. But she had enough faith for the both of us. Mama was my source of strength. *Life is for the living, and so we live,* I repeated silently.

I fell asleep cradling the phone.

Chapter 38 — 911

In the morning, I went to my regular Wednesday appointment with Lynn. I wasn't so excited to see her this morning because we were working on a letter to Cliff. Lynn thought it would be helpful for me to write him about the breakdown. She thought that revealing to him that I had been ill would help me deal with my guilt over the affair, and allow me to realize that his rigidity had something to do with our demise.

Sure, sure. Typical psychologist crap, I thought to myself. *Cliff would only end up congratulating himself after reading the letter when he came to realize that he had rid himself of an incompetent and crazy wife.*

At our session Lynn suggested — once again — that I was not always responsible for the behavior of others, which is what I always seemed to think when a love relationship did not work out for me. "Mila, people have a lot going on in their lives. You are not always the reason for their behavior. You and Cliff broke up not only because of the affair. He had a very black-and white-view of relationships and of you."

"Yes, well, it was hard for him, Lynn. He didn't ask for me to meet Dominic."

"No, he did not. But many couples do get over an affair. Affairs happen. Cliff could have chosen forgiveness. It would have been hard, sure, but not impossible."

"I know. I know. Many people stay together through and after an affair. There are many books and talk show discussions about this very thing," I responded. But although I could say this out loud to Lynn with what seemed to be perfect confidence, inside I still wavered: *Could Cliff have truly forgiven me, given how close we were? Maybe it would have been possible if we had not been best friends who had shared every secret with one another. Could such an intense relationship not weather such a betrayal?*

My head hurt from all this thinking and rethinking, and I felt the back of my neck sweating. "Lynn, can I go get some water? My throat feels very dry." When she nodded yes, I got up and went into the bathroom. I looked at myself in the mirror and said firmly: "It's not always about you, Mila," a few times.

I knew this statement to be empirically true, and maybe if I said it enough, it would sink in. There was something perverse, too, in thinking you were so important that you consistently affected the behavior of others.

After the therapy session ended, I walked to work mouthing, *"It is not always my fault. It is not always my fault."*

When I got to my office, I found I was still thirsty. I drank two large glasses of water and sat down at my computer. As I picked up the phone to retrieve my messages, I noticed that my hand was shaking slightly. Hmmm. That was a little strange. I wondered whether shakiness was a side effect of the increased doses of anti-depressants I had been on since January, or whether the Depakote part of the cocktail was finally showing its effects as well. How frustrating, this whole trying to get the right medicine combination was. I understood now that psychiatry was an art as much as a science. Dr. G. had explained that the right drug treatment would be one that would give me some mood stability – without too much depression and too much excitement overall. But I also had to be careful of potential side effects: weight gain, hair loss, rashes, and dry mouth. We didn't want the cure to be more harmful than the illness.

I Googled the drug Depakote to see whether dry mouth and hand tremors were some of the side effects. But the ring of the phone interrupted my search, and I started talking to my friend Roxanna. And that's when I thought, *Okay, I'll just relax and talk to my friend.*

But then I started saying the wrong stuff. To be exact, my thoughts suddenly began to find themselves as words – without my will. I noticed this when I heard myself telling Roxanna – with whom I hadn't spoken with in a while – that I was dating Alexander Paris. Yet right before I said this, I had thought to myself, *Don't tell her yet about having dinner with Alexander Paris.* I didn't want to mention him because I wasn't in the mood to go into all the details right now, especially as there was a good chance we would not go out again. Besides, this was a new behavior I was anxious to try on – not going exhaustingly into all the details of a new relationship. But just as I was thinking, *Don't tell her,* I heard my voice saying, "I went out to dinner with that guy from the temple."

Aaarph, what had just happened? Why had I said something I had consciously intended not to say? How did those words come out without my wanting them to?

I felt hot and panicky, and I rushed off the phone. Then I got up and shut the door to my office. Again I noticed I felt parched again, and that now both my hands were now trembling noticeably. *What the hell was happening?*

I decided to throw my mind on work, but when I tried to log onto the computer, I could not type my password in correctly. After a few failed attempts, I called Dr. G. to ask him about these symptoms. I told him I was feeling thirsty, shaky, and way too chatty. Together we decided that I should leave work and go home to take some Klonopin, the sedative part of the medicine cocktail, then go to see him uptown for an evaluation.

I hung up and put on my coat. And then I took it off. On with the coat; off with the coat. This happened a few more times. *Why couldn't I just leave my coat on?! How frustrating! Would I be able to leave my office at all?*

Panicked, I called Dr. G. again and told him that I was still in the office. I told him that it was like I was paralyzed into inaction, even though my brain was racing inside with thought upon thought upon thought. Dr. G. said he would stay on the cell with me until I actually left and went downstairs; that he would remind me again and again that I was leaving so I would not return to my office to take off my coat.

"Good idea, Dr. G.," I responded. Then I told him I was worried about encountering my secretary on my way out; what should I say to her? I practiced his suggestion, saying it over and over again into my cell phone: "I am feeling ill and going to the doctor. I'll call a little later."

Forcing myself to move, I floated past my secretary mouthing this phrase without waiting for her to ask me anything more, as I could not trust myself to respond correctly. When I turned down the corner of the hallway, I felt relieved. *Almost out,* I thought. "Almost out," I heard come out of my mouth. "Damn it, I am thinking out loud," I thought/said either to the cell phone or to myself. "Dr. G.?"

"Yes?"

"Good, you're still there. I am almost by the elevator lobby. But I feel so sad. I don't understand what's happening."

"I'm here, Mila. Keep on going," Dr. Gold encouraged me.

"But, I have forgotten what I am doing! Where am I going again?" I asked, completely perplexed.

"Home."

"That's right, home. *Home.* I am going *home*," I emphasized, trying to remember this. But I couldn't. My short-term memory was shot.

"Dr. G., can you keep reminding me?" I begged. I needed him to keep whispering into my ear over the phone.

"Sure."

I felt a tear come. And then another. I quickly wiped at my eyes. This was freaky! I didn't want to cry right now! "Dr. G, why am I so weepy?" I asked.

"Why don't you think of something that makes you happy. Imagine it very specifically, and try not to let your mind wander from it," he counseled.

I thought of a gold star. "How about a star?"

"A star is fine, Mila."

And so I repeated the word "star" to myself so that I would not burst into tears. "Star, star, I love stars, Dr. G. You know, I draw them on all my papers. Lots of them, over and over."

When I got on the elevator, Paula, the secretary of the partner with whom I had been working with recently, was there.

"Hello, how are you?" Paula greeted me.

Oh God, no questions! Given that I was on the phone, I did not really have to talk to her, and so I smiled instead. But I also said the word "star" out loud to her.

"Excuse me; I didn't get that?" Paula asked.

I said the word "star" again before I realized I had to make something up. "My boyfriend and I are talking because he is buying me a beautiful star necklace; isn't that great? I am trying to decide which one right now."

The elevator arrived at the lobby: *Whew!*

"Good luck," called Paula over her shoulder as she too exited the building.

"Thanks!" Had I made it out of the office? "Dr. G.?" There was no answer; I must have hung up. Okay, well, I could call him back from my apartment.

I now had to walk two blocks to my building, then make it past my elevator lobby with its zoo of doormen. But I was beginning to feel more and more confused.

Dr. Gold called back.

"Hi, Dr. G.," I answered. "I am outside. Just a short block to go."

"Good, are you almost home?"

"Yes, I am getting close to my lobby; what should I do, Dr. G.?"

"Just walk in and smile; you don't have to say anything."

"OK, I will smile and think of the necklace. But Dr. G.? Can you continue telling me to smile so that I don't forget?" I requested, unable to keep track of anything in the short term.

And so I walked and held the phone to my ear as Dr. G. told me, over and over again to, "smile and walk through the lobby; smile and walk through the lobby..." I smiled and walked, but also said the words "star necklace" to the doorman who greeted me.

"What, Ms. Mila?" said Raj, the doorman.

"A star necklace, Raj! I am excited about this star necklace I am getting for my birthday."

"Great, Ms. Mila. I hope you enjoy that necklace, Ms. Mila."

"Thanks, Raj," I responded, somewhat aware I was floating in and out of lucidity. For two or three seconds, I could understand I was in my elevator and was going to my apartment to get Klonopin and then take a cab to Dr. G., and then the next second, I would forget. At some point, Dr. G. must have been satisfied that I was in my apartment and knew what I had to do, because we got off the phone.

The light outside was now less bright. Kids were home from school; I could see them playing on the monkey bars below my window. Small dots of bright colors – red, blue, green coats and hats, bopping happily around the playground. In the apartment, time disappeared. When my phone rang the next time, it was Lynn. I realized then that I was sitting on my bed holding the Klonopin. Knowing I was in the safety of my apartment, I really broke down.

"Lynn, something is very wrong! I am very sad, and I am not sure what is happening. I am thinking out loud."

Then my brain got stuck.

"Lynn, I hate this law work. It's all work, work, work! And hate dating. I love Cliff! I miss Cliff! Why, Lynn, why did this shit have to happen? Lynn!"

I was screaming and incoherent, and vaguely I knew this.

"Mila, Dr. Gold left me a message saying you were going to take some Klonopin and then that you are going to go to see him."

"I am, Lynn. But, I just was thinking, Lynn, about something we talked about. About how I never listen to advice; do you remember?"

"Yes, Mila," she spoke in soothing tone.

"Remember, I told you my mother was begging me to stop talking to Dominic and to go to Los Angeles over New Year's and I was so cocky and I didn't listen. I never listen to her, and I'm not sure why. Just like you keep telling me I should go to sleep by twelve every night, but I am staying out late at these ridiculous nightclubs with guys who I know don't even like me."

"Mila, have you found the Klonopin?" she directed.

"I'll look for it," I promised, rummaging through my medicine cabinet. "Oh – I am holding it still, actually!"

"Mila, do you remember the correct dose to take? I will call Dr. G and have him call you again. Just stay put. I have to go now; there is a patient waiting. I also think we should meet tomorrow, okay? I will call you later about the time."

"Thanks, Lynn," I said as we hung up. Then I stared at the Klonopin I had found. *What I was supposed to do with it?* I lay down on my bed.

The phone range; it was Dr. Gold.

"Mila, it's Dr. Gold. Did you take the Klonopin pill? Are you on your way?"

That's right, I was here to get the Klonopin, and then go to Dr. G.

"Hi, Dr. G! Wow, I am sorry, I must have lost track of time. One pill of Klonopin. Got it. I'll go down to see you right now. I'm already out the door," I promised.

And I went down past Raj and the other doormen, smiling at them. I walked to the corner and tried to flag down a cab. However, when the driver pulled over, I got into the cab and then out again.

"Hey, lady, do you want the cab or not?" the annoyed driver hollered at me.

"Uh, no, that's okay."

I let this cab go and tried again. I was walking in a small circle on the street when a taxi almost ran me over. The driver leaned out the window, and began gesticulating wildly. I got into his cab and then right back out. "Sorry!" I yelled to the cabby.

Fuck! What the hell!

I went back to my lobby, and up to my place. In my apartment, I dropped the Klonopin on the floor – I couldn't remember now what to do with it. I tried to call Dr. G. to tell him I couldn't make it. But I could not figure out how to press call. *Why was everything so goddamn difficult! Why couldn't I pull Dr. Gold up from my contacts list?*

I lay down on my floor and threw the phone down, then let out a loud scream of frustration.

The phone rang; I still knew how to answer it, and I did.

"Mila, are you on your way?"

"Dr. G.! I was trying to call you but my fingers are not working right," I said. Then a flood of thoughts simply spilled out of my mouth. "Dr. G., I want you to understand that up until this morning, I was fine. This thing right now is very bizarre; I don't get it. Maybe being at Lynn's earlier did something to me? I am angry at Lynn – Do you get what I'm saying?"

"I do."

"No, do you really get it?" I yelled at Dr. G.

"Yes, Mila," he said in a consoling tone.

My brain and thoughts accelerated even more. "Hey, Dr. Gold, do you know that I never listen to ANYONE? I don't listen to my parents, ever. My mom told me not to switch French for Spanish in college and to go live in France for one year, and I didn't, and who knows how different my life would be if I had!" *Why was I suddenly fixating on this stupid college language issue?* "My mom says every night to me, 'If you keep on crying for Cliff, you won't forget him, and he is not crying for you; he has forgotten you completely. It's been TWO years, Mila.' My mom says all the time that I need to stop dating, because my brain can't handle another bad date. And all of you doctors say to me, 'No dating!' But I am still dating, Dr. G.! And every night, before I go to sleep my mother cautions me that I might end up in the madhouse like our distant relative who ended up in a psych hospital with acute manic episodes – she has very severe manic depression, you know, like you were telling me; not exactly my diagnosis, right? But still, this is so fucking scary. I know that I am much more normal than all this, so what is going on today? I will be okay, right Dr. G., right?"

"Mila, you will be okay."

"Do you promise?" I sobbed.

"Yes, I promise," he said gently.

"How do you know? I am scared, Dr. G." I heard my voice getting louder and louder and more aggressive, but I couldn't control it. "Why should I believe you, Dr. G.? Why should I believe Lynn? I am bored of all this therapy crap! Russians don't even believe in psychotherapy, you know! How do you know you will help me? Are you going to help me? Are you going to help me? Are you going to help me? ARE YOU GOING TO HELP ME?" I shouted.

I hung up on Dr. G. The phone rang. It was Dr. G. again. He told me he was going to call 911 and that they would help me to come to see him. I agreed to this.

But by the time the emergency medical technicians came to my apartment in response to Dr. G.'s 911 call, I forgot that I had agreed to allow them to take me to Cornell hospital where Dr. Gold saw some of his patients and was waiting for me. When they knocked on my door and I opened it, I told them I refused to leave. I sat down on my couch and said I was not going anywhere. I don't remember the exact exchange between me and the six or so men who flooded into my small living room, but I do recall that it took several of them to physically restrain me and get me into a wheelchair.

Not knowing where to take me either, the ambulance driver sped to the default destination: Bellevue.

CHAPTER 39 – AT BELLEVUE

After a terrible night's sleep, I woke up early. It was just seven a.m., according to one of the many nurses milling around, and I was now utterly logical and rational. By eight a.m., I was bored out of my mind. I made my way to the lounge where some patients and a nurse sat at a long table. The only reading material I could find were some ancient issues of *Time* and *People*. On the television, a cooking show was playing, just as it had been the night before.

Breakfast arrived in the lounge; it sucked. It was dry cereal, something I never ate as a rule. Even though I was starving, I just drank the weak coffee. I noticed that some social activity was encouraged even if all the participants were perhaps slightly (or not so slightly) socially strange at this exact moment. All I could think of now was getting out. But the key to my escape was held by doctors who hadn't yet arrived.

A nurse came to get me when it was my turn to be seen. She brought me to a doctor's office where a young man in a white coat held out his hand.

"Mila? I'm Dr. Kahn."

I shook his hand, making sure to make eye contact, as one would in a business meeting. Dr. Kahn was tall and cute and really nice. He asked me how I was feeling. I told him that I was totally fine now, although quite bewildered by both the speed of my earlier deterioration and my subsequent recovery.

"I really have to get back to work today, Dr. Kahn," I emphasized. "But I don't have my Blackberry because they took it away with my purse. I haven't told anyone at the office I might be out today. And I can't use the pay phone to call and alert the office because all the necessary contact numbers are stored in my cell. Plus I am very worried about what my parents are going to think when they can't reach me!"

I hoped Dr. Kahn understood my main point: I had real responsibilities, and my incarceration here at Bellevue was a terrible mistake!

"I'll do what I can for you, Mila, but we need to talk first. As for your parents, they were here already and will be back. Your doctor and your psychologist have called as well. A lot of people are concerned about you," he told me with a smile.

My poor parents knew already! Oh, how harsh these last few years had been for them — and now they had to add a check-in at Bellevue to the laundry list of shitty events. What a disappointing daughter I was turning out to be. So much for all that early promise I had showed.

I had to learn to be tough, like other Russian women. And I should be able to do this: I had tough women in my family. *So I could do it,* I thought, giving myself a pep talk.

"Do you remember what happened yesterday?" Dr. Kahn asked.

"Of course! Pretty hard to forget!" I joked.

Dead silence. The doctor waited for me to fill in the silence; I suppose he wanted to make sure I actually knew the details.

"I woke up on Wednesday — that's yesterday! Wow, can't believe that was yesterday... anyway, that's a digression," I pointed out. It was important that he know that I knew that I was getting off the point, as rambling could be seen as a manic behavior. "Anyway, in the morning, I was feeling fine. I had seen this opera the night before, *Mazeppa*, which was beautiful. I don't know if you've seen it?"

"No."

"Well, actually, there was a scene in it in which the heroine goes mad. It disturbed me..." I paused here, then decided that I didn't want to go into detail on the subject of madness. I probably could find safer topics of conversation.

"Mila?"

"Sorry, Dr. Kahn. So, the opera had upset me. I have a perfectly normal phone call in the morning with my mom, then I went to see Lynn — she's my therapist — for my weekly appointment."

"Yes? And then?"

"Well, then, our therapy session upset me; we were talking about why my marriage had broken up. And afterwards, I had my first anxiety or panic attack ever, and I didn't know how to stop it."

"Hmmm...Do you know we had to give you two shots of Halidol to sedate you once you got here?" Dr. Kahn asked me.

"Oh," I responded, a bit quietly. I had never heard of Halidol, but it certainly sounded serious.

"You were extremely agitated and loud, and resisted the emergency personnel."

"I know. That's funny, as I'm actually not a very agitated or loud person."

"And how do you feel now?" Dr. Kahn continued. I noticed he was taking notes and checking off boxes. I reminded myself this was a formal evaluation, and to sound serious and together.

"I feel perfectly normal," I responded.

"Really?"

"Yes. Really. Seriously, Doctor Kahn, I am fully recovered, so being here is really hard for me. You know, if you're feeling well, it's very boring here. There is nothing to do but talk to the other people and..." I didn't finish. I wanted to say that many of them seemed off, but that seemed mean. "I would like to go home, take a shower, and go to work. I haven't even checked my Blackberry since yesterday, so that makes me nervous. I am working with this new partner. I am an attorney."

"Yes, I know that." He looked at me carefully and nodded his head. He did seem genuinely caring. I allowed myself to feel a bit of hope.

"So... can I can go home with my parents?" I urged. "I'd be much better off resting there. It's easier to sleep if there aren't any fluorescent lights."

Turned out it wouldn't be that easy or quick: Dr. Kahn answered that he has been trying to find a bed for me over at Cornell Hospital, but it was crowded there right now.

"But I don't need a bed at Cornell. Or anywhere. I can leave today! I'm fine, really, I am," I insisted.

"All of us would prefer to watch you for a few days until we all are convinced you are really one hundred percent all right," he said carefully.

"What do you mean, 'all of us;' do you mean Dr. Gold too?" I asked. The very idea made me panic slightly: could Dr. G. possibly be turning on me? He hadn't even spoken to me today. And if he did, he would see that I was totally fine! I realized I needed to talk to him as soon as possible. "Please, Dr. Kahn, I realize I was very 'out there' yesterday. But that was bizarre and unusual... I have never acted like that, ever. I'm taking some new medicine combination, so maybe it was the drugs that helped cause the anxiety. I am certain I am fine now. I am certain too that I'd be better off with my parents, in their backyard in New Jersey. I've recuperated there before; it's a much nicer place than a hospital." *Ooops, I didn't want to suggest I'd had other mental breakdowns!* "I mean, after the bad break-up with my husband, I stayed with them," I quickly corrected. "Why waste any bed space on me when there is someone who could use it much more?"

"I am sorry, but no. Now, unless, we hear back from Cornell shortly, we will arrange for you to go to Gracie Hospital for a day."

"What? Another day? But then it would be Friday already! Dr. Kahn, I really don't think that's necessary," I pleaded with him.

Dr. Kahn sat quietly for a moment, and I saw in his eyes that he was deliberating. I stayed silent, letting him see my ability to stay calm and patient.

"Well, let's see what some of the other doctors think," he hedged.

"Thanks, Doctor."

Great! I had passed round one.

....

I had to convince three other doctors that I was fully recovered and could be released to my parents. I used my best oral advocacy skills, trying to show them I was completely sane and safe. Each of them stared into my eyes, as if searching for some spark of weirdness. But I really was back to myself, so there was nothing for them to see. And I bet my parents' wanting to watch me, and Dr. Gold's informing the doctors that he'd see me first thing on Friday morning, had a lot to do with my being set free.

The senior doctor on duty gave me the good news: "A lot of people are looking out for you, so we are releasing you. We are amazed at your quick recovery; it is truly a remarkable trajectory. If you saw yourself how we saw you yesterday, you too would find it very hard to believe."

"Thank you, doctor! Thank you very much," I said. And I felt just then as if I'd won a big cash prize or got into the college of my choice. I was almost OUT! *See ya later, crazies!* In a few hours, I would escape the fluorescent lighting, the bad soap, the tired-looking guard, and the old publications and reruns. This very weekend, I could window shop, read *The New York Times*, eat a tasty croissant, and drink real coffee with cream and sugar. I could take a Pilates class and blow-dry my hair and dab on some sexy perfume and go eat at Nobu. Yes, all the superficial things I loved about this city would be welcoming me back with open arms.

Later, I could think on a deeper level about what had gone on. But over the past forty-eight hours, I'd experienced enough, uhh, *depth*, to last me some time. Fun now, depth later.

Chapter 40 — Mazel Tov!

The depth came, soon enough: Lynn and Dr. G. and I tried to figure out what had happened over and over again. Perhaps the session with Lynn had unleashed severe panic? Perhaps the Wellbutrin I took after my January crash was too high a dose? As a result of our discussions, Dr. Gold drastically lowered my dose, and prescribed a stronger medicine to induce calmness. I noticed as I started taking the new sedative, my thoughts felt heavy and slow. I needed many hours of sleep.

Lynn and I continued to work on the letter to Cliff. I included the dramatic night at Bellevue in the story. I told him about the therapists, and the confusing diagnoses. I told him I was sorry he could never forgive me. That I was sorry. And then we actually sent the letter.

Cliff didn't respond. Lynn told me that wasn't the point of writing it, and she was right: After I sent the letter, a weight lifted.

I focused on work, dull but calming in its routine. I took the medicine as Dr. Gold had prescribed. When I noticed hair loss, I told Dr. G, and he switched up the cocktail once again. There was a continuous process of titration involved, he explained. Even when something works, it could just stop working some point down the line.

But I wondered whether anything was working: Basically I felt the same as I had before. A bit less energetic and a bit less anxious, but not truly different. And, since I was no longer constantly meeting new guys but casually dating only Alexander Paris, there were no ups and downs. Casually, because Alexander didn't call every day. Or even every other day. But this suited my new discipline. I found the relative emotional calm more healing than any medicine.

One Friday night, a few weeks after Bellevue, I went with Alexander to a nightclub. We met his Argentinian friend Juan there. Juan was trying to quit his heavy drug habit. I wasn't sure if it was coke or heroin or both, but I knew it was something bad. Alexander and Juan smoked cigarettes nonstop and did shots of vodka as Juan complained about the girl who stood him up. Apparently, her husband wanted her to spend the night at home.

Nursing a diet Coke, I felt tired. I didn't belong at a nightclub tonight – I would have rather been reading a novel and taking a bubble bath. We stayed out until four a.m., and I was thrilled when we all got up to leave.

That Monday, Lynn warned me about going clubbing after I had so recently been in Bellevue. She accused me of being reckless: "Mila, you must adhere to a schedule, have a curfew. Give your mind an opportunity to heal," she said sternly. "Do you get it?"

I almost got it; what she was saying wasn't rocket science. But a part of me didn't get it either: Bellevue felt far away, like a bad dream. Still, after our conversation, I hung a schedule on my refrigerator. Up at eight a.m. Swimming, work, in bed by ten p.m.

And so a few weeks went by, quiet and regular. My mother checked in more often than ever before: She wanted to make sure that I didn't disappear into the emergency ward at Bellevue one more time. I saw Alexander only once or twice during this time.

One morning, on a Friday in May, Alexander texted me. "Hockey tonite?" I had no plans. "Great!" I texted back immediately. It sounded fun, not heavy, or reckless.

Alexander and I went to the Rangers game at Madison Square Garden. Afterwards, we met some friends for drinks at a Polish dance bar. We drank vodka cranberries as we smiled at each other. Later, we slept together. It was quick, over in just about three minutes, and Alexander went out on the balcony to smoke a post-sex cigarette.

We didn't use protection.

....

Memorial Day again, and again, I had no special plans for the long weekend. This came as no surprise – the men I was dating casually were too casual even for holiday plans, and my friends with families were going away. Fortunately, my parents were always happy to welcome me home. So this Memorial Day weekend, I would go home on Saturday afternoon. I planned on my usual Saturday routine in the morning: a croissant and a coffee with half-and-half on the side at Duane Street Patisserie bakery in Tribeca while I read *The New York Times*, and then a Pilates class. Then, my dad would arrive and pick me up to go to New Jersey.

But as my alarm went off at eight a.m. on this Saturday, I sat straight up in bed, suddenly wide awake. My period was due today, and it wasn't here. Did I really have anything to worry about, though? When I was married to Cliff and we had tried for a family, my old ob/gyn had been certain I couldn't get pregnant without taking hormones. I couldn't recall now what had made him so certain about this. But, he had been. Still, I was worried. I counted back the days to when Alexander and I had had sex on that Friday after the hockey game. I recalled we had no condoms.

I could have waited. I hadn't even missed my period yet; it was just due today. But, since there had been that one instance of unprotected sex, I wanted to make sure. I determined to take a pregnancy test.

On my way to the bakery, I picked up a test. After my Pilates class, I rushed back to my apartment to take it, knowing my father would be there to pick me up any minute.

I was just getting in the door of my apartment when the phone rang. Papa was downstairs. "I'll be down in a minute, Papa; just getting my stuff together!" I said and hustled off the phone. I quickly peed on the white plastic stick. In two minutes, the double pink line appeared. I was pregnant.

I started crying. This was not how I had imagined it. I had thought Cliff and I would have a baby together. But this baby's daddy was Alexander, and he and I weren't in love. Why was this amazing miracle happening now when I couldn't rejoice in it? I called my father to tell him it would just be a few more minutes before I came downstairs.

I needed to share the news with someone. I called my mother. "Mama, I have to tell you something."

"What is it, Mila?" she asked, sounding quite worried.

"I am pregnant!" I blurted out, and I waited for her to share my dismay.

"Mazel Tov!" she practically screamed in her too-loud phone voice. *Mazel Tov?* Those were happy words.

My mother's words reverberated in my mind all day.

....

As soon as I got to my parents' house, I called my current ob/gyn. Dr. Eisenberg suggested I terminate the pregnancy sooner rather than later, since early on, it was possible to terminate using only some pills. So I made an appointment to see Dr. Eisenberg right after the long holiday weekend. During those three days of Memorial Day weekend, the fact sunk in: *I was pregnant. And soon, I wouldn't be.*

'Mazel Tov,' my mother had said. And in many ways, it did feel like a blessing. Over the weekend, I touched my belly and imagined a small cell growing into two cells, then into four cells, then into a tiny little pea-sized thing. It would grow from a pea to an egg to a grapefruit. This thing would become a baby.

On Monday morning, I woke up with a clear thought: "Life is for the living." What is more living than giving birth, than having and raising a child? I realized I had to do some thinking. When I saw Dr. Eisenberg, I told him I wasn't ready to take the pills yet. He said I had a few weeks to think about it, as forty-nine days was the window for this method of terminating a pregnancy.

My mother told my father what was going on. He had mixed feelings; he was an old-fashioned man. "Your life will become too hard, Milochka," he advised me in a heavy voice full of suffering. I resolved not to talk to him any more about my news; I wanted to spare him any more heartache.

I consulted with Dr. G and Lynn about the pregnancy. I found out that as I had been off the strong meds when I got pregnant, I did not have to worry about them damaging the fetus in any way. The bigger issue was whether, if I decided to keep the baby, I could handle the stress of being a single mother if Alexander decided not to participate.

Lynn expressed her concern as to whether I'd recovered enough from the instability of the last two years. She said a baby would rely totally on me, and I couldn't let the baby down. I couldn't disappear for a day or two or three, the way I had after Jake, after Ezra, after Henry, after Adam. I told Lynn she didn't know me before – before I had become so sad. Or before my breakup with Cliff. Sure, I hadn't been always so ready to fall. I was not immune to ups-and-downs – most women aren't – but I had not been living on the edge the way I had been as a result of failed romances. I truly thought I could get back to that state of stability again. Already I felt stronger; it had just taken time – and some time off from romance. Okay, maybe the doctors' advice of "no dating" had been right! Besides, could Lynn, a single mother herself, tell me that the joy of her baby boy had not become the greatest joy of her life? Upon hearing my words, she quietly nodded. She couldn't deny the truth behind them.

When Alexander returned to New York from a trip to Ibiza, I told him on the phone while he was out to dinner with a friend. His reaction was to immediately ask if I was telling him the truth. I was insulted, and I asked him why someone would lie about something like this. He then asked if I knew for sure the baby was his. And I did: I wasn't sleeping with anyone else. So Alexander asked me to meet for a drink to discuss things.

We met in the dark lobby of the Tribeca Grand. Candles flickered on small pedestal tables as a female DJ entertained the few guests present. I was already sitting when Alexander walked in. He looked big and angry, his thin lips set in a determined line and his black eyes and eyebrows narrowed and full of accusation. He started the conversation by asking if I wanted money to "…take care of it." I told him I wasn't sure that I would "…take care of it."

Taken aback, he vented, "What kind of Jew are you? Jews don't have babies without marriage. And I don't think you and I want to get married to each other."

"That doesn't mean that the baby doesn't deserve a life, Alexander," I responded quietly but steadily. "When this happened, I myself didn't know how I would feel. Or that I would even want this child. I didn't realize I would have such a hard time even thinking of 'taking care'…" Here I stopped, simply unable to finish the sentence. I wiped a tear off my face.

"If this baby is born, it will never have a father! I promise you that, Mila," Alexander said angrily in response. "Why don't you call me when you really want to talk sensibly about this?" And he got up off his chair and stormed out.

....

I called Alexander to meet one more time. I wanted to discuss my options. He agreed to meet me at Café Noir, a French restaurant in Soho. It was quiet that Sunday. The vendors on Grand Street were just setting up their jewelry and art stalls. Alexander walked into the restaurant confidently, flaunting his height and size. He was a mountain of a man, and a mountain of opinion. I wasn't sure how I would succeed in asserting any small thought of mine.

Alexander asked what I was thinking, and I told him I was still thinking. So he listed all the negatives of having a baby with him. I ate my croque-monsieur, and he his quiche. I offered him a bite of my meal, and he laughed in response. "See, what kind of baby would we have," he asked, "if you don't even know I'm Kosher?" Well, I had known; I had just forgotten in that particular moment. But his comment planted seeds of uncertainty once more.

After sitting by myself in a park later that day, I thought about it, and decided Alexander was right. I didn't even know the father. How could I come to love this baby of ours? I couldn't. And just like that, I decided I would not have the baby. I called my parents, and they said they supported whatever choice I made.

"Do you really, Mama?" I asked a bit fearfully.

"Of course we do, darling," my mother replied without an ounce of hesitation. "You are our baby. We support you first."

I called my ob/gyn to tell him I would come in to get started with the pills termination procedure. It was the last week I could have it without having to go through the more traditional surgical route. That afternoon, I called my long-time friend Jessica and told her. She agreed my life would be easier without a baby. "But whatever you decide," she said with conviction, "when you look back, remember you made the best choice under the circumstances." As she spoke, I heard her children yelling and laughing in the background.

The night before my appointment, I tossed and turned; I couldn't sleep. Jessica's words were stuck in my mind. I imagined what would make me feel worse – looking back on the decision to have a baby, or the decision to have an abortion. As usual when I couldn't make up my mind, I called my mother. She suggested I call her psychic (I didn't know she had one!).

So I asked the psychic – a woman named Rachel, who lived in Brooklyn and had a thick New Yawk accent – whether she could help me. I expected something specific, something I could follow. She didn't do that. She only reflected with me on some potential problems and benefits. Frustrated, I asked her if she had a child. "Yes, my Lola." I pressed for more information. Rachel told me she was divorced and lived with her daughter, the greatest gift of her life. She told me Lola was a bright girl who wanted to be a doctor. As Rachel spoke, I could hear the pride in her voice, and feel the love she held for her child. I didn't need to talk further with her. I told Rachel I would send her check in the mail.

In the morning, I skipped my appointment with the ob/gyn for the induced miscarriage. I realized I needed more time to decide. I just couldn't stop this life in me so easily – not after so much sadness. Here was a breath of joy.

Chapter 41 – Riga

Time passed, until there was just a month left before it became too late to get an abortion. I knew I was leaning toward keeping the baby. I began to look pregnant too: My stomach flared out in a way that didn't just seem like excess weight. I started to wear a loose denim jacket to hide the small bulge so only I could tell.

Since it was now August and it had been a year since I went anywhere outside of New York, my mother suggested we take a vacation together. "But where should we go, Mama?" I asked. We went through some alternatives: Cape May. Martha's Vineyard.

Then my mother said, "We can go to Riga, Milochka, to the Baltic Sea."

Riga. Our old city. When I thought of it, I went back in time.

I was four years old, and in the park with my favorite uncle when I fell as I was running. Sporting a big bump on my head, I rode a carousel horse as someone snapped a picture.

I was five years old, and playing a fox in the school play. I was happy to wear a glittery orange skirt and a fox mask as I gave out New Year's gifts to the little children.

I was six years old, and riding with my parents in the back of our best friends' new Zhiguli, the classic Communist car. Feeling sick, I threw up all over my friend Diana's lap. "Why couldn't you throw up the other way, on your mom?" she screamed at me.

I was seven years old and in art class in school. I was painting scenes from fairy tales – Cinderella, Zolushka. The teacher wrote a big 5+ (A+) in red on the back of my paper.

I was eight years old on New Year's, the big holiday for us. I read my favorite Astrid Lindgren book, Karlsson-on-the-Roof, and helped Babushka whip fresh cream and mix dough for the Napoleon that was her specialty.

I was eight, and my parents told me we were leaving in a few weeks for America, the land of roller coasters and jeans and opportunity. I wasn't to tell anyone; it was a secret.

Only our best friends could know. For a whole week, I kept quiet. Then, after math class one day, I whispered I had a secret to a pig-tailed girl named Marina. As I walked home, I realized I had done something terribly wrong. Marina would guess my secret and tell someone else, maybe the teacher. Then, my parents' plans, which Mama and Papa had whispered about all year and were finally close to execution, would be ruined. I worried for days, but nothing happened, and the day came when we shipped our ten boxes of books and our piano. We sold or gave away everything else, packing a few matreshka dolls to sell in Italy where we would stop to wait for our American visas.

The day we left, there was a lot of drizzling rain and my grandmother crying at the train as she hugged my father, one of her two sons and the one whom she wouldn't be following to a new land. She had said she was too old for so much change.

Then my grandmother had hugged me hard, a sweet smell of flour and sugar on her skin as always. "My donenka, my baby," she had said to me. I had kissed her on her soft white hair and by her twinkling eyes. We were leaving and could not come back. This was goodbye. Even though I was only nine years old, I had understood this was a forever goodbye.

When my father and my mother and I stepped on the train, my babushka waved from the platform. Everything in the past then became gray to me.

But now the former Baltic Republics were a destination for cruise ships. Our lovely European Riga, a city we were proud of even during the Soviet Era, was even lovelier now. Helped by the influx of money from wealthy Muscovites, it was a perfect vacation destination. Especially for now: it would be somewhere peaceful where I could reflect. I agreed to go, and brought some baby naming books along – even though my mind was not completely made up.

My Uncle Lev met us at the airport. Lev was the son of my mother's Uncle Elia, the man who had helped her out when her parents had died when she was young. It was Elia who had paid for my mother's wedding, and it was to Elia's farm in Rezekne, a village near Riga, that we had gone during our summers.

Lev was now a successful businessman. He was large and gregarious, with kind eyes. He lived with his second wife Irina and their two kids in a new apartment in Riga, but they also had a dacha in Jurmala, a resort town on the Baltic Sea. And that was where my mother and I would visit with them.

In Jurmala, we ate the full-fat dairy items for which Riga was famous: yogurt, yogurt shakes, kefir, cheeses, farmer cheese, and the *sirochki* I loved. We nibbled on the berries and chanterelle mushrooms that we found in the pine forests near the beach. We drank tea late into the night as we caught up, telling stories of now and yesterday. Latvia had become as modern now as America – Lev's kids went online, listened to the same types of music, and traveled overseas. I was grateful my relatives didn't ask much about Cliff or the divorce. Anyway, with thoughts of the baby occupying my mind, I found that any thoughts of Cliff were receding. I didn't tell my relatives that I was pregnant, although my bulge was beginning to show even more now.

During the days, we walked on the beach with the soft white sands I had loved as a child. In the center of the now glamorous Jurmala, the Riga hotel stood tall, and my mother and I went to the spa there. I swam laps while my mother waited in a lounge chair. Another swimmer was doing laps in the pool too – a very pregnant and gorgeous woman.

As I swam, I thought of my amazing mother, and suddenly I felt both happy and sad. My mother was always there for me – but if I had the baby, I would be having a baby by myself. I got this now.

That night, I told my mother I was jealous of Lev and Irina and their marriage; jealous of the pregnant Russian woman in the pool. I was scared I couldn't do it all alone. "Everyone's life is different, Milochka," my mother advised. "Some people are married but very alone. Don't judge from the outside." I thought of my parents' marriage and all its ups and downs. But my parents had stuck through it all together. Yes, Mama spoke from experience – marriage was hardly easy.

My mother and I visited the town of Rezekne to see the house where she had grown up. The house was tiny, much smaller than I had imagined. I imagined my mother as a little girl imagining what her life would be like: Had she ever thought she would end up in America? There was so much history here. So much family history – my great-grandparents had lived here. They were the grandparents my mother had never met because they were shot and buried in the mass grave here in Rezekne during the Holocaust.

In Riga, we went to Mama's parents' graves at the Jewish cemetery. My mother paid yearly for the caretaker to keep their plots clean. Mama stood at the grave of her parents holding some wildflowers she had purchased at the entrance to the cemetery. She slowly walked up to the pictures of her mother and father that were engraved on the headstones. As she stood gazing at them, I realized what a long time it has been since Mama could be a child instead of a mother.

At the cemetery, I thought about how much I loved my mother. And I recognized I too wanted to give my love to someone else in a way only a mother could give to a child.

I will keep this baby.

This thought just floated into my brain and grew until I felt that I was practically shouting the sentence out loud.

I will keep this baby.

At dinner that night, I told Lev and Irina I was expecting a baby. "Mazel Tov!" Lev said, raising a toast and not skipping a beat. They were suspecting as much, of course, as my baggy shirts hardly hid this good news.

I returned to New York with a sense of calm even though I was off all medication. Instead of dating books, I read baby name books. Lynn and Dr. Gold told me how surprised they were at how well I was doing.

I wasn't. I always knew that I was in there, somewhere. And so did my mama.

Epilogue

Six months later, it was just after one a.m., and I was wincing in pain in a taxi. My driver was highly agitated: "Are you going to make it to the hospital, lady?" he asked as the cab sped from Battery Park to the Upper East Side. "Sure, I will," I said immediately, as I focused on my breathing. There was no time to be anxious; all my attention was on my body and willing it not to have the baby in the car. I managed to dial my mother, of course; in my log of recent calls, the last twenty were from her. My parents sped in from New Jersey, getting to the hospital just slightly later than I did.

Once there, Mama stayed by my side like a sentry as I wailed and waited for my doctor to arrive from his country house.

By three a.m., my doctor hadn't yet arrived, and I walked back and forth desperate for an epidural. Tears of pain streamed down my face. Mama sat nearby, her bright red hair matted, and her brick-brown lipstick on crooked.

"I have treats for after," she whispered suddenly, and took out the chocolate marzipan we both loved. I smiled just as a searing contraction ripped through my body; it felt like it split me in two.

Later, after the doctor finally came and gave me the blessed epidural in the delivery room, Mama fed me ice chips and patted my sweaty head. "Just a bit more, Milochka!" she cheered with each push I made. When I cried out, Mama said, "It's okay, Mila," as she held my hand. "You'll be fine." I took her words as a prophecy.

....

It took twelve hours of labor before the baby arrived, screaming and scrunching her nose, her head covered with black hair just like her father's. I imagined texting this dad of hers who wasn't excited; I'd write, "Bb is here. Signed, Hot Stuff." But I wasn't angry at him; rather, I was grateful to join a sacred female society, happy for the unexpected key to its gates.

The labor nurse took the baby. I hadn't yet chosen a name; I liked Sonya, a name from Chekhov's *Uncle Vanya* and one of my favorite roles from my acting days. But Sonya also reminded me of perfumed elderly aunts from Queens, puffy from years of potatoes and pastries.

Mama walked me to the recovery room, where I drifted off to sleep imagining a hundred crying babies. In my dream I wandered lost through a huge hospital ward full of identical baby dolls with labels. Ecstatic couples stood over all of them except for a small doll that lay in the corner without a label. As nurses argued about who she was, I frantically tried to reach her to hold her. My baby.

When I woke up for the first time after delivering the baby, Mama wasn't there. So I walked by myself to the newborn nursery.

Just as in my dream, there were rows of swaddled babies in striped hats lining the room. The bracelet on my baby said only, "Baby Simon." She was a tiny being with dark slits for eyes, and a crinkled red face. I peered at her, hoping to feel a bond. But she only seemed like a wild animal. Fear flashed through me again: *Was this the right decision after all?*

I turned sharply away and walked into a man pushing a baby in a bassinet. He was tall and broad-shouldered, with sandy hair touched by flecks of gray. An old college boyfriend whom I hadn't seen in years.

"Robert?"

"Mila?" he questioned back as he noticed my maternity-ward robe and bracelet.

"What a coincidence!" I said, in shock.

"Congratulations, you just had...?"

"A baby girl," I answered quickly. "And you?"

"A boy," he said. "Charles."

"Oh, a boy! That's wonderful," I stammered as I thought, *Of all the places to run into an old boyfriend!*

"And who is your little one?"

"She doesn't have a name. I haven't yet – I mean, we haven't finalized it yet."

And I wasn't lying. There was a "We." Mama and I. It turned out I wasn't at all as alone as I thought I would be, even in this. Mama was with me for this scary new and serious undertaking. And, of course, so was Papa.

Robert nodded. "I better go. My wife is waiting."

When I got back to my hospital room, Mama was sitting there holding a coffee. She must have had such a headache by now: It had been a long night, and she needed her caffeine first thing in the morning. Usually she made up instant Taster's Choice with condensed milk – just as she had in our Latvia days.

My mother had told me she wanted to call this baby Nina. I realized how I loved the name: Like Sonya, Nina was also a character in Chekhov – from *The Seagull,* and a name that meant *graceful* and *strong.* And more than anything, I wanted my baby to grow into a strong woman. I'd felt so weak at times this year, and I didn't want that for my baby.

"Okay, Mama," I said out loud. "Nina it is!"

Mama was exhausted; I could see the years on her face. But just then, a smile creased across her face at my words.

"Milochka, *solnyshko,*" she said.

As I walked past Mama to get back into my hospital bed, I kissed the top of my mother's head.

ACKNOWLEDGEMENTS

My heartfelt gratitude to the many friends, colleagues, and mentors who helped: My editor Elizabeth Zack, whose superb work gave my first novel better flow, and me hope! Scarlett Rugers – Beautiful book cover design by Scarlett Rugers Design www.scarlettrugers.com. Charles Salzberg, for inspiring me to work on a novel and teaching me how. Anna Vladi – a very special thank you for your energy and your invaluable help from Excel spreadsheets to book-launch planning. Ladies of the Salon for helping me stick with it – you are my inspiration. Cindy – thank you for all the advice, (some) taken. Adrienne Peres – grateful for all your support and the many phone calls throughout the years. Natasha and Jonas Steinman – friends who kept reminding me there was a project to finish. Stephanie Jones – thanks for believing in this story. The Stars of FL – my lovely Book Club friends – appreciate the enthusiasm, friendship, and fun stories.

 The many friends and family who have continued to believe in me: Yasmine Mahdavi & Patrick Campbell, Arina Lekhel and Vadik Astrakhan, Luci Teixeira, Virginia Friedman, Isaac and Rina Silverman, Oren and Jonathan Silverman, Ira Tager, Boria Tager, and family. My "aunts": Rachel Cherfas, Ada Margolin, Lilia Goldin, Asya Smotkin, Giza Mendlovich, Mila Sakevich, Inna Kulek, Maya Tsimanis – strong Russian women all!

 This novel would not exist without the following dear people: My amazing parents Celia and Simon – thank you for your love, love, and love. Thank you, really, for everything – even if everything is sometimes hard to take! As Mama says, family is family. Marlene Swinton – an inspiration in every which way possible – thank you for your support. Most of all, to my children Ava, Alexa, & Maxim for motivating me and allowing me to steal away a minute (or two or three or more) when all mayhem prevailed, so I could teach by example that getting things done is a valuable mission in life! And of course - my multi-talented husband/best friend Rolfe, for whom few things are hard, and action is the rule, not the exception. Big Kiss for inspiring me and for your love, patience, encouragement, and humor.

To my readers – thank you for giving your time to Mila's story!

About the Author:

INNA SWINTON was born in Riga, Latvia and immigrated to the United States as a child. After graduating from Yale University with a B.A. in literature, she received her J.D. from New York University School of Law. She has worked as a lawyer, a professional actress, and a standup comedienne. Inna currently lives in the New York area with her husband, three children, and a dachshund. This is her debut novel.

CPSIA information can be obtained at www.ICGtesting.com
Printed in the USA
LVOW11s1940020414

380032LV00016B/1356/P